T0144368

Salammbô
Gustave Flaubert

MINT EDITIONS

Salammbô was first published in 1862.

This edition published by Mint Editions 2021.

ISBN 9781513279503 | E-ISBN 9781513284521

Published by Mint Editions®

 MINT
EDITIONS

minteditionbooks.com

Publishing Director: Jennifer Newens
Design & Production: Rachel Lopez Metzger
Project Manager: Micaela Clark
Typesetting: Westchester Publishing Services

Salammbô

Contents

I

The Feast

It was at Megara, a suburb of Carthage, in the gardens of Hamilcar. The soldiers whom he had commanded in Sicily were having a great feast to celebrate the anniversary of the battle of Eryx, and as the master was away, and they were numerous, they ate and drank with perfect freedom.

The captains, who wore bronze cothurni, had placed themselves in the central path, beneath a gold-fringed purple awning, which reached from the wall of the stables to the first terrace of the palace; the common soldiers were scattered beneath the trees, where numerous flat-roofed buildings might be seen, wine-presses, cellars, storehouses, bakeries, and arsenals, with a court for elephants, dens for wild beasts, and a prison for slaves.

Fig-trees surrounded the kitchens; a wood of sycamores stretched away to meet masses of verdure, where the pomegranate shone amid the white tufts of the cotton-plant; vines, grape-laden, grew up into the branches of the pines; a field of roses bloomed beneath the plane-trees; here and there lilies rocked upon the turf; the paths were strewn with black sand mingled with powdered coral, and in the centre the avenue of cypress formed, as it were, a double colonnade of green obelisks from one extremity to the other.

Far in the background stood the palace, built of yellow mottled Numidian marble, broad courses supporting its four terraced stories. With its large, straight, ebony staircase, bearing the prow of a vanquished galley at the corners of every step, its red doors quartered with black crosses, its brass gratings protecting it from scorpions below, and its trellises of gilded rods closing the apertures above, it seemed to the soldiers in its haughty opulence as solemn and impenetrable as the face of Hamilcar.

The Council had appointed his house for the holding of this feast; the convalescents lying in the temple of Eschmoun had set out at daybreak and dragged themselves thither on their crutches. Every minute others were arriving. They poured in ceaselessly by every path like torrents rushing into a lake; through the trees the slaves of the kitchens might be seen running scared and half-naked; the gazelles fled bleating on the lawns; the sun was setting, and the perfume of citron trees rendered the exhalation from the perspiring crowd heavier still.

Men of all nations were there, Ligurians, Lusitanians, Balearians, Negroes, and fugitives from Rome. Beside the heavy Dorian dialect were audible the resonant Celtic syllables rattling like chariots of war, while Ionian terminations conflicted with consonants of the desert as harsh as the jackal's cry. The Greek might be recognised by his slender figure, the Egyptian by his elevated shoulders, the Cantabrian by his broad calves. There were Carians proudly nodding their helmet plumes, Cappadocian archers displaying large flowers painted on their bodies with the juice of herbs, and a few Lydians in women's robes, dining in slippers and earrings. Others were ostentatiously daubed with vermilion, and resembled coral statues.

They stretched themselves on the cushions, they ate squatting round large trays, or lying face downwards they drew out the pieces of meat and sated themselves, leaning on their elbows in the peaceful posture of lions tearing their prey. The last comers stood leaning against the trees watching the low tables half hidden beneath the scarlet coverings, and awaiting their turn.

Hamilcar's kitchens being insufficient, the Council had sent them slaves, ware, and beds, and in the middle of the garden, as on a battle-field when they burn the dead, large bright fires might be seen, at which oxen were roasting. Anise-sprinkled loaves alternated with great cheeses heavier than discuses, crateras filled with wine, and cantharuses filled with water, together with baskets of gold filigree-work containing flowers. Every eye was dilated with the joy of being able at last to gorge at pleasure, and songs were beginning here and there.

First they were served with birds and green sauce in plates of red clay relieved by drawings in black, then with every kind of shell-fish that is gathered on the Punic coasts, wheaten porridge, beans and barley, and snails dressed with cumin on dishes of yellow amber.

Afterwards the tables were covered with meats, antelopes with their horns, peacocks with their feathers, whole sheep cooked in sweet wine, haunches of she-camels and buffaloes, hedgehogs with garum, fried grasshoppers, and preserved dormice. Large pieces of fat floated in the midst of saffron in bowls of Tamrapanni wood. Everything was running over with wine, truffles, and asafotida. Pyramids of fruit were crumbling upon honeycombs, and they had not forgotten a few of those

GUSTAVE FLAUBERT

plump little dogs with pink silky hair and fattened on olive lees,—a Carthaginian dish held in abhorrence among other nations. Surprise at the novel fare excited the greed of the stomach. The Gauls with their long hair drawn up on the crown of the head, snatched at the watermelons and lemons, and crunched them up with the rind. The Negroes, who had never seen a lobster, tore their faces with its red prickles. But the shaven Greeks, whiter than marble, threw the leavings of their plates behind them, while the herdsmen from Brutium, in their wolf-skin garments, devoured in silence with their faces in their portions.

Night fell. The velarium, spread over the cypress avenue, was drawn back, and torches were brought.

The apes, sacred to the moon, were terrified on the cedar tops by the wavering lights of the petroleum as it burned in the porphyry vases. They uttered screams which afforded mirth to the soldiers.

Oblong flames trembled in cuirasses of brass. Every kind of scintillation flashed from the gem-incrusted dishes. The crateras with their borders of convex mirrors multiplied and enlarged the images of things; the soldiers thronged around, looking at their reflections with amazement, and grimacing to make themselves laugh. They tossed the ivory stools and golden spatulas to one another across the tables. They gulped down all the Greek wines in their leathern bottles, the Campanian wine enclosed in amphoras, the Cantabrian wines brought in casks, with the wines of the jujube, cinnamomum and lotus. There were pools of these on the ground that made the foot slip. The smoke of the meats ascended into the foliage with the vapour of the breath. Simultaneously were heard the snapping of jaws, the noise of speech, songs, and cups, the crash of Campanian vases shivering into a thousand pieces, or the limpid sound of a large silver dish.

In proportion as their intoxication increased they more and more recalled the injustice of Carthage. The Republic, in fact, exhausted by the war, had allowed all the returning bands to accumulate in the town. Gisco, their general, had however been prudent enough to send them back severally in order to facilitate the liquidation of their pay, and the Council had believed that they would in the end consent to some reduction. But at present ill-will was caused by the inability to pay them. This debt was confused in the minds of the people with the 3200 Euboic talents exacted by Lutatius, and equally with Rome they were regarded as enemies to Carthage. The Mercenaries understood this, and their indignation found vent in threats and outbreaks. At last they demanded permission to assemble to celebrate one of their victories, and the peace party yielded, at the same time revenging themselves on Hamilcar who had so strongly upheld the war. It had been terminated notwithstanding all his efforts, so that, despairing of Carthage, he had entrusted the government of the Mercenaries to Gisco. To appoint his palace for their reception was to draw upon him something of the hatred which was borne to them. Moreover, the expense must be excessive, and he would incur nearly the whole.

Proud of having brought the Republic to submit, the Mercenaries thought that they were at last about to return to their homes with the payment for their blood in the hoods of their cloaks. But as seen through the mists of intoxication, their fatigues seemed to them prodigious and but ill-rewarded. They showed one another their wounds, they told of their combats, their travels and the hunting in their native lands. They imitated the cries and the leaps of wild beasts. Then came unclean wagers; they buried their heads in the amphoras and drank on without interruption, like thirsty dromedaries. A Lusitanian of gigantic stature ran over the tables, carrying a man in each hand at arm's length, and spitting out fire through his nostrils. Some Lacedæmonians, who had not taken off their cuirasses, were leaping with a heavy step. Some advanced like women, making obscene gestures; others stripped naked to fight amid the cups after the fashion of gladiators, and a company of Greeks danced around a vase whereon nymphs were to be seen, while a Negro tapped with an ox-bone on a brazen buckler.

Suddenly they heard a plaintive song, a song loud and soft, rising and falling in the air like the wing-beating of a wounded bird.

It was the voice of the slaves in the ergastulum. Some soldiers rose at a bound to release them and disappeared.

They returned, driving through the dust amid shouts, twenty men, distinguished by their greater paleness of face. Small black felt caps of conical shape covered their shaven heads; they all wore wooden shoes, and yet made a noise as of old iron like driving chariots.

They reached the avenue of cypress, where they were lost among the crowd of those questioning them. One of them remained apart, standing. Through the rents in his tunic his shoulders could be seen striped with long scars. Drooping his chin, he looked round him with distrust, closing his eyelids somewhat against the dazzling light of the torches, but when he saw that none of the armed men were unfriendly to him, a great sigh escaped from his breast; he stammered, he sneered through the bright tears that bathed his face. At last he seized a brimming cantharus by its rings, raised it straight up into the air with his outstretched arms, from which his chains hung down, and then looking to heaven, and still holding the cup he said:

"Hail first to thee, Baal-Eschmoun, the deliverer, whom the people of my country call Æsculapius! and to you, genii of the fountains, light, and woods! and to you, ye gods hidden beneath the mountains and in the caverns of the earth! and to you, strong men in shining armour who have set me free!"

Then he let fall the cup and related his history. He was called Spendius. The Carthaginians had taken him in the battle of Æginusæ, and he thanked the Mercenaries once more in Greek, Ligurian and Punic; he kissed their hands; finally, he congratulated them on the banquet, while expressing his surprise at not perceiving the cups of the Sacred Legion. These cups, which bore an emerald vine on each of their six golden faces, belonged to a corps composed exclusively of young patricians of the tallest stature. They were a privilege, almost a sacerdotal distinction, and accordingly nothing among the treasures of the Republic was more coveted by the Mercenaries. They detested the Legion on this account, and some of them had been known to risk their lives for the inconceivable pleasure of drinking out of these cups.

Accordingly they commanded that the cups should be brought. They were in the keeping of the Syssitia, companies of traders, who had a common table. The slaves returned. At that hour all the members of the Syssitia were asleep.

"Let them be awakened!" responded the Mercenaries.

After a second excursion it was explained to them that the cups were shut up in a temple.

"Let it be opened!" they replied.

And when the slaves confessed with trembling that they were in the possession of Gisco, the general, they cried out:

"Let him bring them!"

Gisco soon appeared at the far end of the garden with an escort of the Sacred Legion. His full, black cloak, which was fastened on his head to a golden mitre starred with precious stones, and which hung all about him down to his horse's hoofs, blended in the distance with the colour of the night. His white beard, the radiancy of his head-dress, and his triple necklace of broad blue plates beating against his breast, were alone visible.

When he entered, the soldiers greeted him with loud shouts, all crying:

"The cups! The cups!"

He began by declaring that if reference were had to their courage, they were worthy of them.

The crowd applauded and howled with joy.

He knew it, he who had commanded them over yonder, and had returned with the last cohort in the last galley!

"True! True!" said they.

Nevertheless, Gisco continued, the Republic had respected their national divisions, their customs, and their modes of worship; in Carthage they were free! As to the cups of the Sacred Legion, they were private property. Suddenly a Gaul, who was close to Spendius, sprang over the tables and ran straight up to Gisco, gesticulating and threatening him with two naked swords.

Without interrupting his speech, the General struck him on the head with his heavy ivory staff, and the Barbarian fell. The Gauls howled, and their frenzy, which was spreading to the others, would soon have swept away the legionaries. Gisco shrugged his shoulders as he saw them growing pale. He thought that his courage would be useless against these exasperated brute beasts. It would be better to revenge himself upon them by some artifice later; accordingly, he signed to his soldiers and slowly withdrew. Then, turning in the gateway towards the Mercenaries, he cried to them that they would repent of it.

The feast recommenced. But Gisco might return, and by surrounding the suburb, which was beside the last ramparts, might crush them against the walls. Then they felt themselves alone in spite of their crowd, and the great town sleeping beneath them in the shade suddenly made them afraid, with its piles of staircases, its lofty black houses, and its vague gods fiercer even than its people. In the distance a few ships'-lanterns were gliding across the harbour, and there were lights in the temple of Khamon. They thought of Hamilcar. Where was he? Why had he forsaken them when peace was concluded? His differences with the Council were doubtless but a pretence in order to destroy them. Their unsatisfied hate recoiled upon him, and they cursed him, exasperating one another with their own anger. At this juncture they collected together beneath the plane-trees to see a slave who, with eyeballs fixed, neck contorted, and lips covered with foam, was rolling on the ground, and beating the soil with his limbs. Some one cried out that he was poisoned. All then believed themselves poisoned. They fell upon the slaves, a terrible clamour was raised, and a vertigo of destruction came like a whirlwind upon the drunken army. They struck about them at random, they smashed, they slew; some hurled torches into the foliage; others, leaning over the lions' balustrade, massacred the animals with arrows; the most daring ran to the elephants, desiring to cut down their trunks and eat ivory.

Some Balearic slingers, however, who had gone round the corner of the palace, in order to pillage more conveniently, were checked by a lofty barrier, made of Indian cane. They cut the lock-straps with their daggers, and then found themselves beneath the front that faced Carthage, in another garden full of trimmed vegetation. Lines of white flowers all following one another in regular succession formed long parabolas like star-rockets on the azure-coloured earth. The gloomy bushes exhaled warm and honied odours. There were trunks of trees smeared with cinnabar, which resembled columns covered with blood. In the centre were twelve pedestals, each supporting a great glass ball, and these hollow globes were indistinctly filled with reddish lights, like enormous and still palpitating eyeballs. The soldiers lighted themselves with torches as they stumbled on the slope of the deeply laboured soil.

But they perceived a little lake divided into several basins by walls of blue stones. So limpid was the wave that the flames of the torches quivered in it at the very bottom, on a bed of white pebbles and golden dust. It began to bubble, luminous spangles glided past, and great fish with gems about their mouths, appeared near the surface.

With much laughter the soldiers slipped their fingers into the gills and brought them to the tables. They were the fish of the Barca family, and were all descended from those primordial lotes which had hatched the mystic egg wherein the goddess was concealed. The idea of committing a sacrilege revived the greediness of the Mercenaries; they speedily placed fire beneath some brazen vases, and amused themselves by watching the beautiful fish struggling in the boiling water.

The surge of soldiers pressed on. They were no longer afraid. They commenced to drink again. Their ragged tunics were wet with the perfumes that flowed in large drops from their foreheads, and resting both fists on the tables, which seemed to them to be rocking like ships, they rolled their great drunken eyes around to devour by sight what they could not take. Others walked amid the dishes on the purple table covers, breaking ivory stools, and phials of Tyrian glass to pieces with their feet. Songs mingled with the death-rattle of the slaves expiring amid the broken cups. They demanded wine, meat, gold. They cried out for women. They raved in a hundred languages. Some thought that they were at the vapour baths on account of the steam which floated around them, or else, catching sight of the foliage, imagined that they were at the chase, and rushed upon their companions as upon wild beasts. The conflagration spread to all the trees, one after another, and the lofty mosses of verdure, emitting long white spirals, looked like volcanoes beginning to smoke. The clamour redoubled; the wounded lions roared in the shade.

In an instant the highest terrace of the palace was illuminated, the central door opened, and a woman, Hamilcar's daughter herself, clothed in black garments, appeared on the threshold. She descended the first staircase, which ran obliquely along the first story, then the second, and the third, and stopped on the last terrace at the head of the galley staircase. Motionless and with head bent, she gazed upon the soldiers.

Behind her, on each side, were two long shadows of pale men, clad in white, red-fringed robes, which fell straight to their feet. They had no beard, no hair, no eyebrows. In their hands, which sparkled with rings, they carried enormous lyres, and with shrill voice they sang a hymn to the divinity of Carthage. They were the eunuch priests of the temple of Tanith, who were often summoned by Salammbô to her house.

At last she descended the galley staircase. The priests followed her. She advanced into the avenue of cypress, and walked slowly through the tables of the captains, who drew back somewhat as they watched her pass.

Her hair, which was powdered with violet sand, and combined into the form of a tower, after the fashion of the Chanaanite maidens, added to her height. Tresses of pearls were fastened to her temples, and fell to the corners of her mouth, which was as rosy as a half-open pomegranate. On her breast was a collection of luminous stones, their variegation imitating the scales of the murena. Her arms were adorned with diamonds, and issued naked from her sleeveless tunic, which was starred with red flowers on a perfectly black ground. Between her ankles she wore a golden chainlet to regulate her steps, and her large dark purple mantle, cut of an unknown material, trailed behind her, making, as it were, at each step, a broad wave which followed her.

The priests played nearly stifled chords on their lyres from time to time, and in the intervals of the music might be heard the tinkling of the little golden chain, and the regular patter of her papyrus sandals.

No one as yet was acquainted with her. It was only known that she led a retired life, engaged in pious practices. Some soldiers had seen her in the night on the summit of her palace kneeling before the stars amid the eddyings from kindled perfuming-pans. It was the moon that had made her so pale, and there was something from the gods that enveloped her like a subtle vapour. Her eyes seemed to gaze far beyond terrestrial space. She bent her head as she walked, and in her right hand she carried a little ebony lyre.

They heard her murmur:

"Dead! All dead! No more will you come obedient to my voice as when, seated on the edge of the lake, I used to through seeds of the watermelon into your mouths! The mystery of Tanith ranged in the depths of your eyes that were more limpid than the globules of rivers." And she called them by their names, which were those of the months—"Siv! Sivan! Tammouz, Eloul, Tischri, Schebar! Ah! have pity on me, goddess!"

The soldiers thronged about her without understanding what she said. They wondered at her attire, but she turned a long frightened look upon them all, then sinking her head beneath her shoulders, and waving her arms, she repeated several times:

"What have you done? what have you done?

"Yet you had bread, and meats and oil, and all the malobathrum of the granaries for your enjoyment! I had brought oxen from Hecatompylos; I had sent hunters into the desert!" Her voice swelled; her cheeks purpled. She added, "Where, pray, are you now? In a conquered town, or in the palace of a master? And what master? Hamilcar the Suffet, my father, the servant of the Baals! It was he who withheld from Lutatius those arms of yours, red now with the blood of his slaves! Know you of any in your own lands more skilled in the conduct of battles? Look! our palace steps are encumbered with our victories! Ah! desist not! burn it! I will carry away with me the genius of my house, my black serpent slumbering up yonder on lotus leaves! I will whistle and he will follow me, and if I embark in a galley he will speed in the wake of my ship over the foam of the waves."

Her delicate nostrils were quivering. She crushed her nails against the gems on her bosom. Her eyes drooped, and she resumed:

"Ah! poor Carthage! lamentable city! No longer hast thou for thy protection the strong men of former days who went beyond the oceans to build temples on their shores. All the lands laboured about thee, and the sea-plains, ploughed by thine oars, rocked with thy harvests." Then she began to sing the adventures of Melkarth, the god of the Sidonians, and the father of her family.

She told of the ascent of the mountains of Ersiphonia, the journey to Tartessus, and the war against Masisabal to avenge the queen of the serpents:

"He pursued the female monster, whose tail undulated over the dead leaves like a silver brook, into the forest, and came to a plain where women with dragon-croups were round a great fire, standing erect on the points of their tails. The blood-coloured moon was shining within a pale circle, and their scarlet tongues, cloven like the harpoons of fishermen, reached curling forth to the very edge of the flame."

Then Salammbô, without pausing, related how Melkarth, after vanquishing Masisabal, placed her severed head on the prow of his ship. "At each throb of the waves it sank beneath the foam, but the sun embalmed it; it became harder than gold; nevertheless the eyes ceased not to weep, and the tears fell into the water continually."

She sang all this in an old Chanaanite idiom, which the Barbarians did not understand. They asked one another what she could be saying to them with those frightful gestures which accompanied her speech, and mounted round about her on the tables, beds, and sycamore boughs, they strove with open mouths and craned necks to grasp the vague stories hovering before their imaginations, through the dimness of the theogonies, like phantoms wrapped in cloud.

Only the beardless priests understood Salammbô; their wrinkled hands, which hung over the strings of their lyres, quivered, and from time to time they would draw forth a mournful chord; for, feebler than old women, they trembled at once with mystic emotion, and with the fear inspired by men. The Barbarians heeded them not, but listened continually to the maiden's song.

None gazed at her like a young Numidian chief, who was placed at the captains' tables among soldiers of his own nation. His girdle so bristled with darts that it formed a swelling in his ample cloak, which was fastened on his temples with a leather lace. The cloth parted asunder as it fell upon his shoulders, and enveloped his countenance in shadow, so that only the fires of his two fixed eyes could be seen. It was by chance that he was at the feast, his father having domiciled him with the Barca family, according to the custom by which kings used to send their children into the households of the great in order to pave the way for alliances; but Narr' Havas had lodged there for six months without having hitherto seen Salammbô, and now, seated on his heels, with his head brushing the handles of his javelins, he was watching her with dilated nostrils, like a leopard crouching among the bamboos.

On the other side of the tables was a Libyan of colossal stature, and with short black curly hair. He had retained only his military jacket, the brass plates of which were tearing the purple of the couch. A necklace of silver moons was tangled in his hairy breast. His face was stained with splashes of blood; he was leaning on his left elbow with a smile on his large, open mouth.

Salammbô had abandoned the sacred rhythm. With a woman's subtlety she was simultaneously employing all the dialects of the Barbarians in order to appease their anger. To the Greeks she spoke Greek; then she turned to the Ligurians, the Campanians, the Negroes, and listening to her each one found again in her voice the sweetness of his native land. She now, carried away by the memories of Carthage, sang of the ancient battles against Rome; they applauded. She kindled at the gleaming of the naked swords, and cried aloud with outstretched arms. Her lyre fell, she was silent; and, pressing both hands upon her heart, she remained for some minutes with closed eyelids enjoying the agitation of all these men.

Matho, the Libyan, leaned over towards her. Involuntarily she approached him, and impelled by grateful pride, poured him a long stream of wine into a golden cup in order to conciliate the army.

"Drink!" she said.

He took the cup, and was carrying it to his lips when a Gaul, the same that had been hurt by Gisco, struck him on the shoulder, while in a jovial manner he gave utterance to pleasantries in his native tongue. Spendius was not far off, and he volunteered to interpret them.

"Speak!" said Matho.

"The gods protect you; you are going to become rich. When will the nuptials be?"

"What nuptials?"

"Yours! for with us," said the Gaul, "when a woman gives drink to a soldier, it means that she offers him her couch."

He had not finished when Narr' Havas, with a bound, drew a javelin from his girdle, and, leaning his right foot upon the edge of the table, hurled it against Matho.

The javelin whistled among the cups, and piercing the Lybian's arm, pinned it so firmly to the cloth, that the shaft quivered in the air.

Matho quickly plucked it out; but he was weaponless and naked; at last he lifted the over-laden table with both arms, and flung it against Narr' Havas into the very centre of the crowd that rushed between them. The soldiers and Numidians pressed together so closely that they were unable to draw their swords. Matho advanced dealing great blows with his head. When he raised it, Narr' Havas had disappeared. He sought for him with his eyes. Salammbô also was gone.

Then directing his looks to the palace he perceived the red door with the black cross closing far above, and he darted away.

They saw him run between the prows of the galleys, and then reappear along the three staircases until he reached the red door against which he dashed his whole body. Panting, he leaned against the wall to keep himself from falling.

But a man had followed him, and through the darkness, for the lights of the feast were hidden by the corner of the palace, he recognised Spendius.

"Begone!" said he.

The slave without replying began to tear his tunic with his teeth; then kneeling beside Matho he tenderly took his arm, and felt it in the shadow to discover the wound.

By a ray of the moon which was then gliding between the clouds, Spendius perceived a gaping wound in the middle of the arm. He rolled the piece of stuff about it, but the other said irritably, "Leave me! leave me!"

"Oh no!" replied the slave. "You released me from the ergastulum. I am yours! you are my master! command me!"

Matho walked round the terrace brushing against the walls. He strained his ears at every step, glancing down into the silent apartments through the spaces between the gilded reeds. At last he stopped with a look of despair.

"Listen!" said the slave to him. "Oh! do not despise me for my feebleness! I have lived in the palace. I can wind like a viper through the walls. Come! in the Ancestor's Chamber there is an ingot of gold beneath every flagstone; an underground path leads to their tombs."

"Well! what matters it?" said Matho.

Spendius was silent.

They were on the terrace. A huge mass of shadow stretched before them, appearing as if it contained vague accumulations, like the gigantic billows of a black and petrified ocean.

But a luminous bar rose towards the East; far below, on the left, the canals of Megara were beginning to stripe the verdure of the gardens with their windings of white. The conical roofs of the heptagonal temples, the staircases, terraces, and ramparts were being carved by degrees upon the paleness of the dawn; and a girdle of white foam rocked around the Carthaginian peninsula, while the emerald sea appeared as if it were curdled in the freshness of the morning. Then as the rosy sky grew larger, the lofty houses, bending over the sloping soil, reared and massed themselves like a herd of black goats coming down from the mountains. The deserted streets lengthened; the palm-trees that topped the walls here and there were motionless; the brimming cisterns seemed like silver bucklers lost in the courts; the beacon on the promontory of Hermæum was beginning to grow pale. The horses of Eschmoun, on the very summit of the Acropolis in the cypress wood, feeling that the light was coming, placed their hoofs on the marble parapet, and neighed towards the sun.

It appeared, and Spendius raised his arms with a cry.

Everything stirred in a diffusion of red, for the god, as if he were rending himself, now poured full-rayed upon Carthage the golden rain of his veins. The beaks of the galleys sparkled, the roof of Khamon appeared to be all in flames, while far within the temples, whose doors were opening, glimmerings of light could be seen. Large chariots, arriving from the country, rolled their wheels over the flagstones in the streets. Dromedaries, baggage-laden, came down the ramps. Money-changers raised the pent-houses of their shops at the cross ways, storks took to flight, white sails fluttered. In the wood of Tanith might be heard the tabourines of the sacred courtesans, and the furnaces for baking the clay coffins were beginning to smoke on the Mappalian point.

Spendius leaned over the terrace; his teeth chattered and he repeated:

"Ah! yes—yes—master! I understand why you scorned the pillage of the house just now."

Matho was as if he had just been awaked by the hissing of his voice, and did not seem to understand. Spendius resumed:

"Ah! what riches! and the men who possess them have not even the steel to defend them!"

Then, pointing with his right arm outstretched to some of the populace who were crawling on the sand outside the mole to look for gold dust:

"See!" he said to him, "the Republic is like these wretches: bending on the brink of the ocean, she buries her greedy arms in every shore, and the noise of the billows so fills her ear that she cannot hear behind her the tread of a master's heel!"

He drew Matho to quite the other end of the terrace, and showed him the garden, wherein the soldiers' swords, hanging on the trees, were like mirrors in the sun.

"But here there are strong men whose hatred is roused! and nothing binds them to Carthage, neither families, oaths nor gods!"

Matho remained leaning against the wall; Spendius came close, and continued in a low voice:

"Do you understand me, soldier? We should walk purple-clad like satraps. We should bathe in perfumes; and I should in turn have slaves! Are you not weary of sleeping on hard ground, of drinking the vinegar of the camps, and of continually hearing the trumpet? But you will rest later, will you not? When they pull off your cuirass to cast your corpse to the vultures! or perhaps blind, lame, and weak you will go, leaning on a stick, from door to door to tell of your youth to pickle-sellers and little children. Remember all the injustice of your chiefs, the campings in the snow, the marchings in the sun, the tyrannies of discipline, and the everlasting menace of the cross! And after all this misery they have given you a necklace of honour, as they hang a girdle of bells round the breast of an ass to deafen it on its journey, and prevent it from feeling fatigue. A man like you, braver than Pyrrhus! If only you had wished it! Ah! how happy will you be in large cool halls, with the sound of lyres, lying on flowers, with women and buffoons! Do not tell me that the enterprise is impossible. Have not the Mercenaries already possessed Rhegium and other fortified places in Italy? Who is to prevent you? Hamilcar is away; the people execrate the rich; Gisco can do nothing with the cowards who surround him. Command them! Carthage is ours; let us fall upon it!"

"No!" said Matho, "the curse of Moloch weighs upon me. I felt it in her eyes, and just now I saw a black ram retreating in a temple." Looking around him he added: "But where is she?"

Then Spendius understood that a great disquiet possessed him, and did not venture to speak again.

GUSTAVE FLAUBERT

The trees behind them were still smoking; half-burned carcasses of apes dropped from their blackened boughs from time to time into the midst of the dishes. Drunken soldiers snored open-mouthed by the side of the corpses, and those who were not asleep lowered their heads dazzled by the light of day. The trampled soil was hidden beneath splashes of red. The elephants poised their bleeding trunks between the stakes of their pens. In the open granaries might be seen sacks of spilled wheat, below the gate was a thick line of chariots which had been heaped up by the Barbarians, and the peacocks perched in the cedars were spreading their tails and beginning to utter their cry.

Matho's immobility, however, astonished Spendius; he was even paler than he had recently been, and he was following something on the horizon with fixed eyeballs, and with both fists resting on the edge of the terrace. Spendius crouched down, and so at last discovered at what he was gazing. In the distance a golden speck was turning in the dust on the road to Utica; it was the nave of a chariot drawn by two mules; a slave was running at the end of the pole, and holding them by the bridle. Two women were seated in the chariot. The manes of the animals were puffed between the ears after the Persian fashion, beneath a network of blue pearls. Spendius recognised them, and restrained a cry.

A large veil floated behind in the wind.

II

AT SICCA

Two days afterwards the Mercenaries left Carthage.

They had each received a piece of gold on the condition that they should go into camp at Sicca, and they had been told with all sorts of caresses:

"You are the saviours of Carthage! But you would starve it if you remained there; it would become insolvent. Withdraw! The Republic will be grateful to you later for all this condescension. We are going to levy taxes immediately; your pay shall be in full, and galleys shall be equipped to take you back to your native lands."

They did not know how to reply to all this talk. These men, accustomed as they were to war, were wearied by residence in a town; there was difficulty in convincing them, and the people mounted the walls to see them go away.

They defiled through the street of Khamon, and the Cirta gate, pell-mell, archers with hoplites, captains with soldiers, Lusitanians with Greeks. They marched with a bold step, rattling their heavy cothurni on the paving stones. Their armour was dented by the catapult, and their faces blackened by the sunburn of battles. Hoarse cries issued from their thick beards, their tattered coats of mail flapped upon the pommels of their swords, and through the holes in the brass might be seen their naked limbs, as frightful as engines of war. sarissæ, axes, spears, felt caps and bronze helmets, all swung together with a single motion. They filled the street thickly enough to have made the walls crack, and the long mass of armed soldiers overflowed between the lofty bitumen-smeared houses six storys high. Behind their gratings of iron or reed the women, with veiled heads, silently watched the Barbarians pass.

The terraces, fortifications, and walls were hidden beneath the crowd of Carthaginians, who were dressed in garments of black. The sailors' tunics showed like drops of blood among the dark multitude, and nearly naked children, whose skin shone beneath their copper bracelets, gesticulated in the foliage of the columns, or amid the branches of a palm tree. Some of the Ancients were posted on the platform of the towers, and people did not know why a personage with a long beard stood thus in a dreamy attitude here and there. He appeared in the distance against the background of the sky, vague as a phantom and motionless as stone.

All, however, were oppressed with the same anxiety; it was feared that the Barbarians, seeing themselves so strong, might take a fancy to stay. But they were leaving with so much good faith that the Carthaginians grew bold and mingled with the soldiers. They overwhelmed them with protestations and embraces. Some with exaggerated politeness and audacious hypocrisy even sought to induce them not to leave the city. They threw perfumes, flowers, and pieces of silver to them. They gave them amulets to avert sickness; but they had spit upon them three times to attract death, or had enclosed jackal's hair within them to put cowardice into their hearts. Aloud, they invoked Melkarth's favour, and in a whisper, his curse.

Then came the mob of baggage, beasts of burden, and stragglers. The sick groaned on the backs of dromedaries, while others limped along leaning on broken pikes. The drunkards carried leathern bottles, and the greedy quarters of meat, cakes, fruits, butter wrapped in fig leaves, and snow in linen bags. Some were to be seen with parasols in their hands, and parrots on their shoulders. They had mastiffs, gazelles, and panthers following behind them. Women of Libyan race, mounted on asses, inveighed against the Negresses who had forsaken the lupanaria of Malqua for the soldiers; many of them were suckling children suspended on their bosoms by leathern thongs. The mules were goaded out at the point of the sword, their backs bending beneath the load of tents, while there were numbers of serving-men and water-carriers, emaciated, jaundiced with fever, and filthy with vermin, the scum of the Carthaginian populace, who had attached themselves to the Barbarians.

When they had passed, the gates were shut behind them, but the people did not descend from the walls. The army soon spread over the breadth of the isthmus.

It parted into unequal masses. Then the lances appeared like tall blades of grass, and finally all was lost in a train of dust; those of the soldiers who looked back towards Carthage could now only see its long walls with their vacant battlements cut out against the edge of the sky.

Then the Barbarians heard a great shout. They thought that some from among them (for they did not know their own number) had remained in the town, and were amusing themselves by pillaging a temple. They laughed a great deal at the idea of this, and then continued their journey.

They were rejoiced to find themselves, as in former days, marching all together in the open country, and some of the Greeks sang the old song of the Mamertines:

"With my lance and sword I plough and reap; I am master of the house! The disarmed man falls at my feet and calls me Lord and Great King."

They shouted, they leaped, the merriest began to tell stories; the time of their miseries was past. As they arrived at Tunis, some of them remarked that a troop of Balearic slingers was missing. They were doubtless not far off; and no further heed was paid to them.

Some went to lodge in the houses, others camped at the foot of the walls, and the townspeople came out to chat with the soldiers.

During the whole night fires were seen burning on the horizon in the direction of Carthage; the light stretched like giant torches across the motionless lake. No one in the army could tell what festival was being celebrated.

On the following day the Barbarians passed through a region that was covered with cultivation. The domains of the patricians succeeded one another along the border of the route; channels of water flowed through woods of palm; there were long, green lines of olive-trees; rose-coloured vapours floated in the gorges of the hills, while blue mountains reared themselves behind. A warm wind was blowing. Chameleons were crawling on the broad leaves of the cactus.

The Barbarians slackened their speed.

They marched on in isolated detachments, or lagged behind one another at long intervals. They ate grapes along the margin of the vines. They lay on the grass and gazed with stupefaction upon the large, artificially twisted horns of the oxen, the sheep clothed with skins to protect their wool, the furrows crossing one another so as to form lozenges, and the ploughshares like ships' anchors, with the pomegranate trees that were watered with silphium. Such wealth of the soil and such inventions of wisdom dazzled them.

In the evening they stretched themselves on the tents without unfolding them; and thought with regret of Hamilcar's feast, as they fell asleep with their faces towards the stars.

In the middle of the following day they halted on the bank of a river, amid clumps of rose-bays. Then they quickly threw aside lances, bucklers and belts. They bathed with shouts, and drew water in their helmets, while others drank lying flat on their stomachs, and all in the midst of the beasts of burden whose baggage was slipping from them.

Spendius, who was seated on a dromedary stolen in Hamilcar's parks, perceived Matho at a distance, with his arm hanging against his breast, his head bare, and his face bent down, giving his mule drink, and watching the water flow. Spendius immediately ran through the crowd calling him, "Master! master!"

Matho gave him but scant thanks for his blessings, but Spendius paid no heed to this, and began to march behind him, from time to time turning restless glances in the direction of Carthage.

He was the son of a Greek rhetor and a Campanian prostitute. He had at first grown rich by dealing in women; then, ruined by a shipwreck, he had made war against the Romans with the herdsmen of Samnium. He had been taken and had escaped; he had been retaken, and had worked in the quarries, panted in the vapour-baths, shrieked under torture, passed through the hands of many masters, and experienced every frenzy. At last, one day, in despair, he had flung himself into the sea from the top of a trireme where he was working at the oar. Some of Hamilcar's sailors had picked him up when at the point of death, and had brought him to the ergastulum of Megara, at Carthage. But, as fugitives were to be given back to the Romans, he had taken advantage of the confusion to fly with the soldiers.

During the whole of the march he remained near Matho; he brought him food, assisted him to dismount, and spread a carpet in the evening beneath his head. Matho at last was touched by these attentions, and by degrees unlocked his lips.

He had been born in the gulf of Syrtis. His father had taken him on a pilgrimage to the temple of Ammon. Then he had hunted elephants in the forests of the Garamantes. Afterwards he had entered the service of Carthage. He had been appointed tetrarch at the capture of Drepanum. The Republic owed him four horses, twenty-three medimni of wheat, and a winter's pay. He feared the gods, and wished to die in his native land.

Spendius spoke to him of his travels, and of the peoples and temples that he had visited. He knew many things: he could make sandals, boar-spears and nets; he could tame wild beasts and could cook fish.

Sometimes he would interrupt himself, and utter a hoarse cry from the depths of his throat; Matho's mule would quicken his pace, and others would hasten after them, and then Spendius would begin again though still torn with agony. This subsided at last on the evening of the fourth day.

They were marching side by side to the right of the army on the side of a hill; below them stretched the plain lost in the vapours of the night. The lines of soldiers also were defiling below, making undulations in the shade. From time to time these passed over eminences lit up by the moon; then stars would tremble on the points of the pikes, the helmets would glimmer for an instant, all would disappear, and others would come on continually. Startled flocks bleated in the distance, and a something of infinite sweetness seemed to sink upon the earth.

Spendius, with his head thrown back and his eyes half-closed, inhaled the freshness of the wind with great sighs; he spread out his arms, moving his fingers that he might the better feel the cares that streamed over his body. Hopes of vengeance came back to him and transported him. He pressed his hand upon his mouth to check his sobs, and half-swooning with intoxication, let go the halter of his dromedary, which was proceeding with long, regular steps. Matho had relapsed into his former melancholy; his legs hung down to the ground, and the grass made a continuous rustling as it beat against his cothurni.

The journey, however, spread itself out without ever coming to an end. At the extremity of a plain they would always reach a round-shaped plateau; then they would descend again into a valley, and the mountains which seemed to block up the horizon would, in proportion as they were approached, glide as it were from their positions. From time to time a river would appear amid the verdure of tamarisks to lose itself at the turning of the hills. Sometimes a huge rock would tower aloft like the prow of a vessel or the pedestal of some vanished colossus.

At regular intervals they met with little quadrangular temples, which served as stations for the pilgrims who repaired to Sicca. They were closed like tombs. The Libyans struck great blows upon the doors to have them opened. But no one inside responded.

Then the cultivation became more rare. They suddenly entered upon belts of sand bristling with thorny thickets. Flocks of sheep were browsing among the stones; a woman with a blue fleece about her waist was watching them. She fled screaming when she saw the soldiers' pikes among the rocks.

They were marching through a kind of large passage bordered by two chains of reddish coloured hillocks, when their nostrils were greeted with a nauseous odour, and they thought that they could see something extraordinary on the top of a carob tree: a lion's head reared itself above the leaves.

They ran thither. It was a lion with his four limbs fastened to a cross like a criminal. His huge muzzle fell upon his breast, and his two fore-paws, half-hidden beneath the abundance of his mane, were spread out wide like the wings of a bird. His ribs stood severally out beneath his distended skin; his hind legs, which were nailed against each other, were raised somewhat, and the black blood, flowing through his hair, had collected in stalactites at the end of his tail, which hung down perfectly straight along the cross. The soldiers made merry around; they called him consul, and Roman citizen, and threw pebbles into his eyes to drive away the gnats.

But a hundred paces further on they saw two more, and then there suddenly appeared a long file of crosses bearing lions. Some had been so long dead that nothing was left against the wood but the remains of their skeletons; others which were half eaten away had their jaws twisted into horrible grimaces; there were some enormous ones; the shafts of the crosses bent beneath them, and they swayed in the wind, while bands of crows wheeled ceaselessly in the air above their heads. It was thus that the Carthaginian peasants avenged themselves when they captured a wild beast; they hoped to terrify the others by such an example. The Barbarians ceased their laughter, and were long lost in amazement. "What people is this," they thought, "that amuses itself by crucifying lions!"

They were, besides, especially the men of the North, vaguely uneasy, troubled, and already sick. They tore their hands with the darts of the aloes; great mosquitoes buzzed in their ears, and dysentry was breaking out in the army. They were weary at not yet seeing Sicca. They were afraid of losing themselves and of reaching the desert, the country of sands and terrors. Many even were unwilling to advance further. Others started back to Carthage.

At last on the seventh day, after following the base of a mountain for a long time, they turned abruptly to the right, and there then appeared a line of walls resting on white rocks and blending with them. Suddenly the entire city rose; blue, yellow, and white veils moved on the walls in the redness of the evening. These were the priestesses of Tanith, who had hastened hither to receive the men. They stood ranged along the rampart, striking tabourines, playing lyres, and shaking crotala, while the rays of the sun, setting behind them in the mountains of Numidia, shot between the strings of their lyres over which their naked arms were stretched. At intervals their instruments would become suddenly still, and a cry would break forth strident, precipitate, frenzied, continuous, a sort of barking which they made by striking both corners of the mouth with the tongue. Others, more motionless than the Sphynx, rested on their elbows with their chins on their hands, and darted their great black eyes upon the army as it ascended.

Although Sicca was a sacred town it could not hold such a multitude; the temple alone, with its appurtenances, occupied half of it. Accordingly the Barbarians established themselves at their ease on the plain; those who were disciplined in regular troops, and the rest according to nationality or their own fancy.

The Greeks ranged their tents of skin in parallel lines; the Iberians placed their canvas pavilions in a circle; the Gauls made themselves huts of planks; the Libyans cabins of dry stones, while the Negroes with their nails hollowed out trenches in the sand to sleep in. Many, not knowing where to go, wandered about among the baggage, and at nightfall lay down in their ragged mantles on the ground.

The plain, which was wholly bounded by mountains, expanded around them. Here and there a palm tree leaned over a sand hill, and pines and oaks flecked the sides of the precipices: sometimes the rain of a storm would hang from the sky like a long scarf, while the country everywhere was still covered with azure and serenity; then a warm wind would drive before it tornadoes of dust, and a stream would descend in cascades from the heights of Sicca, where, with its roofing of gold on its columns of brass, rose the temple of the Carthaginian Venus, the mistress of the land. She seemed to fill it with her soul. In such convulsions of the soil, such alternations of temperature, and such plays of light would she manifest the extravagance of her might with the beauty of her eternal smile. The mountains at their summits were crescent-shaped; others were like women's bosoms presenting their swelling breasts, and the Barbarians felt a heaviness that was full of delight weighing down their fatigues.

Spendius had bought a slave with the money brought him by his dromedary. The whole day long he lay asleep stretched before Matho's tent. Often he would awake, thinking in his dreams that he heard the whistling of the thongs; with a smile he would pass his hands over the scars on his legs at the place where the fetters had long been worn, and then he would fall asleep again.

Matho accepted his companionship, and when he went out Spendius would escort him like a lictor with a long sword on his thigh; or perhaps Matho would rest his arm carelessly on the other's shoulder, for Spendius was small.

One evening when they were passing together through the streets in the camp they perceived some men covered with white cloaks; among them was Narr' Havas, the prince of the Numidians. Matho started.

"Your sword!" he cried; "I will kill him!"

"Not yet!" said Spendius, restraining him. Narr' Havas was already advancing towards him.

He kissed both thumbs in token of alliance, showing nothing of the anger which he had experienced at the drunkenness of the feast; then he spoke at length against Carthage, but did not say what brought him among the Barbarians.

"Was it to betray them, or else the Republic?" Spendius asked himself; and as he expected to profit by every disorder, he felt grateful to Narr' Havas for the future perfidies of which he suspected him.

The chief of the Numidians remained amongst the Mercenaries. He appeared desirous of attaching Matho to himself. He sent him fat goats, gold dust, and ostrich feathers. The Libyan, who was amazed at such caresses, was in doubt whether to respond to them or to become exasperated at them. But Spendius pacified him, and Matho allowed himself to be ruled by the slave, remaining ever irresolute and in an unconquerable torpor, like those who have once taken a draught of which they are to die.

One morning when all three went out lion-hunting, Narr' Havas concealed a dagger in his cloak. Spendius kept continually behind him, and when they returned the dagger had not been drawn.

Another time Narr' Havas took them a long way off, as far as the boundaries of his kingdom. They came to a narrow gorge, and Narr' Havas smiled as he declared that he had forgotten the way. Spendius found it again.

But most frequently Matho would go off at sunrise, as melancholy as an augur, to wander about the country. He would stretch himself on the sand, and remain there motionless until the evening.

He consulted all the soothsayers in the army one after the other,— those who watch the trail of serpents, those who read the stars, and those who breathe upon the ashes of the dead. He swallowed galbanum, seseli, and viper's venom which freezes the heart; Negro women, singing barbarous words in the moonlight, pricked the skin of his forehead with golden stylets; he loaded himself with necklaces and charms; he invoked in turn Baal-Khamon, Moloch, the seven Kabiri, Tanith, and the Venus of the Greeks. He engraved a name upon a copper plate, and buried it in the sand at the threshold of his tent. Spendius used to hear him groaning and talking to himself.

One night he went in.

Matho, as naked as a corpse, was lying on a lion's skin flat on his stomach, with his face in both his hands; a hanging lamp lit up his armour, which was hooked on to the tent-pole above his head.

"You are suffering?" said the slave to him. "What is the matter with you? Answer me?" And he shook him by the shoulder calling him several times, "Master! master!"

At last Matho lifted large troubled eyes towards him.

"Listen!" he said in a low voice, and with a finger on his lips. "It is the wrath of the Gods! Hamilcar's daughter pursues me! I am afraid of her, Spendius!" He pressed himself close against his breast like a child terrified by a phantom. "Speak to me! I am sick! I want to get well! I have tried everything! But you, you perhaps know some stronger gods, or some resistless invocation?"

"For what purpose?" asked Spendius.

Striking his head with both his fists, he replied:

"To rid me of her!"

Then speaking to himself with long pauses he said:

"I am no doubt the victim of some holocaust which she has promised to the gods?—She holds me fast by a chain which people cannot see. If I walk, it is she that is advancing; when I stop, she is resting! Her eyes burn me, I hear her voice. She encompasses me, she penetrates me. It seems to me that she has become my soul!

"And yet between us there are, as it were, the invisible billows of a boundless ocean! She is far away and quite inaccessible! The splendour of her beauty forms a cloud of light around her, and at times I think that I have never seen her—that she does not exist—and that it is all a dream!"

Matho wept thus in the darkness; the Barbarians were sleeping. Spendius, as he looked at him, recalled the young men who once used to entreat him with golden cases in their hands, when he led his herd of courtesans through the towns; a feeling of pity moved him, and he said—

"Be strong, my master! Summon your will, and beseech the gods no more, for they turn not aside at the cries of men! Weeping like a coward! And you are not humiliated that a woman can cause you so much suffering?"

"Am I a child?" said Matho. "Do you think that I am moved by their faces and songs? We kept them at Drepanum to sweep out our stables. I have embraced them amid assaults, beneath falling ceilings, and while the catapult was still vibrating!—But she, Spendius, she!—"

The slave interrupted him:

"If she were not Hanno's daughter—"

"No!" cried Matho. "She has nothing in common with the daughters of other men! Have you seen her great eyes beneath her great eyebrows, like suns beneath triumphal arches? Think: when she appeared all the torches grew pale. Her naked breast shone here and there through the diamonds of her necklace; behind her you perceived as it were the odour of a temple, and her whole being emitted something that was sweeter than wine and more terrible than death. She walked, however, and then she stopped."

He remained gaping with his head cast down and his eyeballs fixed.

"But I want her! I need her! I am dying for her! I am transported with frenzied joy at the thought of clasping her in my arms, and yet I hate her, Spendius! I should like to beat her! What is to be done? I have a mind to sell myself and become her slave! You have been that! You were able to get sight of her; speak to me of her! Every night she ascends to the terrace of her palace, does she not? Ah! the stones must quiver beneath her sandals, and the stars bend down to see her!"

He fell back in a perfect frenzy, with a rattling in his throat like a wounded bull.

Then Matho sang: "He pursued into the forest the female monster, whose tail undulated over the dead leaves like a silver brook." And with lingering tones he imitated Salammbô's voice, while his outspread hands were held like two light hands on the strings of a lyre.

To all the consolations offered by Spendius, he repeated the same words; their nights were spent in these wailings and exhortations.

Matho sought to drown his thoughts in wine. After his fits of drunkenness he was more melancholy still. He tried to divert himself at huckle-bones, and lost the gold plates of his necklace one by one. He had himself taken to the servants of the Goddess; but he came down the hill sobbing, like one returning from a funeral.

Spendius, on the contrary, became more bold and gay. He was to be seen in the leafy taverns discoursing in the midst of the soldiers. He mended old cuirasses. He juggled with daggers. He went and gathered herbs in the fields for the sick. He was facetious, dexterous, full of invention and talk; the Barbarians grew accustomed to his services, and he came to be loved by them.

However, they were awaiting an ambassador from Carthage to bring them mules laden with baskets of gold; and ever beginning the same calculation over again, they would trace figures with their fingers in the sand. Every one was arranging his life beforehand; they would have concubines, slaves, lands; others intended to bury their treasure, or risk it on a vessel. But their tempers were provoked by want of employment; there were constant disputes between horse-soldiers and foot-soldiers, Barbarians and Greeks, while there was a never-ending din of shrill female voices.

Every day men came flocking in nearly naked, and with grass on their heads to protect them from the sun; they were the debtors of the rich Carthaginians and had been forced to till the lands of the latter, but had escaped. Libyans came pouring in with peasants ruined by the taxes, outlaws, and malefactors. Then the horde of traders, all the dealers in wine and oil, who were furious at not being paid, laid the blame upon the Republic. Spendius declaimed against it. Soon the provisions ran low; and there was talk of advancing in a body upon Carthage, and calling in the Romans.

One evening, at supper-time, dull cracked sounds were heard approaching, and something red appeared in the distance among the undulations of the soil.

It was a large purple litter, adorned with ostrich feathers at the corners. Chains of crystal and garlands of pearls beat against the closed hangings. It was followed by camels sounding the great bells that hung at their breasts, and having around them horsemen clad from shoulder to heel in armour of golden scales.

They halted three hundred paces from the camp to take their round bucklers, broad swords, and Boeotian helmets out of the cases which they carried behind their saddles. Some remained with the camels, while the others resumed their march. At last the ensigns of the Republic appeared, that is to say, staves of blue wood terminated in horses' heads or fir cones. The Barbarians all rose with applause; the women rushed towards the guards of the Legion and kissed their feet.

The litter advanced on the shoulders of twelve Negroes who walked in step with short, rapid strides; they went at random to right or left, being embarrassed by the tent-ropes, the animals that were straying about, or the tripods where food was being cooked. Sometimes a fat hand, laden with rings, would partially open the litter, and a hoarse voice would utter loud reproaches; then the bearers would stop and take a different direction through the camp.

But the purple curtains were raised, and a human head, impassible and bloated, was seen resting on a large pillow; the eyebrows, which were like arches of ebony, met each other at the points; golden dust sparkled in the frizzled hair, and the face was so wan that it looked as if it had been powdered with marble raspings. The rest of the body was concealed beneath the fleeces which filled the litter.

In the man so reclining the soldiers recognised the Suffet Hanno, he whose slackness had assisted to lose the battle of the Ægatian islands; and as to his victory at Hecatompylos over the Libyans, even if he did behave with clemency, thought the Barbarians, it was owing to cupidity, for he had sold all the captives on his own account, although he had reported their deaths to the Republic.

After seeking for some time a convenient place from which to harangue the soldiers, he made a sign; the litter stopped, and Hanno, supported by two slaves, put his tottering feet to the ground.

He wore boots of black felt strewn with silver moons. His legs were swathed in bands like those wrapped about a mummy, and the flesh crept through the crossings of the linen; his stomach came out beyond the scarlet jacket which covered his thighs; the folds of his neck fell down to his breast like the dewlaps of an ox; his tunic, which was painted with flowers, was bursting at the arm-pits; he wore a scarf, a girdle, and an ample black cloak with laced double-sleeves. But the abundance of his garments, his great necklace of blue stones, his golden clasps, and heavy earrings only rendered his deformity still more hideous. He might have been taken for some big idol rough-hewn in a block of stone; for a pale leprosy, which was spread over his whole body, gave him the appearance of an inert thing. His nose, however, which was hooked like a vulture's beak, was violently dilated to breathe in the air, and his little eyes, with their gummed lashes, shone with a hard and metallic lustre. He held a spatula of aloe-wood in his hand wherewith to scratch his skin.

At last two heralds sounded their silver horns; the tumult subsided, and Hanno commenced to speak.

He began with an eulogy of the gods and the Republic; the Barbarians ought to congratulate themselves on having served it. But they must show themselves more reasonable; times were hard, "and if a master has only three olives, is it not right that he should keep two for himself?"

The old Suffet mingled his speech in this way with proverbs and apologues, nodding his head the while to solicit some approval.

He spoke in Punic, and those surrounding him (the most alert, who had hastened thither without their arms), were Campanians, Gauls, and Greeks, so that no one in the crowd understood him. Hanno, perceiving this, stopped and reflected, swaying himself heavily from one leg to the other.

It occurred to him to call the captains together; then his heralds shouted the order in Greek, the language which, from the time of Xanthippus, had been used for commands in the Carthaginian armies.

The guards dispersed the mob of soldiers with strokes of the whip; and the captains of the Spartan phalanxes and the chiefs of the Barbarian cohorts soon arrived with the insignia of their rank, and in the armour of their nation. Night had fallen, a great tumult was spreading throughout the plain; fires were burning here and there; and the soldiers kept going from one to another asking what the matter was, and why the Suffet did not distribute the money?

He was setting the infinite burdens of the Republic before the captains. Her treasury was empty. The tribute to Rome was crushing her. "We are quite at a loss what to do! She is much to be pitied!"

From time to time he would rub his limbs with his aloe-wood spatula, or perhaps he would break off to drink a ptisan made of the ashes of a weasel and asparagus boiled in vinegar from a silver cup handed to him by a slave; then he would wipe his lips with a scarlet napkin and resume:

"What used to be worth a shekel of silver is now worth three shekels of gold, while the cultivated lands which were abandoned during the war bring in nothing! Our purpura fisheries are nearly gone, and even pearls are becoming exhorbitant; we have scarcely unguents enough for the service of the gods! As for the things of the table, I shall say nothing about them; it is a calamity! For want of galleys we are without spices, and it is a matter of great difficulty to procure silphium on account of the rebellions on the Cyrenian frontier. Sicily, where so many slaves used to be had, is now closed to us! Only yesterday I gave more money for a bather and four scullions than I used at one time to give for a pair of elephants!"

He unrolled a long piece of papyrus; and, without omitting a single figure, read all the expenses that the government had incurred; so much for repairing the temples, for paving the streets, for the construction of vessels, for the coral-fisheries, for the enlargement of the Syssitia, and for engines in the mines in the country of the Cantabrians.

But the captains understood Punic as little as the soldiers, although the Mercenaries saluted one another in that language. It was usual to place a few Carthaginian officers in the Barbarian armies to act as interpreters; after the war they had concealed themselves through fear of vengeance, and Hanno had not thought of taking them with him; his hollow voice, too, was lost in the wind.

The Greeks, girthed in their iron waist-belts, strained their ears as they strove to guess at his words, while the mountaineers, covered with furs like bears, looked at him with distrust, or yawned as they leaned on their brass-nailed clubs. The heedless Gauls sneered as they shook their lofty heads of hair, and the men of the desert listened motionless, cowled in their garments of grey wool; others kept coming up behind; the guards, crushed by the mob, staggered on their horses; the Negroes held out burning fir branches at arm's length; and the big Carthaginian, mounted on a grassy hillock, continued his harangue.

The Barbarians, however, were growing impatient; murmuring arose, and every one apostrophized him. Hanno gesticulated with his spatula; and those who wished the others to be quiet shouted still more loudly, thereby adding to the din.

Suddenly a man of mean appearance bounded to Hanno's feet, snatched up a herald's trumpet, blew it, and Spendius (for it was he) announced that he was going to say something of importance. At this declaration, which was rapidly uttered in five different languages, Greek, Latin, Gallic, Libyan and Balearic, the captains, half laughing and half surprised, replied: "Speak! Speak!"

Spendius hesitated; he trembled; at last, addressing the Libyans who were the most numerous, he said to them:

"You have all heard this man's horrible threats!"

Hanno made no exclamation, therefore he did not understand Libyan; and, to carry on the experiment, Spendius repeated the same phrase in the other Barbarian dialects.

They looked at one another in astonishment; then, as by a tacit agreement, and believing perhaps that they had understood, they bent their heads in token of assent.

Then Spendius began in vehement tones:

"He said first that all the Gods of the other nations were but dreams besides the Gods of Carthage! He called you cowards, thieves, liars, dogs, and the sons of dogs! But for you (he said that!) the Republic would not be forced to pay excessive tribute to the Romans; and through your excesses you have drained it of perfumes, aromatics, slaves, and silphium, for you are in league with the nomads on the Cyrenian frontier! But the guilty shall be punished! He read the enumeration of their torments; they shall be made to work at the paving of the streets, at the equipment of the vessels, at the adornment of the Syssitia, while the rest shall be sent to scrape the earth in the mines in the country of the Cantabrians."

Spendius repeated the same statements to the Gauls, Greeks, Campanians and Balearians. The Mercenaries, recognising several of the proper names which had met their ears, were convinced that he was accurately reporting the Suffet's speech. A few cried out to him, "You lie!" but their voices were drowned in the tumult of the rest; Spendius added:

"Have you not seen that he has left a reserve of his horse-soldiers outside the camp? At a given signal they will hasten hither to slay you all."

The Barbarians turned in that direction, and as the crowd was then scattering, there appeared in the midst of them, and advancing with the slowness of a phantom, a human being, bent, lean, entirely naked, and covered down to his flanks with long hair bristling with dried leaves, dust and thorns. About his loins and his knees he had wisps of straw and linen rags; his soft and earthy skin hung on his emaciated limbs like tatters on dried boughs; his hands trembled with a continuous quivering, and as he walked he leaned on a staff of olive-wood.

He reached the Negroes who were bearing the torches. His pale gums were displayed in a sort of idiotic titter; his large, scared eyes gazed upon the crowd of Barbarians around him.

But uttering a cry of terror he threw himself behind them, shielding himself with their bodies. "There they are! There they are!" he stammered out, pointing to the Suffet's guards, who were motionless in their glittering armour. Their horses, dazzled by the light of the torches which crackled in the darkness, were pawing the ground; the human spectre struggled and howled:

"They have killed them!"

At these words, which were screamed in Balearic, some Balearians came up and recognised him; without answering them he repeated:

"Yes, all killed, all! crushed like grapes! The fine young men! the slingers! my companions and yours!"

They gave him wine to drink, and he wept; then he launched forth into speech.

Spendius could scarcely repress his joy, as he explained the horrors related by Zarxas to the Greeks and Libyans; he could not believe them, so appropriately did they come in. The Balearians grew pale as they learned how their companions had perished.

It was a troop of three hundred slingers who had disembarked the evening before, and had on that day slept too late. When they reached the square of Khamon the Barbarians were gone, and they found themselves defenceless, their clay bullets having been put on the camels with the rest of the baggage. They were allowed to advance into the street of Satheb as far as the brass sheathed oaken gate; then the people with a single impulse had sprung upon them.

Indeed, the soldiers remembered a great shout; Spendius, who was flying at the head of the columns, had not heard it.

Then the corpses were placed in the arms of the Patæc gods that fringed the temple of Khamon. They were upbraided with all the crimes of the Mercenaries; their gluttony, their thefts, their impiety, their disdain, and the murder of the fishes in Salammbô's garden. Their bodies were subjected to infamous mutilations; the priests burned their hair in order to torture their souls; they were hung up in pieces in the meat-shops; some even buried their teeth in them, and in the evening funeral-piles were kindled at the cross-ways to finish them.

These were the flames that had gleamed from a distance across the lake. But some houses having taken fire, any dead or dying that remained were speedily thrown over the walls; Zarxas had remained among the reeds on the edge of the lake until the following day; then he had wandered about through the country, seeking for the army by the footprints in the dust. In the morning he hid himself in caves; in the evening he resumed his march with his bleeding wounds, famished, sick, living on roots and carrion; at last one day he perceived lances on the horizon, and he had followed them, for his reason was disturbed through his terrors and miseries.

The indignation of the soldiers, restrained so long as he was speaking, broke forth like a tempest; they were going to massacre the guards together with the Suffet. A few interposed, saying that they ought to hear him and know at least whether they should be paid. Then they all cried: "Our money!" Hanno replied that he had brought it.

They ran to the outposts, and the Suffet's baggage arrived in the midst of the tents, pressed forward by the Barbarians. Without waiting for the slaves, they very quickly unfastened the baskets; in them they found hyacinth robes, sponges, scrapers, brushes, perfumes, and antimony pencils for painting the eyes—all belonging to the guards, who were rich men and accustomed to such refinements. Next they uncovered a large bronze tub on a camel: it belonged to the Suffet who had it for bathing in during his journey; for he had taken all manner of precautions, even going so far as to bring caged weasels from Hecatompylos, which were burnt alive to make his ptisan. But, as his malady gave him a great appetite, there were also many comestibles and many wines, pickle, meats and fishes preserved in honey, with little pots of Commagene, or melted goose-fat covered with snow and chopped straw. There was a considerable supply of it; the more they opened the baskets the more they found, and laughter arose like conflicting waves.

As to the pay of the Mercenaries it nearly filled two esparto-grass baskets; there were even visible in one of them some of the leathern discs which the Republic used to economise its specie; and as the Barbarians appeared greatly surprised, Hanno told them that, their accounts being very difficult, the Ancients had not had leisure to examine them. Meanwhile they had sent them this.

Then everything was in disorder and confusion: mules, serving men, litter, provisions, and baggage. The soldiers took the coin in the bags to stone Hanno. With great difficulty he was able to mount an ass; and he fled, clinging to its hair, howling, weeping, shaken, bruised, and calling down the curse of all the gods upon the army. His broad necklace of precious stones rebounded up to his ears. His cloak which was too long, and which trailed behind him, he kept on with his teeth, and from afar the Barbarians shouted at him, "Begone coward! pig! sink of Moloch! sweat your gold and your plague! quicker! quicker!" The routed escort galloped beside him.

But the fury of the Barbarians did not abate. They remembered that several of them who had set out for Carthage had not returned; no doubt they had been killed. So much injustice exasperated them, and they began to pull up the stakes of their tents, to roll up their cloaks, and to bridle their horses; every one took his helmet and sword, and instantly all was ready. Those who had no arms rushed into the woods to cut staves.

Day dawned; the people of Sicca were roused, and stirring in the streets. "They are going to Carthage," said they, and the rumour of this soon spread through the country.

From every path and every ravine men arose. Shepherds were seen running down from the mountains.

Then, when the Barbarians had set out, Spendius circled the plain, riding on a Punic stallion, and attended by his slave, who led a third horse.

A single tent remained. Spendius entered it.

"Up, master! rise! we are departing!"

"And where are you going?" asked Matho.

"To Carthage!" cried Spendius.

Matho bounded upon the horse which the slave held at the door.

III

Salammbô

The moon was rising just above the waves, and on the town which was still wrapped in darkness there glittered white and luminous specks:—the pole of a chariot, a dangling rag of linen, the corner of a wall, or a golden necklace on the bosom of a god. The glass balls on the roofs of the temples beamed like great diamonds here and there. But ill-defined ruins, piles of black earth, and gardens formed deeper masses in the gloom, and below Malqua fishermen's nets stretched from one house to another like gigantic bats spreading their wings. The grinding of the hydraulic wheels which conveyed water to the highest storys of the palaces, was no longer heard; and the camels, lying ostrich fashion on their stomachs, rested peacefully in the middle of the terraces. The porters were asleep in the streets on the thresholds of the houses; the shadows of the colossuses stretched across the deserted squares; occasionally in the distance the smoke of a still burning sacrifice would escape through the bronze tiling, and the heavy breeze would waft the odours of aromatics blended with the scent of the sea and the exhalation from the sun-heated walls. The motionless waves shone around Carthage, for the moon was spreading her light at once upon the mountain-circled gulf and upon the lake of Tunis, where flamingoes formed long rose-coloured lines amid the banks of sand, while further on beneath the catacombs the great salt lagoon shimmered like a piece of silver. The blue vault of heaven sank on the horizon in one direction into the dustiness of the plains, and in the other into the mists of the sea, and on the summit of the Acropolis, the pyramidal cypress trees, fringing the temple of Eschmoun, swayed murmuring like the regular waves that beat slowly along the mole beneath the ramparts.

Salammbô ascended to the terrace of her palace, supported by a female slave who carried an iron dish filled with live coals.

In the middle of the terrace there was a small ivory bed covered with lynx skins, and cushions made with the feathers of the parrot, a fatidical animal consecrated to the gods; and at the four corners rose four long perfuming-pans filled with nard, incense, cinnamomum, and myrrh. The slave lit the perfumes. Salammbô looked at the polar star; she slowly saluted the four points of heaven, and knelt down on the ground in the azure dust which was strewn with golden stars in imitation of the firmament. Then with both elbows against her sides, her fore-arms straight and her hands open, she threw back her head beneath the rays of the moon, and said:

"O Rabetna!—Baalet!—Tanith!" and her voice was lengthened in a plaintive fashion as if calling to some one. "Anaïtis! Astarte! Derceto! Astoreth! Mylitta! Athara! Elissa! Tiratha!—By the hidden symbols, by the resounding sistra,—by the furrows of the earth,—by the eternal silence and by the eternal fruitfulness,—mistress of the gloomy sea and of the azure shores, O Queen of the watery world, all hail!"

She swayed her whole body twice or thrice, and then cast herself face downwards in the dust with both arms outstretched.

But the slave nimbly raised her, for according to the rites someone must catch the suppliant at the moment of his prostration; this told him that the gods accepted him, and Salammbô's nurse never failed in this pious duty.

Some merchants from Darytian Gætulia had brought her to Carthage when quite young, and after her enfranchisement she would not forsake her old masters, as was shown by her right ear, which was pierced with a large hole. A petticoat of many-coloured stripes fitted closely on her hips, and fell to her ankles, where two tin rings clashed together. Her somewhat flat face was yellow like her tunic. Silver bodkins of great length formed a sun behind her head. She wore a coral button on the nostril, and she stood beside the bed more erect than a Hermes, and with her eyelids cast down.

Salammbô walked to the edge of the terrace; her eyes swept the horizon for an instant, and then were lowered upon the sleeping town, while the sigh that she heaved swelled her bosom, and gave an undulating movement to the whole length of the long white simar which hung without clasp or girdle about her. Her curved and painted sandals were hidden beneath a heap of emeralds, and a net of purple thread was filled with her disordered hair.

But she raised her head to gaze upon the moon, and murmured, mingling her speech with fragments of hymns:

"How lightly turnest thou, supported by the impalpable ether! It brightens about thee, and 'Tis the stir of thine agitation that distributes the winds and fruitful dews. According as thou dost wax and wane the eyes of cats and spots of panthers lengthen or grow short. Wives shriek thy name in the pangs of childbirth! Thou makest the shells to swell, the wine to bubble, and the corpse to putrefy! Thou formest the pearls at the bottom of the sea!

"And every germ, O goddess! ferments in the dark depths of thy moisture.

"When thou appearest, quietness is spread abroad upon the earth; the flowers close, the waves are soothed, wearied man stretches his breast toward thee, and the world with its oceans and mountains looks at itself in thy face as in a mirror. Thou art white, gentle, luminous, immaculate, helping, purifying, serene!"

The crescent of the moon was then over the mountain of the Hot Springs, in the hollow formed by its two summits, on the other side of the gulf. Below it there was a little star, and all around it a pale circle. Salammbô went on:

"But thou art a terrible mistress!—Monsters, terrifying phantoms, and lying dreams come from thee; thine eyes devour the stones of buildings, and the apes are ever ill each time thou growest young again.

"Whither goest thou? Why dost thou change thy forms continually? Now, slender and curved thou glidest through space like a mastless galley; and then, amid the stars, thou art like a shepherd keeping his flock. Shining and round, thou dost graze the mountain-tops like the wheel of a chariot.

"O Tanith! thou dost love me? I have looked so much on thee! But no! thou sailest through thine azure, and I—I remain on the motionless earth.

"Taanach, take your nebal and play softly on the silver string, for my heart is sad!"

The slave lifted a sort of harp of ebony wood, taller than herself, and triangular in shape like a delta; she fixed the point in a crystal globe, and with both hands began to play.

The sounds followed one another hurried and deep, like the buzzing of bees, and with increasing sonorousness floated away into the night with the complaining of the waves, and the rustling of the great trees on the summit of the Acropolis.

"Hush!" cried Salammbô.

"What ails you, mistress? The blowing of the breeze, the passing of a cloud, everything disquiets you just now!"

"I do not know," she said.

"You are wearied with too long prayers!"

"Oh! Tanaach, I would fain be dissolved in them like a flower in wine!"

"Perhaps it is the smoke of your perfumes?"

"No!" said Salammbô; "the spirit of the gods dwells in fragrant odours."

Then the slave spoke to her of her father. It was thought that he had gone towards the amber country, behind the pillars of Melkarth. "But if he does not return," she said, "you must nevertheless, since it was his will, choose a husband among the sons of the Ancients, and then your grief will pass away in a man's arms."

"Why?" asked the young girl. All those that she had seen had horrified her with their fallow-deer laughter and their coarse limbs.

"Sometimes, Tanaach, from the depths of my being there exhale as it were hot fumes heavier than the vapours from a volcano. Voices call me, a globe of fire rolls and mounts within my bosom, it stifles me, I am at the point of death; and then, something sweet, flowing from my brow to my feet, passes through my flesh—it is a caress enfolding me, and I feel myself crushed as if some god were stretched upon me. Oh! would that I could lose myself in the mists of the night, the waters of the fountains, the sap of the trees, that I could issue from my body, and be but a breath, or a ray, and glide, mount up to thee, O Mother!"

She raised her arms to their full length, arching her form, which in its long garment was as pale and light as the moon. Then she fell back, panting, on the ivory couch; but Taanach passed an amber necklace with dolphin's teeth about her neck to banish terrors, and Salammbô said in an almost stifled voice: "Go and bring me Schahabarim."

Her father had not wished her to enter the college of priestesses, nor even to be made at all acquainted with the popular Tanith. He was reserving her for some alliance that might serve his political ends; so that Salammbô lived alone in the midst of the palace. Her mother was long since dead.

She had grown up with abstinences, fastings and purifications, always surrounded by grave and exquisite things, her body saturated with perfumes, and her soul filled with prayers. She had never tasted wine, nor eaten meat, nor touched an unclean animal, nor set her heels in the house of death.

She knew nothing of obscene images, for as each god was manifested in different forms, the same principle often received the witness of contradictory cults, and Salammbô worshipped the goddess in her sidereal presentation. An influence had descended upon the maiden from the moon; when the planet passed diminishing away, Salammbô grew weak. She languished the whole day long, and revived at evening. During an eclipse she nearly died.

But Rabetna, in jealousy, revenged herself for the virginity withdrawn from her sacrifices, and she tormented Salammbô with possessions, all the stronger for being vague, which were spread through this belief and excited by it.

Unceasingly was Hamilcar's daughter disquieted about Tanith. She had learned her adventures, her travels, and all her names, which she would repeat without their having any distinct signification for her. In order to penetrate into the depths of her dogma, she wished to become acquainted, in the most secret part of the temple, with the old idol in the magnificent mantle, whereon depended the destinies of Carthage, for the idea of a god did not stand out clearly from his representation, and to hold, or even see the image of one, was to take away part of his virtue, and in a measure to rule him.

But Salammbô turned around. She had recognised the sound of the golden bells which Schahabarim wore at the hem of his garment.

He ascended the staircases; then at the threshold of the terrace he stopped and folded his arms.

His sunken eyes shone like the lamps of a sepulchre; his long thin body floated in its linen robe which was weighted by the bells, the latter alternating with balls of emeralds at his heels. He had feeble limbs, an oblique skull and a pointed chin; his skin seemed cold to the touch, and his yellow face, which was deeply furrowed with wrinkles, was as if it contracted in a longing, in an everlasting grief.

He was the high priest of Tanith, and it was he who had educated Salammbô.

"Speak!" he said. "What will you?"

"I hoped—you had almost promised me—" She stammered and was confused; then suddenly: "Why do you despise me? what have I forgotten in the rites? You are my master, and you told me that no one was so accomplished in the things pertaining to the goddess as I; but there are some of which you will not speak. Is it so, O father?"

Schahabarim remembered Hamilcar's orders, and replied:

"No, I have nothing more to teach you!"

"A genius," she resumed, "impels me to this love. I have climbed the steps of Eschmoun, god of the planets and intelligences; I have slept beneath the golden olive of Melkarth, patron of the Tyrian colonies; I have pushed open the doors of Baal-Khamon, the enlightener and fertiliser; I have sacrificed to the subterranean Kabiri, to the gods of woods, winds, rivers and mountains; but, can you understand? they are all too far away, too high, too insensible, while she—I feel her mingled in my life; she fills my soul, and I quiver with inward startings, as though she were leaping in order to escape. Methinks I am about to hear her voice, and see her face, lightnings dazzle me and then I sink back again into the darkness."

Schahabarim was silent. She entreated him with suppliant looks. At last he made a sign for the dismissal of the slave, who was not of Chanaanitish race. Taanach disappeared, and Schahabarim, raising one arm in the air, began:

"Before the gods darkness alone was, and a breathing stirred dull and indistinct as the conscience of a man in a dream. It contracted, creating Desire and Cloud, and from Desire and Cloud there issued primitive Matter. This was a water, muddy, black, icy and deep. It contained senseless monsters, incoherent portions of the forms to be born, which are painted on the walls of the sanctuaries.

"Then Matter condensed. It became an egg. It burst. One half formed the earth and the other the firmament. Sun, moon, winds and clouds appeared, and at the crash of the thunder intelligent creatures awoke. Then Eschmoun spread himself in the starry sphere; Khamon beamed in the sun; Melkarth thrust him with his arms behind Gades; the Kabiri descended beneath the volcanoes, and Rabetna like a nurse bent over the world pouring out her light like milk, and her night like a mantle."

"And then?" she said.

He had related the secret of the origins to her, to divert her from sublimer prospects; but the maiden's desire kindled again at his last words, and Schahabarim, half yielding resumed:

"She inspires and governs the loves of men."

"The loves of men!" repeated Salammbô dreamily.

"She is the soul of Carthage," continued the priest; "and although she is everywhere diffused, it is here that she dwells, beneath the sacred veil."

"O father!" cried Salammbô, "I shall see her, shall I not? you will bring me to her! I had long been hesitating; I am devoured with curiosity to see her form. Pity! help me! let us go?"

He repulsed her with a vehement gesture that was full of pride.

"Never! Do you not know that it means death? The hermaphrodite Baals are unveiled to us alone who are men in understanding and women in weakness. Your desire is sacrilege; be satisfied with the knowledge that you possess!"

She fell upon her knees placing two fingers against her ears in token of repentance; and crushed by the priest's words, and filled at once with anger against him, with terror and humiliation, she burst into sobs. Schahabarim remained erect, and more insensible than the stones of the terrace. He looked down upon her quivering at his feet, and felt a kind of joy on seeing her suffer for his divinity whom he himself could not wholly embrace. The birds were already singing, a cold wind was blowing, and little clouds were drifting in the paling sky.

Suddenly he perceived on the horizon, behind Tunis, what looked like slight mists trailing along the ground; then these became a great curtain of dust extending perpendicularly, and, amid the whirlwinds of the thronging mass, dromedaries' heads, lances and shields appeared. It was the army of the Barbarians advancing upon Carthage.

IV

Beneath the Walls of Carthage

S ome country people, riding on asses or running on foot, arrived in the town, pale, breathless, and mad with fear. They were flying before the army. It had accomplished the journey from Sicca in three days, in order to reach Carthage and wholly exterminate it.

The gates were shut. The Barbarians appeared almost immediately; but they stopped in the middle of the isthmus, on the edge of the lake.

At first they made no hostile announcement. Several approached with palm branches in their hands. They were driven back with arrows, so great was the terror.

In the morning and at nightfall prowlers would sometimes wander along the walls. A little man carefully wrapped in a cloak, and with his face concealed beneath a very low visor, was especially noticed. He would remain whole hours gazing at the aqueduct, and so persistently that he doubtless wished to mislead the Carthaginians as to his real designs. Another man, a sort of giant who walked bareheaded, used to accompany him.

But Carthage was defended throughout the whole breadth of the isthmus: first by a trench, then by a grassy rampart, and lastly by a wall thirty cubits high, built of freestone, and in two storys. It contained stables for three hundred elephants with stores for their caparisons, shackles, and food; other stables again for four thousand horses with supplies of barley and harness, and barracks for twenty thousand soldiers with armour and all materials of war. Towers rose from the second story, all provided with battlements, and having bronze bucklers hung on cramps on the outside.

This first line of wall gave immediate shelter to Malqua, the sailors' and dyers' quarter. Masts might be seen whereon purple sails were drying, and on the highest terraces clay furnaces for heating the pickle were visible.

Behind, the lofty houses of the city rose in an ampitheatre of cubical form. They were built of stone, planks, shingle, reeds, shells, and beaten earth. The woods belonging to the temples were like lakes of verdure in this mountain of diversely-coloured blocks. It was levelled at unequal distances by the public squares, and was cut from top to bottom by countless intersecting lanes. The enclosures of the three old quarters which are now lost might be distinguished; they rose here and there like great reefs, or extended in enormous fronts, blackened, half-covered with flowers, and broadly striped by the casting of filth, while streets passed through their yawning apertures like rivers beneath bridges.

The hill of the Acropolis, in the centre of Byrsa, was hidden beneath a disordered array of monuments. There were temples with wreathed columns bearing bronze capitals and metal chains, cones of dry stones with bands of azure, copper cupolas, marble architraves, Babylonian buttresses, obelisks poised on their points like inverted torches. Peristyles reached to pediments; volutes were displayed through colonnades; granite walls supported tile partitions; the whole mounting, half-hidden, the one above the other in a marvellous and incomprehensible fashion. In it might be felt the succession of the ages, and, as it were, the memorials of forgotten fatherlands.

Behind the Acropolis the Mappalian road, which was lined with tombs, extended through red lands in a straight line from the shore to the catacombs; then spacious dwellings occurred at intervals in the gardens, and this third quarter, Megara, which was the new town, reached as far as the edge of the cliff, where rose a giant pharos that blazed forth every night.

In this fashion was Carthage displayed before the soldiers quartered in the plain.

They could recognise the markets and crossways in the distance, and disputed with one another as to the sites of the temples. Khamon's, fronting the Syssitia, had golden tiles; Melkarth, to the left of Eschmoun, had branches of coral on its roofing; beyond, Tanith's copper cupola swelled among the palm trees; the dark Moloch was below the cisterns, in the direction of the pharos. At the angles of the pediments, on the tops of the walls, at the corners of the squares, everywhere, divinities with hideous heads might be seen, colossal or squat, with enormous bellies, or immoderately flattened, opening their jaws, extending their arms, and holding forks, chains or javelins in their hands; while the blue of the sea stretched away behind the streets which were rendered still steeper by the perspective.

They were filled from morning till evening with a tumultuous people; young boys shaking little bells, shouted at the doors of the baths; the shops for hot drinks smoked, the air resounded with the noise of anvils, the white cocks, sacred to the Sun, crowed on the terraces, the oxen that were being slaughtered bellowed in the temples, slaves ran about with baskets on their heads; and in the depths of the porticoes a priest would sometimes appear, draped in a dark cloak, barefooted, and wearing a pointed cap.

The spectacle afforded by Carthage irritated the Barbarians; they admired it and execrated it, and would have liked both to annihilate it and to dwell in it. But what was there in the Military Harbour defended by a triple wall? Then behind the town, at the back of Megara, and higher than the Acropolis, appeared Hamilcar's palace.

Matho's eyes were directed thither every moment. He would ascend the olive trees and lean over with his hand spread out above his eyebrows. The gardens were empty, and the red door with its black cross remained constantly shut.

More than twenty times he walked round the ramparts, seeking some breach by which he might enter. One night he threw himself into the gulf and swam for three hours at a stretch. He reached the foot of the Mappalian quarter and tried to climb up the face of the cliff. He covered his knees with blood, broke his nails, and then fell back into the waves and returned.

His impotence exasperated him. He was jealous of this Carthage which contained Salammbô, as if of some one who had possessed her. His nervelessness left him to be replaced by a mad and continual eagerness for action. With flaming cheek, angry eyes, and hoarse voice, he would walk with rapid strides through the camp; or seated on the shore he would scour his great sword with sand. He shot arrows at the passing vultures. His heart overflowed into frenzied speech.

"Give free course to your wrath like a runaway chariot," said Spendius. "Shout, blaspheme, ravage and slay. Grief is allayed with blood, and since you cannot sate your love, gorge your hate; it will sustain you!"

Matho resumed the command of his soldiers. He drilled them pitilessly. He was respected for his courage and especially for his strength. Moreover he inspired a sort of mystic dread, and it was believed that he conversed at night with phantoms. The other captains were animated by his example. The army soon grew disciplined. From their houses the Carthaginians could hear the bugle-flourishes that regulated their exercises. At last the Barbarians drew near.

To crush them in the isthmus it would have been necessary for two armies to take them simultaneously in the rear, one disembarking at the end of the gulf of Utica, and the second at the mountain of the Hot Springs. But what could be done with the single sacred Legion, mustering at most six thousand men? If the enemy bent towards the east they would join the nomads and intercept the commerce of the desert. If they fell back to the west, Numidia would rise. Finally, lack of provisions would sooner or later lead them to devastate the surrounding country like grasshoppers, and the rich trembled for their fine country-houses, their vineyards and their cultivated lands.

Hanno proposed atrocious and impracticable measures, such as promising a heavy sum for every Barbarian's head, or setting fire to their camp with ships and machines. His colleague Gisco, on the other hand, wished them to be paid. But the Ancients detested him owing to his popularity; for they dreaded the risk of a master, and through terror of monarchy strove to weaken whatever contributed to it or might re-establish it.

Outside the fortification there were people of another race and of unknown origin, all hunters of the porcupine, and eaters of shell-fish and serpents. They used to go into caves to catch hyenas alive, and amuse themselves by making them run in the evening on the sands of Megara between the stelæ of the tombs. Their huts, which were made of mud and wrack, hung on the cliff like swallows' nests. There they lived, without government and without gods, pell-mell, completely naked, at once feeble and fierce, and execrated by the people of all time on account of their unclean food. One morning the sentries perceived that they were all gone.

At last some members of the Great Council arrived at a decision. They came to the camp without necklaces or girdles, and in open sandals like neighbours. They walked at a quiet pace, waving salutations to the captains, or stopped to speak to the soldiers, saying that all was finished and that justice was about to be done to their claims.

Many of them saw a camp of Mercenaries for the first time. Instead of the confusion which they had pictured to themselves, there prevailed everywhere terrible silence and order. A grassy rampart formed a lofty wall round the army immovable by the shock of catapults. The ground in the streets was sprinkled with fresh water; through the holes in the tents they could perceive tawny eyeballs gleaming in the shade. The piles of pikes and hanging panoplies dazzled them like mirrors. They conversed in low tones. They were afraid of upsetting something with their long robes.

The soldiers requested provisions, undertaking to pay for them out of the money that was due.

Oxen, sheep, guinea fowl, fruit and lupins were sent to them, with smoked scombri, that excellent scombri which Carthage dispatched to every port. But they walked scornfully around the magnificent cattle, and disparaging what they coveted, offered the worth of a pigeon for a ram, or the price of a pomegranate for three goats. The Eaters of Uncleanness came forward as arbitrators, and declared that they were being duped. Then they drew their swords with threats to slay.

Commissaries of the Great Council wrote down the number of years for which pay was due to each soldier. But it was no longer possible to know how many Mercenaries had been engaged, and the Ancients were dismayed at the enormous sum which they would have to pay. The reserve of silphium must be sold, and the trading towns taxed; the Mercenaries would grow impatient; Tunis was already with them; and the rich, stunned by Hanno's ragings and his colleague's reproaches, urged any citizens who might know a Barbarian to go to see him immediately in order to win back his friendship, and to speak him fair. Such a show of confidence would soothe them.

Traders, scribes, workers in the arsenal, and whole families visited the Barbarians.

The soldiers allowed all the Carthaginians to come in, but by a single passage so narrow that four men abreast jostled one another in it. Spendius, standing against the barrier, had them carefully searched; facing him Matho was examining the multitude, trying to recognise some one whom he might have seen at Salammbô's palace.

The camp was like a town, so full of people and of movement was it. The two distinct crowds mingled without blending, one dressed in linen or wool, with felt caps like fir-cones, and the other clad in iron and wearing helmets. Amid serving men and itinerant vendors there moved women of all nations, as brown as ripe dates, as greenish as olives, as yellow as oranges, sold by sailors, picked out of dens, stolen from caravans, taken in the sacking of towns, women that were jaded with love so long as they were young, and plied with blows when they were old, and that died in routs on the roadsides among the baggage and the abandoned beasts of burden. The wives of the nomads had square, tawny robes of dromedary's hair swinging at their heels; musicians from Cyrenaica, wrapped in violet gauze and with painted eyebrows, sang, squatting on mats; old Negresses with hanging breasts gathered the animals' dung that was drying in the sun to light their fires; the Syracusan women had golden plates in their hair; the Lusitanians had necklaces of shells; the Gauls wore wolf skins upon their white bosoms; and sturdy children, vermin-covered, naked and uncircumcised, butted with their heads against passers-by, or came behind them like young tigers to bite their hands.

The Carthaginians walked through the camp, surprised at the quantities of things with which it was running over. The most miserable were melancholy, and the rest dissembled their anxiety.

The soldiers struck them on the shoulder, and exhorted them to be gay. As soon as they saw any one, they invited him to their amusements. If they were playing at discus, they would manage to crush his feet, or if at boxing to fracture his jaw with the very first blow. The slingers terrified the Carthaginians with their slings, the Psylli with their vipers, and the horsemen with their horses, while their victims, addicted as they were to peaceful occupations, bent their heads and tried to smile at all these outrages. Some, in order to show themselves brave, made signs that they should like to become soldiers. They were set to split wood and to curry mules. They were buckled up in armour, and rolled like casks through the streets of the camp. Then, when they were about to leave, the Mercenaries plucked out their hair with grotesque contortions.

But many, from foolishness or prejudice, innocently believed that all the Carthaginians were very rich, and they walked behind them entreating them to grant them something. They requested everything that they thought fine: a ring, a girdle, sandals, the fringe of a robe, and when the despoiled Carthaginian cried—"But I have nothing left. What do you want?" they would reply, "Your wife!" Others even said, "Your life!"

The military accounts were handed to the captains, read to the soldiers, and definitively approved. Then they claimed tents; they received them. Next the polemarchs of the Greeks demanded some of the handsome suits of armour that were manufactured at Carthage; the Great Council voted sums of money for their purchase. But it was only fair, so the horsemen pretended, that the Republic should indemnify them for their horses; one had lost three at such a siege, another, five during such a march, another, fourteen in the precipices. Stallions from Hecatompylos were offered to them, but they preferred money.

Next they demanded that they should be paid in money (in pieces of money, and not in leathern coins) for all the corn that was owing to them, and at the highest price that it had fetched during the war; so that they exacted four hundred times as much for a measure of meal as they had given for a sack of wheat. Such injustice was exasperating; but it was necessary, nevertheless, to submit.

Then the delegates from the soldiers and from the Great Council swore renewed friendship by the Genius of Carthage and the gods of the Barbarians. They exchanged excuses and caresses with oriental demonstrativeness and verbosity. Then the soldiers claimed, as a proof of friendship, the punishment of those who had estranged them from the Republic.

Their meaning, it was pretended, was not understood, and they explained themselves more clearly by saying that they must have Hanno's head.

Several times a day, they left their camp, and walked along the foot of the walls, shouting a demand that the Suffet's head should be thrown to them, and holding out their robes to receive it.

The Great Council would perhaps have given way but for a last exaction, more outrageous than the rest; they demanded maidens, chosen from illustrious families, in marriage for their chiefs. It was an idea which had emanated from Spendius, and which many thought most simple and practicable. But the assumption of their desire to mix with Punic blood made the people indignant; and they were bluntly told that they were to receive no more. Then they exclaimed that they had been deceived, and that if their pay did not arrive within three days, they would themselves go and take it in Carthage.

The bad faith of the Mercenaries was not so complete as their enemies thought. Hamilcar had made them extravagant promises, vague, it is true, but at the same time solemn and reiterated. They might have believed that when they disembarked at Carthage the town would be abandoned to them, and that they should have treasures divided among them; and when they saw that scarcely their wages would be paid, the disillusion touched their pride no less than their greed.

Had not Dionysius, Pyrrhus, Agathocles, and the generals of Alexander furnished examples of marvellous good fortune? Hercules, whom the Chanaanites confounded with the sun, was the ideal which shone on the horizon of armies. They knew that simple soldiers had worn diadems, and the echoes of crumbling empires would furnish dreams to the Gaul in his oak forest, to the Ethiopian amid his sands. But there was a nation always ready to turn courage to account; and the robber driven from his tribe, the patricide wandering on the roads, the perpetrator of sacrilege pursued by the gods, all who were starving or in despair strove to reach the port where the Carthaginian broker was recruiting soldiers. Usually the Republic kept its promises. This time, however, the eagerness of its avarice had brought it into perilous disgrace. Numidians, Libyans, the whole of Africa was about to fall upon Carthage. Only the sea was open to it, and there it met with the Romans; so that, like a man assailed by murderers, it felt death all around it.

It was quite necessary to have recourse to Gisco, and the Barbarians accepted his intervention. One morning they saw the chains of the harbour lowered, and three flat-bottomed boats passing through the canal of Tænia entered the lake.

Gisco was visible on the first at the prow. Behind him rose an enormous chest, higher than a catafalque, and furnished with rings like hanging crowns. Then appeared the legion of interpreters, with their hair dressed like sphinxes, and with parrots tattooed on their breasts. Friends and slaves followed, all without arms, and in such numbers that they shouldered one another. The three long, dangerously-loaded barges advanced amid the shouts of the onlooking army.

As soon as Gisco disembarked the soldiers ran to him. He had a sort of tribune erected with knapsacks, and declared that he should not depart before he had paid them all in full.

There was an outburst of applause, and it was a long time before he was able to speak.

Then he censured the wrongs done to the Republic, and to the Barbarians; the fault lay with a few mutineers who had alarmed Carthage by their violence. The best proof of good intention on the part of the latter was that it was he, the eternal adversary of the Suffet Hanno, who was sent to them. They must not credit the people with the folly of desiring to provoke brave men, nor with ingratitude enough not to recognise their services; and Gisco began to pay the soldiers, commencing with the Libyans. As they had declared that the lists were untruthful, he made no use of them.

They defiled before him according to nationality, opening their fingers to show the number of their years of service; they were marked in succession with green paint on the left arm; the scribes dipped into the yawning coffer, while others made holes with a style on a sheet of lead.

A man passed walking heavily like an ox.

"Come up beside me," said the Suffet, suspecting some fraud; "how many years have you served?"

"Twelve," replied the Libyan.

Gisco slipped his fingers under his chin, for the chin-piece of the helmet used in course of time to occasion two callosities there; these were called carobs, and "to have the carobs" was an expression used to denote a veteran.

"Thief!" exclaimed the Suffet, "your shoulders ought to have what your face lacks!" and tearing off his tunic he laid bare is back which was covered with a bleeding scab; he was a labourer from Hippo-Zarytus. Hootings were raised, and he was decapitated.

As soon as night fell, Spendius went and roused the Libyans, and said to them:

"When the Ligurians, Greeks, Balearians, and men of Italy are paid, they will return. But as for you, you will remain in Africa, scattered through your tribes, and without any means of defence! It will be then that the Republic will take its revenge! Mistrust the journey! Are you going to believe everything that is said? Both the Suffets are agreed, and this one is imposing on you! Remember the Island of Bones, and Xanthippus, whom they sent back to Sparta in a rotten galley!"

"How are we to proceed?" they asked.

"Reflect!" said Spendius.

The two following days were spent in paying the men of Magdala, Leptis, and Hecatompylos; Spendius went about among the Gauls.

"They are paying off the Libyans, and then they will discharge the Greeks, the Balearians, the Asiatics and all the rest! But you, who are few in number, will receive nothing! You will see your native lands no more! You will have no ships, and they will kill you to save your food!"

The Gauls came to the Suffet. Autaritus, he whom he had wounded at Hamilcar's palace, put questions to him, but was repelled by the slaves, and disappeared swearing he would be revenged.

The demands and complaints multiplied. The most obstinate penetrated at night into the Suffet's tent; they took his hands and sought to move him by making him feel their toothless mouths, their wasted arms, and the scars of their wounds. Those who had not yet been paid were growing angry, those who had received the money demanded more for their horses; and vagabonds and outlaws assumed soldiers' arms and declared that they were being forgotten. Every minute there arrived whirlwinds of men, as it were; the tents strained and fell; the multitude, thick pressed between the ramparts of the camp, swayed with loud shouts from the gates to the centre. When the tumult grew excessively violent Gisco would rest one elbow on his ivory sceptre and stand motionless looking at the sea with his fingers buried in his beard.

Matho frequently went off to speak with Spendius; then he would again place himself in front of the Suffet, and Gisco could feel his eyes continually like two flaming phalaricas darted against him. Several times they hurled reproaches at each other over the heads of the crowd, but without making themselves heard. The distribution, meanwhile, continued, and the Suffet found expedients to remove every obstacle.

The Greeks tried to quibble about differences in currency, but he furnished them with such explanations that they retired without a murmur. The Negroes demanded white shells such as are used for trading in the interior of Africa, but when he offered to send to Carthage for them they accepted money like the rest.

But the Balearians had been promised something better, namely, women. The Suffet replied that a whole caravan of maidens was expected for them, but the journey was long and would require six moons more. When they were fat and well rubbed with benjamin they should be sent in ships to the ports of the Balearians.

Suddenly Zarxas, now handsome and vigorous, leaped like a mountebank upon the shoulders of his friends and cried:

"Have you reserved any of them for the corpses?" at the same time pointing to the gate of Khamon in Carthage.

The brass plates with which it was furnished from top to bottom shone in the sun's latest fires, and the Barbarians believed that they could discern on it a trail of blood. Every time that Gisco wished to speak their shouts began again. At last he descended with measured steps, and shut himself up in his tent.

When he left it at sunrise his interpreters, who used to sleep outside, did not stir; they lay on their backs with their eyes fixed, their tongues between their teeth, and their faces of a bluish colour. White mucus flowed from their nostrils, and their limbs were stiff, as if they had all been frozen by the cold during the night. Each had a little noose of rushes round his neck.

From that time onward the rebellion was unchecked. The murder of the Balearians which had been recalled by Zarxas strengthened the distrust inspired by Spendius. They imagined that the Republic was always trying to deceive them. An end must be put to it! The interpreters should be dispensed with! Zarxas sang war songs with a sling around his head; Autaritus brandished his great sword; Spendius whispered a word to one or gave a dagger to another. The boldest endeavoured to pay themselves, while those who were less frenzied wished to have the distribution continued. No one now relinquished his arms, and the anger of all combined into a tumultuous hatred of Gisco.

Some got up beside him. So long as they vociferated abuse they were listened to with patience; but if they tried to utter the least word in his behalf they were immediately stoned, or their heads were cut off by a sabre-stroke from behind. The heap of knapsacks was redder than an altar.

They became terrible after their meal and when they had drunk wine! This was an enjoyment forbidden in the Punic armies under pain of death, and they raised their cups in the direction of Carthage in derision of its discipline. Then they returned to the slaves of the exchequer and again began to kill. The word strike, though different in each language, was understood by all.

Gisco was well aware that he was being abandoned by his country; but in spite of its ingratitude he would not dishonour it. When they reminded him that they had been promised ships, he swore by Moloch to provide them himself at his own expense, and pulling off his necklace of blue stones he threw it into the crowd as the pledge of his oath.

Then the Africans claimed the corn in accordance with the engagements made by the Great Council. Gisco spread out the accounts of the Syssitia traced in violet pigment on sheep skins; and read out all that had entered Carthage month by month and day by day.

Suddenly he stopped with gaping eyes, as if he had just discovered his sentence of death among the figures.

The Ancients had, in fact, fraudulently reduced them, and the corn sold during the most calamitous period of the war was set down at so low a rate that, blindness apart, it was impossible to believe it.

"Speak!" they shouted. "Louder! Ah! he is trying to lie, the coward! Don't trust him."

For some time he hesitated. At last he resumed his task.

The soldiers, without suspecting that they were being deceived, accepted the accounts of the Syssitia as true. But the abundance that had prevailed at Carthage made them furiously jealous. They broke open the sycamore chest; it was three parts empty. They had seen such sums coming out of it, that they thought it inexhaustible; Gisco must have buried some in his tent. They scaled the knapsacks. Matho led them, and as they shouted "The money! the money!" Gisco at last replied:

"Let your general give it to you!"

He looked them in the face without speaking, with his great yellow eyes, and his long face that was paler than his beard. An arrow, held by its feathers, hung from the large gold ring in his ear, and a stream of blood was trickling from his tiara upon his shoulder.

At a gesture from Matho all advanced. Gisco held out his arms; Spendius tied his wrists with a slip knot; another knocked him down, and he disappeared amid the disorder of the crowd which was stumbling over the knapsacks.

They sacked his tent. Nothing was found in it except things indispensable to life; and, on a closer search, three images of Tanith, and, wrapped up in an ape's skin, a black stone which had fallen from the moon. Many Carthaginians had chosen to accompany him; they were eminent men, and all belonged to the war party.

They were dragged outside the tents and thrown into the pit used for the reception of filth. They were tied with iron chains around the body to solid stakes, and were offered food at the point of the javelin.

Autaritus overwhelmed them with invectives as he inspected them, but being quite ignorant of his language they made no reply; and the Gaul from time to time threw pebbles at their faces to make them cry out.

The next day a sort of languor took possession of the army. Now that their anger was over they were seized with anxiety. Matho was suffering from vague melancholy. It seemed to him that Salammbô had indirectly been insulted. These rich men were a kind of appendage to her person. He sat down in the night on the edge of the pit, and recognised in their groanings something of the voice of which his heart was full.

All, however, upbraided the Libyans, who alone had been paid. But while national antipathies revived, together with personal hatreds, it was felt that it would be perilous to give way to them. Reprisals after such an outrage would be formidable. It was necessary, therefore, to anticipate the vengeance of Carthage. Conventions and harangues never ceased. Every one spoke, no one was listened to; Spendius, usually so loquacious, shook his head at every proposal.

One evening he asked Matho carelessly whether there were not springs in the interior of the town.

"Not one!" replied Matho.

The next day Spendius drew him aside to the bank of the lake.

"Master!" said the former slave, "If your heart is dauntless, I will bring you into Carthage."

"How?" repeated the other, panting.

"Swear to execute all my commands and to follow me like a shadow!"

Then Matho, raising his arm towards the planet of Chabar, exclaimed:

"By Tanith, I swear!"

Spendius resumed:

"To-morrow after sunset you will wait for me at the foot of the aqueduct between the ninth and tenth arcades. Bring with you an iron pick, a crestless helmet, and leathern sandals."

The aqueduct of which he spoke crossed the entire isthmus obliquely,—a considerable work, afterwards enlarged by the Romans. In spite of her disdain of other nations, Carthage had awkwardly borrowed this novel invention from them, just as Rome herself had built Punic galleys; and five rows of superposed arches, of a dumpy kind of architecture, with buttresses at their foot and lions' heads at the top, reached to the western part of the Acropolis, where they sank beneath the town to incline what was nearly a river into the cisterns of Megara.

Spendius met Matho here at the hour agreed upon. He fastened a sort of harpoon to the end of a cord and whirled it rapidly like a sling; the iron instrument caught fast, and they began to climb up the wall, the one after the other.

But when they had ascended to the first story the cramp fell back every time that they threw it, and in order to discover some fissure they had to walk along the edge of the cornice. At every row of arches they found that it became narrower. Then the cord relaxed. Several times it nearly broke.

At last they reached the upper platform. Spendius stooped down from time to time to feel the stones with his hand.

"Here it is," he said; "let us begin!" And leaning on the pick which Matho had brought they succeeded in dislodging one of the flagstones.

In the distance they perceived a troop of horse-men galloping on horses without bridles. Their golden bracelets leaped in the vague drapings of their cloaks. A man could be seen in front crowned with ostrich feathers, and galloping with a lance in each hand.

"Narr' Havas!" exclaimed Matho.

"What matter?" returned Spendius, and he leaped into the hole which they had just made by removing the flagstone.

Matho at his command tried to thrust out one of the blocks. But he could not move his elbows for want of room.

"We shall return," said Spendius; "go in front." Then they ventured into the channel of water.

It reached to their waists. Soon they staggered, and were obliged to swim. Their limbs knocked against the walls of the narrow duct. The water flowed almost immediately beneath the stones above, and their faces were torn by them. Then the current carried them away. Their breasts were crushed with air heavier than that of a sepulchre, and stretching themselves out as much as possible with their heads between their arms and their legs close together, they passed like arrows into the darkness, choking, gurgling, and almost dead. Suddenly all became black before them, and the speed of the waters redoubled. They fell.

When they came to the surface again, they remained for a few minutes extended on their backs, inhaling the air delightfully. Arcades, one behind another, opened up amid large walls separating the various basins. All were filled, and the water stretched in a single sheet throughout the length of the cisterns. Through the air-holes in the cupolas on the ceiling there fell a pale brightness which spread upon the waves discs, as it were, of light, while the darkness round about thickened towards the walls and threw them back to an indefinite distance. The slightest sound made a great echo.

Spendius and Matho commenced to swim again, and passing through the opening of the arches, traversed several chambers in succession. Two other rows of smaller basins extended in a parallel direction on each side. They lost themselves; they turned, and came back again. At last something offered a resistance to their heels. It was the pavement of the gallery that ran along the cisterns.

Then, advancing with great precautions, they felt along the wall to find an outlet. But their feet slipped, and they fell into the great centre-basins. They had to climb up again, and there they fell again. They experienced terrible fatigue, which made them feel as if all their limbs had been dissolved in the water while swimming. Their eyes closed; they were in the agonies of death.

Spendius struck his hand against the bars of a grating. They shook it, it gave way, and they found themselves on the steps of a staircase. A door of bronze closed it above. With the point of a dagger they moved the bar, which was opened from without, and suddenly the pure open air surrounded them.

The night was filled with silence, and the sky seemed at an extraordinary height. Clusters of trees projected over the long lines of walls. The whole town was asleep. The fires of the outposts shone like lost stars.

Spendius, who had spent three years in the ergastulum, was but imperfectly acquainted with the different quarters. Matho conjectured that to reach Hamilcar's palace they ought to strike to the left and cross the Mappalian district.

"No," said Spendius, "take me to the temple of Tanith."

Matho wished to speak.

"Remember!" said the former slave, and raising his arm he showed him the glittering planet of Chabar.

Then Matho turned in silence towards the Acropolis.

They crept along the nopal hedges which bordered the paths. The water trickled from their limbs upon the dust. Their damp sandals made no noise; Spendius, with eyes that flamed more than torches, searched the bushes at every step;—and he walked behind Matho with his hands resting on the two daggers which he carried on his arms, and which hung from below the armpit by a leathern band.

V

Tanith

After leaving the gardens Matho and Spendius found themselves checked by the rampart of Megara. But they discovered a breach in the great wall and passed through.

The ground sloped downwards, forming a kind of very broad valley. It was an exposed place.

"Listen," said Spendius, "and first of all fear nothing! I shall fulfil my promise—"

He stopped abruptly, and seemed to reflect as though searching for words,—"Do you remember that time at sunrise when I showed Carthage to you on Salammbô's terrace? We were strong that day, but you would listen to nothing!" Then in a grave voice: "Master, in the sanctuary of Tanith there is a mysterious veil, which fell from heaven and which covers the goddess."

"I know," said Matho.

Spendius resumed: "It is itself divine, for it forms part of her. The gods reside where their images are. It is because Carthage possesses it that Carthage is powerful." Then leaning over to his ear: "I have brought you with me to carry it off!"

Matho recoiled in horror. "Begone! look for some one else! I will not help you in this execrable crime!"

"But Tanith is your enemy," retorted Spendius; "she is persecuting you and you are dying through her wrath. You will be revenged upon her. She will obey you, and you will become almost immortal and invincible."

Matho bent his head. Spendius continued:

"We should succumb; the army would be annihilated of itself. We have neither flight, nor succour, nor pardon to hope for! What chastisement from the gods can you be afraid of since you will have their power in your own hands? Would you rather die on the evening of a defeat, in misery beneath the shelter of a bush, or amid the outrages of the populace and the flames of funeral piles? Master, one day you will enter Carthage among the colleges of the pontiffs, who will kiss your sandals; and if the veil of Tanith weighs upon you still, you will reinstate it in its temple. Follow me! come and take it."

Matho was consumed by a terrible longing. He would have liked to possess the veil while refraining from the sacrilege. He said to himself that perhaps it would not be necessary to take it in order to monopolise its virtue. He did not go to the bottom of his thought but stopped at the boundary, where it terrified him.

"Come on!" he said; and they went off with rapid strides, side by side, and without speaking.

The ground rose again, and the dwellings were near. They turned again into the narrow streets amid the darkness. The strips of esparto-grass with which the doors were closed, beat against the walls. Some camels were ruminating in a square before heaps of cut grass. Then they passed beneath a gallery covered with foliage. A pack of dogs were barking. But suddenly the space grew wider and they recognised the western face of the Acropolis. At the foot of Byrsa there stretched a long black mass: it was the temple of Tanith, a whole made up of monuments and galleries, courts and fore-courts, and bounded by a low wall of dry stones. Spendius and Matho leaped over it.

This first barrier enclosed a wood of plane-trees as a precaution against plague and infection in the air. Tents were scattered here and there, in which, during the daytime, depilatory pastes, perfumes, garments, moon-shaped cakes, and images of the goddess with representations of the temple hollowed out in blocks of alabaster, were on sale.

They had nothing to fear, for on nights when the planet did not appear, all rites were suspended; nevertheless Matho slackened his speed, and stopped before the three ebony steps leading to the second enclosure.

"Forward!" said Spendius.

Pomegranate, almond trees, cypresses and myrtles alternated in regular succession; the path, which was paved with blue pebbles, creaked beneath their footsteps, and full-blown roses formed a hanging bower over the whole length of the avenue. They arrived before an oval hole protected by a grating. Then Matho, who was frightened by the silence, said to Spendius:

"It is here that they mix the fresh water and the bitter."

"I have seen all that," returned the former slave, "in Syria, in the town of Maphug"; and they ascended into the third enclosure by a staircase of six silver steps.

A huge cedar occupied the centre. Its lowest branches were hidden beneath scraps of material and necklaces hung upon them by the faithful. They walked a few steps further on, and the front of the temple was displayed before them.

Two long porticoes, with their architraves resting on dumpy pillars, flanked a quadrangular tower, the platform of which was adorned with the crescent of a moon. On the angles of the porticoes and at the four corners of the tower stood vases filled with kindled aromatics. The capitals were laden with pomegranates and coloquintidas. Twining knots, lozenges, and rows of pearls alternated on the walls, and a hedge of silver filigree formed a wide semicircle in front of the brass staircase which led down from the vestibule.

There was a cone of stone at the entrance between a stela of gold and one of emerald, and Matho kissed his right hand as he passed beside it.

The first room was very lofty; its vaulted roof was pierced by numberless apertures, and if the head were raised the stars might be seen. All round the wall rush baskets were heaped up with the first fruits of adolescence in the shape of beards and curls of hair; and in the centre of the circular apartment the body of a woman issued from a sheath which was covered with breasts. Fat, bearded, and with eyelids downcast, she looked as though she were smiling, while her hands were crossed upon the lower part of her big body, which was polished by the kisses of the crowd.

Then they found themselves again in the open air in a transverse corridor, wherein there was an altar of small dimensions leaning against an ivory door. There was no further passage; the priests alone could open it; for the temple was not a place of meeting for the multitude, but the private abode of a divinity.

"The enterprise is impossible," said Matho. "You had not thought of this! Let us go back!" Spendius was examining the walls.

He wanted the veil, not because he had confidence in its virtue (Spendius believed only in the Oracle), but because he was persuaded that the Carthaginians would be greatly dismayed on seeing themselves deprived of it. They walked all round behind in order to find some outlet.

Aedicules of different shapes were visible beneath clusters of turpentine trees. Here and there rose a stone phallus, and large stags roamed peacefully about, spurning the fallen fir-cones with their cloven hoofs.

But they retraced their steps between two long galleries which ran parallel to each other. There were small open cells along their sides, and tabourines and cymbals hung against their cedar columns from top to bottom. Women were sleeping stretched on mats outside the cells. Their bodies were greasy with unguents, and exhaled an odour of spices and extinguished perfuming-pans; while they were so covered with tattooings, necklaces, rings, vermilion, and antimony that, but for the motion of their breasts, they might have been taken for idols as they lay thus on the ground. There were lotus-trees encircling a fountain in which fish like Salammbô's were swimming; and then in the background, against the wall of the temple, spread a vine, the branches of which were of glass and the grape-bunches of emerald, the rays from the precious stones making a play of light through the painted columns upon the sleeping faces.

Matho felt suffocated in the warm atmosphere pressed down upon him by the cedar partitions. All these symbols of fecundation, these perfumes, radiations, and breathings overwhelmed him. Through all the mystic dazzling he kept thinking of Salammbô. She became confused with the goddess herself, and his loved unfolded itself all the more, like the great lotus-plants blooming upon the depths of the waters.

Spendius was calculating how much money he would have made in former days by the sale of these women; and with a rapid glance he estimated the weight of the golden necklaces as he passed by.

The temple was impenetrable on this side as on the other, and they returned behind the first chamber. While Spendius was searching and ferreting, Matho was prostrate before the door supplicating Tanith. He besought her not to permit the sacrilege, and strove to soften her with caressing words, such as are used to an angry person.

Spendius noticed a narrow aperture above the door.

"Rise!" he said to Matho, and he made him stand erect with his back against the wall. Placing one foot in his hands, and then the other upon his head, he reached up to the air-hole, made his way into it and disappeared. Then Matho felt a knotted cord—that one which Spendius had rolled around his body before entering the cisterns—fall upon his shoulders, and bearing upon it with both hands he soon found himself by the side of the other in a large hall filled with shadow.

Such an attempt was something extraordinary. The inadequacy of the means for preventing it was a sufficient proof that it was considered impossible. The sanctuaries were protected by terror more than by their walls. Matho expected to die at every step.

However a light was flickering far back in the darkness, and they went up to it. It was a lamp burning in a shell on the pedestal of a statue which wore the cap of the Kabiri. Its long blue robe was strewn with diamond discs, and its heels were fastened to the ground by chains which sank beneath the pavement. Matho suppressed a cry. "Ah! there she is! there she is!" he stammered out. Spendius took up the lamp in order to light himself.

"What an impious man you are!" murmured Matho, following him nevertheless.

The apartment which they entered had nothing in it but a black painting representing another woman. Her legs reached to the top of the wall, and her body filled the entire ceiling; a huge egg hung by a thread from her navel, and she fell head downwards upon the other wall, reaching as far as the level of the pavement, which was touched by her pointed fingers.

They drew a hanging aside, in order to go on further; but the wind blew and the light went out.

Then they wandered about, lost in the complications of the architecture. Suddenly they felt something strangely soft beneath their feet. Sparks crackled and leaped; they were walking in fire. Spendius touched the ground and perceived that it was carefully carpeted with lynx skins; then it seemed to them that a big cord, wet, cold, and viscous, was gliding between their legs. Through some fissures cut in the wall there fell thin white rays, and they advanced by this uncertain light. At last they distinguished a large black serpent. It darted quickly away and disappeared.

"Let us fly!" exclaimed Matho. "It is she! I feel her; she is coming."

"No, no," replied Spendius, "the temple is empty."

Then a dazzling light made them lower their eyes. Next they perceived all around them an infinite number of beasts, lean, panting, with bristling claws, and mingled together one above another in a mysterious and terrifying confusion. There were serpents with feet, and bulls with wings, fishes with human heads were devouring fruit, flowers were blooming in the jaws of crocodiles, and elephants with uplifted trunks were sailing proudly through the azure like eagles. Their incomplete or multiplied limbs were distended with terrible exertion. As they thrust out their tongues they looked as though they would fain give forth their souls; and every shape was to be found among them as if the germ-receptacle had been suddenly hatched and had burst, emptying itself upon the walls of the hall.

Round the latter were twelve globes of blue crystal, supported by monsters resembling tigers. Their eyeballs were starting out of their heads like those of snails, with their dumpy loins bent they were turning round towards the background where the supreme Rabbet, the Omnifecund, the last invented, shone splendid in a chariot of ivory.

She was covered with scales, feathers, flowers, and birds as high as the waist. For earrings she had silver cymbals, which flapped against her cheeks. Her large fixed eyes gazed upon you, and a luminous stone, set in an obscene symbol on her brow, lighted the whole hall by its reflection in red copper mirrors above the door.

Matho stood a step forward; but a flag stone yielded beneath his heels and immediately the spheres began to revolve and the monsters to roar; music rose melodious and pealing, like the harmony of the planets; the tumultuous soul of Tanith was poured streaming forth. She was about to arise, as lofty as the hall and with open arms. Suddenly the monsters closed their jaws and the crystal globes revolved no more.

Then a mournful modulation lingered for a time through the air and at last died away.

"And the veil?" said Spendius.

Nowhere could it be seen. Where was it to be found? How could it be discovered? What if the priests had hidden it? Matho experienced anguish of heart and felt as though he had been deceived in his belief.

"This way!" whispered Spendius. An inspiration guided him. He drew Matho behind Tanith's chariot, where a cleft a cubit wide ran down the wall from top to bottom.

Then they penetrated into a small and completely circular room, so lofty that it was like the interior of a pillar. In the centre there was a big black stone, of semispherical shape like a tabourine; flames were burning upon it; an ebony cone, bearing a head and two arms, rose behind.

But beyond it seemed as though there were a cloud wherein were twinkling stars; faces appeared in the depths of its folds—Eschmoun with the Kabiri, some of the monsters that had already been seen, the sacred beasts of the Babylonians, and others with which they were not acquainted. It passed beneath the idol's face like a mantle, and spread fully out was drawn up on the wall to which it was fastened by the corners, appearing at once bluish as the night, yellow as the dawn, purple as the sun, multitudinous, diaphanous, sparkling light. It was the mantle of the goddess, the holy zaïmph which might not be seen.

Both turned pale.

"Take it!" said Matho at last.

Spendius did not hesitate, and leaning upon the idol he unfastened the veil, which sank to the ground. Matho laid his hand upon it; then he put his head through the opening, then he wrapped it about his body, and he spread out his arms the better to view it.

"Let us go!" said Spendius.

Matho stood panting with his eyes fixed upon the pavement. Suddenly he exclaimed:

"But what if I went to her? I fear her beauty no longer! What could she do to me? I am now more than a man. I could pass through flames or walk upon the sea! I am transported! Salammbô! Salammbô! I am your master!"

His voice was like thunder. He seemed to Spendius to have grown taller and transformed.

A sound of footsteps drew near, a door opened, and a man appeared, a priest with lofty cap and staring eyes. Before he could make a gesture Spendius had rushed upon him, and clasping him in his arms had buried both his daggers in his sides. His head rang upon the pavement.

Then they stood for a while, as motionless as the corpse, listening. Nothing could be heard but the murmuring of the wind through the half-opened door.

The latter led into a narrow passage. Spendius advanced along it, Matho followed him, and they found themselves almost immediately in the third enclosure, between the lateral porticoes, in which were the dwellings of the priests.

Behind the cells there must be a shorter way out. They hastened along.

Spendius squatted down at the edge of the fountain and washed his bloodstained hands. The women slept. The emerald vine shone. They resumed their advance.

But something was running behind them under the trees; and Matho, who bore the veil, several times felt that it was being pulled very gently from below. It was a large cynocephalus, one of those which dwelt at liberty within the enclosure of the goddess. It clung to the mantle as though it had been conscious of the theft. They did not dare to strike it, however, fearing that it might redouble its cries; suddenly its anger subsided, and it trotted close beside them swinging its body with its long hanging arms. Then at the barrier it leaped at a bound into a palm tree.

When they had left the last enclosure they directed their steps towards Hamilcar's palace, Spendius understanding that it would be useless to try to dissuade Matho.

They went by the street of the Tanners, the square of Muthumbal, the green market and the crossways of Cynasyn. At the angle of a wall a man drew back frightened by the sparkling thing which pierced the darkness.

"Hide the zaïmph!" said Spendius.

Other people passed them, but without perceiving them.

At last they recognised the houses of Megara.

The pharos, which was built behind them on the summit of the cliff, lit up the heavens with a great red brightness, and the shadow of the palace, with its rising terraces, projected a monstrous pyramid, as it were, upon the gardens. They entered through the hedge of jujube-trees, beating down the branches with blows of the dagger.

The traces of the feast of the Mercenaries were everywhere still manifest. The parks were broken up, the trenches drained, the doors of the ergastulum open. No one was to be seen about the kitchens or cellars. They wondered at the silence, which was occasionally broken by the hoarse breathing of the elephants moving in their shackles, and the crepitation of the pharos, in which a pile of aloes was burning.

Matho, however, kept repeating:

"But where is she? I wish to see her! Lead me!"

"It is a piece of insanity!" Spendius kept saying. "She will call, her slaves will run up, and in spite of your strength you will die!"

They reached thus the galley staircase. Matho raised his head, and thought that he could perceive far above a vague brightness, radiant and soft. Spendius sought to restrain him, but he dashed up the steps.

As he found himself again in places where he had already seen her, the interval of the days that had passed was obliterated from his memory. But now had she been singing among the tables; she had disappeared, and he had since been continually ascending this staircase. The sky above his head was covered with fires; the sea filled the horizon; at each step he was surrounded by a still greater immensity, and he continued to climb upward with that strange facility which we experience in dreams.

The rustling of the veil as it brushed against the stones recalled his new power to him; but in the excess of his hope he could no longer tell what he was to do; this uncertainty alarmed him.

From time to time he would press his face against the quadrangular openings in the closed apartments, and he thought that in several of the latter he could see persons asleep.

The last story, which was narrower, formed a sort of dado on the summit of the terraces. Matho walked round it slowly.

A milky light filled the sheets of talc which closed the little apertures in the wall, and in their symmetrical arrangement they looked in the darkness like rows of delicate pearls. He recognised the red door with the black cross. The throbbing of his heart increased. He would fain have fled. He pushed the door and it opened.

A galley-shaped lamp hung burning in the back part of the room, and three rays, emitted from its silver keel, trembled on the lofty wainscots, which were painted red with black bands. The ceiling was an assemblage of small beams, with amethysts and topazes amid their gilding in the knots of the wood. On both the great sides of the apartment there stretched a very low bed made with white leathern straps; while above, semi-circles like shells, opened in the thickness of the wall, suffered a garment to come out and hang down to the ground.

There was an oval basin with a step of onyx round it; delicate slippers of serpent skin were standing on the edge, together with an alabaster flagon. The trace of a wet footstep might be seen beyond. Exquisite scents were evaporating.

Matho glided over the pavement, which was encrusted with gold, mother-of-pearl, and glass; and, in spite of the polished smoothness of the ground, it seemed to him that his feet sank as though he were walking on sand.

Behind the silver lamp he had perceived a large square of azure held in the air by four cords from above, and he advanced with loins bent and mouth open.

Flamingoes' wings, fitted on branches of black coral, lay about among purple cushions, tortoiseshell strigils, cedar boxes, and ivory spatulas. There were antelopes' horns with rings and bracelets strung upon them; and clay vases were cooling in the wind in the cleft of the wall with a lattice-work of reeds. Several times he struck his foot, for the ground had various levels of unequal height, which formed a succession of apartments, as it were, in the room. In the background there were silver balustrades surrounding a carpet strewn with painted flowers. At last he came to the hanging bed beside an ebony stool serving to get into it.

GUSTAVE FLAUBERT

But the light ceased at the edge;—and the shadow, like a great curtain, revealed only a corner of the red mattress with the extremity of a little naked foot lying upon its ankle. Then Matho took up the lamp very gently.

She was sleeping with her cheek in one hand and with the other arm extended. Her ringlets were spread about her in such abundance that she appeared to be lying on black feathers, and her ample white tunic wound in soft draperies to her feet following the curves of her person. Her eyes were just visible beneath her half-closed eyelids. The curtains, which stretched perpendicularly, enveloped her in a bluish atmosphere, and the motion of her breathing, communicating itself to the cords, seemed to rock her in the air. A long mosquito was buzzing.

Matho stood motionless holding the silver lamp at arm's length; but on a sudden the mosquito-net caught fire and disappeared, and Salammbô awoke.

The fire had gone out of itself. She did not speak. The lamp caused great luminous moires to flicker on the wainscots.

"What is it?" she said.

He replied:

"'Tis the veil of the goddess!"

"The veil of the goddess!" cried Salammbô, and supporting herself on both clenched hands she leaned shuddering out. He resumed:

"I have been in the depths of the sanctuary to seek it for you! Look!" The zaïmph shone a mass of rays.

"Do you remember it?" said Matho. "You appeared at night in my dreams, but I did not guess the mute command of your eyes!" She put out one foot upon the ebony stool. "Had I understood I should have hastened hither, I should have forsaken the army, I should not have left Carthage. To obey you I would go down through the caverns of Hadrumetum into the kingdom of the shades!—Forgive me! it was as though mountains were weighing upon my days; and yet something drew me on! I tried to come to you! Should I ever have dared this without the Gods!—Let us go! You must follow me! or, if you do not wish to do so, I will remain. What matters it to me!—Drown my soul in your breath! Let my lips be crushed with kissing your hands!"

"Let me see it!" she said. "Nearer! nearer!"

Day was breaking, and the sheets of talc in the walls were filled with a vinous colour. Salammbô leaned fainting against the cushions of the bed.

"I love you!" cried Matho.

"Give it!" she stammered out, and they drew closer together.

She kept advancing, clothed in her white trailing simar, and with her large eyes fastened on the veil. Matho gazed at her, dazzled by the splendours of her head, and, holding out the zaïmph towards her, was about to enfold her in an embrace. She was stretching out her arms. Suddenly she stopped, and they stood looking at each other, open-mouthed.

Then without understanding the meaning of his solicitation a horror seized upon her. Her delicate eyebrows rose, her lips opened; she trembled. At last she struck one of the brass pateras which hung at the corners of the red mattress, crying:

"To the rescue! to the rescue! Back, sacrilegious man! infamous and accursed! Help, Taanach, Kroum, Ewa, Micipsa, Schaoul!"

And the scared face of Spendius, appearing in the wall between the clay flagons, cried out these words:

"Fly! they are hastening hither!"

A great tumult came upwards shaking the staircases, and a flood of people, women, serving-men, and slaves, rushed into the room with stakes, tomahawks, cutlasses, and daggers. They were nearly paralysed with indignation on perceiving a man; the female servants uttered funeral wailings, and the eunuchs grew pale beneath their black skins.

Matho was standing behind the balustrades. With the zaïmph which was wrapped about him, he looked like a sidereal god surrounded by the firmament. The slaves were going to fall upon him, but she stopped them:

"Touch it not! It is the mantle of the goddess!"

She had drawn back into a corner; but she took a step towards him, and stretched forth her naked arm:

"A curse upon you, you who have plundered Tanith! Hatred, vengeance, massacre, and grief! May Gurzil, god of battles, rend you! may Mastiman, god of the dead, stifle you! and may the Other—he who may not be named—burn you!"

Matho uttered a cry as though he had received a sword-thrust. She repeated several times: "Begone! begone!"

The crowd of servants spread out, and Matho, with hanging head, passed slowly through the midst of them; but at the door he stopped, for the fringe of the zaïmph had caught on one of the golden stars with which the flagstones were paved. He pulled it off abruptly with a movement of his shoulder and went down the staircases.

Spendius, bounding from terrace to terrace, and leaping over the hedges and trenches, had escaped from the gardens. He reached the foot of the pharos. The wall was discontinued at this spot, so inaccessible was the cliff. He advanced to the edge, lay down on his back, and let himself slide, feet foremost, down the whole length of it to the bottom; then by swimming he reached the Cape of the Tombs, made a wide circuit of the salt lagoon, and re-entered the camp of the Barbarians in the evening.

The sun had risen; and, like a retreating lion, Matho went down the paths, casting terrible glances about him.

A vague clamour reached his ears. It had started from the palace, and it was beginning afresh in the distance, towards the Acropolis. Some said that the treasure of the Republic had been seized in the temple of Moloch; others spoke of the assassination of a priest. It was thought, moreover, that the Barbarians had entered the city.

Matho, who did not know how to get out of the enclosures, walked straight before him. He was seen, and an outcry was raised. Every one understood; and there was consternation, then immense wrath.

From the bottom of the Mappalian quarter, from the heights of the Acropolis, from the catacombs, from the borders of the lake, the multitude came in haste. The patricians left their palaces, and the traders left their shops; the women forsook their children; swords, hatchets, and sticks were seized; but the obstacle which had stayed Salammbô stayed them. How could the veil be taken back? The mere sight of it was a crime; it was of the nature of the gods, and contact with it was death.

The despairing priests wrung their hands on the peristyles of the temples. The guards of the Legion galloped about at random; the people climbed upon the houses, the terraces, the shoulders of the colossuses, and the masts of the ships. He went on, nevertheless, and the rage, and the terror also, increased at each of his steps; the streets cleared at his approach, and the torrent of flying men streamed on both sides up to the tops of the walls. Everywhere he could perceive only eyes opened widely as if to devour him, chattering teeth and outstretched fists, and Salammbô's imprecations resounded many times renewed.

Suddenly a long arrow whizzed past, then another, and stones began to buzz about him; but the missiles, being badly aimed (for there was the dread of hitting the zaïmph), passed over his head. Moreover, he made a shield of the veil, holding it to the right, to the left, before him and behind him; and they could devise no expedient. He quickened his steps more and more, advancing through the open streets. They were barred with cords, chariots, and snares; and all his windings brought him back again. At last he entered the square of Khamon where the Balearians had perished, and stopped, growing pale as one about to die. This time he was surely lost, and the multitude clapped their hands.

He ran up to the great gate, which was closed. It was very high, made throughout of heart of oak, with iron nails and sheathed with brass. Matho flung himself against it. The people stamped their feet with joy when they saw the impotence of his fury; then he took his sandal, spit upon it, and beat the immovable panels with it. The whole city howled. The veil was forgotten now, and they were about to crush him. Matho gazed with wide vacant eyes upon the crowd. His temples were throbbing with violence enough to stun him, and he felt a numbness as of intoxication creeping over him. Suddenly he caught sight of the long chain used in working the swinging of the gate. With a bound he grasped it, stiffening his arms, and making a buttress of his feet, and at last the huge leaves partly opened.

Then when he was outside he took the great zaïmph from his neck, and raised it as high as possible above his head. The material, upborne by the sea breeze, shone in the sunlight with its colours, its gems, and the figures of its gods. Matho bore it thus across the whole plain as far as the soldiers' tents, and the people on the walls watched the fortune of Carthage depart.

GUSTAVE FLAUBERT

VI

Hanno

I ought to have carried her off!" Matho said in the evening to Spendius. "I should have seized her, and torn her from her house! No one would have dared to touch me!"

Spendius was not listening to him. Stretched on his back he was taking delicious rest beside a large jar filled with honey-coloured water, into which he would dip his head from time to time in order to drink more copiously.

Matho resumed:

"What is to be done? How can we re-enter Carthage?"

"I do not know," said Spendius.

Such impassibility exasperated Matho and he exclaimed:

"Why! the fault is yours! You carry me away, and then you forsake me, coward that you are! Why, pray, should I obey you? Do you think that you are my master? Ah! you prostituter, you slave, you son of a slave!" He ground his teeth and raised his broad hand above Spendius.

The Greek did not reply. An earthen lamp was burning gently against the tent-pole, where the zaïmph shone amid the hanging panoply. Suddenly Matho put on his cothurni, buckled on his brazen jacket of mail, and took his helmet.

"Where are you going?" asked Spendius.

"I am returning! Let me alone! I will bring her back! And if they show themselves I will crush them like vipers! I will put her to death, Spendius! Yes," he repeated, "I will kill her! You shall see, I will kill her!"

But Spendius, who was listening eagerly, snatched up the zaïmph abruptly and threw it into a corner, heaping up fleeces above it. A murmuring of voices was heard, torches gleamed, and Narr' Havas entered, followed by about twenty men.

They wore white woollen cloaks, long daggers, copper necklaces, wooden earrings, and boots of hyena skin; and standing on the threshold they leaned upon their lances like herdsmen resting themselves. Narr' Havas was the handsomest of all; his slender arms were bound with straps ornamented with pearls. The golden circlet which fastened his ample garment about his head held an ostrich feather which hung down behind his shoulder; his teeth were displayed in a continual smile; his eyes seemed sharpened like arrows, and there was something observant and airy about his whole demeanour.

He declared that he had come to join the Mercenaries, for the Republic had long been threatening his kingdom. Accordingly he was interested in assisting the Barbarians, and he might also be of service to them.

"I will provide you with elephants (my forests are full of them), wine, oil, barley, dates, pitch and sulphur for sieges, twenty thousand foot-soldiers and ten thousand horses. If I address myself to you, Matho, it is because the possession of the zaïmph has made you chief man in the army. Moreover," he added, "we are old friends."

Matho, however, was looking at Spendius, who, seated on the sheep-skins, was listening, and giving little nods of assent the while. Narr' Havas continued speaking. He called the gods to witness he cursed Carthage. In his imprecations he broke a javelin. All his men uttered simultaneously a loud howl, and Matho, carried away by so much passion, exclaimed that he accepted the alliance.

A white bull and a black sheep, the symbols of day and night, were then brought, and their throats were cut on the edge of a ditch. When the latter was full of blood they dipped their arms into it. Then Narr' Havas spread out his hand upon Matho's breast, and Matho did the same to Narr' Havas. They repeated the stain upon the canvas of their tents. Afterwards they passed the night in eating, and the remaining portions of the meat were burnt together with the skin, bones, horns, and hoofs.

Matho had been greeted with great shouting when he had come back bearing the veil of the goddess; even those who were not of the Chanaanitish religion were made by their vague enthusiasm to feel the arrival of a genius. As to seizing the zaïmph, no one thought of it, for the mysterious manner in which he had acquired it was sufficient in the minds of the Barbarians to justify its possession; such were the thoughts of the soldiers of the African race. The others, whose hatred was not of such long standing, did not know how to make up their minds. If they had had ships they would immediately have departed.

Spendius, Narr' Havas, and Matho despatched men to all the tribes on Punic soil.

Carthage was sapping the strength of these nations. She wrung exorbitant taxes from them, and arrears or even murmurings were punished with fetters, the axe, or the cross. It was necessary to cultivate whatever suited the Republic, and to furnish what she demanded; no one had the right of possessing a weapon; when villages rebelled the inhabitants were sold; governors were esteemed like wine-presses, according to the quantity which they succeeded in extracting. Then beyond the regions immediately subject to Carthage extended the allies roamed the Nomads, who might be let loose upon them. By this system the crops were always abundant, the studs skilfully managed, and the plantations superb.

The elder Cato, a master in the matters of tillage and slaves, was amazed at it ninety-two years later, and the death-cry which he repeated continually at Rome was but the exclamation of jealous greed.

During the last war the exactions had been increased, so that nearly all the towns of Libya had surrendered to Regulus. To punish them, a thousand talents, twenty thousand oxen, three hundred bags of gold dust, and considerable advances of grain had been exacted from them, and the chiefs of the tribes had been crucified or thrown to the lions.

Tunis especially execrated Carthage! Older than the metropolis, it could not forgive her her greatness, and it fronted her walls crouching in the mire on the water's edge like a venomous beast watching her. Transportation, massacres, and epidemics did not weaken it. It had assisted Archagathas, the son of Agathocles, and the Eaters of Uncleanness found arms there at once.

The couriers had not yet set out when universal rejoicing broke out in the provinces. Without waiting for anything they strangled the comptrollers of the houses and the functionaries of the Republic in the baths; they took the old weapons that had been concealed out of the caves; they forged swords with the iron of the ploughs; the children sharpened javelins at the doors, and the women gave their necklaces, rings, earrings, and everything that could be employed for the destruction of Carthage. Piles of lances were heaped up in the country towns like sheaves of maize. Cattle and money were sent off. Matho speedily paid the Mercenaries their arrears, and owing to this, which was Spendius's idea, he was appointed commander-in-chief—the schalishim of the Barbarians.

Reinforcements of men poured in at the same time. The aborigines appeared first, and were followed by the slaves from the country; caravans of Negroes were seized and armed, and merchants on their way to Carthage, despairing of any more certain profit, mingled with the Barbarians. Numerous bands were continually arriving. From the heights of the Acropolis the growing army might be seen.

But the guards of the Legion were posted as sentries on the platform of the aqueduct, and near them rose at intervals brazen vats, in which floods of asphalt were boiling. Below in the plain the great crowd stirred tumultuously. They were in a state of uncertainty, feeling the embarrassment with which Barbarians are always inspired when they meet with walls.

Utica and Hippo-Zarytus refused their alliance. Phonician colonies like Carthage, they were self-governing, and always had clauses inserted in the treaties concluded by the Republic to distinguish them from the latter. Nevertheless they respected this strong sister of theirs who protected them, and they did not think that she could be vanquished by a mass of Barbarians; these would on the contrary be themselves exterminated. They desired to remain neutral and to live at peace.

But their position rendered them indispensable. Utica, at the foot of the gulf, was convenient for bringing assistance to Carthage from without. If Utica alone were taken, Hippo-Zarytus, six hours further distant along the coast, would take its place, and the metropolis, being revictualled in this way, would be impregnable.

Spendius wished the siege to be undertaken immediately. Narr' Havas was opposed to this: an advance should first be made upon the frontier. This was the opinion of the veterans, and of Matho himself, and it was decided that Spendius should go to attack Utica, and Matho Hippo-Zarytus, while in the third place the main body should rest on Tunis and occupy the plain of Carthage, Autaritus being in command. As to Narr' Havas, he was to return to his own kingdom to procure elephants and to scour the roads with his cavalry.

The women cried out loudly against this decision; they coveted the jewels of the Punic ladies. The Libyans also protested. They had been summoned against Carthage, and now they were going away from it! The soldiers departed almost alone. Matho commanded his own companions, together with the Iberians, Lusitanians, and the men of the West, and of the islands; all those who spoke Greek had asked for Spendius on account of his cleverness.

Great was the stupefaction when the army was seen suddenly in motion; it stretched along beneath the mountain of Ariana on the road to Utica beside the sea. A fragment remained before Tunis, the rest disappeared to re-appear on the other shore of the gulf on the outskirts of the woods in which they were lost.

They were perhaps eighty thousand men. The two Tyrian cities would offer no resistance, and they would return against Carthage. Already there was a considerable army attacking it from the base of the isthmus, and it would soon perish from famine, for it was impossible to live without the aid of the provinces, the citizens not paying contributions as they did at Rome. Carthage was wanting in political genius. Her eternal anxiety for gain prevented her from having the prudence which results from loftier ambitions. A galley anchored on the Libyan sands, it was with toil that she maintained her position. The nations roared like billows around her, and the slightest storm shook this formidable machine.

The treasury was exhausted by the Roman war and by all that had been squandered and lost in the bargaining with the Barbarians. Nevertheless soldiers must be had, and not a government would trust the Republic! Ptolemæus had lately refused it two thousand talents. Moreover the rape of the veil disheartened them. Spendius had clearly foreseen this.

But the nation, feeling that it was hated, clasped its money and its gods to its heart, and its patriotism was sustained by the very constitution of its government.

First, the power rested with all, without any one being strong enough to engross it. Private debts were considered as public debts, men of Chanaanitish race had a monopoly of commerce, and by multiplying the profits of piracy with those of usury, by hard dealings in lands and slaves and with the poor, fortunes were sometimes made. These alone opened up all the magistracies, and although authority and money were perpetuated in the same families, people tolerated the oligarchy because they hoped ultimately to share in it.

The societies of merchants, in which the laws were elaborated, chose the inspectors of the exchequer, who on leaving office nominated the hundred members of the Council of the Ancients, themselves dependent on the Grand Assembly, or general gathering of all the rich. As to the two Suffets, the relics of the monarchy and the less than consuls, they were taken from distinct families on the same day. All kinds of enmities were contrived between them, so that they might mutually weaken each other. They could not deliberate concerning war, and when they were vanquished the Great Council crucified them.

The power of Carthage emanated, therefore, from the Syssitia, that is to say, from a large court in the centre of Malqua, at the place, it was said, where the first bark of Phonician sailors had touched, the sea having retired a long way since then. It was a collection of little rooms of archaic architecture, built of palm trunks with corners of stone, and separated from one another so as to accommodate the various societies separately. The rich crowded there all day to discuss their own concerns and those of the government, from the procuring of pepper to the extermination of Rome. Thrice in a moon they would have their beds brought up to the lofty terrace running along the wall of the court, and they might be seen from below at table in the air, without cothurni or cloaks, with their diamond-covered fingers wandering over the dishes, and their large earrings hanging down among the flagons,—all fat and lusty, half-naked, smiling and eating beneath the blue sky, like great sharks sporting in the sea.

But just now they were unable to dissemble their anxiety; they were too pale for that. The crowd which waited for them at the gates escorted them to their palaces in order to obtain some news from them. As in times of pestilence, all the houses were shut; the streets would fill and suddenly clear again; people ascended the Acropolis or ran to the harbour, and the Great Council deliberated every night. At last the people were convened in the square of Khamon, and it was decided to leave the management of things to Hanno, the conqueror of Hecatompylos.

He was a true Carthaginian, devout, crafty, and pitiless towards the people of Africa. His revenues equalled those of the Barcas. No one had such experience in administrative affairs.

He decreed the enrolment of all healthy citizens, he placed catapults on the towers, he exacted exorbitant supplies of arms, he even ordered the construction of fourteen galleys which were not required, and he desired everything to be registered and carefully set down in writing. He had himself conveyed to the arsenal, the pharos, and the treasuries of the temples; his great litter was continually to be seen swinging from step to step as it ascended the staircases of the Acropolis. And then in his palace at night, being unable to sleep, he would yell out warlike manouvres in terrible tones so as to prepare himself for the fray.

In their extremity of terror all became brave. The rich ranged themselves in line along the Mappalian district at cockcrow, and tucking up their robes practised themselves in handling the pike. But for want of an instructor they had disputes about it. They would sit down breathless upon the tombs and then begin again. Several even dieted themselves. Some imagined that it was necessary to eat a great deal in order to acquire strength, while others who were inconvenienced by their corpulence weakened themselves with fasts in order to become thin.

Utica had already called several times upon Carthage for assistance; but Hanno would not set out until the engines of war had been supplied with the last screws. He lost three moons more in equipping the one hundred and twelve elephants that were lodged in the ramparts. They were the conquerors of Regulus; the people loved them; it was impossible to treat such old friends too well. Hanno had the brass plates which adorned their breasts recast, their tusks gilt, their towers enlarged, and caparisons, edged with very heavy fringes, cut out of the handsomest purple. Finally, as their drivers were called Indians (after the first ones, no doubt, who came from the Indies) he ordered them all to be costumed after the Indian fashion; that is to say, with white pads round their temples, and small drawers of byssus, which with their transverse folds looked like two valves of a shell applied to the hips.

The army under Autaritus still remained before Tunis. It was hidden behind a wall made with mud from the lake, and protected on the top by thorny brushwood. Some Negroes had planted tall sticks here and there bearing frightful faces,—human masks made with birds' feathers, and jackals' or serpents' heads,—which gaped towards the enemy for the purpose of terrifying him; and the Barbarians, reckoning themselves invincible through these means, danced, wrestled, and juggled, convinced that Carthage would perish before long. Any one but Hanno would easily have crushed such a multitude, hampered as it was with herds and women. Moreover, they knew nothing of drill, and Autaritus was so disheartened that he had ceased to require it.

They stepped aside when he passed by rolling his big blue eyes. Then on reaching the edge of the lake he would draw back his sealskin cloak, unfasten the cord which tied up his long red hair, and soak the latter in the water. He regretted that he had not deserted to the Romans along with the two thousand Gauls of the temple of Eryx.

Often the sun would suddenly lose his rays in the middle of the day. Then the gulf and the open sea would seem as motionless as molten lead. A cloud of brown dust stretching perpendicularly would speed whirling along; the palm trees would bend and the sky disappear, while stones would be heard rebounding on the animals' cruppers; and the Gaul, his lips glued against the holes in his tent, would gasp with exhaustion and melancholy. His thoughts would be of the scent of the pastures on autumn mornings, of snowflakes, or of the bellowing of the urus lost in the fog, and closing his eyelids he would in imagination behold the fires in long, straw-roofed cottages flickering on the marshes in the depths of the woods.

Others regretted their native lands as well as he, even though they might not be so far away. Indeed the Carthaginian captives could distinguish the velaria spread over the courtyards of their houses, beyond the gulf on the slopes of Byrsa. But sentries marched round them continually. They were all fastened to a common chain. Each one wore an iron carcanet, and the crowd was never weary of coming to gaze at them. The women would show their little children the handsome robes hanging in tatters on their wasted limbs.

Whenever Autaritus looked at Gisco he was seized with rage at the recollection of the insult that he had received, and he would have killed him but for the oath which he had taken to Narr' Havas. Then he would go back into his tent and drink a mixture of barley and cumin until he swooned away from intoxication,—to awake afterwards in broad daylight consumed with horrible thirst.

Matho, meanwhile, was besieging Hippo-Zarytus. But the town was protected by a lake, communicating with the sea. It had three lines of circumvallation, and upon the heights which surrounded it there extended a wall fortified with towers. He had never commanded in such an enterprise before. Moreover, he was beset with thoughts of Salammbô, and he raved in the delight of her beauty as in the sweetness of a vengeance that transported him with pride. He felt an acrid, frenzied, permanent want to see her again. He even thought of presenting himself as the bearer of a flag of truce, in the hope that once within Carthage he might make his way to her. Often he would cause the assault to be sounded and waiting for nothing rush upon the mole which it was sought to construct in the sea. He would snatch up the stones with his hands, overturn, strike, and deal sword-thrusts everywhere. The Barbarians would dash on pell-mell; the ladders would break with a loud crash, and masses of men would tumble into the water, causing it to fly up in red waves against the walls. Finally the tumult would subside, and the soldiers would retire to make a fresh beginning.

Matho would go and seat himself outside the tents, wipe his blood-splashed face with his arm, and gaze at the horizon in the direction of Carthage.

GUSTAVE FLAUBERT

In front of him, among the olives, palms, myrtles and planes, stretched two broad ponds which met another lake, the outlines of which could not be seen. Behind one mountain other mountains reared themselves, and in the middle of the immense lake rose an island perfectly black and pyramidal in form. On the left, at the extremity of the gulf, were sand-heaps like arrested waves, large and pale, while the sea, flat as a pavement of lapis-lazuli, ascended by insensible degrees to the edge of the sky. The verdure of the country was lost in places beneath long sheets of yellow; carobs were shining like knobs of coral; vine branches drooped from the tops of the sycamores; the murmuring of the water could be heard; crested larks were hopping about, and the sun's latest fires gilded the carapaces of the tortoises as they came forth from the reeds to inhale the breeze.

Matho would heave deep sighs. He would lie flat on his face, with his nails buried in the soil, and weep; he felt wretched, paltry, forsaken. Never would he possess her, and he was unable even to take a town.

At night when alone in his tent he would gaze upon the zaïmph. Of what use to him was this thing which belonged to the gods?—and doubt crept into the Barbarian's thoughts. Then, on the contrary, it would seem to him that the vesture of the goddess was depending from Salammbô, and that a portion of her soul hovered in it, subtler than a breath; and he would feel it, breathe it in, bury his face in it, and kiss it with sobs. He would cover his shoulders with it in order to delude himself that he was beside her.

Sometimes he would suddenly steal away, stride in the starlight over the sleeping soldiers as they lay wrapped in their cloaks, spring upon a horse on reaching the camp gates, and two hours later be at Utica in Spendius's tent.

At first he would speak of the siege, but his coming was only to ease his sorrow by talking about Salammbô. Spendius exhorted him to be prudent.

"Drive away these trifles from your soul, which is degraded by them! Formerly you were used to obey; now you command an army, and if Carthage is not conquered we shall at least be granted provinces. We shall become kings!"

But how was it that the possession of the zaïmph did not give them the victory? According to Spendius they must wait.

Matho fancied that the veil affected people of Chanaanitish race exclusively, and, in his Barbarian-like subtlety, he said to himself: "The zaïmph will accordingly do nothing for me, but since they have lost it, it will do nothing for them."

Afterwards a scruple troubled him. He was afraid of offending Moloch by worshipping Aptouknos, the god of the Libyans, and he timidly asked Spendius to which of the gods it would be advisable to sacrifice a man.

"Keep on sacrificing!" laughed Spendius.

Matho, who could not understand such indifference, suspected the Greek of having a genius of whom he did not speak.

All modes of worship, as well as all races, were to be met with in these armies of Barbarians, and consideration was had to the gods of others, for they too, inspired fear. Many mingled foreign practices with their native religion. It was to no purpose that they did not adore the stars; if a constellation were fatal or helpful, sacrifices were offered to it; an unknown amulet found by chance at a moment of peril became a divinity; or it might be a name and nothing more, which would be repeated without any attempt to understand its meaning. But after pillaging temples, and seeing numbers of nations and slaughters, many ultimately ceased to believe in anything but destiny and death;—and every evening these would fall asleep with the placidity of wild beasts. Spendius had spit upon the images of Jupiter Olympius; nevertheless he dreaded to speak aloud in the dark, nor did he fail every day to put on his right boot first.

He reared a long quadrangular terrace in front of Utica, but in proportion as it ascended the rampart was also heightened, and what was thrown down by the one side was almost immediately raised again by the other. Spendius took care of his men; he dreamed of plans and strove to recall the stratagems which he had heard described in his travels. But why did Narr' Havas not return? There was nothing but anxiety.

Hanno had at last concluded his preparations. One night when there was no moon he transported his elephants and soldiers on rafts across the Gulf of Carthage. Then they wheeled round the mountain of the Hot Springs so as to avoid Autaritus, and continued their march so slowly that instead of surprising the Barbarians in the morning, as the Suffet had calculated, they did not reach them until it was broad daylight on the third day.

Utica had on the east a plain which extended to the large lagoon of Carthage; behind it a valley ran at right angles between two low and abruptly terminated mountains; the Barbarians were encamped further to the left in such a way as to blockade the harbour; and they were sleeping in their tents (for on that day both sides were too weary to fight and were resting) when the Carthaginian army appeared at the turning of the hills.

Some camp followers furnished with slings were stationed at intervals on the wings. The first line was formed of the guards of the Legion in golden scale-armour, mounted on their big horses, which were without mane, hair, or ears, and had silver horns in the middle of their foreheads to make them look like rhinoceroses. Between their squadrons were youths wearing small helmets and swinging an ashen javelin in each hand. The long files of the heavy infantry marched behind. All these traders had piled as many weapons upon their bodies as possible. Some might be seen carrying an axe, a lance, a club, and two swords all at once; others bristled with darts like porcupines, and their arms stood out from their cuirasses in sheets of horn or iron plates. At last the scaffoldings of the lofty engines appeared: carrobalistas, onagers, catapults and scorpions, rocking on chariots drawn by mules and quadrigas of oxen; and in proportion as the army drew out, the captains ran panting right and left to deliver commands, close up the files, and preserve the intervals. Such of the Ancients as held commands had come in purple cassocks, the magnificent fringes of which tangled in the white straps of their cothurni. Their faces, which were smeared all over with vermilion, shone beneath enormous helmets surmounted with images of the gods; and, as they had shields with ivory borders covered with precious stones, they might have been taken for suns passing over walls of brass.

But the Carthaginians manouvred so clumsily that the soldiers in derision urged them to sit down. They called out that they were just going to empty their big stomachs, to dust the gilding of their skin, and to give them iron to drink.

A strip of green cloth appeared at the top of the pole planted before Spendius's tent: it was the signal. The Carthaginian army replied to it with a great noise of trumpets, cymbals, flutes of asses' bones, and tympanums. The Barbarians had already leaped outside the palisades, and were facing their enemies within a javelin's throw of them.

A Balearic slinger took a step forward, put one of his clay bullets into his thong, and swung round his arm. An ivory shield was shivered, and the two armies mingled together.

The Greeks made the horses rear and fall back upon their masters by pricking their nostrils with the points of their lances. The slaves who were to hurl stones had picked such as were too big, and they accordingly fell close to them. The Punic foot-soldiers exposed the right side in cutting with their long swords. The Barbarians broke their lines; they slaughtered them freely; they stumbled over the dying and dead, quite blinded by the blood that spurted into their faces. The confused heap of pikes, helmets, cuirasses and swords turned round about, widening out and closing in with elastic contractions. The gaps increased more and more in the Carthaginian cohorts, the engines could not get out of the sand; and finally the Suffet's litter (his grand litter with crystal pendants), which from the beginning might have been seen tossing among the soldiers like a bark on the waves, suddenly foundered. He was no doubt dead. The Barbarians found themselves alone.

The dust around them fell and they were beginning to sing, when Hanno himself appeared on the top of an elephant. He sat bare-headed beneath a parasol of byssus which was carried by a Negro behind him. His necklace of blue plates flapped against the flowers on his black tunic; his huge arms were compressed within circles of diamonds, and with open mouth he brandished a pike of inordinate size, which spread out at the end like a lotus, and flashed more than a mirror. Immediately the earth shook,—and the Barbarians saw all the elephants of Carthage, with their gilt tusks and blue-painted ears, hastening up in single line, clothed with bronze and shaking the leathern towers which were placed above their scarlet caparisons, in each of which were three archers bending large bows.

The soldiers were barely in possession of their arms; they had taken up their positions at random. They were frozen with terror; they stood undecided.

Javelins, arrows, phalaricas, and masses of lead were already being showered down upon them from the towers. Some clung to the fringes of the caparisons in order to climb up, but their hands were struck off with cutlasses and they fell backwards upon the swords' points. The pikes were too weak and broke, and the elephants passed through the phalanxes like wild boars through tufts of grass; they plucked up the stakes of the camp with their trunks, and traversed it from one end to the other, overthrowing the tents with their breasts. All the Barbarians had fled. They were hiding themselves in the hills bordering the valley by which the Carthaginians had come.

The victorious Hanno presented himself before the gates of Utica. He had a trumpet sounded. The three Judges of the town appeared in the opening of the battlements on the summit of a tower.

But the people of Utica would not receive such well-armed guests. Hanno was furious. At last they consented to admit him with a feeble escort.

The streets were too narrow for the elephants. They had to be left outside.

As soon as the Suffet was in the town the principal men came to greet him. He had himself taken to the vapour baths, and called for his cooks.

Three hours afterwards he was still immersed in the oil of cinnamomum with which the basin had been filled; and while he bathed he ate flamingoes' tongues with honied poppy-seeds on a spread ox-hide. Beside him was his Greek physician, motionless, in a long yellow robe, directing the re-heating of the bath from time to time, and two young boys leaned over the steps of the basin and rubbed his legs. But attention to his body did not check his love for the commonwealth, for he was dictating a letter to be sent to the Great Council, and as some prisoners had just been taken he was asking himself what terrible punishment could be devised.

"Stop!" said he to a slave who stood writing in the hollow of his hand. "Let some of them be brought to me! I wish to see them!"

And from the bottom of the hall, full of a whitish vapour on which the torches cast red spots, three Barbarians were thrust forward: a Samnite, a Spartan, and a Cappadocian.

"Proceed!" said Hanno.

"Rejoice, light of the Baals! your Suffet has exterminated the ravenous hounds! Blessings on the Republic! Give orders for prayers!" He perceived the captives and burst out laughing: "Ah! ha! my fine fellows of Sicca! You are not shouting so loudly to-day! It is I! Do you recognise me? And where are your swords? What really terrible fellows!" and he pretended to be desirous to hide himself as if he were afraid of them. "You demanded horses, women, estates, magistracies, no doubt, and priesthoods! Why not? Well, I will provide you with the estates, and such as you will never come out of! You shall be married to gibbets that are perfectly new! Your pay? it shall be melted in your mouths in leaden ingots! and I will put you into good and very exalted positions among the clouds, so as to bring you close to the eagles!"

The three long-haired and ragged Barbarians looked at him without understanding what he said. Wounded in the knees, they had been seized by having ropes thrown over them, and the ends of the great chains on their hands trailed upon the pavement. Hanno was indignant at their impassibility.

"On your knees! on your knees! jackals! dust! vermin! excrements! And they make no reply! Enough! be silent! Let them be flayed alive! No! presently!"

He was breathing like a hippopotamus and rolling his eyes. The perfumed oil overflowed beneath the mass of his body, and clinging to the scales on his skin, made it look pink in the light of the torches.

He resumed:

"For four days we suffered greatly from the sun. Some mules were lost in crossing the Macaras. In spite of their position, the extraordinary courage—Ah! Demonades! how I suffer! Have the bricks reheated, and let them be red-hot!"

A noise of rakes and furnaces was heard. The incense smoked more strongly in the large perfuming pans, and the shampooers, who were quite naked and were sweating like sponges, crushed a paste composed of wheat, sulphur, black wine, bitch's milk, myrrh, galbanum and storax upon his joints. He was consumed with incessant thirst, but the yellow-robed man did not yield to this inclination, and held out to him a golden cup in which viper broth was smoking.

"Drink!" said he, "that strength of sun-born serpents may penetrate into the marrow of your bones, and take courage, O reflection of the gods! You know, moreover, that a priest of Eschmoun watches those cruel stars round the Dog from which your malady is derived. They are growing pale like the spots on your skin, and you are not to die from them."

"Oh! yes, that is so, is it not?" repeated the Suffet, "I am not to die from them!" And his violaceous lips gave forth a breath more nauseous than the exhalation from a corpse. Two coals seemed to burn in the place of his eyes, which had lost their eyebrows; a mass of wrinkled skin hung over his forehead; both his ears stood out from his head and were beginning to increase in size; and the deep lines forming semicircles round his nostrils gave him a strange and terrifying appearance, the look of a wild beast. His unnatural voice was like a roar; he said:

"Perhaps you are right, Demonades. In fact there are many ulcers here which have closed. I feel robust. Here! look how I am eating!"

And less from greediness than from ostentation, and the desire to prove to himself that he was in good health, he cut into the forcemeats of cheese and marjoram, the boned fish, gourds, oysters with eggs, horseradishes, truffles, and brochettes of small birds. As he looked at the prisoners he revelled in the imagination of their tortures. Nevertheless he remembered Sicca, and the rage caused by all his woes found vent in the abuse of these three men.

"Ah! traitors! ah! wretches! infamous, accursed creatures! And you outraged me!—me! the Suffet! Their services, the price of their blood, say they! Ah! yes! their blood! their blood!" Then speaking to himself:— "All shall perish! not one shall be sold! It would be better to bring them to Carthage! I should be seen—but doubtless, I have not brought chains enough? Write: Send me—How many of them are there? go and ask Muthumbal! Go! no pity! and let all their hands be cut off and brought to me in baskets!"

But strange cries at once hoarse and shrill penetrated into the hall above Hanno's voice and the rattling of the dishes that were being placed around him. They increased, and suddenly the furious trumpeting of the elephants burst forth as if the battle were beginning again. A great tumult was going on around the town.

The Carthaginians had not attempted to pursue the Barbarians. They had taken up their quarters at the foot of the walls with their baggage, mules, serving men, and all their train of satraps; and they made merry in their beautiful pearl-bordered tents, while the camp of the Mercenaries was now nothing but a heap of ruins in the plain. Spendius had recovered his courage. He dispatched Zarxas to Matho, scoured the woods, rallied his men (the losses had been inconsiderable),—and they were re-forming their lines enraged at having been conquered without a fight, when they discovered a vat of petroleum which had no doubt been abandoned by the Carthaginians. Then Spendius had some pigs carried off from the farms, smeared them with bitumen, set them on fire, and drove them towards Utica.

The elephants were terrified by the flames and fled. The ground sloped upwards, javelins were thrown at them, and they turned back;—and with great blows of ivory and trampling feet they ripped up the Carthaginians, stifled them, flattened them. The Barbarians descended the hill behind them; the Punic camp, which was without entrenchments was sacked at the first rush, and the Carthaginians were crushed against the gates, which were not opened through fear of the Mercenaries.

Day broke, and Matho's foot-soldiers were seen coming up from the west. At the same time horsemen appeared; they were Narr' Havas with his Numidians. Leaping ravines and bushes they ran down the fugitives like greyhounds pursuing hares. This change of fortune interrupted the Suffet. He called out to be assisted to leave the vapour bath.

The three captives were still before him. Then a Negro (the same who had carried his parasol in the battle) leaned over to his ear.

"Well?" replied the Suffet slowly. "Ah! kill them!" he added in an abrupt tone.

The Ethiopian drew a long dagger from his girdle and the three heads fell. One of them rebounded among the remains of the feast, and leaped into the basin, where it floated for some time with open mouth and staring eyes. The morning light entered through the chinks in the wall; the three bodies streamed with great bubbles like three fountains, and a sheet of blood flowed over the mosaics with their powdering of blue dust. The Suffet dipped his hand into this hot mire and rubbed his knees with it: it was a cure.

When evening had come he stole away from the town with his escort, and made his way into the mountain to rejoin his army.

He succeeded in finding the remains of it.

Four days afterward he was on the top of a defile at Gorza, when the troops under Spendius appeared below. Twenty stout lances might easily have checked them by attacking the head of their column, but the Carthaginians watched them pass by in a state of stupefaction. Hanno recognised the king of the Numidians in the rearguard; Narr' Havas bowed to him, at the same time making a sign which he did not understand.

The return to Carthage took place amid all kinds of terrors. They marched only at night, hiding in the olive woods during the day. There were deaths at every halting-place; several times they believed themselves lost. At last they reached Cape Hermæum, where vessels came to receive them.

Hanno was so fatigued, so desperate—the loss of the elephants in particular overwhelmed him—that he demanded poison from Demonades in order to put an end to it all. Moreover he could already feel himself stretched upon the cross.

Carthage had not strength enough to be indignant with him. Its losses had amounted to one hundred thousand nine hundred and seventy-two shekels of silver, fifteen thousand six hundred and twenty-three shekels of gold, eighteen elephants, fourteen members of the Great Council, three hundred of the rich, eight thousand citizens, corn enough for three moons, a considerable quantity of baggage, and all the engines of war! The defection of Narr' Havas was certain, and both sieges were beginning again. The army under Autaritus now extended from Tunis to Rhades. From the top of the Acropolis long columns of smoke might be seen in the country ascending to the sky; they were the mansions of the rich, which were on fire.

One man alone could have saved the Republic. People repented that they had slighted him, and the peace party itself voted holocausts for Hamilcar's return.

The sight of the zaïmph had upset Salammbô. At night she thought that she could hear the footsteps of the goddess, and she would awake terrified and shrieking. Every day she sent food to the temples. Taanach was worn out with executing her orders, and Schahabarim never left her.

VII

Hamilcar Barca

The Announcer of the Moons, who watched on the summit of the temple of Eschmoun every night in order to signal the disturbances of the planet with his trumpet, one morning perceived towards the west something like a bird skimming the surface of the sea with its long wings.

It was a ship with three tiers of oars and with a horse carved on the prow. The sun was rising; the Announcer of the Moons put up his hand before his eyes, and then grasping his clarion with outstretched arms sounded a loud brazen cry over Carthage.

People came out of every house; they would not believe what was said; they disputed with one another; the mole was covered with people. At last they recognised Hamilcar's trireme.

It advanced in fierce and haughty fashion, cleaving the foam around it, the lateen-yard quite square and the sail bulging down the whole length of the mast; its gigantic oars kept time as they beat the water; every now and then the extremity of the keel, which was shaped like a plough-share, would appear, and the ivory-headed horse, rearing both its feet beneath the spur which terminated the prow, would seem to be speeding over the plains of the sea.

As it rounded the promontory the wind ceased, the sail fell, and a man was seen standing bareheaded beside the pilot. It was he, Hamilcar, the Suffet! About his sides he wore gleaming sheets of steel; a red cloak, fastened to his shoulders, left his arms visible; two pearls of great length hung from his ears, and his black, bushy beard rested on his breast.

The galley, however, tossing amid the rocks, was proceeding along the side of the mole, and the crowd followed it on the flag-stones, shouting:

"Greeting! blessing! Eye of Khamon! ah! deliver us! 'Tis the fault of the rich! they want to put you to death! Take care of yourself, Barca!"

He made no reply, as if the loud clamour of oceans and battles had completely deafened him. But when he was below the staircase leading down from the Acropolis, Hamilcar raised his head, and looked with folded arms upon the temple of Eschmoun. His gaze mounted higher still, to the great pure sky; he shouted an order in a harsh voice to his sailors; the trireme leaped forward; it grazed the idol set up at the corner of the mole to stay the storms; and in the merchant harbour, which was full of filth, fragments of wood, and rinds of fruit, it pushed aside and crushed against the other ships moored to stakes and terminating in crocodiles' jaws. The people hastened thither, and some threw themselves into the water to swim to it. It was already at the very end before the gate which bristled with nails. The gate rose, and the trireme disappeared beneath the deep arch.

The Military Harbour was completely separated from the town; when ambassadors arrived, they had to proceed between two walls through a passage which had its outlet on the left in front of the temple of Khamon. This great expanse of water was as round as a cup, and was bordered with quays on which sheds were built for sheltering the ships. Before each of these rose two pillars bearing the horns of Ammon on their capitals and forming continuous porticoes all round the basin. On an island in the centre stood a house for the marine Suffet.

The water was so limpid that the bottom was visible with its paving of white pebbles. The noise of the streets did not reach so far, and Hamilcar as he passed recognised the triremes which he had formerly commanded.

Not more than twenty perhaps remained, under shelter on the land, leaning over on their sides or standing upright on their keels, with lofty poops and swelling prows, and covered with gildings and mystic symbols. The chimaeras had lost their wings, the Patæc Gods their arms, the bulls their silver horns;—and half-painted, motionless, and rotten as they were, yet full of associations, and still emitting the scent of voyages, they all seemed to say to him, like mutilated soldiers on seeing their master again, "'Tis we! 'Tis we! and you too are vanquished!"

No one excepting the marine Suffet might enter the admiral's house. So long as there was no proof of his death he was considered as still in existence. In this way the Ancients avoided a master the more, and they had not failed to comply with the custom in respect to Hamilcar.

The Suffet proceeded into the deserted apartments. At every step he recognised armour and furniture—familiar objects which nevertheless astonished him, and in a perfuming-pan in the vestibule there even remained the ashes of the perfumes that had been kindled at his departure for the conjuration of Melkarth. It was not thus that he had hoped to return. Everything that he had done, everything that he had seen, unfolded itself in his memory: assaults, conflagrations, legions, tempests, Drepanum, Syracuse, Lilybæum, Mount Etna, the plateau of Eryx, five years of battles,—until the fatal day when arms had been laid down and Sicily had been lost. Then he once more saw the woods of citron-trees, and herdsmen with their goats on grey mountains; and his heart leaped at the thought of the establishment of another Carthage down yonder. His projects and his recollections buzzed through his head, which was still dizzy from the pitching of the vessel; he was overwhelmed with anguish, and, becoming suddenly weak, he felt the necessity of drawing near to the gods.

Then he went up to the highest story of his house, and taking a nail-studded staple from a golden shell, which hung on his arm, he opened a small oval chamber.

It was softly lighted by means of delicate black discs let into the wall and as transparent as glass. Between the rows of these equal discs, holes, like those for the urns in columbaria, were hollowed out. Each of them contained a round dark stone, which appeared to be very heavy. Only people of superior understanding honoured these abaddirs, which had fallen from the moon. By their fall they denoted the stars, the sky, and fire; by their colour dark night, and by their density the cohesion of terrestrial things. A stifling atmosphere filled this mystic place. The round stones lying in the niches were whitened somewhat with sea-sand which the wind had no doubt driven through the door. Hamilcar counted them one after another with the tip of his finger; then he hid his face in a saffron-coloured veil, and, falling on his knees, stretched himself on the ground with both arms extended.

The daylight outside was beginning to strike on the folding shutters of black lattice-work. Arborescences, hillocks, eddies, and ill-defined animals appeared in their diaphanous thickness; and the light came terrifying and yet peaceful as it must be behind the sun in the dull spaces of future creations. He strove to banish from his thoughts all forms, and all symbols and appellations of the gods, that he might the better apprehend the immutable spirit which outward appearances took away. Something of the planetary vitalities penetrated him, and he felt withal a wiser and more intimate scorn of death and of every accident. When he rose he was filled with serene fearlessness and was proof against pity or dread, and as his chest was choking he went to the top of the tower which overlooked Carthage.

The town sank downwards in a long hollow curve, with its cupolas, its temples, its golden roofs, its houses, its clusters of palm trees here and there, and its glass balls with streaming rays, while the ramparts formed, as it were, the gigantic border of this horn of plenty which poured itself out before him. Far below he could see the harbours, the squares, the interiors of the courts, the plan of the streets, and the people, who seemed very small and but little above the level of the pavement. Ah! if Hanno had not arrived too late on the morning of the Ægatian islands! He fastened his eyes on the extreme horizon and stretched forth his quivering arms in the direction of Rome.

The steps of the Acropolis were occupied by the multitude. In the square of Khamon the people were pressing forwards to see the Suffet come out, and the terraces were gradually being loaded with people; a few recognised him, and he was saluted; but he retired in order the better to excite the impatience of the people.

Hamilcar found the most important men of his party below in the hall: Istatten, Subeldia, Hictamon, Yeoubas and others. They related to him all that had taken place since the conclusion of the peace: the greed of the Ancients, the departure of the soldiers, their return, their demands, the capture of Gisco, the theft of the zaïmph, the relief and subsequent abandonment of Utica; but no one ventured to tell him of the events which concerned himself. At last they separated, to meet again during the night at the assembly of the Ancients in the temple of Moloch.

They had just gone out when a tumult arose outside the door. Some one was trying to enter in spite of the servants; and as the disturbance was increasing Hamilcar ordered the stranger to be shown in.

An old Negress made her appearance, broken, wrinkled, trembling, stupid-looking, wrapped to the heels in ample blue veils. She advanced face to face with the Suffet, and they looked at each other for some time; suddenly Hamilcar started; at a wave of his hand the slaves withdrew. Then, signing to her to walk with precaution, he drew her by the arm into a remote apartment.

The Negress threw herself upon the floor to kiss his feet; he raised her brutally.

"Where have you left him, Iddibal?"

"Down there, Master;" and extricating herself from her veils, she rubbed her face with her sleeve; the black colour, the senile trembling, the bent figure disappeared, and there remained a strong old man whose skin seemed tanned by sand, wind, and sea. A tuft of white hair rose on his skull like the crest of a bird; and he indicated his disguise, as it lay on the ground, with an ironic glance.

"You have done well, Iddibal! 'Tis well!" Then piercing him, as it were, with his keen gaze: "No one yet suspects?"

The old man swore to him by the Kabiri that the mystery had been kept. They never left their cottage, which was three days' journey from Hadrumetum, on a shore peopled with turtles, and with palms on the dune. "And in accordance with your command, O Master! I teach him to hurl the javelin and to drive a team."

"He is strong, is he not?"

"Yes, Master, and intrepid as well! He has no fear of serpents, or thunder, or phantoms. He runs bare-footed like a herdsman along the brinks of precipices."

"Speak! speak!"

"He invents snares for wild beasts. Would you believe it, that last moon he surprised an eagle; he dragged it away, and the bird's blood and the child's were scattered in the air in large drops like driven roses. The animal in its fury enwrapped him in the beating of its wings; he strained it against his breast, and as it died his laughter increased, piercing and proud like the clashing of swords."

Hamilcar bent his head, dazzled by such presages of greatness.

"But he has been for some time restless and disturbed. He gazes at the sails passing far out at sea; he is melancholy, he rejects bread, he inquires about the gods, and he wishes to become acquainted with Carthage."

"No, no! not yet!" exclaimed the Suffet.

The old slave seemed to understand the peril which alarmed Hamilcar, and he resumed:

"How is he to be restrained? Already I am obliged to make him promises, and I have come to Carthage only to buy him a dagger with a silver handle and pearls all around it." Then he told how, having perceived the Suffet on the terrace, he had passed himself off on the warders of the harbour as one of Salammbô's women, so as to make his way in to him.

Hamilcar remained for a long time apparently lost in deliberation; at last he said:

"To-morrow you will present yourself at sunset behind the purple factories in Megara, and imitate a jackal's cry three times. If you do not see me, you will return to Carthage on the first day of every moon. Forget nothing! Love him! You may speak to him now about Hamilcar."

The slave resumed his costume, and they left the house and the harbour together.

Hamilcar went on his way alone on foot and without an escort, for the meetings of the Ancients were, under extraordinary circumstances, always secret, and were resorted to mysteriously.

At first he went along the western front of the Acropolis, and then passed through the Green Market, the galleries of Kinisdo, and the Perfumers' suburb. The scattered lights were being extinguished, the broader streets grew still, then shadows glided through the darkness. They followed him, others appeared, and like him they all directed their course towards the Mappalian district.

The temple of Moloch was built at the foot of a steep defile in a sinister spot. From below nothing could be seen but lofty walls rising indefinitely like those of a monstrous tomb. The night was gloomy, a greyish fog seemed to weigh upon the sea, which beat against the cliff with a noise as of death-rattles and sobs; and the shadows gradually vanished as if they had passed through the walls.

But as soon as the doorway was crossed one found oneself in a vast quadrangular court bordered by arcades. In the centre rose a mass of architecture with eight equal faces. It was surmounted by cupolas which thronged around a second story supporting a kind of rotunda, from which sprang a cone with a re-entrant curve and terminating in a ball on the summit.

Fires were burning in cylinders of filigree-work fitted upon poles, which men were carrying to and fro. These lights flickered in the gusts of wind and reddened the golden combs which fastened their plaited hair on the nape of the neck. They ran about calling to one another to receive the Ancients.

Here and there on the flag-stones huge lions were couched like sphinxes, living symbols of the devouring sun. They were slumbering with half-closed eyelids. But roused by the footsteps and voices they rose slowly, came towards the Ancients, whom they recognised by their dress, and rubbed themselves against their thighs, arching their backs with sonorous yawns; the vapour of their breath passed across the light of the torches. The stir increased, doors closed, all the priests fled, and the Ancients disappeared beneath the columns which formed a deep vestibule round the temple.

These columns were arranged in such a way that their circular ranks, which were contained one within another, showed the Saturnian period with its years, the years with their months, and the months with their days, and finally reached to the walls of the sanctuary.

Here it was that the Ancients laid aside their sticks of narwhal's-horn,—for a law which was always observed inflicted the punishment of death upon any one entering the meeting with any kind of weapon. Several wore a rent repaired with a strip of purple at the bottom of their garment, to show that they had not been economical in their dress when mourning for their relatives, and this testimony to their affliction prevented the slit from growing larger. Others had their beards inclosed in little bags of violet skin, and fastened to their ears by two cords. They all accosted one another by embracing breast to breast. They surrounded Hamilcar with congratulations; they might have been taken for brothers meeting their brother again.

These men were generally thick-set, with curved noses like those of the Assyrian colossi. In a few, however, the more prominent cheek-bone, the taller figure, and the narrower foot, betrayed an African origin and nomad ancestors. Those who lived continually shut up in their counting-houses had pale faces; others showed in theirs the severity of the desert, and strange jewels sparkled on all the fingers of their hands, which were burnt by unknown suns. The navigators might be distinguished by their rolling gait, while the men of agriculture smelt of the wine-press, dried herbs, and the sweat of mules. These old pirates had lands under tillage, these money-grubbers would fit out ships, these proprietors of cultivated lands supported slaves who followed trades. All were skilled in religious discipline, expert in strategy, pitiless and rich. They looked wearied of prolonged cares. Their flaming eyes expressed distrust, and their habits of travelling and lying, trafficking and commanding, gave an appearance of cunning and violence, a sort of discreet and convulsive brutality to their whole demeanour. Further, the influence of the god cast a gloom upon them.

They first passed through a vaulted hall which was shaped like an egg. Seven doors, corresponding to the seven planets, displayed seven squares of different colours against the wall. After traversing a long room they entered another similar hall.

A candelabrum completely covered with chiselled flowers was burning at the far end, and each of its eight golden branches bore a wick of byssus in a diamond chalice. It was placed upon the last of the long steps leading to a great altar, the corners of which terminated in horns of brass. Two lateral staircases led to its flattened summit; the stones of it could not be seen; it was like a mountain of heaped cinders, and something indistinct was slowly smoking at the top of it. Then further back, higher than the candelabrum, and much higher than the altar, rose the Moloch, all of iron, and with gaping apertures in his human breast. His outspread wings were stretched upon the wall, his tapering hands reached down to the ground; three black stones bordered by yellow circles represented three eyeballs on his brow, and his bull's head was raised with a terrible effort as if in order to bellow.

Ebony stools were ranged round the apartment. Behind each of them was a bronze shaft resting on three claws and supporting a torch. All these lights were reflected in the mother-of-pearl lozenges which formed the pavement of the hall. So lofty was the latter that the red colour of the walls grew black as it rose towards the vaulted roof, and the three eyes of the idol appeared far above like stars half lost in the night.

The Ancients sat down on the ebony stools after putting the trains of their robes over their heads. They remained motionless with their hands crossed inside their broad sleeves, and the mother-of-pearl pavement seemed like a luminous river streaming from the altar to the door and flowing beneath their naked feet.

The four pontiffs had their places in the centre, sitting back to back on four ivory seats which formed a cross, the high-priest of Eschmoun in a hyacinth robe, the high-priest of Tanith in a white linen robe, the high-priest of Khamon in a tawny woollen robe, and the high-priest of Moloch in a purple robe.

Hamilcar advanced towards the candelabrum. He walked all round it, looking at the burning wicks; then he threw a scented powder upon them, and violet flames appeared at the extremities of the branches.

Then a shrill voice rose; another replied to it, and the hundred Ancients, the four pontiffs, and Hamilcar, who remained standing, simultaneously intoned a hymn, and their voices—ever repeating the same syllables and strengthening the sounds—rose, grew loud, became terrible, and then suddenly were still.

There was a pause for some time. At last Hamilcar drew from his breast a little three-headed statuette, as blue as sapphire, and placed it before him. It was the image of Truth, the very genius of his speech. Then he replaced it in his bosom, and all, as if seized with sudden wrath, cried out:

"They are good friends of yours, are the Barbarians! Infamous traitor! You come back to see us perish, do you not? Let him speak!—No! no!"

They were taking their revenge for the constraint to which political ceremonial had just obliged them; and even though they had wished for Hamilcar's return, they were now indignant that he had not anticipated their disasters, or rather that he had not endured them as well as they.

When the tumult had subsided, the pontiff of Moloch rose:

"We ask you why you did not return to Carthage?"

"What is that to you?" replied the Suffet disdainfully.

Their shouts were redoubled.

"Of what do you accuse me? I managed the war badly, perhaps! You have seen how I order my battles, you who conveniently allow Barbarians—"

"Enough! enough!"

He went on in a low voice so as to make himself the better listened to:

"Oh! that is true! I am wrong, lights of the Baals; there are intrepid men among you! Gisco, rise!" And surveying the step of the altar with half-closed eyelids, as if he sought for some one, he repeated:

"Rise, Gisco! You can accuse me; they will protect you! But where is he?" Then, as if he remembered himself: "Ah! in his house, no doubt! surrounded by his sons, commanding his slaves, happy, and counting on the wall the necklaces of honour which his country has given to him!"

They moved about raising their shoulders as if they were being scourged with thongs. "You do not even know whether he is living or dead!" And without giving any heed to their clamours he said that in deserting the Suffet they had deserted the Republic. So, too, the peace with Rome, however advantageous it might appear to them, was more fatal than twenty battles. A few—those who were the least rich of the Council and were suspected of perpetual leanings towards the people or towards tyranny—applauded. Their opponents, chiefs of the Syssitia and administrators, triumphed over them in point of numbers; and the more eminent of them had ranged themselves close to Hanno, who was sitting at the other end of the hall before the lofty door, which was closed by a hanging of hyacinth colour.

He had covered the ulcers on his face with paint. But the gold dust in his hair had fallen upon his shoulders, where it formed two brilliant sheets, so that his hair appeared whitish, fine, and frizzled like wool. His hands were enveloped in linen soaked in a greasy perfume, which dripped upon the pavement, and his disease had no doubt considerably increased, for his eyes were hidden beneath the folds of his eyelids. He had thrown back his head in order to see. His partisans urged him to speak. At last in a hoarse and hideous voice he said:

"Less arrogance, Barca! We have all been vanquished! Each one supports his own misfortune! Be resigned!"

"Tell us rather," said Hamilcar, smiling, "how it was that you steered your galleys into the Roman fleet?"

"I was driven by the wind," replied Hanno.

"You are like a rhinoceros trampling on his dung: you are displaying your own folly! be silent!" And they began to indulge in recriminations respecting the battle of the Ægatian islands.

Hanno accused him of not having come to meet him.

"But that would have left Eryx undefended. You ought to have stood out from the coast; what prevented you? Ah! I forgot! all elephants are afraid of the sea!"

Hamilcar's followers thought this jest so good that they burst out into loud laughter. The vault rang with it like the beating of tympanums.

Hanno denounced the unworthiness of such an insult; the disease had come upon him from a cold taken at the siege of Hecatompylos, and tears flowed down his face like winter rain on a ruined wall.

Hamilcar resumed:

"If you had loved me as much as him there would be great joy in Carthage now! How many times did I not call upon you! and you always refused me money!"

"We had need of it," said the chiefs of the Syssitia.

"And when things were desperate with me—we drank mules' urine and ate the straps of our sandals; when I would fain have had the blades of grass soldiers and made battalions with the rottenness of our dead, you recalled the vessels that I had left!"

"We could not risk everything," replied Baat-Baal, who possessed gold mines in Darytian Gætulia.

"But what did you do here, at Carthage, in your houses, behind your walls? There are Gauls on the Eridanus, who ought to have been roused, Chanaanites at Cyrene who would have come, and while the Romans send ambassadors to Ptolemæus—"

"Now he is extolling the Romans to us!" Some one shouted out to him: "How much have they paid you to defend them?"

"Ask that of the plains of Brutium, of the ruins of Locri, of Metapontum, and of Heraclea! I have burnt all their trees, I have pillaged all their temples, and even to the death of their grandchildren's grandchildren—"

"Why, you disclaim like a rhetor!" said Kapouras, a very illustrious merchant. "What is it that you want?"

"I say that we must be more ingenious or more terrible! If the whole of Africa rejects your yoke the reason is, my feeble masters, that you do not know how to fasten it to her shoulders! Agathocles, Regulus, Copio, any bold man has only to land and capture her; and when the Libyans in the east concert with the Numidians in the west, and the Nomads come from the south, and the Romans from the north"—a cry of horror rose—"Oh! you will beat your breasts, and roll in the dust, and tear your cloaks! No matter! you will have to go and turn the mill-stone in the Suburra, and gather grapes on the hills of Latium."

They smote their right thighs to mark their sense of the scandal, and the sleeves of their robes rose like large wings of startled birds. Hamilcar, carried away by a spirit, continued his speech, standing on the highest step of the altar, quivering and terrible; he raised his arms, and the rays from the candelabrum which burned behind him passed between his fingers like javelins of gold.

"You will lose your ships, your country seats, your chariots, your hanging beds, and the slaves who rub your feet! The jackal will crouch in your palaces, and the ploughshare will upturn your tombs. Nothing will be left but the eagles' scream and a heap of ruins. Carthage, thou wilt fall!"

The four pontiffs spread out their hands to avert the anathema. All had risen. But the marine Suffet, being a sacerdotal magistrate under the protection of the Sun, was inviolate so long as the assembly of the rich had not judged him. Terror was associated with the altar. They drew back.

Hamilcar had ceased speaking, and was panting with eye fixed, his face as pale as the pearls of his tiara, almost frightened at himself, and his spirit lost in funereal visions. From the height on which he stood, all the torches on the bronze shafts seemed to him like a vast crown of fire laid level with the pavement; black smoke issuing from them mounted up into the darkness of the vault; and for some minutes the silence was so profound that they could hear in the distance the sound of the sea.

Then the Ancients began to question one another. Their interests, their existence, were attacked by the Barbarians. But it was impossible to conquer them without the assistance of the Suffet, and in spite of their pride this consideration made them forget every other. His friends were taken aside. There were interested reconciliations, understandings, and promises. Hamilcar would not take any further part in any government. All conjured him. They besought him; and as the word treason occurred in their speech, he fell into a passion. The sole traitor was the Great Council, for as the enlistment of the soldiers expired with the war, they became free as soon as the war was finished; he even exalted their bravery and all the advantages which might be derived from interesting them in the Republic by donations and privileges.

Then Magdassin, a former provincial governor, said, as he rolled his yellow eyes:

"Truly Barca, with your travelling you have become a Greek, or a Latin, or something! Why speak you of rewards for these men? Rather let ten thousand Barbarians perish than a single one of us!"

The Ancients nodded approval, murmuring:—"Yes, is there need for so much trouble? They can always be had?"

"And they can be got rid of conveniently, can they not? They are deserted as they were by you in Sardinia. The enemy is apprised of the road which they are to take, as in the case of those Gauls in Sicily, or perhaps they are disembarked in the middle of the sea. As I was returning I saw the rock quite white with their bones!"

"What a misfortune!" said Kapouras impudently.

"Have they not gone over to the enemy a hundred times?" cried the others.

"Why, then," exclaimed Hamilcar, "did you recall them to Carthage, notwithstanding your laws? And when they are in your town, poor and numerous amid all your riches, it does not occur to you to weaken them by the slightest division! Afterwards you dismiss the whole of them with their women and children, without keeping a single hostage! Did you expect that they would murder themselves to spare you the pain of keeping your oaths? You hate them because they are strong! You hate me still more, who am their master! Oh! I felt it just now when you were kissing my hands and were all putting a constraint upon yourselves not to bite them!"

If the lions that were sleeping in the court had come howling in, the uproar could not have been more frightful. But the pontiff of Eschmoun rose, and, standing perfectly upright, with his knees close together, his elbows pressed to his body, and his hands half open, he said:

"Barca, Carthage has need that you should take the general command of the Punic forces against the Mercenaries!"

"I refuse," replied Hamilcar.

"We will give you full authority," cried the chiefs of the Syssitia.

"No!"

"With no control, no partition, all the money that you want, all the captives, all the booty, fifty zereths of land for every enemy's corpse."

"No! no! because it is impossible to conquer with you!"

"He is afraid!"

"Because you are cowardly, greedy, ungrateful, pusillanimous and mad!"

"He is careful of them!"

"In order to put himself at their head," said some one.

"And return against us," said another; and from the bottom of the hall Hanno howled:

"He wants to make himself king!"

Then they bounded up, overturning the seats and the torches: the crowd of them rushed towards the altar; they brandished daggers. But Hamilcar dived into his sleeves and drew from them two broad cutlasses; and half stooping, his left foot advanced, his eyes flaming and his teeth clenched, he defied them as he stood there beneath the golden candelabrum.

Thus they had brought weapons with them as a precaution; it was a crime; they looked with terror at one another. As all were guilty, every one became quickly reassured; and by degrees they turned their backs on the Suffet and came down again maddened with humiliation. For the second time they recoiled before him. They remained standing for some time. Several who had wounded their fingers put them to their mouths or rolled them gently in the hem of their mantles, and they were about to depart when Hamilcar heard these words:

"Why! it is a piece of delicacy to avoid distressing his daughter!"

A louder voice was raised:

"No doubt, since she takes her lovers from among the Mercenaries!"

At first he tottered, then his eye rapidly sought for Schahabarim. But the priest of Tanith had alone remained in his place; and Hamilcar could see only his lofty cap in the distance. All were sneering in his face. In proportion as his anguish increased their joy redoubled, and those who were behind shouted amid the hootings:

"He was seen coming out of her room!"

"One morning in the month of Tammouz!"

"It was the thief who stole the zaïmph!"

"A very handsome man!"

"Taller than you!"

He snatched off the tiara, the ensign of his rank—his tiara with its eight mystic rows, and with an emerald shell in the centre—and with both hands and with all his strength dashed it to the ground; the golden circles rebounded as they broke, and the pearls rang upon the pavement. Then they saw a long scar upon the whiteness of his brow; it moved like a serpent between his eyebrows; all his limbs trembled. He ascended one of the lateral staircases which led on to the altar, and walked upon the latter! This was to devote himself to the god, to offer himself as a holocaust. The motion of his mantle agitated the lights of the candelabrum, which was lower than his sandals, and the fine dust raised by his footsteps surrounded him like a cloud as high as the waist. He stopped between the legs of the brass colossus. He took up two handfuls of the dust, the mere sight of which made every Carthaginian shudder with horror, and said:

"By the hundred torches of your Intelligences! by the eight fires of the Kabiri! by the stars, the meteors, and the volcanoes! by everything that burns! by the thirst of the desert and the saltness of the ocean! by the cave of Hadrumetum and the empire of Souls! by extermination! by the ashes of your sons and the ashes of the brothers of your ancestors with which I now mingle my own!—you, the Hundred of the Council of Carthage, have lied in your accusation of my daughter! And I, Hamilcar Barca, marine Suffet, chief of the rich and ruler of the people, in the presence of bull-headed Moloch, I swear"—they expected something frightful, but he resumed in a loftier and calmer tone—"that I will not even speak to her about it!"

The sacred servants entered wearing their golden combs, some with purple sponges and others with branches of palm. They raised the hyacinth curtain which was stretched before the door; and through the opening of this angle there was visible behind the other halls the great pink sky which seemed to be a continuation of the vault and to rest at the horizon upon the blue sea. The sun was issuing from the waves and mounting upwards. It suddenly struck upon the breast of the brazen colossus, which was divided into seven compartments closed by gratings. His red-toothed jaws opened in a horrible yawn; his enormous nostrils were dilated, the broad daylight animated him, and gave him a terrible and impatient aspect, as if he would fain have leaped without to mingle with the star, the god, and together traverse the immensities.

The torches, however, which were scattered on the ground, were still burning, while here and there on the mother-of-pearl pavement was stretched from them what looked like spots of blood. The Ancients were reeling from exhaustion; they filled their lungs inhaling the freshness of the air; the sweat flowed down their livid faces; they had shouted so much that they could now scarcely make their voices heard. But their wrath against the Suffet was not at all abated; they hurled menaces at him by way of farewells, and Hamilcar answered them again.

"Until the next night, Barca, in the temple of Eschmoun!"

"I shall be there!"

"We will have you condemned by the rich!"

"And I you by the people!"

"Take care that you do not end on the cross!"

"And you that you are not torn to pieces in the streets!"

As soon as they were on the threshold of the court they again assumed a calm demeanour.

Their runners and coachmen were waiting for them at the door. Most of them departed on white mules. The Suffet leaped into his chariot and took the reins; the two animals, curving their necks, and rhythmically beating the resounding pebbles, went up the whole of the Mappalian Way at full gallop, and the silver vulture at the extremity of the pole seemed to fly, so quickly did the chariot pass along.

The road crossed a field planted with slabs of stone, which were painted on the top like pyramids, and had open hands carved out in the centre as if all the dead men lying beneath had stretched them out towards heaven to demand something. Next there came scattered cabins built of earth, branches, and bulrush-hurdles, and all of a conical shape. These dwellings, which became constantly denser as the road ascended towards the Suffet's gardens, were irregularly separated from one another by little pebble walls, trenches of spring water, ropes of esparto-grass, and nopal hedges. But Hamilcar's eyes were fastened on a great tower, the three storys of which formed three monster cylinders—the first being built of stone, the second of brick, and the third all of cedar—supporting a copper cupola upon twenty-four pillars of juniper, from which slender interlacing chains of brass hung down after the manner of garlands. This lofty edifice overlooked the buildings—the emporiums and mercantile houses—which stretched to the right, while the women's palace rose at the end of the cypress trees, which were ranged in line like two walls of bronze.

When the echoing chariot had entered through the narrow gateway it stopped beneath a broad shed in which there were shackled horses eating from heaps of chopped grass.

All the servants hastened up. They formed quite a multitude, those who worked on the country estates having been brought to Carthage through fear of the soldiers. The labourers, who were clad in animals' skins, had chains riveted to their ankles and trailing after them; the workers in the purple factories had arms as red as those of executioners; the sailors wore green caps; the fishermen coral necklaces; the huntsmen carried nets on their shoulders; and the people belonging to Megara wore black or white tunics, leathern drawers, and caps of straw, felt or linen, according to their service or their different occupations.

Behind pressed a tattered populace. They lived without employment remote from the apartments, slept at night in the gardens, ate the refuse from the kitchens,—a human mouldiness vegetating in the shadow of the palace. Hamilcar tolerated them from foresight even more than from scorn. They had all put a flower in the ear in token of their joy, and many of them had never seen him.

But men with head-dresses like the Sphinx's, and furnished with great sticks, dashed into the crowd, striking right and left. This was to drive back the slaves, who were curious to see their master, so that he might not be assailed by their numbers or inconvenienced by their smell.

Then they all threw themselves flat on the ground, crying:

"Eye of Baal, may your house flourish!" And through these people as they lay thus on the ground in the avenue of cypress trees, Abdalonim, the Steward of the stewards, waving a white miter, advanced towards Hamilcar with a censer in his hand.

Salammbô was then coming down the galley staircases. All her slave women followed her; and, at each of her steps, they also descended. The heads of the Negresses formed big black spots on the line of the bands of the golden plates clasping the foreheads of the Roman women. Others had silver arrows, emerald butterflies, or long bodkins set like suns in their hair. Rings, clasps, necklaces, fringes, and bracelets shone amid the confusion of white, yellow, and blue garments; a rustling of light material became audible; the pattering of sandals might be heard together with the dull sound of naked feet as they were set down on the wood;—and here and there a tall eunuch, head and shoulders above them, smiled with his face in air. When the shouting of the men had subsided they hid their faces in their sleeves, and together uttered a strange cry like the howling of a she-wolf, and so frenzied and strident was it that it seemed to make the great ebony staircase, with its thronging women, vibrate from top to bottom like a lyre.

The wind lifted their veils, and the slender stems of the papyrus plant rocked gently. It was the month of Schebaz and the depth of winter. The flowering pomegranates swelled against the azure of the sky, and the sea disappeared through the branches with an island in the distance half lost in the mist.

Hamilcar stopped on perceiving Salammbô. She had come to him after the death of several male children. Moreover, the birth of daughters was considered a calamity in the religions of the Sun. The gods had afterwards sent him a son; but he still felt something of the betrayal of his hope, and the shock, as it were, of the curse which he had uttered against her. Salammbô, however, continued to advance.

Long bunches of various-coloured pearls fell from her ears to her shoulders, and as far as her elbows. Her hair was crisped so as to simulate a cloud. Round her neck she wore little quadrangular plates of gold, representing a woman between two rampant lions; and her costume was a complete reproduction of the equipment of the goddess. Her broad-sleeved hyacinth robe fitted close to her figure, widening out below. The vermilion on her lips gave additional whiteness to her teeth, and the antimony on her eyelids greater length to her eyes. Her sandals, which were cut out in bird's plumage, had very high heels, and she was extraordinarily pale, doubtless on account of the cold.

At last she came close to Hamilcar, and without looking at him, without raising her head to him:

"Greeting, eye of Baalim, eternal glory! triumph! leisure! satisfaction! riches! Long has my heart been sad and the house drooping. But the returning master is like reviving Tammouz; and beneath your gaze, O father, joyfulness and a new existence will everywhere prevail!"

And taking from Taanach's hands a little oblong vase wherein smoked a mixture of meal, butter, cardamom, and wine: "Drink freely," said she, "of the returning cup, which your servant has prepared!"

He replied: "A blessing upon you!" and he mechanically grasped the golden vase which she held out to him.

He scanned her, however, with such harsh attention, that Salammbô was troubled and stammered out:

"They have told you, O Master!"

"Yes! I know!" said Hamilcar in a low voice.

Was this a confession, or was she speaking of the Barbarians? And he added a few vague words upon the public embarrassments which he hoped by his sole efforts to clear away.

"O father!" exclaimed Salammbô, "you will not obliterate what is irreparable!"

Then he drew back and Salammbô was astonished at his amazement; for she was not thinking of Carthage but of the sacrilege in which she found herself implicated. This man, who made legions tremble and whom she hardly knew, terrified her like a god; he had guessed, he knew all, something awful was about to happen. "Pardon!" she cried.

Hamilcar slowly bowed his head.

Although she wished to accuse herself she dared not open her lips; and yet she felt stifled with the need of complaining and being comforted. Hamilcar was struggling against a longing to break his oath. He kept it out of pride or from the dread of putting an end to his uncertainty; and he looked into her face with all his might so as to lay hold on what she kept concealed at the bottom of her heart.

By degrees the panting Salammbô, crushed by such heavy looks, let her head sink below her shoulders. He was now sure that she had erred in the embrace of a Barbarian; he shuddered and raised both his fists. She uttered a shriek and fell down among her women, who crowded around her.

Hamilcar turned on his heel. All the stewards followed him.

The door of the emporiums was opened, and he entered a vast round hall form which long passages leading to other halls branched off like the spokes from the nave of a wheel. A stone disc stood in the centre with balustrades to support the cushions that were heaped up upon carpets.

The Suffet walked at first with rapid strides; he breathed noisily, he struck the ground with his heel, and drew his hand across his forehead like a man annoyed by flies. But he shook his head, and as he perceived the accumulation of his riches he became calm; his thoughts, which were attracted by the vistas in the passages, wandered to the other halls that were full of still rarer treasures. Bronze plates, silver ingots, and iron bars alternated with pigs of tin brought from the Cassiterides over the Dark Sea; gums from the country of the Blacks were running over their bags of palm bark; and gold dust heaped up in leathern bottles was insensibly creeping out through the worn-out seams. Delicate filaments drawn from marine plants hung amid flax from Egypt, Greece, Taprobane and Judæa; mandrepores bristled like large bushes at the foot of the walls; and an indefinable odour—the exhalation from perfumes, leather, spices, and ostrich feathers, the latter tied in great bunches at the very top of the vault—floated through the air. An arch was formed above the door before each passage with elephants' teeth placed upright and meeting together at the points.

At last he ascended the stone disc. All the stewards stood with arms folded and heads bent while Abdalonim reared his pointed mitre with a haughty air.

Hamilcar questioned the Chief of the Ships. He was an old pilot with eyelids chafed by the wind, and white locks fell to his hips as if dashing foam of the tempests had remained on his beard.

He replied that he had sent a fleet by Gades and Thymiamata to try to reach Eziongaber by doubling the Southern Horn and the promontory of Aromata.

Others had advanced continuously towards the west for four moons without meeting with any shore; but the ships prows became entangled in weeds, the horizon echoed continually with the noise of cataracts, blood-coloured mists darkened the sun, a perfume-laden breeze lulled the crews to sleep; and their memories were so disturbed that they were now unable to tell anything. However, expeditions had ascended the rivers of the Scythians, had made their way into Colchis, and into the countries of the Jugrians and of the Estians, had carried off fifteen hundred maidens in the Archipelago, and sunk all the strange vessels sailing beyond Cape Oestrymon, so that the secret of the routes should not be known. King Ptolemæus was detaining the incense from Schesbar; Syracuse, Elathia, Corsica, and the islands had furnished nothing, and the old pilot lowered his voice to announce that a trireme was taken at Rusicada by the Numidians,—"for they are with them, Master."

Hamilcar knit his brows; then he signed to the Chief of the Journeys to speak. This functionary was enveloped in a brown, ungirdled robe, and had his head covered with a long scarf of white stuff which passed along the edge of his lips and fell upon his shoulder behind.

The caravans had set out regularly at the winter equinox. But of fifteen hundred men directing their course towards the extreme boundaries of Ethiopia with excellent camels, new leathern bottles, and supplies of painted cloth, but one had reappeared at Carthage—the rest having died of fatigue or become mad through the terror of the desert;—and he said that far beyond the Black Harousch, after passing the Atarantes and the country of the great apes, he had seen immense kingdoms, wherein the pettiest utensils were all of gold, a river of the colour of milk and as broad as the sea, forests of blue trees, hills of aromatics, monsters with human faces vegetating on the rocks with eyeballs which expanded like flowers to look at you; and then crystal mountains supporting the sun behind lakes all covered with dragons. Others had returned from India with peacocks, pepper, and new textures. As to those who go by way of the Syrtes and the temple of Ammon to purchase chalcedony, they had no doubt perished in the sands. The caravans from Gætulia and Phazzana had furnished their usual supplies; but he, the Chief of the Journeys, did not venture to fit one out just now.

Hamilcar understood; the Mercenaries were in occupation of the country. He leaned upon his other elbow with a hollow groan; and the Chief of Farms was so afraid to speak that he trembled horribly in spite of his thick shoulders and his big red eyeballs. His face, which was as snub-nosed as a mastiff's, was surmounted by a net woven of threads of bark. He wore a waist-belt of hairy leopard's skin, wherein gleamed two formidable cutlasses.

As soon as Hamilcar turned away he began to cry aloud and invoke all the Baals. It was not his fault! he could not help it! He had watched the temperature, the soil, the stars, had planted at the winter solstice and pruned at the waning of the moon, had inspected the slaves and had been careful of their clothes.

But Hamilcar grew angry at this loquacity. He clacked his tongue, and the man with the cutlasses went on in rapid tones:

"Ah, Master! they have pillaged everything! sacked everything! destroyed everything! Three thousand trees have been cut down at Maschala, and at Ubada the granaries have been looted and the cisterns filled up! At Tedes they have carried off fifteen hundred gomors of meal; at Marrazana they have killed the shepherds, eaten the flocks, burnt your house—your beautiful house with its cedar beams, which you used to visit in the summer! The slaves at Tuburbo who were reaping barley fled to the mountains; and the asses, the mules both great and small, the oxen from Taormina, and the antelopes,—not a single one left! all carried away! It is a curse! I shall not survive it!" He went on again in tears: "Ah! if you knew how full the cellars were, and how the ploughshares shone! Ah! the fine rams! ah! the fine bulls!—"

Hamilcar's wrath was choking him. It burst forth:

"Be silent! Am I a pauper then? No lies! speak the truth! I wish to know all that I have lost to the last shekel, to the last cab! Abdalonim, bring me the accounts of the ships, of the caravans, of the farms, of the house! And if your consciences are not clear, woe be on your heads! Go out!"

All the stewards went out walking backwards, with their fists touching the ground.

Abdalonim went up to a set of pigeon-holes in the wall, and from the midst of them took out knotted cords, strips of linen or papyrus, and sheeps' shoulder-blades inscribed with delicate writing. He laid them at Hamilcar's feet, placed in his hands a wooden frame furnished on the inside with three threads on which balls of gold, silver, and horn were strung, and began:

"One hundred and ninety-two houses in the Mappalian district let to the New Carthaginians at the rate of one bekah a moon."

"No! it is too much! be lenient towards the poor people! and you will try to learn whether they are attached to the Republic, and write down the names of those who appear to you to be the most daring! What next?"

Abdalonim hesitated in surprise at such generosity.

Hamilcar snatched the strips of linen from his hands.

"What is this? three palaces around Khamon at twelve kesitahs a month! Make it twenty! I do not want to be eaten up by the rich."

The Steward of the stewards, after a long salutation, resumed:

"Lent to Tigillas until the end of the season two kikars at three per cent., maritime interest; to Bar-Malkarth fifteen hundred shekels on the security of thirty slaves. But twelve have died in the salt-marshes."

"That is because they were not hardy," said the Suffet, laughing. "No matter! if he is in want of money, satisfy him! We should always lend, and at different rates of interest, according to the wealth of the individual."

Then the servant hastened to read all that had been brought in by the iron-mines of Annaba, the coral fisheries, the purple factories, the farming of the tax on the resident Greeks, the export of silver to Arabia, where it had ten times the value of gold, and the captures of vessels, deduction of a tenth being made for the temple of the goddess. "Each time I declared a quarter less, Master!" Hamilcar was reckoning with the balls; they rang beneath his fingers.

"Enough! What have you paid?"

"To Stratonicles of Corinth, and to three Alexandrian merchants, on these letters here (they have been realised), ten thousand Athenian drachmas, and twelve Syrian talents of gold. The food for the crews, amounting to twenty minæ a month for each trireme—"

"I know! How many lost?"

"Here is the account on these sheets of lead," said the Steward. "As to the ships chartered in common, it has often been necessary to throw the cargo into the seas, and so the unequal losses have been divided among the partners. For the ropes which were borrowed from the arsenals, and which it was impossible to restore, the Syssitia exacted eight hundred kesitahs before the expedition to Utica."

"They again!" said Hamilcar, hanging his head; and he remained for a time as if quite crushed by the weight of all the hatreds that he could feel upon him. "But I do not see the Megara expenses?"

Abdalonim, turning pale, went to another set of pigeon-holes, and took from them some planchettes of sycamore wood strung in packets on leathern strings.

Hamilcar, curious about these domestic details, listened to him and grew calm with the monotony of the tones in which the figures were enumerated. Abdalonim became slower. Suddenly he let the wooden sheets fall to the ground and threw himself flat on his face with his arms stretched out in the position of a condemned criminal. Hamilcar picked up the tablets without any emotion; and his lips parted and his eyes grew larger when he perceived an exorbitant consumption of meat, fish, birds, wines, and aromatics, with broken vases, dead slaves, and spoiled carpets set down as the expense of a single day.

Abdalonim, still prostrate, told him of the feast of the Barbarians. He had not been able to avoid the command of the Ancients. Moreover, Salammbô desired money to be lavished for the better reception of the soldiers.

At his daughter's name Hamilcar leaped to his feet. Then with compressed lips he crouched down upon the cushions, tearing the fringes with his nails, and panting with staring eyes.

"Rise!" said he; and he descended.

Abdalonim followed him; his knees trembled. But seizing an iron bar he began like one distraught to loosen the paving stones. A wooden disc sprang up and soon there appeared throughout the length of the passage several of the large covers employed for stopping up the trenches in which grain was kept.

"You see, Eye of Baal," said the servant, trembling, "they have not taken everything yet! and these are each fifty cubits deep and filled up to the brim! During your voyage I had them dug out in the arsenals, in the gardens, everywhere! your house is full of corn as your heart is full of wisdom."

A smile passed over Hamilcar's face. "It is well, Abdalonim!" Then bending over to his ear: "You will have it brought from Etruria, Brutium, whence you will, and no matter at what price! Heap it and keep it! I alone must possess all the corn in Carthage."

Then when they were alone at the extremity of the passage, Abdalonim, with one of the keys hanging at his girdle, opened a large quadrangular chamber divided in the centre by pillars of cedar. Gold, silver, and brass coins were arranged on tables or packed into niches, and rose as high as the joists of the roof along the four walls. In the corners there were huge baskets of hippopotamus skin supporting whole rows of smaller bags; there were hillocks formed of heaps of bullion on the pavement; and here and there a pile that was too high had given way and looked like a ruined column. The large Carthaginian pieces, representing Tanith with a horse beneath a palm-tree, mingled with those from the colonies, which were marked with a bull, star, globe, or crescent. Then there might be seen pieces of all values, dimensions, and ages arrayed in unequal amounts—from the ancient coins of Assyria, slender as the nail, to the ancient ones of Latium, thicker than the hand, with the buttons of Egina, the tablets of Bactriana, and the short bars of Lacedæmon; many were covered with rust, or had grown greasy, or, having been taken in nets or from among the ruins of captured cities, were green with the water or blackened by fire. The Suffet had speedily calculated whether the sums present corresponded with the gains and losses which had just been read to him; and he was going away when he perceived three brass jars completely empty. Abdalonim turned away his head to mark his horror, and Hamilcar, resigning himself to it, said nothing.

They crossed other passages and other halls, and at last reached a door where, to ensure its better protection and in accordance with a Roman custom lately introduced into Carthage, a man was fastened by the waist to a long chain let into the wall. His beard and nails had grown to an immoderate length, and he swayed himself from right to left with that continual oscillation which is characteristic of captive animals. As soon as he recognised Hamilcar he darted towards him, crying:

"Pardon, Eye of Baal! pity! kill me! For ten years I have not seen the sun! In your father's name, pardon!"

Hamilcar, without answering him, clapped his hands and three men appeared; and all four simultaneously stiffening their arms, drew back from its rings the enormous bar which closed the door. Hamilcar took a torch and disappeared into the darkness.

This was believed to be the family burying-place; but nothing would have been found in it except a broad well. It was dug out merely to baffle robbers, and it concealed nothing. Hamilcar passed along beside it; then stooping down he made a very heavy millstone turn upon its rollers, and through this aperture entered an apartment which was built in the shape of a cone.

The walls were covered with scales of brass; and in the centre, on a granite pedestal, stood the statue of one of the Kabiri called Aletes, the discoverer of the mines in Celtiberia. On the ground, at its base, and arranged in the form of a cross, were large gold shields and monster close-necked silver vases, of extravagant shape and unfitted for use; it was customary to cast quantities of metal in this way, so that dilapidation and even removal should be almost impossible.

With his torch he lit a miner's lamp which was fastened to the idol's cap, and green, yellow, blue, violet, wine-coloured, and blood-coloured fires suddenly illuminated the hall. It was filled with gems which were either in gold calabashes fastened like sconces upon sheets of brass, or were ranged in native masses at the foot of the wall. There were callaides shot away from the mountains with slings, carbuncles formed by the urine of the lynx, glossopetræ which had fallen from the moon, tyanos, diamonds, sandastra, beryls, with the three kinds of rubies, the four kinds of sapphires, and the twelve kinds of emeralds. They gleamed like splashes of milk, blue icicles, and silver dust, and shed their light in sheets, rays, and stars. Ceraunia, engendered by the thunder, sparkled by the side of chalcedonies, which are a cure for poison. There were topazes from Mount Zabarca to avert terrors, opals from Bactriana to prevent abortions, and horns of Ammon, which are placed under the bed to induce dreams.

The fires from the stones and the flames from the lamp were mirrored in the great golden shields. Hamilcar stood smiling with folded arms, and was less delighted by the sight of his riches than by the consciousness of their possession. They were inaccessible, exhaustless, infinite. His ancestors sleeping beneath his feet transmitted something of their eternity to his heart. He felt very near to the subterranean deities. It was as the joy of one of the Kabiri; and the great luminous rays striking upon his face looked like the extremity of an invisible net linking him across the abysses with the centre of the world.

A thought came which made him shudder, and placing himself behind the idol he walked straight up to the wall. Then among the tattooings on his arm he scrutinised a horizontal line with two other perpendicular ones which in Chanaanitish figures expressed the number thirteen. Then he counted as far as the thirteenth of the brass plates and again raised his ample sleeve; and with his right hand stretched out he read other more complicated lines on his arm, at the same time moving his fingers daintily about like one playing on a lyre. At last he struck seven blows with his thumb, and an entire section of the wall turned about in a single block.

It served to conceal a sort of cellar containing mysterious things which had no name and were of incalculable value. Hamilcar went down the three steps, took up a llama's skin which was floating on a black liquid in a silver vat, and then re-ascended.

Abdalonim again began to walk before him. He struck the pavement with his tall cane, the pommel of which was adorned with bells, and before every apartment cried aloud the name of Hamilcar amid eulogies and benedictions.

Along the walls of the circular gallery, from which the passages branched off, were piled little beams of algummim, bags of Lawsonia, cakes of Lemnos-earth, and tortoise carapaces filled with pearls. The Suffet brushed them with his robe as he passed without even looking at some gigantic pieces of amber, an almost divine material formed by the rays of the sun.

A cloud of odorous vapour burst forth.

"Push open the door!"

They went in.

Naked men were kneading pastes, crushing herbs, stirring coals, pouring oil into jars, and opening and shutting the little ovoid cells which were hollowed out all round in the wall, and were so numerous that the apartment was like the interior of a hive. They were brimful of myrobalan, bdellium, saffron, and violets. Gums, powders, roots, glass phials, branches of filipendula, and rose-petals were scattered about everywhere, and the scents were stifling in spite of the cloud-wreaths from the styrax shrivelling on a brazen tripod in the centre.

The Chief of the Sweet Odours, pale and long as a waxen torch, came up to Hamilcar to crush a roll of metopion in his hands, while two others rubbed his heels with leaves of baccharis. He repelled them; they were Cyreneans of infamous morals, but valued on account of the secrets which they possessed.

To show his vigilance the Chief of the Odours offered the Suffet a little malobathrum to taste in an electrum spoon; then he pierced three Indian bezoars with an awl. The master, who knew the artifices employed, took a horn full of balm, and after holding it near the coals inclined it over his robe. A brown spot appeared; it was a fraud. Then he gazed fixedly at the Chief of the Odours, and without saying anything flung the gazelle's horn full in his face.

However indignant he might be at adulterations made to his own prejudice, when he perceived some parcels of nard which were being packed up for countries beyond the sea, he ordered antimony to be mixed with it so as to make it heavier.

Then he asked where three boxes of psagdas designed for his own use were to be found.

The Chief of the Odours confessed that he did not know; some soldiers had come howling in with knives and he had opened the boxes for them.

"So you are more afraid of them then of me!" cried the Suffet; and his eyeballs flashed like torches through the smoke upon the tall, pale man who was beginning to understand. "Abdalonim! you will make him run the gauntlet before sunset: tear him!"

This loss, which was less than the others, had exasperated him; for in spite of his efforts to banish them from his thoughts he was continually coming again across the Barbarians. Their excesses were blended with his daughter's shame, and he was angry with the whole household for knowing of the latter and for not speaking of it to him. But something impelled him to bury himself in his misfortune; and in an inquisitorial fit he visited the sheds behind the mercantile house to see the supplies of bitumen, wood, anchors and cordage, honey and wax, the cloth warehouse, the stores of food, the marble yard and the silphium barn.

He went to the other side of the gardens to make an inspection in their cottages, of the domestic artisans whose productions were sold. There were tailors embroidering cloaks, others making nets, others painting cushions or cutting out sandals, and Egyptian workmen polished papyrus with a shell, while the weavers' shuttles rattled and the armourers' anvils rang.

Hamilcar said to them:

"Beat away at the swords! I shall want them." And he drew the antelope's skin that had been steeped in poisons from his bosom to have it cut into a cuirass more solid than one of brass and unassailable by steel or flame.

As soon as he approached the workmen, Abdalonim, to give his wrath another direction, tried to anger him against them by murmured disparagement of their work. "What a performance! It is a shame! The Master is indeed too good." Hamilcar moved away without listening to him.

He slackened his pace, for the paths were barred by great trees calcined from one end to the other, such as may be met with in woods where shepherds have encamped; and the palings were broken, the water in the trenches was disappearing, while fragments of glass and the bones of apes were to be seen amid the miry puddles. A scrap of cloth hung here and there from the bushes, and the rotten flowers formed a yellow muck-heap beneath the citron trees. In fact, the servants had neglected everything, thinking that the master would never return.

At every step he discovered some new disaster, some further proof of the thing which he had forbidden himself to learn. Here he was soiling his purple boots as he crushed the filth under-foot; and he had not all these men before him at the end of a catapult to make them fly into fragments! He felt humiliated at having defended them; it was a delusion and a piece of treachery; and as he could not revenge himself upon the soldiers, or the Ancients, or Salammbô, or anybody, and his wrath required some victim, he condemned all the slaves of the gardens to the mines at a single stroke.

Abdalonim shuddered each time that he saw him approaching the parks. But Hamilcar took the path towards the mill, from which there might be heard issuing a mournful melopoia.

The heavy mill-stones were turning amid the dust. They consisted of two cones of porphyry laid the one upon the other—the upper one of the two, which carried a funnel, being made to revolve upon the second by means of strong bars. Some men were pushing these with their breasts and arms, while others were yoked to them and were pulling them. The friction of the straps had formed purulent scabs round about their armpits such as are seen on asses' withers, and the end of the limp black rag, which scarcely covered their loins, hung down and flapped against their hams like a long tail. Their eyes were red, the irons on their feet clanked, and all their breasts panted rhythmically. On their mouths they had muzzles fastened by two little bronze chains to render it impossible for them to eat the flour, and their hands were enclosed in gauntlets without fingers, so as to prevent them from taking any.

At the master's entrance the wooden bars creaked still more loudly. The grain grated as it was being crushed. Several fell upon their knees; the others, continuing their work, stepped across them.

He asked for Giddenem, the governor of the slaves, and that personage appeared, his rank being displayed in the richness of his dress. His tunic, which was slit up the sides, was of fine purple; his ears were weighted with heavy rings; and the strips of cloth enfolding his legs were joined together with a lacing of gold which extended from his ankles to his hips, like a serpent winding about a tree. In his fingers, which were laden with rings, he held a necklace of jet beads, so as to recognise the men who were subject to the sacred disease.

Hamilcar signed to him to unfasten the muzzles. Then with the cries of famished animals they all rushed upon the flour, burying their faces in the heaps of it and devouring it.

"You are weakening them!" said the Suffet.

Giddenem replied that such treatment was necessary in order to subdue them.

"It was scarcely worth while sending you to the slaves' school at Syracuse. Fetch the others!"

And the cooks, butlers, grooms, runners, and litter-carriers, the men belonging to the vapour-baths, and the women with their children, all ranged themselves in a single line in the garden from the mercantile house to the deer park. They held their breath. An immense silence prevailed in Megara. The sun was lengthening across the lagoon at the foot of the catacombs. The peacocks were screeching. Hamilcar walked along step by step.

"What am I to do with these old creatures?" he said. "Sell them! There are too many Gauls: they are drunkards! and too many Cretans: they are liars! Buy me some Cappadocians, Asiatics, and Negroes."

He was astonished that the children were so few. "The house ought to have births every year, Giddenem. You will leave the huts open every night to let them mingle freely."

He then had the thieves, the lazy, and the mutinous shown to him. He distributed punishments, with reproaches to Giddenem; and Giddenem, ox-like, bent his low forehead, with its two broad intersecting eyebrows.

"See, Eye of Baal," he said, pointing out a sturdy Libyan, "here is one who was caught with the rope round his neck."

"Ah! you wish to die?" said the Suffet scornfully.

"Yes!" replied the slave in an intrepid tone.

Then, without heeding the precedent or the pecuniary loss, Hamilcar said to the serving-men:

"Away with him!"

Perhaps in his thoughts he intended a sacrifice. It was a misfortune which he inflicted upon himself in order to avert more terrible ones.

Giddenem had hidden those who were mutilated behind the others. Hamilcar perceived them.

"Who cut off your arm?"

"The soldiers, Eye of Baal."

Then to a Samnite who was staggering like a wounded heron:

"And you, who did that to you?"

It was the governor, who had broken his leg with an iron bar.

This silly atrocity made the Suffet indignant; he snatched the jet necklace out of Giddenem's hands.

"Cursed be the dog that injures the flock! Gracious Tanith, to cripple slaves! Ah! you ruin your master! Let him be smothered in the dunghill. And those that are missing? Where are they? Have you helped the soldiers to murder them?"

His face was so terrible that all the women fled. The slaves drew back and formed a large circle around them; Giddenem was frantically kissing his sandals; Hamilcar stood upright with his arms raised above him.

But with his understanding as clear as in the sternest of his battles, he recalled a thousand odious things, ignominies from which he had turned aside; and in the gleaming of his wrath he could once more see all his disasters simultaneously as in the lightnings of a storm. The governors of the country estates had fled through terror of the soldiers, perhaps through collusion with them; they were all deceiving him; he had restrained himself too long.

"Bring them here!" he cried; "and brand them on the forehead with red-hot irons as cowards!"

Then they brought and spread out in the middle of the garden, fetters, carcanets, knives, chains for those condemned to the mines, cippi for fastening the legs, numellæ for confining the shoulders, and scorpions or whips with triple thongs terminating in brass claws.

All were placed facing the sun, in the direction of Moloch the Devourer, and were stretched on the ground on their stomachs or on their backs, those, however, who were sentenced to be flogged standing upright against the trees with two men beside them, one counting the blows and the other striking.

In striking he used both his arms, and the whistling thongs made the bark of the plane-trees fly. The blood was scattered like rain upon the foliage, and red masses writhed with howls at the foot of the trees. Those who were under the iron tore their faces with their nails. The wooden screws could be heard creaking; dull knockings resounded; sometimes a sharp cry would suddenly pierce the air. In the direction of the kitchens, men were brisking up burning coals with fans amid tattered garments and scattered hair, and a smell of burning flesh was perceptible. Those who were under the scourge, swooning, but kept in their positions by the bonds on their arms, rolled their heads upon their shoulders and closed their eyes. The others who were watching them began to shriek with terror, and the lions, remembering the feast perhaps, stretched themselves out yawning against the edge of the dens.

Then Salammbô was seen on the platform of her terrace. She ran wildly about it from left to right. Hamilcar perceived her. It seemed to him that she was holding up her arms towards him to ask for pardon; with a gesture of horror he plunged into the elephants' park.

These animals were the pride of the great Punic houses. They had carried their ancestors, had triumphed in the wars, and they were reverenced as being the favourites of the Sun.

Those of Megara were the strongest in Carthage. Before he went away Hamilcar had required Abdalonim to swear that he would watch over them. But they had died from their mutilations; and only three remained, lying in the middle of the court in the dust before the ruins of their manger.

They recognised him and came up to him. One had its ears horribly slit, another had a large wound in its knee, while the trunk of the third was cut off.

They looked sadly at him, like reasonable creatures; and the one that had lost its trunk tried by stooping its huge head and bending its hams to stroke him softly with the hideous extremity of its stump.

At this caress from the animal two tears started into his eyes. He rushed at Abdalonim.

"Ah! wretch! the cross! the cross!"

Abdalonim fell back swooning upon the ground.

The bark of a jackal rang from behind the purple factories, the blue smoke of which was ascending slowly into the sky; Hamilcar paused.

The thought of his son had suddenly calmed him like the touch of a god. He caught a glimpse of a prolongation of his might, an indefinite continuation of his personality, and the slaves could not understand whence this appeasement had come upon him.

As he bent his steps towards the purple factories he passed before the ergastulum, which was a long house of black stone built in a square pit with a small pathway all round it and four staircases at the corners.

Iddibal was doubtless waiting until the night to finish his signal. "There is no hurry yet," thought Hamilcar; and he went down into the prison. Some cried out to him: "Return"; the boldest followed him.

The open door was flapping in the wind. The twilight entered through the narrow loopholes, and in the interior broken chains could be distinguished hanging from the walls.

This was all that remained of the captives of war!

Then Hamilcar grew extraordinarily pale, and those who were leaning over the pit outside saw him resting one hand against the wall to keep himself from falling.

But the jackal uttered its cry three times in succession. Hamilcar raised his head; he did not speak a word nor make a gesture. Then when the sun had completely set he disappeared behind the nopal hedge, and in the evening he said as he entered the assembly of the rich in the temple of Eschmoun:

"Luminaries of the Baalim, I accept the command of the Punic forces against the army of the Barbarians!"

VIII

The Battle of the Macaras

I n the following day he drew two hundred and twenty-three thousand kikars of gold from the Syssitia, and decreed a tax of fourteen shekels upon the rich. Even the women contributed; payment was made in behalf of the children, and he compelled the colleges of priests to furnish money—a monstrous thing, according to Carthaginian customs.

He demanded all the horses, mules, and arms. A few tried to conceal their wealth, and their property was sold; and, to intimidate the avarice of the rest, he himself gave sixty suits of armour, and fifteen hundred gomers of meal, which was as much as was given by the Ivory Company.

He sent into Liguria to buy soldiers, three thousand mountaineers accustomed to fight with bears; they were paid for six moons in advance at the rate of four minæ a day.

Nevertheless an army was wanted. But he did not, like Hanno, accept all the citizens. First he rejected those engaged in sedentary occupations, and then those who were big-bellied or had a pusillanimous look; and he admitted those of ill-repute, the scum of Malqua, sons of Barbarians, freed men. For reward he promised some of the New Carthaginians complete rights of citizenship.

His first care was to reform the Legion. These handsome young fellows, who regarded themselves as the military majesty of the Republic, governed themselves. He reduced their officers to the ranks; he treated them harshly, made them run, leap, ascend the declivity of Byrsa at a single burst, hurl javelins, wrestle together, and sleep in the squares at night. Their families used to come to see them and pity them.

He ordered shorter swords and stronger buskins. He fixed the number of serving-men, and reduced the amount of baggage; and as there were three hundred Roman pila kept in the temple of Moloch, he took them in spite of the pontiff's protests.

He organised a phalanx of seventy-two elephants with those which had returned from Utica, and others which were private property, and rendered them formidable. He armed their drivers with mallet and chisel to enable them to split their skulls in the fight if they ran away.

He would not allow his generals to be nominated by the Grand Council. The Ancients tried to urge the laws in objection, but he set them aside; no one ventured to murmur again, and everything yielded to the violence of his genius.

He assumed sole charge of the war, the government, and the finances; and as a precaution against accusations he demanded the Suffet Hanno as examiner of his accounts.

He set to work upon the ramparts, and had the old and now useless inner walls demolished in order to furnish stones. But difference of fortune, replacing the hierarchy of race, still kept the sons of the vanquished and those of the conquerors apart; thus the patricians viewed the destruction of these ruins with an angry eye, while the plebeians, scarcely knowing why, rejoiced.

The troops defiled under arms through the streets from morning till night; every moment the sound of trumpets was heard; chariots passed bearing shields, tents, and pikes; the courts were full of women engaged in tearing up linen; the enthusiasm spread from one to another, and Hamilcar's soul filled the Republic.

He had divided his soldiers into even numbers, being careful to place a strong man and a weak one alternately throughout the length of his files, so that he who was less vigorous or more cowardly might be at once led and pushed forward by two others. But with his three thousand Ligurians, and the best in Carthage, he could form only a simple phalanx of four thousand and ninety-six hoplites, protected by bronze helmets, and handling ashen sarissæ fourteen cubits long.

There were two thousand young men, each equipped with a sling, a dagger, and sandals. He reinforced them with eight hundred others armed with round shields and Roman swords.

The heavy cavalry was composed of the nineteen hundred remaining guardsmen of the Legion, covered with plates of vermilion bronze, like the Assyrian Clinabarians. He had further four hundred mounted archers, of those that were called Tarentines, with caps of weasel's skin, two-edged axes, and leathern tunics. Finally there were twelve hundred Negroes from the quarter of the caravans, who were mingled with the Clinabarians, and were to run beside the stallions with one hand resting on the manes. All was ready, and yet Hamilcar did not start.

Often at night he would go out of Carthage alone and make his way beyond the lagoon towards the mouths of the Macaras. Did he intend to join the Mercenaries? The Ligurians encamped in the Mappalian district surrounded his house.

The apprehensions of the rich appeared justified when, one day, three hundred Barbarians were seen approaching the walls. The Suffet opened the gates to them; they were deserters; drawn by fear or by fidelity, they were hastening to their master.

Hamilcar's return had not surprised the Mercenaries; according to their ideas the man could not die. He was returning to fulfil his promise;—a hope by no means absurd, so deep was the abyss between Country and Army. Moreover they did not believe themselves culpable; the feast was forgotten.

The spies whom they surprised undeceived them. It was a triumph for the bitter; even the lukewarm grew furious. Then the two sieges overwhelmed then with weariness; no progress was being made; a battle would be better! Thus many men had left the ranks and were scouring the country. But at news of the arming they returned; Matho leaped for joy. "At last! at last!" he cried.

Then the resentment which he cherished against Salammbô was turned against Hamilcar. His hate could now perceive a definite prey; and as his vengeance grew easier of conception he almost believed that he had realised it and he revelled in it already. At the same time he was seized with a loftier tenderness, and consumed by more acrid desire. He saw himself alternately in the midst of the soldiers brandishing the Suffet's head on a pike, and then in the room with the purple bed, clasping the maiden in his arms, covering her face with kisses, passing his hands over her long, black hair; and the imagination of this, which he knew could never be realised, tortured him. He swore to himself that, since his companions had appointed him schalishim, he would conduct the war; the certainty that he would not return from it urged him to render it a pitiless one.

He came to Spendius and said to him:

"You will go and get your men! I will bring mine! Warn Autaritus! We are lost if Hamilcar attacks us! Do you understand me? Rise!"

Spendius was stupefied before such an air of authority. Matho usually allowed himself to be led, and his previous transports had quickly passed away. But just now he appeared at once calmer and more terrible; a superb will gleamed in his eyes like the flame of sacrifice.

The Greek did not listen to his reasons. He was living in one of the Carthaginian pearl-bordered tents, drinking cool beverages from silver cups, playing at the cottabos, letting his hair grow, and conducting the siege with slackness. Moreover, he had entered into communications with some in the town and would not leave, being sure that it would open its gates before many days were over.

Narr' Havas, who wandered about among the three armies, was at that time with him. He supported his opinion, and even blamed the Libyan for wishing in his excess of courage to abandon their enterprise.

"Go, if you are afraid!" exclaimed Matho; "you promised us pitch, sulphur, elephants, foot-soldiers, horses! where are they?"

Narr' Havas reminded him that he had exterminated Hanno's last cohorts;—as to the elephants, they were being hunted in the woods, he was arming the foot-soldiers, the horses were on their way; and the Numidian rolled his eyes like a woman and smiled in an irritating manner as he stroked the ostrich feather which fell upon his shoulder. In his presence Matho was at a loss for a reply.

But a man who was a stranger entered, wet with perspiration, scared, and with bleeding feet and loosened girdle; his breathing shook his lean sides enough to have burst them, and speaking in an unintelligible dialect he opened his eyes wide as if he were telling of some battle. The king sprang outside and called his horsemen.

They ranged themselves in the plain before him in the form of a circle. Narr' Havas, who was mounted, bent his head and bit his lips. At last he separated his men into two equal divisions, and told the first to wait; then with an imperious gesture he carried off the others at a gallop and disappeared on the horizon in the direction of the mountains.

"Master!" murmured Spendius, "I do not like these extraordinary chances—the Suffet returning, Narr' Havas going away—"

"Why! what does it matter?" said Matho disdainfully.

It was a reason the more for anticipating Hamilcar by uniting with Autaritus. But if the siege of the towns were raised, the inhabitants would come out and attack them in the rear, while they would have the Carthaginians in front. After much talking the following measures were resolved upon and immediately executed.

Spendius proceeded with fifteen thousand men as far as the bridge built across the Macaras, three miles from Utica; the corners of it were fortified with four huge towers provided with catapults; all the paths and gorges in the mountains were stopped up with trunks of trees, pieces of rock, interlacings of thorn, and stone walls; on the summits heaps of grass were made which might be lighted as signals, and shepherds who were able to see at a distance were posted at intervals.

No doubt Hamilcar would not, like Hanno, advance by the mountain of the Hot Springs. He would think that Autaritus, being master of the interior, would close the route against him. Moreover, a check at the opening of the campaign would ruin him, while if he gained a victory he would soon have to make a fresh beginning, the Mercenaries being further off. Again, he could disembark at Cape Grapes and march thence upon one of the towns. But he would then find himself between the two armies, an indiscretion which he could not commit with his scanty forces. Accordingly he must proceed along the base of Mount Ariana, then turn to the left to avoid the mouths of the Macaras, and come straight to the bridge. It was there that Matho expected him.

At night he used to inspect the pioneers by torch-light. He would hasten to Hippo-Zarytus or to the works on the mountains, would come back again, would never rest. Spendius envied his energy; but in the management of spies, the choice of sentries, the working of the engines and all means of defence, Matho listened docilely to his companion. They spoke no more of Salammbô,—one not thinking about her, and the other being prevented by a feeling of shame.

Often he would go towards Carthage, striving to catch sight of Hamilcar's troops. His eyes would dart along the horizon; he would lie flat on the ground, and believe that he could hear an army in the throbbing of his arteries.

He told Spendius that if Hamilcar did not arrive in three days he would go with all his men to meet him and offer him battle. Two further days elapsed. Spendius restrained him; but on the morning of the sixth day he departed.

THE CARTHAGINIANS WERE NO LESS impatient for war than the Barbarians. In tents and in houses there was the same longing and the same distress; all were asking one another what was delaying Hamilcar.

From time to time he would mount to the cupola of the temple of Eschmoun beside the Announcer of the Moons and take note of the wind.

One day—it was the third of the month of Tibby—they saw him descending from the Acropolis with hurried steps. A great clamour arose in the Mappalian district. Soon the streets were astir, and the soldiers were everywhere beginning to arm themselves upon their breasts; then they ran quickly to the square of Khamon to take their places in the ranks. No one was allowed to follow them or even to speak to them, or to approach the ramparts; for some minutes the whole town was silent as a great tomb. The soldiers as they leaned on their lances were thinking, and the others in the houses were sighing.

At sunset the army went out by the western gate; but instead of taking the road to Tunis or making for the mountains in the direction of Utica, they continued their march along the edge of the sea; and they soon reached the Lagoon, where round spaces quite whitened with salt glittered like gigantic silver dishes forgotten on the shore.

Then the pools of water multiplied. The ground gradually became softer, and the feet sank in it. Hamilcar did not turn back. He went on still at their head; and his horse, which was yellow-spotted like a dragon, advanced into the mire flinging froth around him, and with great straining of the loins. Night—a moonless light—fell. A few cried out that they were about to perish; he snatched their arms from them, and gave them to the serving-men. Nevertheless the mud became deeper and deeper. Some had to mount the beasts of burden; others clung to the horses' tails; the sturdy pulled the weak, and the Ligurian corps drove on the infantry with the points of their pikes. The darkness increased. They had lost their way. All stopped.

Then some of the Suffet's slaves went on ahead to look for the buoys which had been placed at intervals by his order. They shouted through the darkness, and the army followed them at a distance.

At last they felt the resistance of the ground. Then a whitish curve became dimly visible, and they found themselves on the bank of the Macaras. In spite of the cold no fires were lighted.

In the middle of the night squalls of wind arose. Hamilcar had the soldiers roused, but not a trumpet was sounded: their captain tapped them softly on the shoulder.

A man of lofty stature went down into the water. It did not come up to his girdle; it was possible to cross.

The Suffet ordered thirty-two of the elephants to be posted in the river a hundred paces further on, while the others, lower down, would check the lines of men that were carried away by the current; and holding their weapons above their heads they all crossed the Macaras as though between two walls. He had noticed that the western wind had driven the sand so as to obstruct the river and form a natural causeway across it.

He was now on the left bank in front of Utica, and in a vast plain, the latter being advantageous for his elephants, which formed the strength of his army.

This feat of genius filled the soldiers with enthusiasm. They recovered extraordinary confidence. They wished to hasten immediately against the Barbarians; but the Suffet bade them rest for two hours. As soon as the sun appeared they moved into the plain in three lines—first came the elephants, and then the light infantry with the cavalry behind it, the phalanx marching next.

The Barbarians encamped at Utica, and the fifteen thousand about the bridge were surprised to see the ground undulating in the distance. The wind, which was blowing very hard, was driving tornadoes of sand before it; they rose as though snatched from the soil, ascended in great light-coloured strips, then parted asunder and began again, hiding the Punic army the while from the Mercenaries. Owing to the horns, which stood up on the edge of the helmets, some thought that they could perceive a herd of oxen; others, deceived by the motion of the cloaks, pretended that they could distinguish wings, and those who had travelled a good deal shrugged their shoulders and explained everything by the illusions of the mirage. Nevertheless something of enormous size continued to advance. Little vapours, as subtle as the breath, ran across the surface of the desert; the sun, which was higher now, shone more strongly: a harsh light, which seemed to vibrate, threw back the depths of the sky, and permeating objects, rendered distance incalculable. The immense plain expanded in every direction beyond the limits of vision; and the almost insensible undulations of the soil extended to the extreme horizon, which was closed by a great blue line which they knew to be the sea. The two armies, having left their tents, stood gazing; the people of Utica were massing on the ramparts to have a better view.

At last they distinguished several transverse bars bristling with level points. They became thicker, larger; black hillocks swayed to and fro; square thickets suddenly appeared; they were elephants and lances. A single shout went up: "The Carthaginians!" and without signal or command the soldiers at Utica and those at the bridge ran pell-mell to fall in a body upon Hamilcar.

Spendius shuddered at the name. "Hamilcar! Hamilcar!" he repeated, panting, and Matho was not there! What was to be done? No means of flight! The suddenness of the event, his terror of the Suffet, and above all, the urgent need of forming an immediate resolution, distracted him;

he could see himself pierced by a thousand swords, decapitated, dead. Meanwhile he was being called for; thirty thousand men would follow him; he was seized with fury against himself; he fell back upon the hope of victory; it was full of bliss, and he believed himself more intrepid than Epaminondas. He smeared his cheeks with vermilion in order to conceal his paleness, then he buckled on his knemids and his cuirass, swallowed a patera of pure wine, and ran after his troops, who were hastening towards those from Utica.

They united so rapidly that the Suffet had not time to draw up his men in battle array. By degrees he slackened his speed. The elephants stopped; they rocked their heavy heads with their chargings of ostrich feathers, striking their shoulders the while with their trunks.

Behind the intervals between them might be seen the cohorts of the velites, and further on the great helmets of the Clinabarians, with steel heads glancing in the sun, cuirasses, plumes, and waving standards. But the Carthaginian army, which amounted to eleven thousand three hundred and ninety-six men, seemed scarcely to contain them, for it formed an oblong, narrow at the sides and pressed back upon itself.

Seeing them so weak, the Barbarians, who were thrice as numerous, were seized with extravagant joy. Hamilcar was not to be seen. Perhaps he had remained down yonder? Moreover what did it matter? The disdain which they felt for these traders strengthened their courage; and before Spendius could command a manouvre they had all understood it, and already executed it.

They were deployed in a long, straight line, overlapping the wings of the Punic army in order to completely encompass it. But when there was an interval of only three hundred paces between the armies, the elephants turned round instead of advancing; then the Clinabarians were seen to face about and follow them; and the surprise of the Mercenaries increased when they saw the archers running to join them. So the Carthaginians were afraid, they were fleeing! A tremendous hooting broke out from among the Barbarian troops, and Spendius exclaimed from the top of his dromedary: "Ah! I knew it! Forward! forward!"

Then javelins, darts, and sling-bullets burst forth simultaneously. The elephants feeling their croups stung by the arrows began to gallop more quickly; a great dust enveloped them, and they vanished like shadows in a cloud.

But from the distance there came a loud noise of footsteps dominated by the shrill sound of the trumpets, which were being blown furiously. The space which the Barbarians had in front of them, which was full of eddies and tumult, attracted like a whirlpool; some dashed into it. Cohorts of infantry appeared; they closed up; and at the same time all the rest saw the foot-soldiers hastening up with the horseman at a gallop.

Hamilcar had, in fact, ordered the phalanx to break its sections, and the elephants, light troops, and cavalry to pass through the intervals so as to bring themselves speedily upon the wings, and so well had he calculated the distance from the Barbarians, that at the moment when they reached him, the entire Carthaginian army formed one long straight line.

In the centre bristled the phalanx, formed of syntagmata or full squares having sixteen men on each side. All the leaders of all the files appeared amid long, sharp lanceheads, which jutted out unevenly around them, for the first six ranks crossed their sarissæ, holding them in the middle, and the ten lower ranks rested them upon the shoulders of their companions in succession before them. Their faces were all half hidden beneath the visors of their helmets; their right legs were all covered with bronze knemids; broad cylindrical shields reached down to their knees; and the horrible quadrangular mass moved in a single body, and seemed to live like an animal and work like a machine. Two cohorts of elephants flanked it in regular array; quivering, they shook off the splinters of the arrows that clung to their black skins. The Indians, squatting on their withers among the tufts of white feathers, restrained them with their spoon-headed harpoons, while the men in the towers, who were hidden up to their shoulders, moved about iron distaffs furnished with lighted tow on the edges of their large bended bows. Right and left of the elephants hovered the slingers, each with a sling around his loins, a second on his head, and a third in his right hand. Then came the Clinabarians, each flanked by a Negro, and pointing their lances between the ears of their horses, which, like themselves, were completely covered with gold. Afterwards, at intervals, came the light armed soldiers with shields of lynx skin, beyond which projected the points of the javelins which they held in their left hands; while the Tarentines, each having two coupled horses, relieved this wall of soldiers at its two extremities.

The army of the Barbarians, on the contrary, had not been able to preserve its line. Undulations and blanks were to be found through its extravagant length; all were panting and out of breath with their running.

The phalanx moved heavily along with thrusts from all its sarissæ; and the too slender line of the Mercenaries soon yielded in the centre beneath the enormous weight.

Then the Carthaginian wings expanded in order to fall upon them, the elephants following. The phalanx, with obliquely pointed lances, cut through the Barbarians; there were two enormous, struggling bodies; and the wings with slings and arrows beat them back upon the phalangites. There was no cavalry to get rid of them, except two hundred Numidians operating against the right squadron of the Clinabarians. All the rest were hemmed in, and unable to extricate themselves from the lines. The peril was imminent, and the need of coming to some resolution urgent.

Spendius ordered attacks to be made simultaneously on both flanks of the phalanx so as to pass clean through it. But the narrower ranks glided below the longer ones and recovered their position, and the phalanx turned upon the Barbarians as terrible in flank as it had just been in front.

They struck at the staves of the sarissæ, but the cavalry in the rear embarrassed their attack; and the phalanx, supported by the elephants, lengthened and contracted, presenting itself in the form of a square, a cone, a rhombus, a trapezium, a pyramid. A twofold internal movement went on continually from its head to its rear; for those who were at the lowest part of the files hastened up to the first ranks, while the latter, from fatigue, or on account of the wounded, fell further back. The Barbarians found themselves thronged upon the phalanx. It was impossible for it to advance; there was, as it were, an ocean wherein leaped red crests and scales of brass, while the bright shields rolled like silver foam. Sometimes broad currents would descend from one extremity to the other, and then go up again, while a heavy mass remained motionless in the centre. The lances dipped and rose alternately. Elsewhere there was so quick a play of naked swords that only the points were visible, while turmæ of cavalry formed wide circles which closed again like whirlwinds behind them.

Above the voices of the captains, the ringing of clarions and the grating of tyres, bullets of lead and almonds of clay whistled through the air, dashing the sword from the hand or the brain out of the skull. The wounded, sheltering themselves with one arm beneath their shields, pointed their swords by resting the pommels on the ground, while others, lying in pools of blood, would turn and bite the heels of those above them. The multitude was so compact, the dust so thick, and the tumult so great that it was impossible to distinguish anything; the cowards who offered to surrender were not even heard. Those whose hands were empty clasped one another close; breasts cracked against cuirasses, and corpses hung with head thrown back between a pair of contracted arms. There was a company of sixty Umbrians who, firm on their hams, their pikes before their eyes, immovable and grinding their teeth, forced two syntagmata to recoil simultaneously. Some Epirote shepherds ran upon the left squadron of the Clinabarians, and whirling their staves, seized the horses by the man; the animals threw their riders and fled across the plain. The Punic slingers scattered here and there stood gaping. The phalanx began to waver, the captains ran to and fro in distraction, the rearmost in the files were pressing upon the soldiers, and the Barbarians had re-formed; they were recovering; the victory was theirs.

But a cry, a terrible cry broke forth, a roar of pain and wrath: it came from the seventy-two elephants which were rushing on in double line, Hamilcar having waited until the Mercenaries were massed together in one spot to let them loose against them; the Indians had goaded them so vigorously that blood was trickling down their broad ears. Their trunks, which were smeared with minium, were stretched straight out in the air like red serpents; their breasts were furnished with spears and their backs with cuirasses; their tusks were lengthened with steel blades curved like sabres,—and to make them more ferocious they had been intoxicated with a mixture of pepper, wine, and incense. They shook their necklaces of bells, and shrieked; and the elephantarchs bent their heads beneath the stream of phalaricas which was beginning to fly from the tops of the towers.

In order to resist them the better the Barbarians rushed forward in a compact crowd; the elephants flung themselves impetuously upon the centre of it. The spurs on their breasts, like ships' prows, clove through the cohorts, which flowed surging back. They stifled the men with their trunks, or else snatching them up from the ground delivered them over their heads to the soldiers in the towers; with their tusks they disembowelled them, and hurled them into the air, and long entrails hung from their ivory fangs like bundles of rope from a mast. The Barbarians strove to blind them, to hamstring them; others would slip beneath their bodies, bury a sword in them up to the hilt, and perish crushed to death; the most intrepid clung to their straps; they would go on sawing the leather amid flames, bullets, and arrows, and the wicker tower would fall like a tower of stone. Fourteen of the animals on the extreme right, irritated by their wounds, turned upon the second rank; the Indians seized mallet and chisel, applied the latter to a joint in the head, and with all their might struck a great blow.

Down fell the huge beasts, falling one above another. It was like a mountain; and upon the heap of dead bodies and armour a monstrous elephant, called "The Fury of Baal," which had been caught by the leg in some chains, stood howling until the evening with an arrow in its eye.

The others, however, like conquerors, delighting in extermination, overthrew, crushed, stamped, and raged against the corpses and the débris. To repel the maniples in serried circles around them, they turned about on their hind feet as they advanced, with a continual rotatory motion. The Carthaginians felt their energy increase, and the battle begin again.

The Barbarians were growing weak; some Greek hoplites threw away all their arms, and terror seized upon the rest. Spendius was seen stooping upon his dromedary, and spurring it on the shoulders with two javelins. Then they all rushed away from the wings and ran towards Utica.

The Clinabarians, whose horses were exhausted, did not try to overtake them. The Ligurians, who were weakened by thirst, cried out for an advance towards the river. But the Carthaginians, who were posted in the centre of the syntagmata, and had suffered less, stamped their feet with longing for the vengeance which was flying from them; and they were already darting forward in pursuit of the Mercenaries when Hamilcar appeared.

He held in his spotted and sweat-covered horse with silver reins. The bands fastened to the horns on his helmet flapped in the wind behind him, and he had placed his oval shield beneath his left thigh. With a motion of his triple-pointed pike he checked the army.

The Tarentines leaped quickly upon their spare horses, and set off right and left towards the river and towards the town.

The phalanx exterminated all the remaining Barbarians at leisure. When the swords appeared they would stretch out their throats and close their eyelids. Others defended themselves to the last, and were knocked down from a distance with flints like mad dogs. Hamilcar had desired the taking of prisoners, but the Carthaginians obeyed him grudgingly, so much pleasure did they derive from plunging their swords into the bodies of the Barbarians. As they were too hot they set about their work with bare arms like mowers; and when they desisted to take breath they would follow with their eyes a horseman galloping across the country after a fleeing soldier. He would succeed in seizing him by the hair, hold him thus for a while, and then fell him with a blow of his axe.

Night fell. Carthaginians and Barbarians had disappeared. The elephants which had taken to flight roamed in the horizon with their fired towers. These burned here and there in the darkness like beacons nearly half lost in the mist; and no movement could be discerned in the plain save the undulation of the river, which was heaped with corpses, and was drifting them away to the sea.

Two hours afterwards Matho arrived. He caught sight in the starlight of long, uneven heaps lying upon the ground.

They were files of Barbarians. He stooped down; all were dead. He called into the distance, but no voice replied.

That very morning he had left Hippo-Zarytus with his soldiers to march upon Carthage. At Utica the army under Spendius had just set out, and the inhabitants were beginning to fire the engines. All had fought desperately. But, the tumult which was going on in the direction of the bridge increasing in an incomprehensible fashion, Matho had struck across the mountain by the shortest road, and as the Barbarians were fleeing over the plain he had encountered nobody.

Facing him were little pyramidal masses rearing themselves in the shade, and on this side of the river and closer to him were motionless lights on the surface of the ground. In fact the Carthaginians had fallen back behind the bridge, and to deceive the Barbarians the Suffet had stationed numerous posts upon the other bank.

Matho, still advancing, thought that he could distinguish Punic engines, for horses' heads which did not stir appeared in the air fixed upon the tops of piles of staves which could not be seen; and further off he could hear a great clamour, a noise of songs, and clashing of cups.

Then, not knowing where he was nor how to find Spendius, assailed with anguish, scared, and lost in the darkness, he returned more impetuously by the same road. The dawn as growing grey when from the top of the mountain he perceived the town with the carcases of the engines blackened by the flames and looking like giant skeletons leaning against the walls.

All was peaceful amid extraordinary silence and heaviness. Among his soldiers on the verge of the tents men were sleeping nearly naked, each upon his back, or with his forehead against his arm which was supported by his cuirass. Some were unwinding bloodstained bandages from their legs. Those who were doomed to die rolled their heads about gently; others dragged themselves along and brought them drink. The sentries walked up and down along the narrow paths in order to warm themselves, or stood in a fierce attitude with their faces turned towards the horizon, and their pikes on their shoulders. Matho found Spendius sheltered beneath a rag of canvas, supported by two sticks set in the ground, his knee in his hands and his head cast down.

They remained for a long time without speaking.

At last Matho murmured: "Conquered!"

Spendius rejoined in a gloomy voice: "Yes, conquered!"

And to all questions he replied by gestures of despair.

Meanwhile sighs and death-rattles reached them. Matho partially opened the canvas. Then the sight of the soldiers reminded him of another disaster on the same spot, and he ground his teeth: "Wretch! once already—"

Spendius interrupted him: "You were not there either."

"It is a curse!" exclaimed Matho. "Nevertheless, in the end I will get at him! I will conquer him! I will slay him! Ah! if I had been there!—" The thought of having missed the battle rendered him even more desperate than the defeat. He snatched up his sword and threw it upon the ground. "But how did the Carthaginians beat you?"

The former slave began to describe the manouvres. Matho seemed to see them, and he grew angry. The army from Utica ought to have taken Hamilcar in the rear instead of hastening to the bridge.

"Ah! I know!" said Spendius.

"You ought to have made your ranks twice as deep, avoided exposing the velites against the phalanx, and given free passage to the elephants. Everything might have been recovered at the last moment; there was no necessity to fly."

Spendius replied:

"I saw him pass along in his large red cloak, with uplifted arms and higher than the dust, like an eagle flying upon the flank of the cohorts; and at every nod they closed up or darted forward; the throng carried us towards each other; he looked at me, and I felt the cold steel as it were in my heart."

"He selected the day, perhaps?" whispered Matho to himself.

They questioned each other, trying to discover what it was that had brought the Suffet just when circumstances were most unfavourable. They went on to talk over the situation, and Spendius, to extenuate his fault, or to revive his courage, asserted that some hope still remained.

"And if there be none, it matters not!" said Matho; "alone, I will carry on the war!"

"And I too!" exclaimed the Greek, leaping up; he strode to and fro, his eyes sparkling, and a strange smile wrinkled his jackal face.

"We will make a fresh start; do not leave me again! I am not made for battles in the sunlight—the flashing of swords troubles my sight; it is a disease, I lived too long in the ergastulum. But give me walls to scale at night, and I will enter the citadels, and the corpses shall be cold before cock-crow! Show me any one, anything, an enemy, a treasure, a woman,—a woman," he repeated, "were she a king's daughter, and I will quickly bring your desire to your feet. You reproach me for having lost the battle against Hanno, nevertheless I won it back again. Confess it! my herd of swine did more for us than a phalanx of Spartans." And yielding to the need that he felt of exalting himself and taking his revenge, he enumerated all that he had done for the cause of the Mercenaries. "It was I who urged on the Gaul in the Suffet's gardens! And later, at Sicca, I maddened them all with fear of the Republic! Gisco was sending them back, but I prevented the interpreters speaking. Ah! how their tongues hung out of their mouths! do you remember? I brought you into Carthage; I stole the zaïmph. I led you to her. I will do more yet: you shall see!" He burst out laughing like a madman.

Matho regarded him with gaping eyes. He felt in a measure uncomfortable in the presence of this man, who was at once so cowardly and so terrible.

The Greek resumed in jovial tones and cracking his fingers:

"Evoe! Sun after run! I have worked in the quarries, and I have drunk Massic wine beneath a golden awning in a vessel of my own like a Ptolemæus. Calamity should help to make us cleverer. By dint of work we may make fortune bend. She loves politicians. She will yield!"

He returned to Matho and took him by the arm.

"Master, at present the Carthaginians are sure of their victory. You have quite an army which has not fought, and your men obey you. Place them in the front: mine will follow to avenge themselves. I have still three thousand Carians, twelve hundred slingers and archers, whole cohorts! A phalanx even might be formed; let us return!"

Matho, who had been stunned by the disaster, had hitherto thought of no means of repairing it. He listened with open mouth, and the bronze plates which circled his sides rose with the leapings of his heart. He picked up his sword, crying:

"Follow me; forward!"

But when the scouts returned, they announced that the Carthaginian dead had been carried off, that the bridge was in ruins, and that Hamilcar had disappeared.

IX

In the Field

Hamilcar had thought that the Mercenaries would await him at Utica, or that they would return against him; and finding his forces insufficient to make or to sustain an attack, he had struck southwards along the right bank of the river, thus protecting himself immediately from a surprise.

He intended first to wink at the revolt of the tribes and to detach them all from the cause of the Barbarians; then when they were quite isolated in the midst of the provinces he would fall upon them and exterminate them.

In fourteen days he pacified the region comprised between Thouccaber and Utica, with the towns of Tignicabah, Tessourah, Vacca, and others further to the west. Zounghar built in the mountains, Assoura celebrated for its temple, Djeraado fertile in junipers, Thapitis, and Hagour sent embassies to him. The country people came with their hands full of provisions, implored his protection, kissed his feet and those of the soldiers, and complained of the Barbarians. Some came to offer him bags containing heads of Mercenaries killed, so they said, by themselves, but which they had cut off corpses; for many had lost themselves in their flight, and were found dead here and there beneath the olive trees and among the vines.

On the morrow of his victory, Hamilcar, to dazzle the people, had sent to Carthage the two thousand captives taken on the battlefield. They arrived in long companies of one hundred men each, all with their arms fastened behind their backs with a bar of bronze which caught them at the nape of the neck, and the wounded, bleeding as they still were, running also along; horsemen followed them, driving them on with blows of the whip.

Then there was a delirium of joy! People repeated that there were six thousand Barbarians killed; the others would not hold out, and the war was finished; they embraced one another in the streets, and rubbed the faces of the Patæc Gods with butter and cinnamomum to thank them. These, with their big eyes, their big bodies, and their arms raised as high as the shoulder, seemed to live beneath their freshened paint, and to participate in the cheerfulness of the people. The rich left their doors open; the city resounded with the noise of the timbrels; the temples were illuminated every night, and the servants of the goddess went down to Malqua and set up stages of sycamore-wood at the corners of the cross-ways, and prostituted themselves there. Lands were voted to the conquerors, holocausts to Melkarth, three hundred gold crowns to the Suffet, and his partisans proposed to decree to him new prerogatives and honours.

He had begged the Ancients to make overtures to Autaritus for exchanging all the Barbarians, if necessary, for the aged Gisco, and the other Carthaginians detained like him. The Libyans and Nomads composing the army under Autaritus knew scarcely anything of these Mercenaries, who were men of Italiote or Greek race; and the offer by the Republic of so many Barbarians for so few Carthaginians, showed that the value of the former was nothing and that of the latter considerable. They dreaded a snare. Autaritus refused.

Then the Ancients decreed the execution of the captives, although the Suffet had written to them not to put them to death. He reckoned upon incorporating the best of them with his own troops and of thus instigating defections. But hatred swept away all circumspection.

The two thousand Barbarians were tied to the stelæ of the tombs in the Mappalian quarter; and traders, scullions, embroiderers, and even women,—the widows of the dead with their children—all who would, came to kill them with arrows. They aimed slowly at them, the better to prolong their torture, lowering the weapon and then raising it in turn; and the multitude pressed forward howling. Paralytics had themselves brought thither in hand-barrows; many took the precaution of bringing their food, and remained on the spot until the evening; others passed the night there. Tents had been set up in which drinking went on. Many gained large sums by hiring out bows.

Then all these crucified corpses were left upright, looking like so many red statues on the tombs, and the excitement even spread to the people of Malqua, who were the descendants of the aboriginal families, and were usually indifferent to the affairs of their country. Out of gratitude for the pleasure it had been giving them they now interested themselves in its fortunes, and felt that they were Carthaginians, and the Ancients thought it a clever thing to have thus blended the entire people in a single act of vengeance.

The sanction of the gods was not wanting; for crows alighted from all quarters of the sky. They wheeled in the air as they flew with loud hoarse cries, and formed a huge cloud rolling continually upon itself. It was seen from Clypea, Rhades, and the promontory of Hermæum. Sometimes it would suddenly burst asunder, its black spirals extending far away, as an eagle clove the centre of it, and then departed again; here and there on the terraces the domes, the peaks of the obelisks, and the pediments of the temples there were big birds holding human fragments in their reddened beaks.

Owing to the smell the Carthaginians resigned themselves to unbind the corpses. A few of them were burnt; the rest were thrown into the sea, and the waves, driven by the north wind, deposited them on the shore at the end of the gulf before the camp of Autaritus.

This punishment had no doubt terrified the Barbarians, for from the top of Eschmoun they could be seen striking their tents, collecting their flocks, and hoisting their baggage upon asses, and on the evening of the same day the entire army withdrew.

IT WAS TO MARCH TO and fro between the mountain of the Hot Springs and Hippo-Zarytus, and so debar the Suffet from approaching the Tyrian towns, and from the possibility of a return to Carthage.

Meanwhile the two other armies were to try to overtake him in the south, Spendius in the east, and Matho in the west, in such a way that all three should unite to surprise and entangle him. Then they received a reinforcement which they had not looked for: Narr' Havas appeared with three hundred camels laden with bitumen, twenty-five elephants, and six thousand horsemen.

To weaken the Mercenaries the Suffet had judged it prudent to occupy his attention at a distance in his own kingdom. From the heart of Carthage he had come to an understanding with Masgaba, a Gætulian brigand who was seeking to found an empire. Strengthened by Punic money, the adventurer had raised the Numidian States with promises of freedom. But Narr' Havas, warned by his nurse's son, had dropped into Cirta, poisoned the conquerors with the water of the cisterns, struck off a few heads, set all right again, and had just arrived against the Suffet more furious than the Barbarians.

The chiefs of the four armies concerted the arrangements for the war. It would be a long one, and everything must be foreseen.

It was agreed first to entreat the assistance of the Romans, and this mission was offered to Spendius, but as a fugitive he dared not undertake it. Twelve men from the Greek colonies embarked at Annaba in a sloop belonging to the Numidians. Then the chiefs exacted an oath of complete obedience from all the Barbarians. Every day the captains inspected clothes and boots; the sentries were even forbidden to use a shield, for they would often lean it against their lance and fall asleep as they stood; those who had any baggage trailing after them were obliged to get rid of it; everything was to be carried, in Roman fashion, on the back. As a precaution against the elephants Matho instituted a corps of cataphract cavalry, men and horses being hidden beneath cuirasses of hippopotamus skin bristling with nails; and to protect the horses' hoofs boots of plaited esparto-grass were made for them.

It was forbidden to pillage the villages, or to tyrannise over the inhabitants who were not of Punic race. But as the country was becoming exhausted, Matho ordered the provisions to be served out to the soldiers individually, without troubling about the women. At first the men shared with them. Many grew weak for lack of food. It was the occasion of many quarrels and invectives, many drawing away the companions of the rest by the bait or even by the promise of their own portion. Matho commanded them all to be driven away pitilessly. They took refuge in the camp of Autaritus; but the Gaulish and Libyan women forced them by their outrageous treatment to depart.

At last they came beneath the walls of Carthage to implore the protection of Ceres and Proserpine, for in Byrsa there was a temple with priests consecrated to these goddesses in expiation of the horrors formerly committed at the siege of Syracuse. The Syssitia, alleging their right to waifs and strays, claimed the youngest in order to sell them; and some fair Lacedæmonian women were taken by New Carthaginians in marriage.

A few persisted in following the armies. They ran on the flank of the syntagmata by the side of the captains. They called to their husbands, pulled them by the cloak, cursed them as they beat their breasts, and held out their little naked and weeping children at arm's length. The sight of them was unmanning the Barbarians; they were an embarrassment and a peril. Several times they were repulsed, but they came back again; Matho made the horsemen belonging to Narr' Havas charge them with the point of the lance; and on some Balearians shouting out to him that they must have women, he replied: "I have none!"

Just now he was invaded by the genius of Moloch. In spite of the rebellion of his conscience, he performed terrible deeds, imagining that he was thus obeying the voice of a god. When he could not ravage the fields, Matho would cast stones into them to render them sterile.

He urged Autaritus and Spendius with repeated messages to make haste. But the Suffet's operations were incomprehensible. He encamped at Eidous, Monchar, and Tehent successively; some scouts believed that they saw him in the neighbourhood of Ischiil, near the frontiers of Narr' Havas, and it was reported that he had crossed the river above Tebourba as though to return to Carthage. Scarcely was he in one place when he removed to another. The routes that he followed always remained unknown. The Suffet preserved his advantages without offering battle, and while pursued by the Barbarians seemed to be leading them.

These marches and counter marches were still more fatiguing to the Carthaginians, and Hamilcar's forces, receiving no reinforcements, diminished from day to day. The country people were now more backward in bringing him provisions. In every direction he encountered taciturn hesitation and hatred; and in spite of his entreaties to the Great Council no succour came from Carthage.

It was said, perhaps it was believed, that he had need of none. It was a trick, or his complaints were unnecessary; and Hanno's partisans, in order to do him an ill turn, exaggerated the importance of his victory. The troops which he commanded he was welcome to; but they were not going to supply his demands continually in that way. The war was quite burdensome enough! it had cost too much, and from pride the patricians belonging to his faction supported him but slackly.

Then Hamilcar, despairing of the Republic, took by force from the tribes all that he wanted for the war—grain, oil, wood, cattle, and men. But the inhabitants were not long in taking flight. The villages passed through were empty, and the cabins were ransacked without anything being discerned in them. The Punic army was soon encompassed by a terrible solitude.

The Carthaginians, who were furious, began to sack the provinces; they filled up the cisterns and fired the houses. The sparks, being carried by the wind, were scattered far off, and whole forests were on fire on the mountains; they bordered the valleys with a crown of flames, and it was often necessary to wait in order to pass beyond them. Then the soldiers resumed their march over the warm ashes in the full glare of the sun.

Sometimes they would see what looked like the eyes of a tiger cat gleaming in a bush by the side of the road. This was a Barbarian crouching upon his heels, and smeared with dust, that he might not be distinguished from the colour of the foliage; or perhaps when passing along a ravine those on the wings would suddenly hear the rolling of stones, and raising their eyes would perceive a bare-footed man bounding along through the openings of the gorge.

Meanwhile Utica and Hippo-Zarytus were free since the Mercenaries were no longer besieging them. Hamilcar commanded them to come to his assistance. But not caring to compromise themselves, they answered him with vague words, with compliments and excuses.

He went up again abruptly into the North, determined to open up one of the Tyrian towns, though he were obliged to lay siege to it. He required a station on the coast, so as to be able to draw supplies and men from the islands or from Cyrene, and he coveted the harbour of Utica as being the nearest to Carthage.

The Suffet therefore left Zouitin and turned the lake of Hippo-Zarytus with circumspection. But he was soon obliged to lengthen out his regiments into column in order to climb the mountain which separates the two valleys. They were descending at sunset into its hollow, funnel-shaped summit, when they perceived on the level of the ground before them bronze she-wolves which seemed to be running across the grass.

Suddenly large plumes arose and a terrible song burst forth, accompanied by the rhythm of flutes. It was the army under Spendius; for some Campanians and Greeks, in their execration of Carthage, had assumed the ensigns of Rome. At the same time long pikes, shields of leopard's skin, linen cuirasses, and naked shoulders were seen on the left. These were the Iberians under Matho, the Lusitanians, Balearians, and Gætulians; the horses of Narr' Havas were heard to neigh; they spread around the hill; then came the loose rabble commanded by Autaritus— Gauls, Libyans, and Nomads; while the Eaters of Uncleanness might be recognised among them by the fish bones which they wore in their hair.

Thus the Barbarians, having contrived their marches with exactness, had come together again. But themselves surprised, they remained motionless for some minutes in consultation.

The Suffet had collected his men into an orbicular mass, in such a way as to offer an equal resistance in every direction. The infantry were surrounded by their tall, pointed shields fixed close to one another in the turf. The Clinabarians were outside and the elephants at intervals further off. The Mercenaries were worn out with fatigue; it was better to wait till next day; and the Barbarians feeling sure of their victory occupied themselves the whole night in eating.

GUSTAVE FLAUBERT

They lighted large bright fires, which, while dazzling themselves, left the Punic army below them in the shade. Hamilcar caused a trench fifteen feet broad and ten cubits deep to be dug in Roman fashion round his camp, and the earth thrown out to be raised on the inside into a parapet, on which sharp interlacing stakes were planted; and at sunrise the Mercenaries were amazed to perceive all the Carthaginians thus entrenched as if in a fortress.

They could recognise Hamilcar in the midst of the tents walking about and giving orders. His person was clad in a brown cuirass cut in little scales; he was followed by his horse, and stopped from time to time to point out something with his right arm outstretched.

Then more than one recalled similar mornings when, amid the din of clarions, he passed slowly before them, and his looks strengthened them like cups of wine. A kind of emotion overcame them. Those, on the contrary, who were not acquainted with Hamilcar, were mad with joy at having caught him.

Nevertheless if all attacked at once they would do one another mutual injury in the insufficiency of space. The Numidians might dash through; but the Clinabarians, who were protected by cuirasses, would crush them. And then how were the palisades to be crossed? As to the elephants, they were not sufficiently well trained.

"You are all cowards!" exclaimed Matho.

And with the best among them he rushed against the entrenchment. They were repulsed by a volley of stones; for the Suffet had taken their abandoned catapults on the bridge.

This want of success produced an abrupt change in the fickle minds of the Barbarians. Their extreme bravery disappeared; they wished to conquer, but with the smallest possible risk. According to Spendius they ought to maintain carefully the position that they held, and starve out the Punic army. But the Carthaginians began to dig wells, and as there were mountains surrounding the hill, they discovered water.

From the summit of their palisade they launched arrows, earth, dung, and pebbles which they gathered from the ground, while the six catapults rolled incessantly throughout the length of the terrace.

But the springs would dry up of themselves; the provisions would be exhausted, and the catapults worn out; the Mercenaries, who were ten times as numerous, would triumph in the end. The Suffet devised negotiations so as to gain time, and one morning the Barbarians found a sheep's skin covered with writing within their lines. He justified himself for his victory: the Ancients had forced him into the war, and to show them that he was keeping his word, he offered them the pillaging of Utica or Hippo-Zarytus at their choice; in conclusion, Hamilcar declared that he did not fear them because he had won over some traitors, and thanks to them would easily manage the rest.

The Barbarians were disturbed: this proposal of immediate booty made them consider; they were apprehensive of treachery, not suspecting a snare in the Suffet's boasting, and they began to look upon one another with mistrust. Words and steps were watched; terrors awaked them in the night. Many forsook their companions and chose their army as fancy dictated, and the Gauls with Autaritus went and joined themselves with the men of Cisalpine Gaul, whose language they understood.

The four chiefs met together every evening in Matho's tent, and squatting round a shield, attentively moved backwards and forwards the little wooden figures invented by Pyrrhus for the representation of manouvres. Spendius would demonstrate Hamilcar's resources, and with oaths by all the gods entreat that the opportunity should not be wasted. Matho would walk about angry and gesticulating. The war against Carthage was his own personal affair; he was indignant that the others should interfere in it without being willing to obey him. Autaritus would divine his speech from his countenance and applaud. Narr' Havas would elevate his chin to mark his disdain; there was not a measure he did not consider fatal; and he had ceased to smile. Sighs would escape him as though he were thrusting back sorrow for an impossible dream, despair for an abortive enterprise.

While the Barbarians deliberated in uncertainty, the Suffet increased his defences: he had a second trench dug within the palisades, a second wall raised, and wooden towers constructed at the corners; and his slaves went as far as the middle of the outposts to drive caltrops into the ground. But the elephants, whose allowances were lessened, struggled in their shackles. To economise the grass he ordered the Clinabarians to kill the least strong among the stallions. A few refused to do so, and he had them decapitated. The horses were eaten. The recollection of this fresh meat was a source of great sadness to them in the days that followed.

From the bottom of the ampitheatre in which they were confined they could see the four bustling camps of the Barbarians all around them on the heights. Women moved about with leathern bottles on their heads, goats strayed bleating beneath the piles of pikes; sentries were being relieved, and eating was going on around tripods. In fact, the tribes furnished them abundantly with provisions, and they did not themselves suspect how much their inaction alarmed the Punic army.

On the second day the Carthaginians had remarked a troop of three hundred men apart from the rest in the camp of the nomads. These were the rich who had been kept prisoners since the beginning of the war. Some Libyans ranged them along the edge of the trench, took their station behind them, and hurled javelins, making themselves a rampart of their bodies. The wretched creatures could scarcely be recognised, so completely were their faces covered with vermin and filth. Their hair had been plucked out in places, leaving bare the ulcers on their heads, and they were so lean and hideous that they were like mummies in tattered shrouds. A few trembled and sobbed with a stupid look; the rest cried out to their friends to fire upon the Barbarians. There was one who remained quite motionless with face cast down, and without speaking; his long white beard fell to his chain-covered hands; and the Carthaginians, feeling as it were the downfall of the Republic in the bottom of their hearts, recognised Gisco. Although the place was a dangerous one they pressed forward to see him. On his head had been placed a grotesque tiara of hippopotamus leather incrusted with pebbles. It was Autaritus's idea; but it was displeasing to Matho.

Hamilcar in exasperation, and resolved to cut his way through in one way or another, had the palisades opened; and the Carthaginians went at a furious rate half way up the hill or three hundred paces. Such a flood of Barbarians descended upon them that they were driven back to their lines. One of the guards of the Legion who had remained outside was stumbling among the stones. Zarxas ran up to him, knocked him down, and plunged a dagger into his throat; he drew it out, threw himself upon the wound—and gluing his lips to it with mutterings of joy, and startings which shook him to the heels, pumped up the blood by breastfuls; then he quietly sat down upon the corpse, raised his face with his neck thrown back the better to breathe in the air, like a hind that has just drunk at a mountain stream, and in a shrill voice began to sing a Balearic song, a vague melody full of prolonged modulations, with interruptions and alternations like echoes answering one another in the mountains; he called upon his dead brothers and invited them to a feast;—then he let his hands fall between his legs, slowly bent his head, and wept. This atrocious occurrence horrified the Barbarians, especially the Greeks.

From that time forth the Carthaginians did not attempt to make any sally; and they had no thought of surrender, certain as they were that they would perish in tortures.

Nevertheless the provisions, in spite of Hamilcar's carefulness, diminished frightfully. There was not left per man more than ten k'hommers of wheat, three hins of millet, and twelve betzas of dried fruit. No more meat, no more oil, no more salt food, and not a grain of barley for the horses, which might be seen stretching down their wasted necks seeking in the dust for blades of trampled straw. Often the sentries on vedette upon the terrace would see in the moonlight a dog belonging to the Barbarians coming to prowl beneath the entrenchment among the heaps of filth; it would be knocked down with a stone, and then, after a descent had been effected along the palisades by means of the straps of a shield, it would be eaten without a word. Sometimes horrible barkings would be heard and the man would not come up again. Three phalangites, in the fourth dilochia of the twelfth syntagmata, killed one another with knives in a dispute about a rat.

All regretted their families, and their houses; the poor their hive-shaped huts, with the shells on the threshold and the hanging net, and the patricians their large halls filled with bluish shadows, where at the most indolent hour of the day they used to rest listening to the vague noise of the streets mingled with the rustling of the leaves as they stirred in their gardens;—to go deeper into the thought of this, and to enjoy it more, they would half close their eyelids, only to be roused by the shock of a wound. Every minute there was some engagement, some fresh alarm; the towers were burning, the Eaters of Uncleanness were leaping across the palisades; their hands would be struck off with axes; others would hasten up; an iron hail would fall upon the tents. Galleries of rushen hurdles were raised as a protection against the projectiles. The Carthaginians shut themselves up within them and stirred out no more.

Every day the sun coming over the hill used, after the early hours, to forsake the bottom of the gorge and leave them in the shade. The grey slopes of the ground, covered with flints spotted with scanty lichen, ascended in front and in the rear, and above their summits stretched the sky in its perpetual purity, smoother and colder to the eye than a metal cupola. Hamilcar was so indignant with Carthage that he felt inclined to throw himself among the Barbarians and lead them against her.

Moreover, the porters, sutlers, and slaves were beginning to murmur, while neither people, nor Great Council, nor any one sent as much as a hope. The situation was intolerable, especially owing to the thought that it would become worse.

AT THE NEWS OF THE disaster Carthage had leaped, as it were, with anger and hate; the Suffet would have been less execrated if he had allowed himself to be conquered from the first.

But time and money were lacking for the hire of other Mercenaries. As to a levy of soldiers in the town, how were they to be equipped? Hamilcar had taken all the arms! and then who was to command them? The best captains were down yonder with him! Meanwhile, some men despatched by the Suffet arrived in the streets with shouts. The Great Council were roused by them, and contrived to make them disappear.

It was an unnecessary precaution; every one accused Barca of having behaved with slackness. He ought to have annihilated the Mercenaries after his victory. Why had he ravaged the tribes? The sacrifices already imposed had been heavy enough! and the patricians deplored their contributions of fourteen shekels, and the Syssitia their two hundred and twenty-three thousand gold kikars; those who had given nothing lamented like the rest. The populace was jealous of the New Carthaginians, to whom he had promised full rights of citizenship; and even the Ligurians, who had fought with such intrepidity, were confounded with the Barbarians and cursed like them; their race became a crime, the proof of complicity. The traders on the threshold of their shops, the workmen passing plumb-line in hand, the vendors of pickle rinsing their baskets, the attendants in the vapour baths and the retailers of hot drinks all discussed the operations of the campaign. They would trace battle-plans with their fingers in the dust, and there was not a sorry rascal to be found who could not have corrected Hamilcar's mistakes.

It was a punishment, said the priests, for his long-continued impiety. He had offered no holocausts; he had not purified his troops; he had even refused to take augurs with him; and the scandal of sacrilege strengthened the violence of restrained hate, and the rage of betrayed hopes. People recalled the Sicilian disasters, and all the burden of his pride that they had borne for so long! The colleges of the pontiffs could not forgive him for having seized their treasure, and they demanded a pledge from the Great Council to crucify him should he ever return.

The heats of the month of Eloul, which were excessive in that year, were another calamity. Sickening smells rose from the borders of the Lake, and were wafted through the air together with the fumes of the aromatics that eddied at the corners of the streets. The sounds of hymns were constantly heard. Crowds of people occupied the staircases of the temples; all the walls were covered with black veils; tapers burnt on the brows of the Patæc Gods, and the blood of camels slain for sacrifice ran along the flights of stairs forming red cascades upon the steps. Carthage was agitated with funereal delirium. From the depths of the narrowest lanes, and the blackest dens, there issued pale faces, men with viper-like profiles and grinding their teeth. The houses were filled with the women's piercing shrieks, which, escaping through the gratings, caused those who stood talking in the squares to turn round. Sometimes it was thought that the Barbarians were arriving; they had been seen behind the mountain of the Hot Springs; they were encamped at Tunis; and the voices would multiply and swell, and be blended into one single clamour. Then universal silence would reign, some remaining where they had climbed upon the frontals of the buildings, screening their eyes with their open hand, while the rest lay flat on their faces at the foot of the ramparts straining their ears. When their terror had passed off their anger would begin again. But the conviction of their own impotence would soon sink them into the same sadness as before.

It increased every evening when all ascended the terraces, and bowing down nine times uttered a loud cry in salutation of the sun, as it sank slowly behind the lagoon, and then suddenly disappeared among the mountains in the direction of the Barbarians.

They were waiting for the thrice holy festival when, from the summit of a funeral pile, an eagle flew heavenwards as a symbol of the resurrection of the year, and a message from the people to their Baal; they regarded it as a sort of union, a method of connecting themselves with the might of the Sun. Moreover, filled as they now were with hatred, they turned frankly towards homicidal Moloch, and all forsook Tanith. In fact, Rabetna, having lost her veil, was as if she had been despoiled of part of her virtue. She denied the beneficence of her waters, she had abandoned Carthage; she was a deserter, an enemy. Some threw stones at her to insult her. But many pitied her while they inveighed against her; she was still beloved, and perhaps more deeply than she had been.

All their misfortunes came, therefore, from the loss of the zaïmph. Salammbô had indirectly participated in it; she was included in the same ill will; she must be punished. A vague idea of immolation spread among the people. To appease the Baalim it was without doubt necessary to offer them something of incalculable worth, a being handsome, young, virgin, of old family, a descendant of the gods, a human star. Every day the gardens of Megara were invaded by strange men; the slaves, trembling on their own account, dared not resist them. Nevertheless, they did not pass beyond the galley staircase. They remained below with their eyes raised to the highest terrace; they were waiting for Salammbô, and they would cry out for hours against her like dogs baying at the moon.

X

The Serpent

These clamourings of the populace did not alarm Hamilcar's daughter. She was disturbed by loftier anxieties: her great serpent, the black python, was drooping; and in the eyes of the Carthaginians, the serpent was at once a national and a private fetish. It was believed to be the offspring of the dust of the earth, since it emerges from its depths and has no need of feet to traverse it; its mode of progression called to mind the undulations of rivers, its temperature the ancient, viscous, and fecund darkness, and the orbit which it describes when biting its tail the harmony of the planets, and the intelligence of Eschmoun.

Salammbô's serpent had several times already refused the four live sparrows which were offered to it at the full moon and at every new moon. Its handsome skin, covered like the firmament with golden spots upon a perfectly black ground, was now yellow, relaxed, wrinkled, and too large for its body. A cottony mouldiness extended round its head; and in the corners of its eyelids might be seen little red specks which appeared to move. Salammbô would approach its silver-wire basket from time to time, and would draw aside the purple curtains, the lotus leaves, and the bird's down; but it was continually rolled up upon itself, more motionless than a withered bind-weed; and from looking at it she at last came to feel a kind of spiral within her heart, another serpent, as it were, mounting up to her throat by degrees and strangling her.

She was in despair of having seen the zaïmph, and yet she felt a sort of joy, an intimate pride at having done so. A mystery shrank within the splendour of its folds; it was the cloud that enveloped the gods, and the secret of the universal existence, and Salammbô, horror-stricken at herself, regretted that she had not raised it.

She was almost always crouching at the back of her apartment, holding her bended left leg in her hands, her mouth half open, her chin sunk, her eye fixed. She recollected her father's face with terror; she wished to go away into the mountains of Phonicia, on a pilgrimage to the temple of Aphaka, where Tanith descended in the form of a star; all kinds of imaginings attracted her and terrified her; moreover, a solitude which every day became greater encompassed her. She did not even know what Hamilcar was about.

Wearied at last with her thoughts she would rise, and trailing along her little sandals whose soles clacked upon her heels at every step, she would walk at random through the large silent room. The amethysts and topazes of the ceiling made luminous spots quiver here and there, and Salammbô as she walked would turn her head a little to see them. She would go and take the hanging amphoras by the neck; she would cool her bosom beneath the broad fans, or perhaps amuse herself by burning cinnamomum in hollow pearls. At sunset Taanach would draw back the black felt lozenges that closed the openings in the wall; then her doves, rubbed with musk like the doves of Tanith, suddenly entered, and their pink feet glided over the glass pavement, amid the grains of barley which she threw to them in handfuls like a sower in a field. But on a sudden she would burst into sobs and lie stretched on the large bed of ox-leather straps without moving, repeating a word that was ever the same, with open eyes, pale as one dead, insensible, cold; and yet she could hear the cries of the apes in the tufts of the palm trees, with the continuous grinding of the great wheel which brought a flow of pure water through the stories into the porphyry centre-basin.

Sometimes for several days she would refuse to eat. She could see in a dream troubled stars wandering beneath her feet. She would call Schahabarim, and when he came she had nothing to say to him.

She could not live without the relief of his presence. But she rebelled inwardly against this domination; her feeling towards the priest was one at once of terror, jealousy, hatred, and a species of love, in gratitude for the singular voluptuousness which she experienced by his side.

He had recognised the influence of Rabbet, being skilful to discern the gods who send diseases; and to cure Salammbô he had her apartment watered with lotions of vervain, and maidenhair; she ate mandrakes every morning; she slept with her head on a cushion filled with aromatics blended by the pontiffs; he had even employed baaras, a fiery-coloured root which drives back fatal geniuses into the North; lastly, turning towards the polar star, he murmured thrice the mysterious name of Tanith; but Salammbô still suffered and her anguish deepened.

No one in Carthage was so learned as he. In his youth he had studied at the College of the Mogbeds, at Borsippa, near Babylon; had then visited Samothrace, Pessinus, Ephesus, Thessaly, Judæa, and the temples of the Nabathæ, which are lost in the sands; and had travelled on foot along the banks of the Nile from the cataracts to the sea. Shaking torches with veil-covered face, he had cast a black cock upon a fire of sandarach before the breast of the Sphinx, the Father of Terror. He had descended into the caverns of Proserpine; he had seen the five hundred pillars of the labyrinth of Lemnos revolve, and the candelabrum of Tarentum, which bore as many sconces on its shaft as there are days in the year, shine in its splendour; at times he received Greeks by night in order to question them. The constitution of the world disquieted him no less than the nature of the gods; he had observed the equinoxes with the armils placed in the portico of Alexandria, and accompanied the bematists of Evergetes, who measure the sky by calculating the number of their steps, as far as Cyrene; so that there was now growing in his thoughts a religion of his own, with no distinct formula, and on that very account full of infatuation and fervour. He no longer believed that the earth was formed like a fir-cone; he believed it to be round, and eternally falling through immensity with such prodigious speed that its fall was not perceived.

From the position of the sun above the moon he inferred the predominance of Baal, of whom the planet itself is but the reflection and figure; moreover, all that he saw in terrestrial things compelled him to recognise the male exterminating principle as supreme. And then he secretly charged Rabbet with the misfortune of his life. Was it not for her that the grand-pontiff had once advanced amid the tumult of cymbals, and with a patera of boiling water taken from him his future virility? And he followed with a melancholy gaze the men who were disappearing with the priestesses in the depths of the turpentine trees.

His days were spent in inspecting the censers, the gold vases, the tongs, the rakes for the ashes of the altar, and all the robes of the statues down to the bronze bodkin that served to curl the hair of an old Tanith in the third aedicule near the emerald vine. At the same hours he would raise the great hangings of the same swinging doors; would remain with his arms outspread in the same attitude; or prayed prostrate on the same flag-stones, while around him a people of priests moved barefooted through the passages filled with an eternal twilight.

But Salammbô was in the barrenness of his life like a flower in the cleft of a sepulchre. Nevertheless he was hard upon her, and spared her neither penances nor bitter words. His condition established, as it were, the equality of a common sex between them, and he was less angry with the girl for his inability to possess her than for finding her so beautiful, and above all so pure. Often he saw that she grew weary of following his thought. Then he would turn away sadder than before; he would feel himself more forsaken, more empty, more alone.

Strange words escaped him sometimes, which passed before Salammbô like broad lightnings illuminating the abysses. This would be at night on the terrace when, both alone, they gazed upon the stars, and Carthage spread below under their feet, with the gulf and the open sea dimly lost in the colour of the darkness.

He would set forth to her the theory of the souls that descend upon the earth, following the same route as the sun through the signs of the zodiac. With outstretched arm he showed the gate of human generation in the Ram, and that of the return to the gods in Capricorn; and Salammbô strove to see them, for she took these conceptions for realities; she accepted pure symbols and even manners of speech as being true in themselves, a distinction not always very clear even to the priest.

"The souls of the dead," said he, "resolve themselves into the moon, as their bodies do into the earth. Their tears compose its humidity; 'Tis a dark abode full of mire, and wreck, and tempest."

She asked what would become of her then.

"At first you will languish as light as a vapour hovering upon the waves; and after more lengthened ordeals and agonies, you will pass into the forces of the sun, the very source of Intelligence!"

He did not speak, however, of Rabbet. Salammbô imagined that it was through some shame for his vanquished goddess, and calling her by a common name which designated the moon, she launched into blessings upon the soft and fertile planet. At last he exclaimed:

"No! no! she draws all her fecundity from the other! Do you not see her hovering about him like an amorous woman running after a man in a field?" And he exalted the virtue of light unceasingly.

Far from depressing her mystic desires, he sought, on the contrary, to excite them, and he even seemed to take joy in grieving her by the revelation of a pitiless doctrine. In spite of the pains of her love Salammbô threw herself upon it with transport.

But the more that Schahabarim felt himself in doubt about Tanith, the more he wished to believe in her. At the bottom of his soul he was arrested by remorse. He needed some proof, some manifestation from the gods, and in the hope of obtaining it the priest devised an enterprise which might save at once his country and his belief.

Thenceforward he set himself to deplore before Salammbô the sacrilege and the misfortunes which resulted from it even in the regions of the sky. Then he suddenly announced the peril of the Suffet, who was assailed by three armies under the command of Matho—for on account of the veil Matho was, in the eyes of the Carthaginians, the king, as it were, of the Barbarians,—and he added that the safety of the Republic and of her father depended upon her alone.

"Upon me!" she exclaimed. "How can I—?"

But the priest, with a smile of disdain said:

"You will never consent!"

She entreated him. At last Schahabarim said to her:

"You must go to the Barbarians and recover the zaïmph!"

She sank down upon the ebony stool, and remained with her arms stretched out between her knees and shivering in all her limbs, like a victim at the altar's foot awaiting the blow of the club. Her temples were ringing, she could see fiery circles revolving, and in her stupor she had lost the understanding of all things save one, that she was certainly going to die soon.

But if Rabbetna triumphed, if the zaïmph were restored and Carthage delivered, what mattered a woman's life? thought Schahabarim. Moreover, she would perhaps obtain the veil and not perish.

He stayed away for three days; on the evening of the fourth she sent for him.

The better to inflame her heart he reported to her all the invectives howled against Hamilcar in open council; he told her that she had erred, that she owed reparation for her crime, and that Rabbetna commanded the sacrifice.

A great uproar came frequently across the Mappalian district to Megara. Schahabarim and Salammbô went out quickly, and gazed from the top of the galley staircase.

There were people in the square of Khamon shouting for arms. The Ancients would not provide them, esteeming such an effort useless; others who had set out without a general had been massacred. At last they were permitted to depart, and as a sort of homage to Moloch, or from a vague need of destruction, they tore up tall cypress trees in the woods of the temples, and having kindled them at the torches of the Kabiri, were carrying them through the streets singing. These monstrous flames advanced swaying gently; they transmitted fires to the glass balls on the crests of the temples, to the ornaments of the colossuses and the beaks of the ships, passed beyond the terraces and formed suns as it were, which rolled through the town. They descended the Acropolis. The gate of Malqua opened.

"Are you ready?" exclaimed Schahabarim, "or have you asked them to tell your father that you abandoned him?" She hid her face in her veils, and the great lights retired, sinking gradually the while to the edge of the waves.

An indeterminate dread restrained her; she was afraid of Moloch and of Matho. This man, with his giant stature, who was master of the zaïmph, ruled Rabbetna as much as did Baal, and seemed to her to be surrounded by the same fulgurations; and then the souls of the gods sometimes visited the bodies of men. Did not Schahabarim in speaking of him say that she was to vanquish Moloch? They were mingled with each other; she confused them together; both of them were pursuing her.

She wished to learn the future, and approached the serpent, for auguries were drawn from the attitudes of serpents. But the basket was empty; Salammbô was disturbed.

She found him with his tail rolled round one of the silver balustrades beside the hanging bed, which he was rubbing in order to free himself from his old yellowish skin, while his body stretched forth gleaming and clear like a sword half out of the sheath.

Then on the days following, in proportion as she allowed herself to be convinced, and was more disposed to succour Tanith, the python recovered and grew; he seemed to be reviving.

The certainty that Salammbô was giving expression to the will of the gods then became established in her conscience. One morning she awoke resolved, and she asked what was necessary to make Matho restore the veil.

"To claim it," said Schahabarim.

"But if he refuses?" she rejoined.

The priest scanned her fixedly with a smile such as she had never seen.

"Yes, what is to be done?" repeated Salammbô.

He rolled between his fingers the extremities of the bands which fell from his tiara upon his shoulders, standing motionless with eyes cast down. At last seeing that she did not understand:

"You will be alone with him."

"Well?" she said.

"Alone in his tent."

"What then?"

Schahabarim bit his lips. He sought for some phrase, some circumlocution.

"If you are to die, that will be later," he said; "later! fear nothing! and whatever he may undertake to do, do not call out! do not be frightened! You will be humble, you understand, and submissive to his desire, which is ordained of heaven!"

"But the veil?"

"The gods will take thought for it," replied Schahabarim.

"Suppose you were to accompany me, O father?" she added.

"No!"

He made her kneel down, and keeping his left hand raised and his right extended, he swore in her behalf to bring back the mantle of Tanith into Carthage. With terrible imprecations she devoted herself to the gods, and each time that Schahabarim pronounced a word she falteringly repeated it.

He indicated to her all the purifications and fastings that she was to observe, and how she was to reach Matho. Moreover, a man acquainted with the routes would accompany her.

She felt as if she had been set free. She thought only of the happiness of seeing the zaïmph again, and she now blessed Schahabarim for his exhortations.

It was the period at which the doves of Carthage migrated to Sicily to the mountain of Eryx and the temple of Venus. For several days before their departure they sought out and called to one another so as to collect together; at last one evening they flew away; the wind blew them along, and the big white cloud glided across the sky high above the sea.

The horizon was filled with the colour of blood. They seemed to descend gradually to the waves; then they disappeared as though swallowed up, and falling of themselves into the jaws of the sun. Salammbô, who watched them retiring, bent her head, and then Taanach, believing that she guessed her sorrow, said gently to her:

"But they will come back, Mistress."

"Yes! I know."

"And you will see them again."

"Perhaps!" she said, sighing.

She had not confided her resolve to any one; in order to carry it out with the greater discretion she sent Taanach to the suburb of Kinisdo to buy all the things that she required instead of requesting them from the stewards: vermilion, aromatics, a linen girdle, and new garments. The old slave was amazed at these preparations, without daring, however, to ask any questions; and the day, which had been fixed by Schahabarim, arrived when Salammbô was to set out.

About the twelfth hour she perceived, in the depths of the sycamore trees, a blind old man with one hand resting on the shoulder of a child who walked before him, while with the other he carried a kind of cithara of black wood against his hip. The eunuchs, slaves, and women had been scrupulously sent away; no one might know the mystery that was preparing.

Taanach kindled four tripods filled with strobus and cadamomum in the corners of the apartment; then she unfolded large Babylonian hangings, and stretched them on cords all around the room, for Salammbô did not wish to be seen even by the walls. The kinnor-player squatted behind the door and the young boy standing upright applied a reed flute to his lips. In the distance the roar of the streets was growing feebler, violet shadows were lengthening before the peristyles of the temples, and on the other side of the gulf the mountain bases, the fields of olive-trees, and the vague yellow lands undulated indefinitely, and were blended together in a bluish haze; not a sound was to be heard, and an unspeakable depression weighed in the air.

Salammbô crouched down upon the onyx step on the edge of the basin; she raised her ample sleeves, fastening them behind her shoulders, and began her ablutions in methodical fashion, according to the sacred rites.

Next Taanach brought her something liquid and coagulated in an alabaster phial; it was the blood of a black dog slaughtered by barren women on a winter's night amid the rubbish of a sepulchre. She rubbed it upon her ears, her heels, and the thumb of her right hand, and even her nail remained somewhat red, as if she had crushed a fruit.

The moon rose; then the cithara and the flute began to play together.

Salammbô unfastened her earrings, her necklace, her bracelets, and her long white simar; she unknotted the band in her hair, shaking the latter for a few minutes softly over her shoulders to cool herself by thus scattering it. The music went on outside; it consisted of three notes ever the same, hurried and frenzied; the strings grated, the flute blew;

Taanach kept time by striking her hands; Salammbô, with a swaying of her whole body, chanted prayers, and her garments fell one after another around her.

The heavy tapestry trembled, and the python's head appeared above the cord that supported it. The serpent descended slowly like a drop of water flowing along a wall, crawled among the scattered stuffs, and then, gluing its tail to the ground, rose perfectly erect; and his eyes, more brilliant than carbuncles, darted upon Salammbô.

A horror of cold, or perhaps a feeling of shame, at first made her hesitate. But she recalled Schahabarim's orders and advanced; the python turned downwards, and resting the centre of its body upon the nape of her neck, allowed its head and tail to hang like a broken necklace with both ends trailing to the ground. Salammbô rolled it around her sides, under her arms and between her knees; then taking it by the jaw she brought the little triangular mouth to the edge of her teeth, and half shutting her eyes, threw herself back beneath the rays of the moon. The white light seemed to envelop her in a silver mist, the prints of her humid steps shone upon the flag-stones, stars quivered in the depth of the water; it tightened upon her its black rings that were spotted with scales of gold. Salammbô panted beneath the excessive weight, her loins yielded, she felt herself dying, and with the tip of its tail the serpent gently beat her thigh; then the music becoming still it fell off again.

Taanach came back to her; and after arranging two candelabra, the lights of which burned in crystal balls filled with water, she tinged the inside of her hands with Lawsonia, spread vermilion upon her cheeks, and antimony along the edge of her eyelids, and lengthened her eyebrows with a mixture of gum, musk, ebony, and crushed legs of flies.

Salammbô seated on a chair with ivory uprights, gave herself up to the attentions of the slave. But the touchings, the odour of the aromatics, and the fasts that she had undergone, were enervating her. She became so pale that Taanach stopped.

"Go on!" said Salammbô, and bearing up against herself, she suddenly revived. Then she was seized with impatience; she urged Taanach to make haste, and the old slave grumbled:

"Well! well! Mistress!—Besides, you have no one waiting for you!"

"Yes!" said Salammbô, "some one is waiting for me."

Taanach drew back in surprise, and in order to learn more about it, said:

GUSTAVE FLAUBERT

"What orders to you give me, Mistress? for if you are to remain away—"

But Salammbô was sobbing; the slave exclaimed:

"You are suffering! what is the matter? Do not go away! take me! When you were quite little and used to cry, I took you to my heart and made you laugh with the points of my breasts; you have drained them, Mistress!" She struck herself upon her dried-up bosom. "Now I am old! I can do nothing for you! you no longer love me! you hide your griefs from me, you despise the nurse!" And tears of tenderness and vexation flowed down her cheeks in the gashes of her tattooing.

"No!" said Salammbô, "no, I love you! be comforted!"

With a smile like the grimace of an old ape, Taanach resumed her task. In accordance with Schahabarim's recommendations, Salammbô had ordered the slave to make her magnificent; and she was obeying her mistress with barbaric taste full at once of refinement and ingenuity.

Over a first delicate and vinous-coloured tunic she passed a second embroidered with birds' feathers. Golden scales clung to her hips, and from this broad girdle descended her blue flowing silver-starred trousers. Next Taanach put upon her a long robe made of the cloth of the country of Seres, white and streaked with green lines. On the edge of her shoulder she fastened a square of purple weighted at the hem with grains of sandastrum; and above all these garments she placed a black mantle with a flowing train; then she gazed at her, and proud of her work could not help saying:

"You will not be more beautiful on the day of your bridal!"

"My bridal!" repeated Salammbô; she was musing with her elbow resting upon the ivory chair.

But Taanach set up before her a copper mirror, which was so broad and high that she could see herself completely in it. Then she rose, and with a light touch of her finger raised a lock of her hair which was falling too low.

Her hair was covered with gold dust, was crisped in front, and hung down behind over her back in long twists ending in pearls. The brightness of the candelabra heightened the paint on her cheeks, the gold on her garments, and whiteness of her skin; around her waist, and on her arms, hands and toes, she had such a wealth of gems that the mirror sent back rays upon her like a sun;—and Salammbô, standing by the side of Taanach, who leaned over to see her, smiled amid this dazzling display.

Then she walked to and fro embarrassed by the time that was still left.

Suddenly the crow of a cock resounded. She quickly pinned a long yellow veil upon her hair, passed a scarf around her neck, thrust her feet into blue leather boots, and said to Taanach:

"Go and see whether there is not a man with two horses beneath the myrtles."

Taanach had scarcely re-entered when she was descending the galley staircase.

"Mistress!" cried the nurse.

Salammbô turned round with one finger on her mouth as a sign for discretion and immobility.

Taanach stole softly along the prows to the foot of the terrace, and from a distance she could distinguish by the light of the moon a gigantic shadow walking obliquely in the cypress avenue to the left of Salammbô, a sign which presaged death.

Taanach went up again into the chamber. She threw herself upon the ground tearing her face with her nails; she plucked out her hair, and uttered piercing shrieks with all her might.

It occurred to her that they might be heard; then she became silent, sobbing quite softly with her head in the hands and her face on the pavement.

XI

In the Tent

The man who guided Salammbô made her ascend again beyond the pharos in the direction of the Catacombs, and then go down the long suburb of Molouya, which was full of steep lanes. The sky was beginning to grow grey. Sometimes palm-wood beams jutting out from the walls obliged them to bend their heads. The two horses which were at the walk would often slip; and thus they reached the Teveste gate.

Its heavy leaves were half open; they passed through, and it closed behind them.

At first they followed the foot of the ramparts for a time, and at the height of the cisterns they took their way along the Tænia, a narrow strip of yellow earth separating the gulf from the lake and extending as far as Rhades.

No one was to be seen around Carthage, whether on the sea or in the country. The slate-coloured waves chopped softly, and the light wind blowing their foam hither and thither spotted them with white rents. In spite of all her veils, Salammbô shivered in the freshness of the morning; the motion and the open air dazed her. Then the sun rose; it preyed on the back of her head, and she involuntarily dozed a little. The two animals rambled along side by side, their feet sinking into the silent sand.

When they had passed the mountain of the Hot Springs, they went on at a more rapid rate, the ground being firmer.

But although it was the season for sowing and ploughing, the fields were as empty as the desert as far as the eye could reach. Here and there were scattered heaps of corn; at other places the barley was shedding its reddened ears. The villages showed black upon the clear horizon, with shapes incoherently carved.

From time to time a half-calcined piece of wall would be found standing on the edge of the road. The roofs of the cottages were falling in, and in the interiors might be distinguished fragments of pottery, rags of clothing, and all kinds of unrecognisable utensils and broken things. Often a creature clothed in tatters, with earthy face and flaming eyes would emerge from these ruins. But he would very quickly begin to run or would disappear into a hole. Salammbô and her guide did not stop.

Deserted plains succeeded one another. Charcoal dust which was raised by their feet behind them, stretched in unequal trails over large spaces of perfectly white soil. Sometimes they came upon little peaceful spots, where a brook flowed amid the long grass; and as they ascended the other bank Salammbô would pluck damp leaves to cool her hands. At the corner of a wood of rose-bays her horse shied violently at the corpse of a man which lay extended on the ground.

The slave immediately settled her again on the cushions. He was one of the servants of the Temple, a man whom Schahabarim used to employ on perilous missions.

With extreme precaution he now went on foot beside her and between the horses; he would whip the animals with the end of a leathern lace wound round his arm, or would perhaps take balls made of wheat, dates, and yolks of eggs wrapped in lotus leaves from a scrip hanging against his breast, and offer them to Salammbô without speaking, and running all the time.

In the middle of the day three Barbarians clad in animals' skins crossed their path. By degrees others appeared wandering in troops of ten, twelve, or twenty-five men; many were driving goats or a limping cow. Their heavy sticks bristled with brass points; cutlasses gleamed in their clothes, which were savagely dirty, and they opened their eyes with a look of menace and amazement. As they passed some sent them a vulgar benediction; others obscene jests, and Schahabarim's man replied to each in his own idiom. He told them that this was a sick youth going to be cured at a distant temple.

However, the day was closing in. Barkings were heard, and they approached them.

Then in the twilight they perceived an enclosure of dry stones shutting in a rambling edifice. A dog was running along the top of the wall. The slave threw some pebbles at him and they entered a lofty vaulted hall.

A woman was crouching in the centre warming herself at a fire of brushwood, the smoke of which escaped through the holes in the ceiling. She was half hidden by her white hair which fell to her knees; and unwilling to answer, she muttered with idiotic look words of vengeance against the Barbarians and the Carthaginians.

The runner ferreted right and left. Then he returned to her and demanded something to eat. The old woman shook her head, and murmured with her eyes fixed upon the charcoal:

"I was the hand. The ten fingers are cut off. The mouth eats no more."

The slave showed her a handful of gold pieces. She rushed upon them, but soon resumed her immobility.

At last he placed a dagger which he had in his girdle beneath her throat. Then, trembling, she went and raised a large stone, and brought back an amphora of wine with fish from Hippo-Zarytus preserved in honey.

Salammbô turned away from this unclean food, and fell asleep on the horses' caparisons which were spread in a corner of the hall.

He awoke her before daylight.

The dog was howling. The slave went up to it quietly, and struck off its head with a single blow of his dagger. Then he rubbed the horses' nostrils with blood to revive them. The old woman cast a malediction at him from behind. Salammbô perceived this, and pressed the amulet which she wore above her heart.

They resumed their journey.

From time to time she asked whether they would not arrive soon. The road undulated over little hills. Nothing was to be heard but the grating of the grasshoppers. The sun heated the yellowed grass; the ground was all chinked with crevices which in dividing formed, as it were, monstrous paving-stones. Sometimes a viper passed, or eagles flew by; the slave still continued running. Salammbô mused beneath her veils, and in spite of the heat did not lay them aside through fear of soiling her beautiful garments.

At regular distances stood towers built by the Carthaginians for the purpose of keeping watch upon the tribes. They entered these for the sake of the shade, and then set out again.

For prudence sake they had made a wide detour the day before. But they met with no one just now; the region being a sterile one, the Barbarians had not passed that way.

Gradually the devastation began again. Sometimes a piece of mosaic would be displayed in the centre of a field, the sole remnant of a vanished mansion; and the leafless olive trees looked at a distance like large bushes of thorns. They passed through a town in which houses were burnt to the ground. Human skeletons might be seen along the walls. There were some, too, of dromedaries and mules. Half-gnawed carrion blocked the streets.

Night fell. The sky was lowering and cloudy.

They ascended again for two hours in a westerly direction, when suddenly they perceived a quantity of little flames before them.

These were shining at the bottom of an ampitheatre. Gold plates, as they displaced one another, glanced here and there. These were the cuirasses of the Clinabarians in the Punic camp; then in the neighbourhood they distinguished other and more numerous lights, for the armies of the Mercenaries, now blended together, extended over a great space.

Salammbô made a movement as though to advance. But Schahabarim's man took her further away, and they passed along by the terrace which enclosed the camp of the Barbarians. A breach became visible in it, and the slave disappeared.

A sentry was walking upon the top of the entrenchment with a bow in his hand and a pike on his shoulder.

Salammbô drew still nearer; the Barbarian knelt and a long arrow pierced the hem of her cloak. Then as she stood motionless and shrieking, he asked her what she wanted.

"To speak to Matho," she replied. "I am a fugitive from Carthage."

He gave a whistle, which was repeated at intervals further away.

Salammbô waited; her frightened horse moved round and round, sniffing.

When Matho arrived the moon was rising behind her. But she had a yellow veil with black flowers over her face, and so many draperies about her person, that it was impossible to make any guess about her. From the top of the terrace he gazed upon this vague form standing up like a phantom in the penumbræ of the evening.

At last she said to him:

"Lead me to your tent! I wish it!"

A recollection which he could not define passed through his memory. He felt his heart beating. The air of command intimidated him.

"Follow me!" he said.

The barrier was lowered, and immediately she was in the camp of the Barbarians.

It was filled with a great tumult and a great throng. Bright fires were burning beneath hanging pots; and their purpled reflections illuminating some places left others completely in the dark. There was shouting and calling; shackled horses formed long straight lines amid the tents; the latter were round and square, of leather or of canvas; there were huts of reeds, and holes in the sand such as are made by dogs. Soldiers were carting faggots, resting on their elbows on the ground, or wrapping themselves up in mats and preparing to sleep; and Salammbô's horse sometimes stretched out a leg and jumped in order to pass over them.

She remembered that she had seen them before; but their beards were longer now, their faces still blacker, and their voices hoarser. Matho, who walked before her, waved them off with a gesture of his arm which raised his red mantle. Some kissed his hands; others bending their spines approached him to ask for orders, for he was now veritable and sole chief of the Barbarians; Spendius, Autaritus, and Narr' Havas had become disheartened, and he had displayed so much audacity and obstinacy that all obeyed him.

Salammbô followed him through the entire camp. His tent was at the end, three hundred feet from Hamilcar's entrenchments.

She noticed a wide pit on the right, and it seemed to her that faces were resting against the edge of it on a level with the ground, as decapitated heads might have done. However, their eyes moved, and from these half-opened mouths groanings escaped in the Punic tongue.

Two Negroes holding resin lights stood on both sides of the door. Matho drew the canvas abruptly aside. She followed him.

It was a deep tent with a pole standing up in the centre. It was lighted by a large lamp-holder shaped like a lotus and full of a yellow oil wherein floated handfuls of burning tow, and military things might be distinguished gleaming in the shade. A naked sword leaned against a stool by the side of a shield; whips of hippopotamus leather, cymbals, bells, and necklaces were displayed pell-mell on baskets of esparto-grass; a felt rug lay soiled with crumbs of black bread; some copper money was carelessly heaped upon a round stone in a corner, and through the rents in the canvas the wind brought the dust from without, together with the smell of the elephants, which might be heard eating and shaking their chains.

"Who are you?" said Matho.

She looked slowly around her without replying; then her eyes were arrested in the background, where something bluish and sparkling fell upon a bed of palm-branches.

She advanced quickly. A cry escaped her. Matho stamped his foot behind her.

"Who brings you here? why do you come?"

"To take it!" she replied, pointing to the zaïmph, and with the other hand she tore the veils from her head. He drew back with his elbows behind him, gaping, almost terrified.

She felt as if she were leaning on the might of the gods; and looking at him face to face she asked him for the zaïmph; she demanded it in words abundant and superb.

Matho did not hear; he was gazing at her, and in his eyes her garments were blended with her body. The clouding of the stuffs, like the splendour of her skin, was something special and belonging to her alone. Her eyes and her diamonds sparkled; the polish of her nails continued the delicacy of the stones which loaded her fingers; the two clasps of her tunic raised her breasts somewhat and brought them closer together, and he in thought lost himself in the narrow interval between them whence there fell a thread holding a plate of emeralds which could be seen lower down beneath the violet gauze. She had as earrings two little sapphire scales, each supporting a hollow pearl filled with liquid scent. A little drop would fall every moment through the holes in the pearl and moisten her naked shoulder. Matho watched it fall.

He was carried away by ungovernable curiosity; and, like a child laying his hand upon a strange fruit, he tremblingly and lightly touched the top of her chest with the tip of his finger: the flesh, which was somewhat cold, yielded with an elastic resistance.

This contact, though scarcely a sensible one, shook Matho to the very depths of his nature. An uprising of his whole being urged him towards her. He would fain have enveloped her, absorbed her, drunk her. His bosom was panting, his teeth were chattering.

Taking her by the wrists he drew her gently to him, and then sat down upon a cuirass beside the palm-tree bed which was covered with a lion's skin. She was standing. He looked up at her, holding her thus between his knees, and repeating:

"How beautiful you are! how beautiful you are!"

His eyes, which were continually fixed upon hers, pained her; and the uncomfortableness, the repugnance increased in so acute a fashion that Salammbô put a constraint upon herself not to cry out. The thought of Schahabarim came back to her, and she resigned herself.

Matho still kept her little hands in his own; and from time to time, in spite of the priest's command, she turned away her face and tried to thrust him off by jerking her arms. He opened his nostrils the better to breathe in the perfume which exhaled from her person. It was a fresh, indefinable emanation, which nevertheless made him dizzy, like the smoke from a perfuming-pan. She smelt of honey, pepper, incense, roses, with another odour still.

But how was she thus with him in his tent, and at his disposal? Some one no doubt had urged her. She had not come for the zaïmph. His arms fell, and he bent his head whelmed in sudden reverie.

GUSTAVE FLAUBERT

To soften him Salammbô said to him in a plaintive voice:

"What have I done to you that you should desire my death?"

"Your death!"

She resumed:

"I saw you one evening by the light of my burning gardens amid fuming cups and my slaughtered slaves, and your anger was so strong that you bounded towards me and I was obliged to fly! Then terror entered into Carthage. There were cries of the devastation of the towns, the burning of the country-seats, the massacre of the soldiery; it was you who had ruined them, it was you who had murdered them! I hate you! Your very name gnaws me like remorse! You are execrated more than the plague, and the Roman war! The provinces shudder at your fury, the furrows are full of corpses! I have followed the traces of your fires as though I were travelling behind Moloch!"

Matho leaped up; his heart was swelling with colossal pride; he was raised to the stature of a god.

With quivering nostrils and clenched teeth she went on:

"As if your sacrilege were not enough, you came to me in my sleep covered with the zaïmph! Your words I did not understand; but I could see that you wished to drag me to some terrible thing at the bottom of an abyss."

Matho, writhing his arms, exclaimed:

"No! no! it was to give it to you! to restore it to you! It seemed to me that the goddess had left her garment for you, and that it belonged to you! In her temple or in your house, what does it matter? are you not all-powerful, immaculate, radiant and beautiful even as Tanith?" And with a look of boundless adoration he added:

"Unless perhaps you are Tanith?"

"I, Tanith!" said Salammbô to herself.

They left off speaking. The thunder rolled in the distance. Some sheep bleated, frightened by the storm.

"Oh! come near!" he went on, "come near! fear nothing!

"Formerly I was only a soldier mingled with the common herd of the Mercenaries, ay, and so meek that I used to carry wood on my back for the others. Do I trouble myself about Carthage! The crowd of its people move as though lost in the dust of your sandals, and all its treasures, with the provinces, fleets, and islands, do not raise my envy like the freshness of your lips and the turn of your shoulders. But I wanted to throw down its walls that I might reach you to possess you! Moreover,

I was revenging myself in the meantime! At present I crush men like shells, and I throw myself upon phalanxes; I put aside the sarissæ with my hands, I check the stallions by the nostrils; a catapult would not kill me! Oh! if you knew how I think of you in the midst of war! Sometimes the memory of a gesture or of a fold of your garment suddenly seizes me and entwines me like a net! I perceive your eyes in the flames of the phalaricas and on the gilding of the shields! I hear your voice in the sounding of the cymbals. I turn aside, but you are not there! and I plunge again into the battle!"

He raised his arms whereon his veins crossed one another like ivy on the branches of a tree. Sweat flowed down his breast between his square muscles; and his breathing shook his sides with his bronze girdle all garnished with thongs hanging down to his knees, which were firmer than marble. Salammbô, who was accustomed to eunuchs, yielded to amazement at the strength of this man. It was the chastisement of the goddess or the influence of Moloch in motion around her in the five armies. She was overwhelmed with lassitude; and she listened in a state of stupor to the intermittent shouts of the sentinels as they answered one another.

The flames of the lamp kindled in the squalls of hot air. There came at times broad lightning flashes; then the darkness increased; and she could only see Matho's eyeballs like two coals in the night. However, she felt that a fatality was surrounding her, that she had reached a supreme and irrevocable moment, and making an effort she went up again towards the zaïmph and raised her hands to seize it.

"What are you doing?" exclaimed Matho.

"I am going back to Carthage," she placidly replied.

He advanced folding his arms and with so terrible a look that her heels were immediately nailed, as it were, to the spot.

"Going back to Carthage!" He stammered, and, grinding his teeth, repeated:

"Going back to Carthage! Ah! you came to take the zaïmph, to conquer me, and then disappear! No, no! you belong to me! and no one now shall tear you from here! Oh! I have not forgotten the insolence of your large tranquil eyes, and how you crushed me with the haughtiness of your beauty! 'Tis my turn now! You are my captive, my slave, my servant! Call, if you like, on your father and his army, the Ancients, the rich, and your whole accursed people! I am the master of three hundred thousand soldiers! I will go and seek them in Lusitania, in the Gauls, and in the depths of the desert, and I will overthrow your town and burn all its temples; the triremes shall float on the waves of blood! I will not have a house, a stone, or a palm tree remaining! And if men fail me I will draw the bears from the mountains and urge on the lions! Seek not to fly or I kill you!"

Pale and with clenched fists he quivered like a harp whose strings are about to burst. Suddenly sobs stifled him, and he sank down upon his hams.

"Ah! forgive me! I am a scoundrel, and viler than scorpions, than mire and dust! Just now while you were speaking your breath passed across my face, and I rejoiced like a dying man who drinks lying flat on the edge of a stream. Crush me, if only I feel your feet! curse me, if only I hear your voice! Do not go! have pity! I love you! I love you!"

He was on his knees on the ground before her; and he encircled her form with both his arms, his head thrown back, and his hands wandering; the gold discs hanging from his ears gleamed upon his bronzed neck; big tears rolled in his eyes like silver globes; he sighed caressingly, and murmured vague words lighter than a breeze and sweet as a kiss.

Salammbô was invaded by a weakness in which she lost all consciousness of herself. Something at once inward and lofty, a command from the gods, obliged her to yield herself; clouds uplifted her, and she fell back swooning upon the bed amid the lion's hair. The zaïmph fell, and enveloped her; she could see Matho's face bending down above her breast.

"Moloch, thou burnest me!" and the soldier's kisses, more devouring than flames, covered her; she was as though swept away in a hurricane, taken in the might of the sun.

He kissed all her fingers, her arms, her feet, and the long tresses of her hair from one end to the other.

"Carry it off," he said, "what do I care? take me away with it! I abandon the army! I renounce everything! Beyond Gades, twenty days' journey into the sea, you come to an island covered with gold dust, verdure, and birds. On the mountains large flowers filled with smoking perfumes rock like eternal censers; in the citron trees, which are higher than cedars, milk-coloured serpents cause the fruit to fall upon the turf with the diamonds in their jaws; the air is so mild that it keeps you from dying. Oh! I shall find it, you will see. We shall live in crystal grottoes cut out at the foot of the hills. No one dwells in it yet, or I shall become the king of the country."

He brushed the dust off her cothurni; he wanted her to put a quarter of a pomegranate between her lips; he heaped up garments behind her head to make a cushion for her. He sought for means to serve her, and to humble himself, and he even spread the zaïmph over her feet as if it were a mere rug.

"Have you still," he said, "those little gazelle's horns on which your necklaces hang? You will give them to me! I love them!" For he spoke as if the war were finished, and joyful laughs broke from him. The Mercenaries, Hamilcar, every obstacle had now disappeared. The moon was gliding between two clouds. They could see it through an opening in the tent. "Ah, what nights have I spent gazing at her! she seemed to me like a veil that hid your face; you would look at me through her; the memory of you was mingled with her beams; then I could no longer distinguish you!" And with his head between her breasts he wept copiously.

"And this," she thought, "is the formidable man who makes Carthage tremble!"

He fell asleep. Then disengaging herself from his arm she put one foot to the ground, and she perceived that her chainlet was broken.

The maidens of the great families were accustomed to respect these shackles as something that was almost religious, and Salammbô, blushing, rolled the two pieces of the golden chain around her ankles.

Carthage, Megara, her house, her room, and the country that she had passed through, whirled in tumultuous yet distinct images through her memory. But an abyss had yawned and thrown them far back to an infinite distance from her.

The storm was departing; drops of water splashing rarely, one by one, made the tent-roof shake.

Matho slept like a drunken man, stretched on his side, and with one arm over the edge of the couch. His band of pearls was raised somewhat, and uncovered his brow; his teeth were parted in a smile; they shone through his black beard, and there was a silent and almost outrageous gaiety in his half-closed eyelids.

Salammbô looked at him motionless, her head bent and her hands crossed.

A dagger was displayed on the table of cypress-wood at the head of the bed; the sight of the gleaming blade fired her with a sanguinary desire. Mournful voices lingered at a distance in the shade, and like a chorus of geniuses urged her on. She approached it; she seized the steel by the handle. At the rustling of her dress Matho half opened his eyes, putting forth his mouth upon her hands, and the dagger fell.

Shouts arose; a terrible light flashed behind the canvas. Matho raised the latter; they perceived the camp of the Libyans enveloped in great flames.

Their reed huts were burning, and the twisting stems burst in the smoke and flew off like arrows; black shadows ran about distractedly on the red horizon. They could hear the shrieks of those who were in the huts; the elephants, oxen, and horses plunged in the midst of the crowd crushing it together with the stores and baggage that were being rescued from the fire. Trumpets sounded. There were calls of "Matho! Matho!" Some people at the door tried to get in.

"Come along! Hamilcar is burning the camp of Autaritus!"

He made a spring. She found herself quite alone.

Then she examined the zaïmph; and when she had viewed it well she was surprised that she had not the happiness which she had once imagined to herself. She stood with melancholy before her accomplished dream.

But the lower part of the tent was raised, and a monstrous form appeared. Salammbô could at first distinguish only the two eyes and a long white beard which hung down to the ground; for the rest of the body, which was cumbered with the rags of a tawny garment, trailed along the earth; and with every forward movement the hands passed into the beard and then fell again. Crawling in this way it reached her feet, and Salammbô recognised the aged Gisco.

In fact, the Mercenaries had broken the legs of the captive Ancients with a brass bar to prevent them from taking to flight; and they were all rotting pell-mell in a pit in the midst of filth. But the sturdiest of them raised themselves and shouted when they heard the noise of platters, and it was in this way that Gisco had seen Salammbô. He had guessed that she was a Carthaginian woman by the little balls of sandastrum flapping against her cothurni; and having a presentiment of an important mystery he had succeeded, with the assistance of his companions, in getting out of the pit; then with elbows and hands he had dragged himself twenty paces further on as far as Matho's tent. Two voices were speaking within it. He had listened outside and had heard everything.

"It is you!" she said at last, almost terrified.

"Yes, it is I!" he replied, raising himself on his wrists. "They think me dead, do they not?"

She bent her head. He resumed:

"Ah! why have the Baals not granted me this mercy!" He approached so close he was touching her. "They would have spared me the pain of cursing you!"

Salammbô sprang quickly back, so much afraid was she of this unclean being, who was as hideous as a larva and nearly as terrible as a phantom.

"I am nearly one hundred years old," he said. "I have seen Agathocles; I have seen Regulus and the eagles of the Romans passing over the harvests of the Punic fields! I have seen all the terrors of battles and the sea encumbered with the wrecks of our fleets! Barbarians whom I used to command have chained my four limbs like a slave that has committed murder. My companions are dying around me, one after the other; the odour of their corpses awakes me in the night; I drive away the birds that come to peck out their eyes; and yet not for a single day have I despaired of Carthage! Though I had seen all the armies of the earth against her, and the flames of the siege overtop the height of the temples, I should have still believed in her eternity! But now all is over! all is lost! The gods execrate her! A curse upon you who have quickened her ruin by your disgrace!"

She opened her lips.

"Ah! I was there!" he cried. "I heard you gurgling with love like a prostitute; then he told you of his desire, and you allowed him to kiss your hands! But if the frenzy of your unchastity urged you to it, you should at least have done as do the fallow deer, which hide themselves in their copulations, and not have displayed your shame beneath your father's very eyes!"

"What?" she said.

"Ah! you did not know that the two entrenchments are sixty cubits from each other and that your Matho, in the excess of his pride, has posted himself just in front of Hamilcar. Your father is there behind you; and could I climb the path which leads to the platform, I should cry to him: 'Come and see your daughter in the Barbarian's arms! She has put on the garment of the goddess to please him; and in yielding her body to him she surrenders with the glory of your name the majesty of the gods, the vengeance of her country, even the safety of Carthage!'" The motion of his toothless mouth moved his beard throughout its length; his eyes were riveted upon her and devoured her; panting in the dust he repeated:

GUSTAVE FLAUBERT

"Ah! sacrilegious one! May you be accursed! accursed! accursed!"

Salammbô had drawn back the canvas; she held it raised at arm's length, and without answering him she looked in the direction of Hamilcar.

"It is this way, is it not?" she said.

"What matters it to you? Turn away! Begone! Rather crush your face against the earth! It is a holy spot which would be polluted by your gaze!"

She threw the zaïmph about her waist, and quickly picked up her veils, mantle, and scarf. "I hasten thither!" she cried; and making her escape Salammbô disappeared.

At first she walked through the darkness without meeting any one, for all were betaking themselves to the fire; the uproar was increasing and great flames purpled the sky behind; a long terrace stopped her.

She turned round to right and left at random, seeking for a ladder, a rope, a stone, something in short to assist her. She was afraid of Gisco, and it seemed to her that shouts and footsteps were pursuing her. Day was beginning to break. She perceived a path in the thickness of the entrenchment. She took the hem of her robe, which impeded her, in her teeth, and in three bounds she was on the platform.

A sonorous shout burst forth beneath her in the shade, the same which she had heard at the foot of the galley staircase, and leaning over she recognised Schahabarim's man with his coupled horses.

He had wandered all night between the two entrenchments; then disquieted by the fire, he had gone back again trying to see what was passing in Matho's camp; and, knowing that this spot was nearest to his tent, he had not stirred from it, in obedience to the priest's command.

He stood up on one of the horses. Salammbô let herself slide down to him; and they fled at full gallop, circling the Punic camp in search of a gate.

Matho had re-entered his tent. The smoky lamp gave but little light, and he also believed that Salammbô was asleep. Then he delicately touched the lion's skin on the palm-tree bed. He called but she did not answer; he quickly tore away a strip of the canvas to let in some light; the zaïmph was gone.

The earth trembled beneath thronging feet. Shouts, neighings, and clashing of armour rose in the air, and clarion flourishes sounded the charge. It was as though a hurricane were whirling around him.

Immoderate frenzy made him leap upon his arms, and he dashed outside.

The long files of the Barbarians were descending the mountain at a run, and the Punic squares were advancing against them with a heavy and regular oscillation. The mist, rent by the rays of the sun, formed little rocking clouds which as they rose gradually discovered standards, helmets, and points of pikes. Beneath the rapid evolutions portions of the earth which were still in the shadow seemed to be displaced bodily; in other places it looked as if huge torrents were crossing one another, while thorny masses stood motionless between them. Matho could distinguish the captains, soldiers, heralds, and even the serving-men, who were mounted on asses in the rear. But instead of maintaining his position in order to cover the foot-soldiers, Narr' Havas turned abruptly to the right, as though he wished himself to be crushed by Hamilcar.

His horsemen outstripped the elephants, which were slackening their speed; and all the horses, stretching out their unbridled heads, galloped at so furious a rate that their bellies seemed to graze the earth. Then suddenly Narr' Havas went resolutely up to a sentry. He threw away his sword, lance, and javelins, and disappeared among the Carthaginians.

The king of the Numidians reached Hamilcar's tent, and pointing to his men, who were standing still at a distance, he said:

"Barca! I bring them to you. They are yours."

Then he prostrated himself in token of bondage, and to prove his fidelity recalled all his conduct from the beginning of the war.

First, he had prevented the siege of Carthage and the massacre of the captives; then he had taken no advantage of the victory over Hanno after the defeat at Utica. As to the Tyrian towns, they were on the frontiers of his kingdom. Finally he had not taken part in the battle of the Macaras; and he had even expressly absented himself in order to evade the obligation of fighting against the Suffet.

Narr' Havas had in fact wished to aggrandise himself by encroachments upon the Punic provinces, and had alternately assisted and forsaken the Mercenaries according to the chances of victory. But seeing that Hamilcar would ultimately prove the stronger, he had gone over to him; and in his desertion there was perhaps something of a grudge against Matho, whether on account of the command or of his former love.

The Suffet listened without interrupting him. The man who thus presented himself with an army where vengeance was his due was not an auxiliary to be despised; Hamilcar at once divined the utility of such an alliance in his great projects. With the Numidians he would get rid of the Libyans. Then he would draw off the West to the conquest of Iberia; and, without asking Narr' Havas why he had not come sooner, or noticing any of his lies, he kissed him, striking his breast thrice against his own.

It was to bring matters to an end and in despair that he had fired the camp of the Libyans. This army came to him like a relief from the gods; dissembling his joy he replied:

"May the Baals favour you! I do not know what the Republic will do for you, but Hamilcar is not ungrateful."

The tumult increased; some captains entered. He was arming himself as he spoke.

"Come, return! You will use your horsemen to beat down their infantry between your elephants and mine. Courage! exterminate them!"

And Narr' Havas was rushing away when Salammbô appeared.

She leaped down quickly from her horse. She opened her ample cloak and spreading out her arms displayed the zaïmph.

The leathern tent, which was raised at the corners, left visible the entire circuit of the mountain with its thronging soldiers, and as it was in the centre Salammbô could be seen on all sides. An immense shouting burst forth, a long cry of triumph and hope. Those who were marching stopped; the dying leaned on their elbows and turned round to bless her. All the Barbarians knew now that she had recovered the zaïmph; they saw her or believed that they saw her from a distance; and other cries, but those of rage and vengeance, resounded in spite of the plaudits of the Carthaginians. Thus did the five armies in tiers upon the mountain stamp and shriek around Salammbô.

Hamilcar, who was unable to speak, nodded her his thanks. His eyes were directed alternately upon the zaïmph and upon her, and he noticed that her chainlet was broken. Then he shivered, being seized with a terrible suspicion. But soon recovering his impassibility he looked sideways at Narr' Havas without turning his face.

The king of the Numidians held himself apart in a discreet attitude; on his forehead he bore a little of the dust which he had touched when prostrating himself. At last the Suffet advanced towards him with a look full of gravity.

"As a reward for the services which you have rendered me, Narr' Havas, I give you my daughter. Be my son," he added, "and defend your father!"

Narr' Havas gave a great gesture of surprise; then he threw himself upon Hamilcar's hands and covered them with kisses.

Salammbô, calm as a statue, did not seem to understand. She blushed a little as she cast down her eyelids, and her long curved lashes made shadows upon her cheeks.

Hamilcar wished to unite them immediately in indissoluble betrothal. A lance was placed in Salammbô's hands and by her offered to Narr' Havas; their thumbs were tied together with a thong of ox-leather; then corn was poured upon their heads, and the grains that fell around them rang like rebounding hail.

XII

THE AQUEDUCT

Twelve hours afterwards all that remained of the Mercenaries was a heap of wounded, dead, and dying.

Hamilcar had suddenly emerged from the bottom of the gorge, and again descended the western slope that looked towards Hippo-Zarytus, and the space being broader at this spot he had taken care to draw the Barbarians into it. Narr' Havas had encompassed them with his horse; the Suffet meanwhile drove them back and crushed them. Then, too, they were conquered beforehand by the loss of the zaïmph; even those who cared nothing about it had experienced anguish and something akin to enfeeblement. Hamilcar, not indulging his pride by holding the field of battle, had retired a little further off on the left to some heights, from which he commanded them.

The shape of the camps could be recognised by their sloping palisades. A long heap of black cinders was smoking on the side of the Libyans; the devastated soil showed undulations like the sea, and the tents with their tattered canvas looked like dim ships half lost in the breakers. Cuirasses, forks, clarions, pieces of wood, iron and brass, corn, straw, and garments were scattered about among the corpses; here and there a phalarica on the point of extinction burned against a heap of baggage; in some places the earth was hidden with shields; horses' carcasses succeeded one another like a series of hillocks; legs, sandals, arms, and coats of mail were to be seen, with heads held in their helmets by the chin-pieces and rolling about like balls; heads of hair were hanging on the thorns; elephants were lying with their towers in pools of blood, with entrails exposed, and gasping. The foot trod on slimy things, and there were swamps of mud although no rain had fallen.

This confusion of dead bodies covered the whole mountain from top to bottom.

Those who survived stirred as little as the dead. Squatting in unequal groups they looked at one another scared and without speaking.

The lake of Hippo-Zarytus shone at the end of a long meadow beneath the setting sun. To the right an agglomeration of white houses extended beyond a girdle of walls; then the sea spread out indefinitely;

and the Barbarians, with their chins in their hands, sighed as they thought of their native lands. A cloud of grey dust was falling.

The evening wind blew; then every breast dilated, and as the freshness increased, the vermin might be seen to forsake the dead, who were colder now, and to run over the hot sand. Crows, looking towards the dying, rested motionless on the tops of the big stones.

When night had fallen yellow-haired dogs, those unclean beasts which followed the armies, came quite softly into the midst of the Barbarians. At first they licked the clots of blood on the still tepid stumps; and soon they began to devour the corpses, biting into the stomachs first of all.

The fugitives reappeared one by one like shadows; the women also ventured to return, for there were still some of them left, especially among the Libyans, in spite of the dreadful massacre of them by the Numidians.

Some took ropes' ends and lighted them to use as torches. Others held crossed pikes. The corpses were placed upon these and were conveyed apart.

They were found lying stretched in long lines, on their backs, with their mouths open, and their lances beside them; or else they were piled up pell-mell so that it was often necessary to dig out a whole heap in order to discover those they were wanting. Then the torch would be passed slowly over their faces. They had received complicated wounds from hideous weapons. Greenish strips hung from their foreheads; they were cut in pieces, crushed to the marrow, blue from strangulation, or broadly cleft by the elephants' ivory. Although they had died at almost the same time there existed differences between their various states of corruption. The men of the North were puffed up with livid swellings, while the more nervous Africans looked as though they had been smoked, and were already drying up. The Mercenaries might be recognised by the tattooing on their hands: the old soldiers of Antiochus displayed a sparrow-hawk; those who had served in Egypt, the head of the cynosephalus; those who had served with the princes of Asia, a hatchet, a pomegranate, or a hammer; those who had served in the Greek republics, the side-view of a citadel or the name of an archon; and some were to be seen whose arms were entirely covered with these multiplied symbols, which mingled with their scars and their recent wounds.

Four great funeral piles were erected for the men of Latin race, the Samnites, Etruscans, Campanians, and Bruttians.

The Greeks dug pits with the points of their swords. The Spartans removed their red cloaks and wrapped them round the dead; the Athenians laid them out with their faces towards the rising sun; the Cantabrians buried them beneath a heap of pebbles; the Nasamonians bent them double with ox-leather thongs, and the Garamantians went and interred them on the shore so that they might be perpetually washed by the waves. But the Latins were grieved that they could not collect the ashes in urns; the Nomads regretted the heat of the sands in which bodies were mummified, and the Celts, the three rude stones beneath a rainy sky at the end of an islet-covered gulf.

Vociferations arose, followed by the lengthened silence. This was to oblige the souls to return. Then the shouting was resumed persistently at regular intervals.

They made excuses to the dead for their inability to honour them as the rites prescribed: for, owing to this deprivation, they would pass for infinite periods through all kinds of chances and metamorphoses; they questioned them and asked them what they desired; others loaded them with abuse for having allowed themselves to be conquered.

The bloodless faces lying back here and there on wrecks of armour showed pale in the light of the great funeral-pile; tears provoked tears, the sobs became shriller, the recognitions and embracings more frantic. Women stretched themselves on the corpses, mouth to mouth and brow to brow; it was necessary to beat them in order to make them withdraw when the earth was being thrown in. They blackened their cheeks; they cut off their hair; they drew their own blood and poured it into the pits; they gashed themselves in imitation of the wounds that disfigured the dead. Roarings burst forth through the crashings of the cymbals. Some snatched off their amulets and spat upon them. The dying rolled in the bloody mire biting their mutilated fists in their rage; and forty-three Samnites, quite a "sacred spring," cut one another's throats like gladiators. Soon wood for the funeral-piles failed, the flames were extinguished, every spot was occupied; and weary from shouting, weakened, tottering, they fell asleep close to their dead brethren, those who still clung to life full of anxieties, and the others desiring never to wake again.

IN THE GREYNESS OF THE dawn some soldiers appeared on the outskirts of the Barbarians, and filed past with their helmets raised on the points of their pikes; they saluted the Mercenaries and asked them whether they had no messages to send to their native lands.

Others approached, and the Barbarians recognised some of their former companions.

The Suffet had proposed to all the captives that they should serve in his troops. Several had fearlessly refused; and quite resolved neither to support them nor to abandon them to the Great Council, he had sent them away with injunctions to fight no more against Carthage. As to those who had been rendered docile by the fear of tortures, they had been furnished with the weapons taken from the enemy; and they were now presenting themselves to the vanquished, not so much in order to seduce them as out of an impulse of pride and curiosity.

At first they told of the good treatment which they had received from the Suffet; the Barbarians listened to them with jealousy although they despised them. Then at the first words of reproach the cowards fell into a passion; they showed them from a distance their own swords and cuirasses and invited them with abuse to come and take them. The Barbarians picked up flints; all took to flight; and nothing more could be seen on the summit of the mountain except the lance-points projecting above the edge of the palisades.

Then the Barbarians were overwhelmed with a grief that was heavier than the humiliation of the defeat. They thought of the emptiness of their courage, and they stood with their eyes fixed and grinding their teeth.

The same thought came to them all. They rushed tumultuously upon the Carthaginian prisoners. It chanced that the Suffet's soldiers had been unable to discover them, and as he had withdrawn from the field of battle they were still in the deep pit.

They were ranged on the ground on a flattened spot. Sentries formed a circle round them, and the women were allowed to enter thirty or forty at a time. Wishing to profit by the short time that was allowed to them, they ran from one to the other, uncertain and panting; then bending over the poor bodies they struck them with all their might like washerwomen beating linen; shrieking their husband's names they tore them with their nails and put out their eyes with the bodkins of their hair. The men came next and tortured them from their feet, which they cut off at the ankles, to their foreheads, from which they took crowns of skin to put upon their own heads. The Eaters of Uncleanness were atrocious in their devices. They envenomed the wounds by pouring into them dust, vinegar, and fragments of pottery; others waited behind; blood flowed, and they rejoiced like vintagers round fuming vats.

Matho, however, was seated on the ground, at the very place where he had happened to be when the battle ended, his elbows on his knees, and his temples in his hands; he saw nothing, heard nothing, and had ceased to think.

At the shrieks of joy uttered by the crowd he raised his head. Before him a strip of canvas caught on a flagpole, and trailing on the ground, sheltered in confused fashion blankets, carpets, and a lion's skin. He recognised his tent; and he riveted his eyes upon the ground as though Hamilcar's daughter, when she disappeared, had sunk into the earth.

The torn canvas flapped in the wind; the long rags of it sometimes passed across his mouth, and he perceived a red mark like the print of a hand. It was the hand of Narr' Havas, the token of their alliance. Then Matho rose. He took a firebrand which was still smoking, and threw it disdainfully upon the wrecks of his tent. Then with the toe of his cothurn he pushed the things which fell out back towards the flame so that nothing might be left.

Suddenly, without any one being able to guess from what point he had sprung up, Spendius reappeared.

The former slave had fastened two fragments of a lance against his thigh; he limped with a piteous look, breathing forth complaints the while.

"Remove that," said Matho to him. "I know that you are a brave fellow!" For he was so crushed by the injustice of the gods that he had not strength enough to be indignant with men.

Spendius beckoned to him and led him to a hollow of the mountain, where Zarxas and Autaritus were lying concealed.

They had fled like the slave, the one although he was cruel, and the other in spite of his bravery. But who, said they, could have expected the treachery of Narr' Havas, the burning of the camp of the Libyans, the loss of the zaïmph, the sudden attack by Hamilcar, and, above all, his manouvres which forced them to return to the bottom of the mountain beneath the instant blows of the Carthaginians? Spendius made no acknowledgement of his terror, and persisted in maintaining that his leg was broken.

At last the three chiefs and the schalischim asked one another what decision should now be adopted.

Hamilcar closed the road to Carthage against them; they were caught between his soldiers and the provinces belonging to Narr' Havas; the Tyrian towns would join the conquerors; the Barbarians would find themselves driven to the edge of the sea, and all those united forces would crush them. This would infallibly happen.

Thus no means presented themselves of avoiding the war. Accordingly they must prosecute it to the bitter end. But how were they to make the necessity of an interminable battle understood by all these disheartened people, who were still bleeding from their wounds.

"I will undertake that!" said Spendius.

Two hours afterwards a man who came from the direction of Hippo-Zarytus climbed the mountain at a run. He waved some tablets at arm's length, and as he shouted very loudly the Barbarians surrounded him.

The tablets had been despatched by the Greek soldiers in Sardinia. They recommended their African comrades to watch over Gisco and the other captives. A Samian trader, one Hipponax, coming from Carthage, had informed them that a plot was being organised to promote their escape, and the Barbarians were urged to take every precaution; the Republic was powerful.

Spendius's stratagem did not succeed at first as he had hoped. This assurance of the new peril, so far from exciting frenzy, raised fears; and remembering Hamilcar's warning, lately thrown into their midst, they expected something unlooked for and terrible. The night was spent in great distress; several even got rid of their weapons, so as to soften the Suffet when he presented himself.

But on the following day, at the third watch, a second runner appeared, still more breathless, and blackened with dust. The Greek snatched from his hand a roll of papyrus covered with Phonician writing. The Mercenaries were entreated not to be disheartened; the brave men of Tunis were coming with large reinforcements.

Spendius first read the letter three times in succession; and held up by two Cappadocians, who bore him seated on their shoulders, he had himself conveyed from place to place and re-read it. For seven hours he harangued.

He reminded the Mercenaries of the promises of the Great Council; the Africans of the cruelties of the stewards, and all the Barbarians of the injustice of Carthage. The Suffet's mildness was only a bait to capture them; those who surrendered would be sold as slaves, and the vanquished would perish under torture. As to flight, what routes could they follow? Not a nation would receive them. Whereas by continuing their efforts they would obtain at once freedom, vengeance, and money! And they would not have long to wait, since the people of Tunis, the whole of Libya, was rushing to relieve them. He showed the unrolled papyrus: "Look at it! read! see their promises! I do not lie."

Dogs were straying about with their black muzzles all plastered with red. The men's uncovered heads were growing hot in the burning sun. A nauseous smell exhaled from the badly buried corpses. Some even projected from the earth as far as the waist. Spendius called them to witness what he was saying; then he raised his fists in the direction of Hamilcar.

Matho, moreover, was watching him, and to cover his cowardice he displayed an anger by which he gradually found himself carried away. Devoting himself to the gods he heaped curses upon the Carthaginians. The torture of the captives was child's play. Why spare them, and be ever dragging this useless cattle after one? "No! we must put an end to it! their designs are known! a single one might ruin us! no pity! Those who are worthy will be known by the speed of their legs and the force of their blows."

Then they turned again upon the captives. Several were still in the last throes; they were finished by the thrust of a heel in the mouth or a stab with the point of a javelin.

Then they thought of Gisco. Nowhere could he be seen; they were disturbed with anxiety. They wished at once to convince themselves of his death and to participate in it. At last three Samnite shepherds discovered him at a distance of fifteen paces from the spot where Matho's tent lately stood. They recognised him by his long beard and they called the rest.

Stretched on his back, his arms against his hips, and his knees close together, he looked like a dead man laid out for the tomb. Nevertheless his wasted sides rose and fell, and his eyes, wide-opened in his pallid face, gazed in a continuous and intolerable fashion.

The Barbarians looked at him at first with great astonishment. Since he had been living in the pit he had been almost forgotten; rendered uneasy by old memories they stood at a distance and did not venture to raise their hands against him.

But those who were behind were murmuring and pressed forward when a Garamantian passed through the crowd; he was brandishing a sickle; all understood his thought; their faces purpled, and smitten with shame they shrieked:

"Yes! yes!"

The man with the curved steel approached Gisco. He took his head, and, resting it upon his knee, sawed it off with rapid strokes; it fell; to great jets of blood made a hole in the dust. Zarxas leaped upon it, and lighter than a leopard ran towards the Carthaginians.

Then when he had covered two thirds of the mountain he drew Gisco's head from his breast by the beard, whirled his arm rapidly several times,—and the mass, when thrown at last, described a long parabola and disappeared behind the Punic entrenchments.

Soon at the edge of the palisades there rose two crossed standards, the customary sign for claiming a corpse.

Then four heralds, chosen for their width of chest, went out with great clarions, and speaking through the brass tubes declared that henceforth there would be between Carthaginians and Barbarians neither faith, pity, nor gods, that they refused all overtures beforehand, and that envoys would be sent back with their hands cut off.

Immediately afterwards, Spendius was sent to Hippo-Zarytus to procure provisions; the Tyrian city sent them some the same evening. They ate greedily. Then when they were strengthened they speedily collected the remains of their baggage and their broken arms; the women massed themselves in the centre, and heedless of the wounded left weeping behind them, they set out along the edge of the shore like a herd of wolves taking its departure.

They were marching upon Hippo-Zarytus, resolved to take it, for they had need of a town.

Hamilcar, as he perceived them at a distance, had a feeling of despair in spite of the pride which he experienced in seeing them fly before him. He ought to have attacked them immediately with fresh troops. Another similar day and the war was over! If matters were protracted they would return with greater strength; the Tyrian towns would join them; his clemency towards the vanquished had been of no avail. He resolved to be pitiless.

The same evening he sent the Great Council a dromedary laden with bracelets collected from the dead, and with horrible threats ordered another army to be despatched.

All had for a long time believed him lost; so that on learning his victory they felt a stupefaction which was almost terror. The vaguely announced return of the zaïmph completed the wonder. Thus the gods and the might of Carthage seemed now to belong to him.

None of his enemies ventured upon complaint or recrimination. Owing to the enthusiasm of some and the pusillanimity of the rest, an army of five thousand men was ready before the interval prescribed had elapsed.

This army promptly made its way to Utica in order to support the Suffet's rear, while three thousand of the most notable citizens embarked in vessels which were to land them at Hippo-Zarytus, whence they were to drive back the Barbarians.

Hanno had accepted the command; but he intrusted the army to his lieutenant, Magdassin, so as to lead the troops which were to be disembarked himself, for he could no longer endure the shaking of the litter. His disease had eaten away his lips and nostrils, and had hollowed out a large hole in his face; the back of his throat could be seen at a distance of ten paces, and he knew himself to be so hideous that he wore a veil over his head like a woman.

Hippo-Zarytus paid no attention to his summonings nor yet to those of the Barbarians; but every morning the inhabitants lowered provisions to the latter in baskets, and shouting from the tops of the towers pleaded the exigencies of the Republic and conjured them to withdraw. By means of signs they addressed the same protestations to the Carthaginians, who were stationed on the sea.

Hanno contented himself with blockading the harbour without risking an attack. However, he permitted the judges of Hippo-Zarytus to admit three hundred soldiers. Then he departed to the Cape Grapes, and made a long circuit so as to hem in the Barbarians, an inopportune and even dangerous operation. His jealousy prevented him from relieving the Suffet; he arrested his spies, impeded him in all his plans, and compromised the success of the enterprise. At last Hamilcar wrote to the Great Council to rid himself of Hanno, and the latter returned to Carthage furious at the baseness of the Ancients and the madness of his colleague. Hence, after so many hopes, the situation was now still more deplorable; but there was an effort not to reflect upon it and even not to talk about it.

As if all this were not sufficient misfortune at one time, news came that the Sardinian Mercenaries had crucified their general, seized the strongholds, and everywhere slaughtered those of Chanaanitish race. The Roman people threatened the Republic with immediate hostilities unless she gave twelve hundred talents with the whole of the island of Sardinia. They had accepted the alliance of the Barbarians, and they despatched to them flat-bottomed boats laden with meal and dried meat. The Carthaginians pursued these, and captured five hundred men; but three days afterwards a fleet coming from Byzacena, and conveying provisions to Carthage, foundered in a storm. The gods were evidently declaring against her.

Upon this the citizens of Hippo-Zarytus, under pretence of an alarm, made Hanno's three hundred men ascend their walls; then coming behind them they took them by the legs, and suddenly threw them over the ramparts. Some who were not killed were pursued, and went and drowned themselves in the sea.

Utica was enduring the presence of soldiers, for Magdassin had acted like Hanno, and in accordance with his orders and deaf to Hamilcar's prayers, was surrounding the town. As for these, they were given wine mixed with mandrake, and were then slaughtered in their sleep. At the same time the Barbarians arrived; Magdassin fled; the gates were opened, and thenceforward the two Tyrian towns displayed an obstinate devotion to their new friends and an inconceivable hatred to their former allies.

This abandonment of the Punic cause was a counsel and a precedent. Hopes of deliverance revived. Populations hitherto uncertain hesitated no longer. Everywhere there was a stir. The Suffet learnt this, and he had no assistance to look for! He was now irrevocably lost.

He immediately dismissed Narr' Havas, who was to guard the borders of his kingdom. As for himself, he resolved to re-enter Carthage in order to obtain soldiers and begin the war again.

The Barbarians posted at Hippo-Zarytus perceived his army as it descended the mountain.

Where could the Carthaginians be going? Hunger, no doubt, was urging them on; and, distracted by their sufferings, they were coming in spite of their weakness to give battle. But they turned to the right: they were fleeing. They might be overtaken and all be crushed. The Barbarians dashed in pursuit of them.

The Carthaginians were checked by the river. It was wide this time and the west wind had not been blowing. Some crossed by swimming, and the rest on their shields. They resumed their march. Night fell. They were out of sight.

The Barbarians did not stop; they went higher to find a narrower place. The people of Tunis hastened thither, bringing those of Utica along with them. Their numbers increased at every bush; and the Carthaginians, as they lay on the ground, could hear the tramping of their feet in the darkness. From time to time Barca had a volley of arrows discharged behind him to check them, and several were killed. When day broke they were in the Ariana Mountains, at the spot where the road makes a bend.

GUSTAVE FLAUBERT

Then Matho, who was marching at the head, thought that he could distinguish something green on the horizon on the summit of an eminence. Then the ground sank, and obelisks, domes, and houses appeared! It was Carthage. He leaned against a tree to keep himself from falling, so rapidly did his heart beat.

He thought of all that had come to pass in his existence since the last time that he had passed that way! It was an infinite surprise, it stunned him. Then he was transported with joy at the thought of seeing Salammbô again. The reasons which he had for execrating her returned to his recollection, but he very quickly rejected them. Quivering and with straining eyeballs he gazed at the lofty terrace of a palace above the palm trees beyond Eschmoun; a smile of ecstasy lighted his face as if some great light had reached him; he opened his arms, and sent kisses on the breeze, and murmured: "Come! come!" A sigh swelled his breast, and two long tears like pearls fell upon his beard.

"What stays you?" cried Spendius. "Make haste! Forward! The Suffet is going to escape us! But your knees are tottering, and you are looking at me like a drunken man!"

He stamped with impatience and urged Matho, his eyes twinkling as at the approach of an object long aimed at.

"Ah! we have reached it! We are there! I have them!"

He had so convinced and triumphant an air that Matho was surprised from his torpor, and felt himself carried away by it. These words, coming when his distress was at its height, drove his despair to vengeance, and pointed to food for his wrath. He bounded upon one of the camels that were among the baggage, snatched up its halter, and with the long rope, struck the stragglers with all his might, running right and left alternately, in the rear of the army, like a dog driving a flock.

At this thundering voice the lines of men closed up; even the lame hurried their steps; the intervening space lessened in the middle of the isthmus. The foremost of the Barbarians were marching in the dust raised by the Carthaginians. The two armies were coming close, and were on the point of touching. But the Malqua gate, the Tagaste gate, and the great gate of Khamon threw wide their leaves. The Punic square divided; three columns were swallowed up, and eddied beneath the porches. Soon the mass, being too tightly packed, could advance no further; pikes clashed in the air, and the arrows of the Barbarians were shivering against the walls.

Hamilcar was to be seen on the threshold of Khamon. He turned round and shouted to his men to move aside. He dismounted from his horse; and pricking it on the croup with the sword which he held, sent it against the Barbarians.

It was a black stallion, which was fed on balls of meal, and would bend its knees to allow its master to mount. Why was he sending it away? Was this a sacrifice?

The noble horse galloped into the midst of the lances, knocked down men, and, entangling its feet in its entrails, fell down, then rose again with furious leaps; and while they were moving aside, trying to stop it, or looking at it in surprise, the Carthaginians had united again; they entered, and the enormous gate shut echoing behind them.

It would not yield. The Barbarians came crushing against it;—and for some minutes there was an oscillation throughout the army, which became weaker and weaker, and at last ceased.

The Carthaginians had placed soldiers on the aqueduct, they began to hurl stones, balls, and beams. Spendius represented that it would be best not to persist. The Barbarians went and posted themselves further off, all being quite resolved to lay siege to Carthage.

THE RUMOUR OF THE WAR, however, had passed beyond the confines of the Punic empire; and from the pillars of Hercules to beyond Cyrene shepherds mused on it as they kept their flocks, and caravans talked about it in the light of the stars. This great Carthage, mistress of the seas, splendid as the sun, and terrible as a god, actually found men who were daring enough to attack her! Her fall even had been asserted several times; and all had believed it for all wished it: the subject populations, the tributary villages, the allied provinces, the independent hordes, those who execrated her for her tyranny or were jealous of her power, or coveted her wealth. The bravest had very speedily joined the Mercenaries. The defeat at the Macaras had checked all the rest. At last they had recovered confidence, had gradually advanced and approached; and now the men of the eastern regions were lying on the sandhills of Clypea on the other side of the gulf. As soon as they perceived the Barbarians they showed themselves.

They were not Libyans from the neighbourhood of Carthage, who had long composed the third army, but nomads from the tableland of Barca, bandits from Cape Phiscus and the promontory of Dernah, from Phazzana and Marmarica. They had crossed the desert, drinking at the brackish wells walled in with camels' bones; the Zuaeces, with their covering of ostrich feathers, had come on quadrigæ; the Garamantians, masked with black veils, rode behind on their painted mares; others were mounted on asses, onagers, zebras, and buffaloes; while some dragged after them the roofs of their sloop-shaped huts together with their families and idols. There were Ammonians with limbs wrinkled by the hot water of the springs; Atarantians, who curse the sun; Troglodytes, who bury their dead with laughter beneath branches of trees; and the hideous Auseans, who eat grass-hoppers; the Achyrmachidæ, who eat lice; and the vermilion-painted Gysantians, who eat apes.

All were ranged along the edge of the sea in a great straight line. Afterwards they advanced like tornadoes of sand raised by the wind. In the centre of the isthmus the throng stopped, the Mercenaries who were posted in front of them, close to the walls, being unwilling to move.

Then from the direction of Ariana appeared the men of the West, the people of the Numidians. In fact, Narr' Havas governed only the Massylians; and, moreover, as they were permitted by custom to abandon their king when reverses were sustained, they had assembled on the Zainus, and then had crossed it at Hamilcar's first movement. First were seen running up all the hunters from Malethut-Baal and Garaphos, clad in lions' skins, and with the staves of their pikes driving small lean horses with long manes; then marched the Gætulians in cuirasses of serpents' skin; then the Pharusians, wearing lofty crowns made of wax and resin; and the Caunians, Macarians, and Tillabarians, each holding two javelins and a round shield of hippopotamus leather. They stopped at the foot of the Catacombs among the first pools of the Lagoon.

But when the Libyans had moved away, the multitude of the Negroes appeared like a cloud on a level with the ground, in the place which the others had occupied. They were there from the White Harousch, the Black Harousch, the desert of Augila, and even from the great country of Agazymba, which is four months' journey south of the Garamantians, and from regions further still! In spite of their red wooden jewels, the filth of their black skin made them look like mulberries that had been long rolling in the dust. They had bark-thread drawers, dried-grass tunics, fallow-deer muzzles on their heads; they shook rods furnished with rings, and brandished cows' tails at the end of sticks, after the fashion of standards, howling the while like wolves.

Then behind the Numidians, Marusians, and Gætulians pressed the yellowish men, who are spread through the cedar forests beyond Taggir. They had cat-skin quivers flapping against their shoulders, and they led in leashes enormous dogs, which were as high as asses, and did not bark.

Finally, as though Africa had not been sufficiently emptied, and it had been necessary to seek further fury in the very dregs of the races, men might be seen behind the rest, with beast-like profiles and grinning with idiotic laughter—wretches ravaged by hideous diseases, deformed pigmies, mulattoes of doubtful sex, albinos whose red eyes blinked in the sun; stammering out unintelligible sounds, they put a finger into their mouths to show that they were hungry.

The confusion of weapons was as great as that of garments and peoples. There was not a deadly invention that was not present—from wooden daggers, stone hatchets and ivory tridents, to long sabres toothed like saws, slender, and formed of a yielding copper blade. They handled cutlasses which were forked into several branches like antelopes' horns, bills fastened to the ends of ropes, iron triangles, clubs and bodkins. The Ethiopians from the Bambotus had little poisoned darts hidden in their hair. Many had brought pebbles in bags. Others, empty handed, chattered with their teeth.

This multitude was stirred with a ceaseless swell. Dromedaries, smeared all over with tar-like streaks, knocked down the women, who carried their children on their hips. The provisions in the baskets were pouring out; in walking, pieces of salt, parcels of gum, rotten dates, and gourou nuts were crushed underfoot; and sometimes on vermin-covered bosoms there would hang a slender cord supporting a diamond that the Satraps had sought, an almost fabulous stone, sufficient to purchase an empire. Most of them did not even know what they desired. They were impelled by fascination or curiosity; and nomads who had never seen a town were frightened by the shadows of the walls.

The isthmus was now hidden by men; and this long surface, whereon the tents were like huts amid an inundation, stretched as far as the first lines of the other Barbarians, which were streaming with steel and were posted symmetrically upon both sides of the aqueduct.

The Carthaginians had not recovered from the terror caused by their arrival when they perceived the siege-engines sent by the Tyrian towns coming straight towards them like monsters and like buildings—with their masts, arms, ropes, articulations, capitals and carapaces, sixty carroballistas, eighty onagers, thirty scorpions, fifty tollenos, twelve rams, and three gigantic catapults which hurled pieces of rock of the weight of fifteen talents. Masses of men clinging to their bases pushed them on; at every step a quivering shook them, and in this way they arrived in front of the walls.

But several days were still needed to finish the preparations for the siege. The Mercenaries, taught by their defeats, would not risk themselves in useless engagements; and on both sides there was no haste, for it was well known that a terrible action was about to open, and that the result of it would be complete victory or complete extermination.

Carthage might hold out for a long time; her broad walls presented a series of re-entrant and projecting angles, an advantageous arrangement for repelling assaults.

Nevertheless a portion had fallen down in the direction of the Catacombs, and on dark nights lights could be seen in the dens of Malqua through the disjointed blocks. These in some places overlooked the top of the ramparts. It was here that the Mercenaries' wives, who had been driven away by Matho, were living with their new husbands. On seeing the men again their hearts could stand it no longer. They waved their scarfs at a distance; then they came and chatted in the darkness with the soldiers through the cleft in the wall, and one morning the Great Council learned that they had all fled. Some had passed through between the stones; others with greater intrepidity had let themselves down with ropes.

At last Spendius resolved to accomplish his design.

The war, by keeping him at a distance, had hitherto prevented him; and since the return to before Carthage, it seemed to him that the inhabitants suspected his enterprise. But soon they diminished the sentries on the aqueduct. There were not too many people for the defence of the walls.

The former slave practised himself for some days in shooting arrows at the flamingoes on the lake. Then one moonlight evening he begged Matho to light a great fire of straw in the middle of the night, while all his men were to shout at the same time; and taking Zarxas with him, he went away along the edge of the gulf in the direction of Tunis.

When on a level with the last arches they returned straight towards the aqueduct; the place was unprotected: they crawled to the base of the pillars.

The sentries on the platform were walking quietly up and down.

Towering flames appeared; clarions rang; and the soldiers on vedette, believing that there was an assault, rushed away in the direction of Carthage.

One man had remained. He showed black against the background of the sky. The moon was shining behind him, and his shadow, which was of extravagant size, looked in the distance like an obelisk proceeding across the plain.

They waited until he was in position just before them. Zarxas seized his sling, but whether from prudence or from ferocity Spendius stopped him. "No, the whiz of the bullet would make a noise! Let me!"

Then he bent his bow with all his strength, resting the lower end of it against the great toe of his left foot; he took aim, and the arrow went off.

The man did not fall. He disappeared.

"If he were wounded we should hear him!" said Spendius; and he mounted quickly from story to story as he had done the first time, with the assistance of a rope and a harpoon. Then when he had reached the top and was beside the corpse, he let it fall again. The Balearian fastened a pick and a mallet to it and turned back.

The trumpets sounded no longer. All was now quiet. Spendius had raised one of the flag-stones and, entering the water, had closed it behind him.

Calculating the distance by the number of his steps, he arrived at the exact spot where he had noticed an oblique fissure; and for three hours until morning he worked in continuous and furious fashion, breathing with difficulty through the interstices in the upper flag-tones, assailed with anguish, and twenty times believing that he was going to die. At last a crack was heard, and a huge stone ricocheting on the lower arches rolled to the ground,—and suddenly a cataract, an entire river, fell from the skies onto the plain. The aqueduct, being cut through in the centre, was emptying itself. It was death to Carthage and victory for the Barbarians.

In an instant the awakened Carthaginians appeared on the walls, the houses, and the temples. The Barbarians pressed forward with shouts. They danced in delirium around the great waterfall, and came up and wet their heads in it in the extravagance of their joy.

A man in a torn, brown tunic was perceived on the summit of the aqueduct. He stood leaning over the very edge with both hands on his hips, and was looking down below him as though astonished at his work.

Then he drew himself up. He surveyed the horizon with a haughty

　　　　　　　　　　　　　　　GUSTAVE FLAUBERT

air which seemed to say: "All that is now mine!" The applause of the Barbarians burst forth, while the Carthaginians, comprehending their disaster at last, shrieked with despair. Then he began to run about the platform from one end to the other,—and like a chariot-driver triumphant at the Olympic Games, Spendius, distraught with pride, raised his arms aloft.

XIII

Moloch

The Barbarians had no need of a circumvallation on the side of Africa, for it was theirs. But to facilitate the approach to the walls, the entrenchments bordering the ditch were thrown down. Matho next divided the army into great semicircles so as to encompass Carthage the better. The hoplites of the Mercenaries were placed in the first rank, and behind them the slingers and horsemen; quite at the back were the baggage, chariots, and horses; and the engines bristled in front of this throng at a distance of three hundred paces from the towers.

Amid the infinite variety of their nomenclature (which changed several times in the course of the centuries) these machines might be reduced to two systems: some acted like slings, and the rest like bows.

The first, which were the catapults, was composed of a square frame with two vertical uprights and a horizontal bar. In its anterior portion was a cylinder, furnished with cables, which held back a great beam bearing a spoon for the reception of projectiles; its base was caught in a skein of twisted thread, and when the ropes were let go it sprang up and struck against the bar, which, checking it with a shock, multiplied its power.

The second presented a more complicated mechanism. A cross-bar had its centre fixed on a little pillar, and from this point of junction there branched off at right angles a short of channel; two caps containing twists of horse-hair stood at the extremities of the cross-bar; two small beams were fastened to them to hold the extremities of a rope which was brought to the bottom of the channel upon a tablet of bronze. This metal plate was released by a spring, and sliding in grooves impelled the arrows.

The catapults were likewise called onagers, after the wild asses which fling up stones with their feet, and the ballistas scorpions, on account of a hook which stood upon the tablet, and being lowered by a blow of the fist, released the spring.

Their construction required learned calculations; the wood selected had to be of the hardest substance, and their gearing all of brass; they were stretched with levers, tackle-blocks, capstans or tympanums; the direction of the shooting was changed by means of strong pivots; they were moved forward on cylinders, and the most considerable of them, which were brought piece by piece, were set up in front of the enemy.

Spendius arranged three great catapults opposite the three principle angles; he placed a ram before every gate, a ballista before every tower, while carroballistas were to move about in the rear. But it was necessary to protect them against the fire thrown by the besieged, and first of all to fill up the trench which separated them from the walls.

They pushed forward galleries formed of hurdles of green reeds, and oaken semicircles like enormous shields gliding on three wheels; the workers were sheltered in little huts covered with raw hides and stuffed with wrack; the catapults and ballistas were protected by rope curtains which had been steeped in vinegar to render them incombustible. The women and children went to procure stones on the strand, and gathered earth with their hands and brought it to the soldiers.

The Carthaginians also made preparations.

Hamilcar had speedily reassured them by declaring that there was enough water left in the cisterns for one hundred and twenty-three days. This assertion, together with his presence, and above all that of the zaïmph among them, gave them good hopes. Carthage recovered from its dejection; those who were not of Chanaanitish origin were carried away by the passion of the rest.

The slaves were armed, the arsenals were emptied, and every citizen had his own post and his own employment. Twelve hundred of the fugitives had survived, and the Suffet made them all captains; and carpenters, armourers, blacksmiths, and goldsmiths were intrusted with the engines. The Carthaginians had kept a few in spite of the conditions of the peace with Rome. These were repaired. They understood such work.

The two northern and eastern sides, being protected by the sea and the gulf, remained inaccessible. On the wall fronting the Barbarians they collected tree-trunks, mill-stones, vases filled with sulphur, and vats filled with oil, and built furnaces. Stones were heaped up on the platforms of the towers, and the houses bordering immediately on the rampart were crammed with sand in order to strengthen it and increase its thickness.

The Barbarians grew angry at the sight of these preparations. They wished to fight at once. The weights which they put into the catapults were so extravagantly heavy that the beams broke, and the attack was delayed.

At last on the thirteenth day of the month of Schabar,—at sunrise,—a great blow was heard at the gate of Khamon.

Seventy-five soldiers were pulling at ropes arranged at the base of a gigantic beam which was suspended horizontally by chains hanging from a framework, and which terminated in a ram's head of pure brass. It had been swathed in ox-hides; it was bound at intervals with iron bracelets; it was thrice as thick as a man's body, one hundred and twenty cubits long, and under the crowd of naked arms pushing it forward and drawing it back, it moved to and fro with a regular oscillation.

The other rams before the other gates began to be in motion. Men might be seen mounting from step to step in the hollow wheels of the tympanums. The pulleys and caps grated, the rope curtains were lowered, and showers of stones and showers of arrows poured forth simultaneously; all the scattered slingers ran up. Some approached the rampart hiding pots of resin under their shields; then they would hurl these with all their might. This hail of bullets, darts, and flames passed above the first ranks in the form of a curve which fell behind the walls. But long cranes, used for masting vessels, were reared on the summit of the ramparts; and from them there descended some of those enormous pincers which terminated in two semicircles toothed on the inside. They bit the rams. The soldiers clung to the beam and drew it back. The Carthaginians hauled in order to pull it up; and the action was prolonged until the evening.

When the Mercenaries resumed their task on the following day, the tops of the walls were completely carpeted with bales of cotton, sails, and cushions; the battlements were stopped up with mats; and a line of forks and blades, fixed upon sticks, might be distinguished among the cranes on the rampart. A furious resistance immediately began.

Trunks of trees fastened to cables fell and rose alternately and battered the rams; cramps hurled by the ballistas tore away the roofs of the huts; and streams of flints and pebbles poured from the platforms of the towers.

At last the rams broke the gates of Khamon and Tagaste. But the Carthaginians had piled up such an abundance of materials on the inside that the leaves did not open. They remained standing.

Then they drove augers against the walls; these were applied to the joints of the blocks, so as to detach the latter. The engines were better managed, the men serving them were divided into squads, and they were worked from morning till evening without interruption and with the monotonous precision of a weaver's loom.

Spendius returned to them untiringly. It was he who stretched the skeins of the ballistas. In order that the twin tensions might completely correspond, the ropes as they were tightened were struck on the right and left alternately until both sides gave out an equal sound. Spendius would mount upon the timbers. He would strike the ropes softly with the extremity of his foot, and strain his ears like a musician tuning a lyre. Then when the beam of the catapult rose, when the pillar of the ballista trembled with the shock of the spring, when the stones were shooting in rays, and the darts pouring in streams, he would incline his whole body and fling his arms into the air as though to follow them.

The soldiers admired his skill and executed his commands. In the gaiety of their work they gave utterance to jests on the names of the machines. Thus the plyers for seizing the rams were called "wolves," and the galleries were covered with "vines"; they were lambs, or they were going to gather the grapes; and as they loaded their pieces they would say to the onagers: "Come, pick well!" and to the scorpions: "Pierce them to the heart!" These jokes, which were ever the same, kept up their courage.

Nevertheless the machines did not demolish the rampart. It was formed of two walls and was completely filled with earth. The upper portions were beaten down, but each time the besieged raised them again. Matho ordered the construction of wooden towers which should be as high as the towers of stone. They cast turf, stakes, pebbles and chariots with their wheels into the trench so as to fill it up the more quickly; but before this was accomplished the immense throng of the Barbarians undulated over the plain with a single movement and came beating against the foot of the walls like an overflowing sea.

They moved forward the rope ladders, straight ladders, and sambucas, the latter consisting of two poles from which a series of bamboos terminating in a moveable bridge were lowered by means of tackling. They formed numerous straight lines resting against the wall, and the Mercenaries mounted them in files, holding their weapons in their hands. Not a Carthaginian showed himself; already two thirds of the rampart had been covered. Then the battlements opened, vomiting flames and smoke like dragon jaws; the sand scattered and entered the joints of their armour; the petroleum fastened on their garments; the liquid lead hopped on their helmets and made holes in their flesh; a rain of sparks splashed against their faces, and eyeless orbits seemed to weep tears as big as almonds. There were men all yellow with oil, with their hair in flames. They began to run and set fire to the rest. They were extinguished in mantles steeped in blood, which were thrown from a distance over their faces. Some who had no wounds remained motionless, stiffer than stakes, their mouths open and their arms outspread.

The assault was renewed for several days in succession, the Mercenaries hoping to triumph by extraordinary energy and audacity.

Sometimes a man raised on the shoulders of another would drive a pin between the stones, and then making use of it as a step to reach further, would place a second and a third; and, protected by the edge of the battlements, which stood out from the wall, they would gradually raise themselves in this way; but on reaching a certain height they always fell back again. The great trench was full to overflowing; the wounded were massed pell-mell with the dead and dying beneath the footsteps of the living. Calcined trunks formed black spots amid opened entrails, scattered brains, and pools of blood; and arms and legs projecting half way out of a heap, would stand straight up like props in a burning vineyard.

The ladders proving insufficient the tollenos were brought into requisition,—instruments consisting of a long beam set transversely upon another, and bearing at its extremity a quadrangular basket which would hold thirty foot-soldiers with their weapons.

Matho wished to ascend in the first that was ready. Spendius stopped him.

Some men bent over a capstan; the great beam rose, became horizontal, reared itself almost vertically, and being overweighted at the end, bent like a huge reed. The soldiers, who were crowded together, were hidden up to their chins; only their helmet-plumes could be seen. At last when it was twenty cubits high in the air it turned several times to the right and to the left, and then was depressed; and like a giant arm holding a cohort of pigmies in its hand, it laid the basketful of men upon the edge of the wall. They leaped into the crowd and never returned.

All the other tollenos were speedily made ready. But a hundred times as many would have been needed for the capture of the town. They were utilised in a murderous fashion: Ethiopian archers were placed in the baskets; then, the cables having been fastened, they remained suspended and shot poisoned arrows. The fifty tollenos commanding the battlements thus surrounded Carthage like monstrous vultures; and the Negroes laughed to see the guards on the rampart dying in grievous convulsions.

Hamilcar sent hoplites to these posts, and every morning made them drink the juice of certain herbs which protected them against the poison.

One evening when it was dark he embarked the best of his soldiers on lighters and planks, and turning to the right of the harbour, disembarked on the Tænia. Then he advanced to the first lines of the Barbarians, and taking them in flank, made a great slaughter. Men hanging to ropes would descend at night from the top of the wall with torches in their hands, burn the works of the Mercenaries, and then mount up again.

Matho was exasperated; every obstacle strengthened his wrath, which led him into terrible extravagances. He mentally summoned Salammbô to an interview; then he waited. She did not come; this seemed to him like a fresh piece of treachery,—and henceforth he execrated her. If he had seen her corpse he would perhaps have gone away. He doubled the outposts, he planted forks at the foot of the rampart, he drove caltrops into the ground, and he commanded the Libyans to bring him a whole forest that he might set it on fire and burn Carthage like a den of foxes.

Spendius went on obstinately with the siege. He sought to invent terrible machines such as had never before been constructed.

The other Barbarians, encamped at a distance on the isthmus, were amazed at these delays; they murmured, and they were let loose.

Then they rushed with their cutlasses and javelins, and beat against the gates with them. But the nakedness of their bodies facilitating the infliction of wounds, the Carthaginians massacred them freely; and the Mercenaries rejoiced at it, no doubt through jealousy about the plunder. Hence there resulted quarrels and combats between them. Then, the country having been ravaged, provisions were soon scarce. They grew disheartened. Numerous hordes went away, but the crowd was so great that the loss was not apparent.

The best of them tried to dig mines, but the earth, being badly supported, fell in. They began again in other places, but Hamilcar always guessed the direction that they were taking by holding his ear against a bronze shield. He bored counter-mines beneath the path along which the wooden towers were to move, and when they were pushed forward they sank into the holes.

At last all recognised that the town was impregnable, unless a long terrace was raised to the same height as the walls, so as to enable them to fight on the same level. The top of it should be paved so that the machines might be rolled along. Then Carthage would find it quite impossible to resist.

THE TOWN WAS BEGINNING TO suffer from thirst. The water which was worth two kesitahs the bath at the opening of the siege was now sold for a shekel of silver; the stores of meat and corn were also becoming exhausted; there was a dread of famine, and some even began to speak of useless mouths, which terrified every one.

From the square of Khamon to the temple of Melkarth the streets were cumbered with corpses; and, as it was the end of the summer, the combatants were annoyed by great black flies. Old men carried off the wounded, and the devout continued the fictitious funerals for their relatives and friends who had died far away during the war. Waxen statues with clothes and hair were displayed across the gates. They melted in the heat of the tapers burning beside them; the paint flowed down upon their shoulders, and tears streamed over the faces of the living, as they chanted mournful songs beside them. The crowd meanwhile ran to and fro; armed bands passed; captains shouted orders, while the shock of the rams beating against the rampart was constantly heard.

The temperature became so heavy that the bodies swelled and would no longer fit into the coffins. They were burned in the centre of the courts. But the fires, being too much confined, kindled the neighbouring walls, and long flames suddenly burst from the houses like blood spurting from an artery. Thus Moloch was in possession of Carthage; he clasped the ramparts, he rolled through the streets, he devoured the very corpses.

Men wearing cloaks made of collected rags in token of despair, stationed themselves at the corners of the cross-ways. They declaimed against the Ancients and against Hamilcar, predicted complete ruin to the people, and invited them to universal destruction and license. The most dangerous were the henbane-drinkers; in their crisis they believed themselves wild beasts, and leaped upon the passers-by to rend them. Mobs formed around them, and the defence of Carthage was forgotten. The Suffet devised the payment of others to support his policy.

In order to retain the genius of the gods within the town their images had been covered with chains. Black veils were placed upon the Patæc gods, and hair-cloths around the altars; and attempts were made to excite the pride and jealousy of the Baals by singing in their ears: "Thou art about to suffer thyself to be vanquished! Are the others perchance more strong? Show thyself! aid us! that the peoples may not say: 'Where are now their gods?'"

The colleges of the pontiffs were agitated by unceasing anxiety. Those of Rabbetna were especially afraid—the restoration of the zaïmph having been of no avail. They kept themselves shut up in the third enclosure which was as impregnable as a fortress. Only one among them, the high priest Schahabarim, ventured to go out.

He used to visit Salammbô. But he would either remain perfectly silent, gazing at her with fixed eyeballs, or else would be lavish of words, and the reproaches that he uttered were harder than ever.

With inconceivable inconsistency he could not forgive the young girl for carrying out his commands; Schahabarim had guessed all, and this haunting thought revived the jealousies of his impotence. He accused her of being the cause of the war. Matho, according to him, was besieging Carthage to recover the zaïmph; and he poured out imprecations and sarcasms upon this Barbarian who pretended to the possession of holy things. Yet it was not this that the priest wished to say.

But just now Salammbô felt no terror of him. The anguish which she used formerly to suffer had left her. A strange peacefulness possessed her. Her gaze was less wandering, and shone with limpid fire.

Meanwhile the python had become ill again; and as Salammbô, on the contrary, appeared to be recovering, old Taanach rejoiced in the conviction that by its decline it was taking away the languor of her mistress.

One morning she found it coiled up behind the bed of ox-hides, colder than marble, and with its head hidden by a heap of worms. Her cries brought Salammbô to the spot. She turned it over for a while with the tip of her sandal, and the slave was amazed at her insensibility.

Hamilcar's daughter no longer prolonged her fasts with so much fervour. She passed whole days on the top of her terrace, leaning her elbows against the balustrade, and amusing herself by looking out before her. The summits of the walls at the end of the town cut uneven zigzags upon the sky, and the lances of the sentries formed what was like a border of corn-ears throughout their length. Further away she could see the manouvres of the Barbarians between the towers; on days when the siege was interrupted she could even distinguish their occupations.

They mended their weapons, greased their hair, and washed their bloodstained arms in the sea; the tents were closed; the beasts of burden were feeding; and in the distance the scythes of the chariots, which were all ranged in a semicircle, looked like a silver scimitar lying at the base of the mountains. Schahabarim's talk recurred to her memory. She was waiting for Narr' Havas, her betrothed. In spite of her hatred she would have liked to see Matho again. Of all the Carthaginians she was perhaps the only one who would have spoken to him without fear.

Her father often came into her room. He would sit down panting on the cushions, and gaze at her with an almost tender look, as if he found some rest from her fatigues in the sight of her. He sometimes questioned her about her journey to the camp of the Mercenaries. He even asked her whether any one had urged her to it; and with a shake of the head she answered, No,—so proud was Salammbô of having saved the zaïmph.

But the Suffet always came back to Matho under pretence of making military inquiries. He could not understand how the hours which she had spent in the tent had been employed. Salammbô, in fact, said nothing about Gisco; for as words had an effective power in themselves, curses, if reported to any one, might be turned against him; and she was silent about her wish to assassinate, lest she should be blamed for not having yielded to it. She said that the schalischim appeared furious, that he had shouted a great deal, and that he had then fallen asleep. Salammbô told no more, through shame perhaps, or else because she was led by her extreme ingenuousness to attach but little importance to the soldier's kisses. Moreover, it all floated through her head in a melancholy and misty fashion, like the recollection of a depressing dream; and she would not have known in what way or in what words to express it.

One evening when they were thus face to face with each other, Taanach came in looking quite scared. An old man with a child was yonder in the courts, and wished to see the Suffet.

Hamilcar turned pale, and then quickly replied:

"Let him come up!"

Iddibal entered without prostrating himself. He held a young boy, covered with a goat's-hair cloak, by the hand, and at once raised the hood which screened his face.

"Here he is, Master! Take him!"

The Suffet and the slave went into a corner of the room.

The child remained in the centre standing upright, and with a gaze of attention rather than of astonishment he surveyed the ceiling, the furniture, the pearl necklaces trailing on the purple draperies, and the majestic maiden who was bending over towards him.

He was perhaps ten years old, and was not taller than a Roman sword. His curly hair shaded his swelling forehead. His eyeballs looked as if they were seeking for space. The nostrils of his delicate nose were broad and palpitating, and upon his whole person was displayed the indefinable splendour of those who are destined to great enterprises. When he had cast aside his extremely heavy cloak, he remained clad in a lynx skin, which was fastened about his waist, and he rested his little naked feet, which were all white with dust, resolutely upon the pavement. But he no doubt divined that important matters were under discussion, for he stood motionless, with one hand behind his back, his chin lowered, and a finger in his mouth.

At last Hamilcar attracted Salammbô with a sign and said to her in a low voice:

"You will keep him with you, you understand! No one, even though belonging to the house, must know of his existence!"

Then, behind the door, he again asked Iddibal whether he was quite sure that they had not been noticed.

"No!" said the slave, "the streets were empty."

As the war filled all the provinces he had feared for his master's son. Then, not knowing where to hide him, he had come along the coasts in a sloop, and for three days Iddibal had been tacking about in the gulf and watching the ramparts. At last, that evening, as the environs of Khamon seemed to be deserted, he had passed briskly through the channel and landed near the arsenal, the entrance to the harbour being free.

But soon the Barbarians posted an immense raft in front of it in order to prevent the Carthaginians from coming out. They were again rearing the wooden towers, and the terrace was rising at the same time.

Outside communications were cut off and an intolerable famine set in.

The besieged killed all the dogs, all the mules, all the asses, and then the fifteen elephants which the Suffet had brought back. The lions of the temple of Moloch had become ferocious, and the hierodules no longer durst approach them. They were fed at first with the wounded Barbarians; then they were thrown corpses that were still warm; they refused them, and they all died. People wandered in the twilight along the old enclosures, and gathered grass and flowers among the stones to boil them in wine, wine being cheaper than water. Others crept as far as the enemy's outposts, and entered the tents to steal food, and the stupefied Barbarians sometimes allowed them to return. At last a day arrived when the Ancients resolved to slaughter the horses of Eschmoun privately. They were holy animals whose manes were plaited by the pontiffs with gold ribbons, and whose existence denoted the motion of the sun—the idea of fire in its most exalted form. Their flesh was cut into equal portions and buried behind the altar. Then every evening the Ancients, alleging some act of devotion, would go up to the temple and regale themselves in secret, and each would take away a piece beneath his tunic for his children. In the deserted quarters remote from the walls, the inhabitants, whose misery was not so great, had barricaded themselves through fear of the rest.

The stones from the catapults, and the demolitions commanded for purposes of defence, had accumulated heaps of ruins in the middle of the streets. At the quietest times masses of people would suddenly rush along with shouts; and from the top of the Acropolis the conflagrations were like purple rags scattered upon the terraces and twisted by the wind.

The three great catapults did not stop in spite of all these works. Their ravages were extraordinary: thus a man's head rebounded from the pediment of the Syssitia; a woman who was being confined in the street of Kinisdo was crushed by a block of marble, and her child was carried with the bed as far as the crossways of Cinasyn, where the coverlet was found.

The most annoying were the bullets of the slingers. They fell upon the roofs, and in the gardens, and in the middle of the courts, while people were at table before a slender meal with their hearts big with sighs. These cruel projectiles bore engraved letters which stamped themselves upon the flesh;—and insults might be read on corpses such as "pig," "jackal," "vermin," and sometimes jests: "Catch it!" or "I have well deserved it!"

The portion of the rampart which extended from the corner of the harbours to the height of the cisterns was broken down. Then the people of Malqua found themselves caught between the old enclosure of Byrsa behind, and the Barbarians in front. But there was enough to be done in thickening the wall and making it as high as possible without troubling about them; they were abandoned; all perished; and although they were generally hated, Hamilcar came to be greatly abhorred.

On the morrow he opened the pits in which he kept stores of corn, and his stewards gave it to the people. For three days they gorged themselves.

Their thirst, however, only became the more intolerable, and they could constantly see before them the long cascade formed by the clear falling water of the aqueduct. A thin vapour, with a rainbow beside it, went up from its base, beneath the rays of the sun, and a little stream curving through the plain fell into the gulf.

Hamilcar did not give way. He was reckoning upon an event, upon something decisive and extraordinary.

His own slaves tore off the silver plates from the temple of Melkarth; four long boats were drawn out of the harbour, they were brought by means of capstans to the foot of the Mappalian quarter, the wall facing the shore was bored, and they set out for the Gauls to buy Mercenaries there at no matter what price. Nevertheless, Hamilcar was distressed at his inability to communicate with the king of the Numidians, for he knew that he was behind the Barbarians, and ready to fall upon them. But Narr' Havas, being too weak, was not going to make any venture alone; and the Suffet had the rampart raised twelve palms higher, all the material in the arsenals piled up in the Acropolis, and the machines repaired once more.

Sinews taken from bulls' necks, or else stags' hamstrings, were commonly employed for the twists of the catapults. However, neither stags nor bulls were in existence in Carthage. Hamilcar asked the Ancients for the hair of their wives; all sacrificed it, but the quantity was not sufficient. In the buildings of the Syssitia there were twelve hundred marriageable slaves destined for prostitution in Greece and Italy, and their hair, having been rendered elastic by the use of unguents, was wonderfully well adapted for engines of war. But the subsequent loss would be too great. Accordingly it was decided that a choice should be made of the finest heads of hair among the wives of the plebeians. Careless of their country's needs, they shrieked in despair when the servants of the Hundred came with scissors to lay hands upon them.

The Barbarians were animated with increased fury. They could be seen in the distance taking fat from the dead to grease their machines, while others pulled out the nails and stitched them end to end to make cuirasses. They devised a plan of putting into the catapults vessels filled with serpents which had been brought by the Negroes; the clay pots broke on the flag-stones, the serpents ran about, seemed to multiply, and, so numerous were they, to issue naturally from the walls. Then the Barbarians, not satisfied with their invention, improved upon it; they hurled all kinds of filth, human excrements, pieces of carrion, corpses. The plague reappeared. The teeth of the Carthaginians fell out of their mouths, and their gums were discoloured like those of camels after too long a journey.

The machines were set up on the terrace, although the latter did not as yet reach everywhere to the height of the rampart. Before the twenty-three towers on the fortification stood twenty-three others of wood. All the tollenos were mounted again, and in the centre, a little further back, appeared the formidable helepolis of Demetrius Poliorcetes, which Spendius had at last reconstructed. Of pyramidical shape, like the pharos of Alexandria, it was one hundred and thirty cubits high and twenty-three wide, with nine stories, diminishing as they approached the summit, and protected by scales of brass; they were pierced with numerous doors and were filled with soldiers, and on the upper platform there stood a catapult flanked by two ballistas.

Then Hamilcar planted crosses for those who should speak of surrender, and even the women were brigaded. The people lay in the streets and waited full of distress.

Then one morning before sunrise (it was the seventh day of the month of Nyssan) they heard a great shout uttered by all the Barbarians simultaneously; the leaden-tubed trumpets pealed, and the great Paphlagonian horns bellowed like bulls. All rose and ran to the rampart.

A forest of lances, pikes, and swords bristled at its base. It leaped against the wall, the ladders grappled them; and Barbarians' heads appeared in the intervals of the battlements.

Beams supported by long files of men were battering at the gates; and, in order to demolish the wall at places where the terrace was wanting, the Mercenaries came up in serried cohorts, the first line crawling, the second bending their hams, and the others rising in succession to the last who stood upright; while elsewhere, in order to climb up, the tallest advanced in front and the lowest in the rear, and all rested their shields upon their helmets with their left arms, joining them together at the edges so tightly that they might have been taken for an assemblage of large tortoises. The projectiles slid over these oblique masses.

The Carthaginians threw down mill-stones, pestles, vats, casks, beds, everything that could serve as a weight and could knock down. Some watched at the embrasures with fisherman's nets, and when the Barbarian arrived he found himself caught in the meshes, and struggled like a fish. They demolished their own battlements; portions of wall fell down raising a great dust; and as the catapults on the terrace were shooting over against one another, the stones would strike together and shiver into a thousand pieces, making a copious shower upon the combatants.

Soon the two crowds formed but one great chain of human bodies; it overflowed into the intervals in the terrace, and, somewhat looser at the two extremities, swayed perpetually without advancing. They clasped one another, lying flat on the ground like wrestlers. They crushed one another. The women leaned over the battlements and shrieked. They were dragged away by their veils, and the whiteness of their suddenly uncovered sides shone in the arms of the Negroes as the latter buried their daggers in them. Some corpses did not fall, being too much pressed by the crowd, and, supported by the shoulders of their companions, advanced for some minutes quite upright and with staring eyes. Some who had both temples pierced by a javelin swayed their heads about like bears. Mouths, opened to shout, remained gaping; severed hands flew through the air. Mighty blows were dealt, which were long talked of by the survivors.

Meanwhile arrows darted from the towers of wood and stone. The tollenos moved their long yards rapidly; and as the Barbarians had sacked the old cemetery of the aborigines beneath the Catacombs, they hurled the tombstones against the Carthaginians. Sometimes the cables broke under the weight of too heavy baskets, and masses of men, all with uplifted arms, would fall from the sky.

Up to the middle of the day the veterans had attacked the Tænia fiercely in order to penetrate into the harbour and destroy the fleet. Hamilcar had a fire of damp straw lit upon the roofing of Khamon, and as the smoke blinded them they fell back to left, and came to swell the horrible rout which was pressing forward in Malqua. Some syntagmata composed of sturdy men, chosen expressly for the purpose, had broken in three gates. They were checked by lofty barriers made of planks studded with nails, but a fourth yielded easily; they dashed over it at a run and rolled into a pit in which there were hidden snares. At the south-west gate Autaritus and his men broke down the rampart, the fissure in which had been stopped up with bricks. The ground behind rose, and they climbed it nimbly. But on the top they found a second wall composed of stones and long beams lying quite flat and alternating like the squares on a chess-board. It was a Gaulish fashion, and had been adapted by the Suffet to the requirements of the situation; the Gauls imagined themselves before a town in their own country. Their attack was weak, and they were repulsed.

All the roundway, from the street of Khamon as far as the Green Market, now belonged to the Barbarians, and the Samnites were finishing off the dying with blows of stakes; or else with one foot on the wall were gazing down at the smoking ruins beneath them, and the battle which was beginning again in the distance.

The slingers, who were distributed through the rear, were still shooting. But the springs of the Acarnanian slings had broken from use, and many were throwing stones with the hand like shepherds; the rest hurled leaden bullets with the handle of a whip. Zarxas, his shoulders covered with his long black hair, went about everywhere, and led on the Barbarians. Two pouches hung at his hips; he thrust his left hand into them continually, while his right arm whirled round like a chariot-wheel.

Matho had at first refrained from fighting, the better to command the Barbarians all at once. He had been seen along the gulf with the Mercenaries, near the lagoon with the Numidians, and on the shores of the lake among the Negroes, and from the back part of the plain he urged forward masses of soldiers who came ceaselessly against the ramparts. By degrees he had drawn near; the smell of blood, the sight of carnage, and the tumult of clarions had at last made his heart leap. Then he had gone back into his tent, and throwing off his cuirass had taken his lion's skin as being more convenient for battle. The snout fitted upon his head, bordering his face with a circle of fangs; the two fore-paws were crossed upon his breast, and the claws of the hinder ones fell beneath his knees.

He had kept on his strong waist-belt, wherein gleamed a two-edged axe, and with his great sword in both hands he had dashed impetuously through the breach. Like a pruner cutting willow-branches and trying to strike off as much as possible so as to make the more money, he marched along mowing down the Carthaginians around him. Those who tried to seize him in flank he knocked down with blows of the pommel; when they attacked him in front he ran them through; if they fled he clove them. Two men leaped together upon his back; he bounded backwards against a gate and crushed them. His sword fell and rose. It shivered on the angle of a wall. Then he took his heavy axe, and front and rear he ripped up the Carthaginians like a flock of sheep. They scattered more and more, and he was quite alone when he reached the second enclosure at the foot of the Acropolis. The materials which had been flung from the summit cumbered the steps and were heaped up higher than the wall. Matho turned back amid the ruins to summons his companions.

He perceived their crests scattered over the multitude; they were sinking and their wearers were about to perish; he dashed towards them; then the vast wreath of red plumes closed in, and they soon rejoined him and surrounded him. But an enormous crowd was discharging from the side streets. He was caught by the hips, lifted up and carried away outside the ramparts to a spot where the terrace was high.

Matho shouted a command and all the shields sank upon the helmets; he leaped upon them in order to catch hold somewhere so as to re-enter Carthage; and, flourishing his terrible axe, ran over the shields, which resembled waves of bronze, like a marine god, with brandished trident, over his billows.

However, a man in a white robe was walking along the edge of the rampart, impassible, and indifferent to the death which surrounded him. Sometimes he would spread out his right hand above his eyes in order to find out some one. Matho happened to pass beneath him. Suddenly his eyeballs flamed, his livid face contracted; and raising both his lean arms he shouted out abuse at him.

Matho did not hear it; but he felt so furious and cruel a look entering his heart that he uttered a roar. He hurled his long axe at him; some people threw themselves upon Schahabarim; and Matho seeing him no more fell back exhausted.

A terrible creaking drew near, mingled with the rhythm of hoarse voices singing together.

It was the great helepolis surrounded by a crowd of soldiers. They were dragging it with both hands, hauling it with ropes, and pushing it with their shoulders,—for the slope rising from the plain to the terrace, although extremely gentle, was found impracticable for machines of such prodigious weight. However, it had eight wheels banded with iron, and it had been advancing slowly in this way since the morning, like a mountain raised upon another. Then there appeared an immense ram issuing from its base. The doors along the three fronts which faced the town fell down, and cuirassed soldiers appeared in the interior like pillars of iron. Some might be seen climbing and descending the two staircases which crossed the stories. Some were waiting to dart out as soon as the cramps of the doors touched the walls; in the middle of the upper platform the skeins of the ballistas were turning, and the great beam of the catapult was being lowered.

Hamilcar was at that moment standing upright on the roof of Melkarth. He had calculated that it would come directly towards him, against what was the most invulnerable place in the wall, which was for that very reason denuded of sentries. His slaves had for a long time been bringing leathern bottles along the roundway, where they had raised with clay two transverse partitions forming a sort of basin. The water was flowing insensibly along the terrace, and strange to say, it seemed to cause Hamilcar no anxiety.

But when the helepolis was thirty paces off, he commanded planks to be placed over the streets between the houses from the cisterns to the rampart; and a file of people passed from hand to hand helmets and amphoras, which were emptied continually. The Carthaginians, however, grew indignant at this waste of water. The ram was demolishing the wall, when suddenly a fountain sprang forth from the disjointed stones. Then the lofty brazen mass, nine stories high, which contained and engaged more than three thousand soldiers, began to rock gently like a ship. In fact, the water, which had penetrated the terrace, had broken up the path before it; its wheels stuck in the mire; the head of Spendius, with distended cheeks blowing an ivory cornet, appeared between leathern curtains on the first story. The great machine, as though convulsively upheaved, advanced perhaps ten paces; but the ground softened more and more, the mire reached to the axles, and the helepolis stopped, leaning over frightfully to one side. The catapult rolled to the edge of the platform, and carried away by the weight of its beam, fell, shattering the lower stories beneath it. The soldiers who were standing on the doors slipped into the abyss, or else held on to the extremities of the long beams, and by their weight increased the inclination of the helepolis, which was going to pieces with creakings in all its joints.

The other Barbarians rushed up to help them, massing themselves into a compact crowd. The Carthaginians descended from the rampart, and, assailing them in the rear, killed them at leisure. But the chariots furnished with sickles hastened up, and galloped round the outskirts of the multitude. The latter ascended the wall again; night came on; and the Barbarians gradually retired.

Nothing could now be seen on the plain but a sort of perfectly black, swarming mass, which extended from the bluish gulf to the purely white lagoon; and the lake, which had received streams of blood, stretched further away like a great purple pool.

The terrace was now so laden with corpses that it looked as though it had been constructed of human bodies. In the centre stood the helepolis covered with armour; and from time to time huge fragments broke off from it, like stones from a crumbling pyramid. Broad tracks made by the streams of lead might be distinguished on the walls. A broken-down wooden tower burned here and there, and the houses showed dimly like the stages of a ruined ampitheatre. Heavy fumes of smoke were rising, and rolling with them sparks which were lost in the dark sky.

THE CARTHAGINIANS, HOWEVER, WHO WERE consumed by thirst, had rushed to the cisterns. They broke open the doors. A miry swamp stretched at the bottom.

What was to be done now? Moreover, the Barbarians were countless, and when their fatigue was over they would begin again.

The people deliberated all night in groups at the corners of the streets. Some said that they ought to send away the women, the sick, and the old men; others proposed to abandon the town, and found a colony far away. But vessels were lacking, and when the sun appeared no decision had been made.

There was no fighting that day, all being too much exhausted. The sleepers looked like corpses.

Then the Carthaginians, reflecting upon the cause of their disasters, remembered that they had not dispatched to Phonicia the annual offering due to Tyrian Melkarth, and a great terror came upon them. The gods were indignant with the Republic, and were, no doubt, about to prosecute their vengeance.

They were considered as cruel masters, who were appeased with supplications and allowed themselves to be bribed with presents. All were feeble in comparison with Moloch the Devourer. The existence, the very flesh of men, belonged to him; and hence in order to preserve it, the Carthaginians used to offer up a portion of it to him, which calmed his fury. Children were burned on the forehead, or on the nape of the neck, with woollen wicks; and as this mode of satisfying Baal brought in much money to the priests, they failed not to recommend it as being easier and more pleasant.

This time, however, the Republic itself was at stake. But as every profit must be purchased by some loss, and as every transaction was regulated according to the needs of the weaker and the demands of the stronger, there was no pain great enough for the god, since he delighted in such as was of the most horrible description, and all were now at his mercy. He must accordingly be fully gratified. Precedents showed that in this way the scourge would be made to disappear. Moreover, it was believed that an immolation by fire would purify Carthage. The ferocity of the people was predisposed towards it. The choice, too, must fall exclusively upon the families of the great.

The Ancients assembled. The sitting was a long one. Hanno had come to it. As he was now unable to sit he remained lying down near the door, half hidden among the fringes of the lofty tapestry; and when the pontiff of Moloch asked them whether they would consent to surrender their children, his voice suddenly broke forth from the shadow like the roaring of a genius in the depths of a cavern. He regretted, he said, that he had none of his own blood to give; and he gazed at Hamilcar, who faced him at the other end of the hall. The Suffet was so much disconcerted by this look that it made him lower his eyes. All successively bent their heads in approval; and in accordance with the rites he had to reply to the high priest: "Yes; be it so." Then the Ancients decreed the sacrifice in traditional circumlocution,—because there are things more troublesome to say than to perform.

The decision was almost immediately known in Carthage, and lamentations resounded. The cries of women might everywhere be heard; their husbands consoled them, or railed at them with remonstrances.

But three hours afterwards extraordinary tidings were spread abroad: the Suffet had discovered springs at the foot of the cliff. There was a rush to the place. Water might be seen in holes dug in the sand, and some were already lying flat on the ground and drinking.

Hamilcar did not himself know whether it was by the determination of the gods or through the vague recollection of a revelation which his father had once made to him; but on leaving the Ancients he had gone down to the shore and had begun to dig the gravel with his slaves.

He gave clothing, boots, and wine. He gave all the rest of the corn that he was keeping by him. He even let the crowd enter his palace, and he opened kitchens, stores, and all the rooms,—Salammbô's alone excepted. He announced that six thousand Gaulish Mercenaries were coming, and that the king of Macedonia was sending soldiers.

But on the second day the springs diminished, and on the evening of the third they were completely dried up. Then the decree of the Ancients passed everywhere from lip to lip, and the priests of Moloch began their task.

Men in black robes presented themselves in the houses. In many instances the owners had deserted them under pretence of some business, or of some dainty that they were going to buy; and the servants of Moloch came and took the children away. Others themselves surrendered them stupidly. Then they were brought to the temple of Tanith, where the priestesses were charged with their amusement and support until the solemn day.

They visited Hamilcar suddenly and found him in his gardens.

"Barca! we come for that that you know of—your son!" They added that some people had met him one evening during the previous moon in the centre of the Mappalian district being led by an old man.

He was as though suffocated at first. But speedily understanding that any denial would be in vain, Hamilcar bowed; and he brought them into the commercial house. Some slaves who had run up at a sign kept watch all round about it.

He entered Salammbô's room in a state of distraction. He seized Hannibal with one hand, snatched up the cord of a trailing garment with the other, tied his feet and hands with it, thrust the end into his mouth to form a gag, and hid him under the bed of the ox-hides by letting an ample drapery fall to the ground.

Afterwards he walked about from right to left, raised his arms, wheeled round, bit his lips. Then he stood still with staring eyelids, and panted as though he were about to die.

But he clapped his hands three times. Giddenem appeared.

"Listen!" he said, "go and take from among the slaves a male child from eight to nine years of age, with black hair and swelling forehead! Bring him here! make haste!"

Giddenem soon entered again, bringing forward a young boy.

He was a miserable child, at once lean and bloated; his skin looked greyish, like the infected rag hanging to his sides; his head was sunk between his shoulders, and with the back of his hand he was rubbing his eyes, which were filled with flies.

How could he ever be confounded with Hannibal! and there was no time to choose another. Hamilcar looked at Giddenem; he felt inclined to strangle him.

"Begone!" he cried; and the master of the slaves fled.

The misfortune which he had so long dreaded was therefore come, and with extravagant efforts he strove to discover whether there was not some mode, some means to escape it.

Abdalonim suddenly spoke from behind the door. The Suffet was being asked for. The servants of Moloch were growing impatient.

Hamilcar repressed a cry as though a red hot iron had burnt him; and he began anew to pace the room like one distraught. Then he sank down beside the balustrade, and, with his elbows on his knees, pressed his forehead into his shut fists.

The porphyry basin still contained a little clear water for Salammbô's ablutions. In spite of his repugnance and all his pride, the Suffet dipped the child into it, and, like a slave merchant, began to wash him and rub him with strigils and red earth. Then he took two purple squares from the receptacles round the wall, placed one on his breast and the other on his back, and joined them together on the collar bones with two diamond clasps. He poured perfume upon his head, passed an electrum necklace around his neck, and put on him sandals with heels of pearl,— sandals belonging to his own daughter! But he stamped with shame and vexation; Salammbô, who busied herself in helping him, was as pale as he. The child, dazzled by such splendour, smiled and, growing bold even, was beginning to clap his hands and jump, when Hamilcar took him away.

He held him firmly by the arm as though he were afraid of losing him, and the child, who was hurt, wept a little as he ran beside him.

When on a level with the ergastulum, under a palm tree, a voice was raised, a mournful and supplicant voice. It murmured: "Master! oh! master!"

Hamilcar turned and beside him perceived a man of abject appearance, one of the wretches who led a haphazard existence in the household.

"What do you want?" said the Suffet.

The slave, who trembled horribly, stammered:

"I am his father!"

Hamilcar walked on; the other followed him with stooping loins, bent hams, and head thrust forward. His face was convulsed with unspeakable anguish, and he was choking with suppressed sobs, so eager was he at once to question him, and to cry: "Mercy!"

At last he ventured to touch him lightly with one finger on the elbow.

"Are you going to—?" He had not the strength to finish, and Hamilcar stopped quite amazed at such grief.

He had never thought—so immense was the abyss separating them from each other—that there could be anything in common between them. It even appeared to him a sort of outrage, an encroachment upon his own privileges. He replied with a look colder and heavier than an executioner's axe; the slave swooned and fell in the dust at his feet. Hamilcar strode across him.

The three black-robed men were waiting in the great hall, and standing against the stone disc. Immediately he tore his garments, and rolled upon the pavement uttering piercing cries.

"Ah! poor little Hannibal! Oh! my son! my consolation! my hope! my life! Kill me also! take me away! Woe! Woe!" He ploughed his face with his nails, tore out his hair, and shrieked like the women who lament at funerals. "Take him away then! my suffering is too great! begone! kill me like him!" The servants of Moloch were astonished that the great Hamilcar was so weak-spirited. They were almost moved by it.

A noise of naked feet became audible, with a broken throat-rattling like the breathing of a wild beast speeding along, and a man, pale, terrible, and with outspread arms appeared on the threshold of the third gallery, between the ivory pots; he exclaimed:

"My child!"

Hamilcar threw himself with a bound upon the slave, and covering the man's mouth with his hand exclaimed still more loudly:

"It is the old man who reared him! he calls him 'my child!' it will make him mad! enough! enough!" And hustling away the three priests and their victim he went out with them and with a great kick shut the door behind him.

Hamilcar strained his ears for some minutes in constant fear of seeing them return. He then thought of getting rid of the slave in order to be quite sure that he would see nothing; but the peril had not wholly disappeared, and, if the gods were provoked at the man's death, it might be turned against his son. Then, changing his intention, he sent him by Taanach the best from his kitchens—a quarter of a goat, beans, and preserved pomegranates. The slave, who had eaten nothing for a long time, rushed upon them; his tears fell into the dishes.

Hamilcar at last returned to Salammbô, and unfastened Hannibal's cords. The child in exasperation bit his hand until the blood came. He repelled him with a caress.

To make him remain quiet Salammbô tried to frighten him with Lamia, a Cyrenian ogress.

"But where is she?" he asked.

He was told that brigands were coming to put him into prison. "Let them come," he rejoined, "and I will kill them!"

Then Hamilcar told him the frightful truth. But he fell into a passion with his father, contending that he was quite able to annihilate the whole people, since he was the master of Carthage.

At last, exhausted by his exertions and anger, he fell into a wild sleep. He spoke in his dreams, his back leaning against a scarlet cushion; his head was thrown back somewhat, and his little arm, outstretched from his body, lay quite straight in an attitude of command.

When the night had grown dark Hamilcar lifted him up gently, and, without a torch, went down the galley staircase. As he passed through the mercantile house he took up a basket of grapes and a flagon of pure water; the child awoke before the statue of Aletes in the vault of gems, and he smiled—like the other—on his father's arm at the brilliant lights which surrounded him.

Hamilcar felt quite sure that his son could not be taken from him. It was an impenetrable spot communicating with the beach by a subterranean passage which he alone knew, and casting his eyes around he inhaled a great draught of air. Then he set him down upon a stool beside some golden shields. No one at present could see him; he had no further need for watching; and he relieved his feelings. Like a mother finding her first-born that was lost, he threw himself upon his son; he clasped him to his breast, he laughed and wept at the same time, he called him by the fondest names and covered him with kisses; little Hannibal was frightened by this terrible tenderness and was silent now.

Hamilcar returned with silent steps, feeling the walls around him, and came into the great hall where the moonlight entered through one of the apertures in the dome; in the centre the slave lay sleeping after his repast, stretched at full length upon the marble pavement. He looked at him and was moved with a sort of pity. With the tip of his cothurn he pushed forward a carpet beneath his head. Then he raised his eyes and gazed at Tanith, whose slender crescent was shining in the sky, and felt himself stronger than the Baals and full of contempt for them.

The arrangements for the sacrifice were already begun.

PART OF A WALL IN the temple of Moloch was thrown down in order to draw out the brazen god without touching the ashes of the altar. Then as soon as the sun appeared the hierodules pushed it towards the square of Khamon.

It moved backwards sliding upon cylinders; its shoulders overlapped the walls. No sooner did the Carthaginians perceive it in the distance than they speedily took to flight, for the Baal could be looked upon with impunity only when exercising his wrath.

A smell of aromatics spread through the streets. All the temples had just been opened simultaneously, and from them there came forth tabernacles borne upon chariots, or upon litters carried by the pontiffs. Great plumes swayed at the corners of them, and rays were emitted from their slender pinnacles which terminated in balls of crystal, gold, silver or copper.

These were the Chanaanitish Baalim, offshoots of the supreme Baal, who were returning to their first cause to humble themselves before his might and annihilate themselves in his splendour.

Melkarth's pavilion, which was of fine purple, sheltered a petroleum flare; on Khamon's, which was of hyacinth colour, there rose an ivory phallus bordered with a circle of gems; between Eschmoun's curtains, which were as blue as the ether, a sleeping python formed a circle with his tail, and the Patæc gods, held in the arms of their priests, looked like great infants in swaddling clothes with their heels touching the ground.

Then came all the inferior forms of the Divinity: Baal-Samin, god of celestial space; Baal-Peor, god of the sacred mountains; Baal-Zeboub, god of corruption, with those of the neighbouring countries and congenerous races: the Iarbal of Libya, the Adramelech of Chaldæa, the Kijun of the Syrians; Derceto, with her virgin's face, crept on her fins, and the corpse of Tammouz was drawn along in the midst of a catafalque among torches and heads of hair. In order to subdue the kings of the firmament to the Sun, and prevent their particular influences from disturbing his, diversely coloured metal stars were brandished at the end of long poles; and all were there, from the dark Neblo, the genius of Mercury, to the hideous Rahab, which is the constellation of the Crocodile. The Abbadirs, stones which had fallen from the moon, were whirling in slings of silver thread; little loaves, representing the female form, were born on baskets by the priests of Ceres; others brought their fetishes and amulets; forgotten idols reappeared, while the mystic symbols had been taken from the very ships as though Carthage wished to concentrate herself wholly upon a single thought of death and desolation.

Before each tabernacle a man balanced a large vase of smoking incense on his head. Clouds hovered here and there, and the hangings, pendants, and embroideries of the sacred pavilions might be distinguished amid the thick vapours. These advanced slowly owing to their enormous weight. Sometimes the axles became fast in the streets; then the pious took advantage of the opportunity to touch the Baalim with their garments, which they preserved afterwards as holy things.

The brazen statue continued to advance towards the square of Khamon. The rich, carrying sceptres with emerald balls, set out from the bottom of Megara; the Ancients, with diadems on their heads, had assembled in Kinisdo, and masters of the finances, governors of provinces, sailors, and the numerous horde employed at funerals, all with the insignia of their magistracies or the instruments of their calling, were making their way towards the tabernacles which were descending from the Acropolis between the colleges of the pontiffs.

Out of deference to Moloch they had adorned themselves with the most splendid jewels. Diamonds sparkled on their black garments; but their rings were too large and fell from their wasted hands,—nor could there have been anything so mournful as this silent crowd where earrings tapped against pale faces, and gold tiaras clasped brows contracted with stern despair.

At last the Baal arrived exactly in the centre of the square. His pontiffs arranged an enclosure with trellis-work to keep off the multitude, and remained around him at his feet.

The priests of Khamon, in tawny woollen robes, formed a line before their temple beneath the columns of the portico; those of Eschmoun, in linen mantles with necklaces of koukouphas' heads and pointed tiaras, posted themselves on the steps of the Acropolis; the priests of Melkarth, in violet tunics, took the western side; the priests of the Abbadirs, clasped with bands of Phrygian stuffs, placed themselves on the east, while towards the south, with the necromancers all covered with tattooings, and the shriekers in patched cloaks, were ranged the curates of the Patæc gods, and the Yidonim, who put the bone of a dead man into their mouths to learn the future. The priests of Ceres, who were dressed in blue robes, had prudently stopped in the street of Satheb, and in low tones were chanting a thesmophorion in the Megarian dialect.

From time to time files of men arrived, completely naked, their arms outstretched, and all holding one another by the shoulders. From the depths of their breasts they drew forth a hoarse and cavernous intonation; their eyes, which were fastened upon the colossus, shone through the dust, and they swayed their bodies simultaneously, and at equal distances, as though they were all affected by a single movement. They were so frenzied that to restore order the hierodules compelled them, with blows of the stick, to lie flat upon the ground, with their faces resting against the brass trellis-work.

Then it was that a man in a white robe advanced from the back of the square. He penetrated the crowd slowly, and people recognised a priest of Tanith—the high-priest Schahabarim. Hootings were raised, for the tyranny of the male principle prevailed that day in all consciences, and the goddess was actually so completely forgotten that the absence of her pontiffs had not been noticed. But the amazement was increased when he was seen to open one of the doors of the trellis-work intended for those who intended to offer up victims. It was an outrage to their god, thought the priests of Moloch, that he had just committed, and they sought with eager gestures to repel him. Fed on the meat of the holocausts, clad in purple like kings, and wearing triple-storied crowns, they despised the pale eunuch, weakened with his macerations, and angry laughter shook their black beards, which were displayed on their breasts in the sun.

Schahabarim walked on, giving no reply, and, traversing the whole enclosure with deliberation, reached the legs of the colossus; then, spreading out both arms, he touched it on both sides, which was a solemn form of adoration. For a long time Rabbet had been torturing him, and in despair, or perhaps for lack of a god that completely satisfied his ideas, he had at last decided for this one.

The crowd, terrified by this act of apostasy, uttered a lengthened murmur. It was felt that the last tie which bound their souls to a merciful divinity was breaking.

But owing to his mutilation, Schahabarim could take no part in the cult of the Baal. The men in the red cloaks shut him out from the enclosure; then, when he was outside, he went round all the colleges in succession, and the priest, henceforth without a god, disappeared into the crowd. It scattered at his approach.

Meanwhile a fire of aloes, cedar, and laurel was burning between the legs of the colossus. The tips of its long wings dipped into the flame; the unguents with which it had been rubbed flowed like sweat over its brazen limbs. Around the circular flagstone on which its feet rested, the children, wrapped in black veils, formed a motionless circle; and its extravagantly long arms reached down their palms to them as though to seize the crown that they formed and carry it to the sky.

The rich, the Ancients, the women, the whole multitude, thronged behind the priests and on the terraces of the houses. The large painted stars revolved no longer; the tabernacles were set upon the ground; and the fumes from the censers ascended perpendicularly, spreading their bluish branches through the azure like gigantic trees.

Many fainted; others became inert and petrified in their ecstasy. Infinite anguish weighed upon the breasts of the beholders. The last shouts died out one by one,—and the people of Carthage stood breathless, and absorbed in the longing of their terror.

At last the high priest of Moloch passed his left hand beneath the children's veils, plucked a lock of hair from their foreheads, and threw it upon the flames. Then the men in the red cloaks chanted the sacred hymn:

"Homage to thee, Sun! king of the two zones, self-generating Creator, Father and Mother, Father and Son, God and Goddess, Goddess and God!" And their voices were lost in the outburst of instruments sounding simultaneously to drown the cries of the victims. The eight-stringed scheminiths, the kinnors which had ten strings, and the nebals which had twelve, grated, whistled, and thundered. Enormous leathern bags, bristling with pipes, made a shrill clashing noise; the tabourines, beaten with all the players' might, resounded with heavy, rapid blows; and, in spite of the fury of the clarions, the salsalim snapped like grasshoppers' wings.

The hierodules, with a long hook, opened the seven-storied compartments on the body of the Baal. They put meal into the highest, two turtle-doves into the second, an ape into the third, a ram into the fourth, a sheep into the fifth, and as no ox was to be had for the sixth, a tawny hide taken from the sanctuary was thrown into it. The seventh compartment yawned empty still.

Before undertaking anything it was well to make trial of the arms of the god. Slender chainlets stretched from his fingers up to his shoulders and fell behind, where men by pulling them made the two hands rise to a level with the elbows, and come close together against the belly; they were moved several times in succession with little abrupt jerks. Then the instruments were still. The fire roared.

The pontiffs of Moloch walked about on the great flagstone scanning the multitude.

An individual sacrifice was necessary, a perfectly voluntary oblation, which was considered as carrying the others along with it. But no one had appeared up to the present, and the seven passages leading from the barriers to the colossus were completely empty. Then the priests, to encourage the people, drew bodkins from their girdles and gashed their faces. The Devotees, who were stretched on the ground outside, were brought within the enclosure. A bundle of horrible irons was thrown to them, and each chose his own torture. They drove in spits between their breasts; they split their cheeks; they put crowns of thorns upon their heads; then they twined their arms together, and surrounded the children in another large circle which widened and contracted in turns. They reached to the balustrade, they threw themselves back again, and then began once more, attracting the crowd to them by the dizziness of their motion with its accompanying blood and shrieks.

By degrees people came into the end of the passages; they flung into the flames pearls, gold vases, cups, torches, all their wealth; the offerings became constantly more numerous and more splendid. At last a man who tottered, a man pale and hideous with terror, thrust forward a child; then a little black mass was seen between the hands of the colossus, and sank into the dark opening. The priests bent over the edge of the great flagstone,—and a new song burst forth celebrating the joys of death and of new birth into eternity.

The children ascended slowly, and as the smoke formed lofty eddies as it escaped, they seemed at a distance to disappear in a cloud. Not one stirred. Their wrists and ankles were tied, and the dark drapery prevented them from seeing anything and from being recognised.

Hamilcar, in a red cloak, like the priests of Moloch, was beside the Baal, standing upright in front of the great toe of its right foot. When the fourteenth child was brought every one could see him make a great gesture of horror. But he soon resumed his former attitude, folded his arms, and looked upon the ground. The high pontiff stood on the other side of the statue as motionless as he. His head, laden with an

Assyrian mitre, was bent, and he was watching the gold plate on his breast; it was covered with fatidical stones, and the flame mirrored in it formed irisated lights. He grew pale and dismayed. Hamilcar bent his brow; and they were both so near the funeral-pile that the hems of their cloaks brushed it as they rose from time to time.

The brazen arms were working more quickly. They paused no longer. Every time that a child was placed in them the priests of Moloch spread out their hands upon him to burden him with the crimes of the people, vociferating: "They are not men but oxen!" and the multitude round about repeated: "Oxen! oxen!" The devout exclaimed: "Lord! eat!" and the priests of Proserpine, complying through terror with the needs of Carthage, muttered the Eleusinian formula: "Pour out rain! bring forth!"

The victims, when scarcely at the edge of the opening, disappeared like a drop of water on a red-hot plate, and white smoke rose amid the great scarlet colour.

Nevertheless, the appetite of the god was not appeased. He ever wished for more. In order to furnish him with a larger supply, the victims were piled up on his hands with a big chain above them which kept them in their place. Some devout persons had at the beginning wished to count them, to see whether their number corresponded with the days of the solar year; but others were brought, and it was impossible to distinguish them in the giddy motion of the horrible arms. This lasted for a long, indefinite time until the evening. Then the partitions inside assumed a darker glow, and burning flesh could be seen. Some even believed that they could descry hair, limbs, and whole bodies.

Night fell; clouds accumulated above the Baal. The funeral-pile, which was flameless now, formed a pyramid of coals up to his knees; completely red like a giant covered with blood, he looked, with his head thrown back, as though he were staggering beneath the weight of his intoxication.

In proportion as the priests made haste, the frenzy of the people increased; as the number of the victims was diminishing, some cried out to spare them, others that still more were needful. The walls, with their burden of people, seemed to be giving way beneath the howlings of terror and mystic voluptuousness. Then the faithful came into the passages, dragging their children, who clung to them; and they beat them in order to make them let go, and handed them over to the men in red. The instrument-players sometimes stopped through exhaustion; then the cries of the mothers might be heard, and the frizzling of the fat as it fell upon the coals. The henbane-drinkers crawled on all fours around the colossus, roaring like tigers; the Yidonim vaticinated, the Devotees sang with their cloven lips; the trellis-work had been broken through, all wished for a share in the sacrifice;—and fathers, whose children had died previously, cast their effigies, their playthings, their preserved bones into the fire. Some who had knives rushed upon the rest. They slaughtered one another. The hierodules took the fallen ashes at the edge of the flagstone in bronze fans, and cast them into the air that the sacrifice might be scattered over the town and even to the region of the stars.

The loud noise and great light had attracted the Barbarians to the foot of the walls; they clung to the wreck of the helepolis to have a better view, and gazed open-mouthed in horror.

XIV

THE PASS OF THE HATCHET

The Carthaginians had not re-entered their houses when the clouds accumulated more thickly; those who raised their heads towards the colossus could feel big drops on their foreheads, and the rain fell.

It fell the whole night plentifully, in floods; the thunder growled; it was the voice of Moloch; he had vanquished Tanith; and she, being now fecundated, opened up her vast bosom in heaven's heights. Sometimes she could be seen in a clear and luminous spot stretched upon cushions of cloud; and then the darkness would close in again as though she were still too weary and wished to sleep again; the Carthaginians, all believing that water is brought forth by the moon, shouted to make her travail easy.

The rain beat upon the terraces and overflowed them, forming lakes in the courts, cascades on the staircases, and eddies at the corners of the streets. It poured in warm heavy masses and urgent streams; big frothy jets leaped from the corners of all the buildings; and it seemed as though whitish cloths hung dimly upon the walls, and the washed temple-roofs shone black in the gleam of the lightning. Torrents descended from the Acropolis by a thousand paths; houses suddenly gave way, and small beams, plaster, rubbish, and furniture passed along in streams which ran impetuously over the pavement.

Amphoras, flagons, and canvases had been placed out of doors; but the torches were extinguished; brands were taken from the funeral-pile of the Baal, and the Carthaginians bent back their necks and opened their mouths to drink. Others by the side of the miry pools, plunged their arms into them up to the armpits, and filled themselves so abundantly with water that they vomited it forth like buffaloes. The freshness gradually spread; they breathed in the damp air with play of limb, and in the happiness of their intoxication boundless hope soon arose. All their miseries were forgotten. Their country was born anew.

They felt the need, as it were, of directing upon others the extravagant fury which they had been unable to employ against themselves. Such a sacrifice could not be in vain; although they felt no remorse they found themselves carried away by the frenzy which results from complicity in irreparable crimes.

The Barbarians had encountered the storm in their ill-closed tents; and they were still quite chilled on the morrow as they tramped through the mud in search of their stores and weapons, which were spoiled and lost.

Hamilcar went himself to see Hanno, and, in virtue of his plenary powers, intrusted the command to him. The old Suffet hesitated for a few minutes between his animosity and his appetite for authority, but he accepted nevertheless.

Hamilcar next took out a galley armed with a catapult at each end. He placed it in the gulf in front of the raft; then he embarked his stoutest troops on board such vessels as were available. He was apparently taking to flight; and running northward before the wind he disappeared into the mist.

But three days afterwards, when the attack was about to begin again, some people arrived tumultuously from the Libyan coast. Barca had come among them. He had carried off provisions everywhere, and he was spreading through the country.

Then the Barbarians were indignant as though he were betraying them. Those who were most weary of the siege, and especially the Gauls, did not hesitate to leave the walls in order to try and rejoin him. Spendius wanted to reconstruct the helepolis; Matho had traced an imaginary line from his tent to Megara, and inwardly swore to follow it, and none of their men stirred. But the rest, under the command of Autaritus, went off, abandoning the western part of the rampart, and so profound was the carelessness exhibited that no one even thought of replacing them.

Narr' Havas spied them from afar in the mountains. During the night he led all his men along the sea-shore on the outer side of the Lagoon, and entered Carthage.

He presented himself as a saviour with six thousand men all carrying meal under their cloaks, and forty elephants laden with forage and dried meat. The people flocked quickly around them; they gave them names. The sight of these strong animals, sacred to Baal, gave the Carthaginians even more joy than the arrival of such relief; it was a token of the tenderness of the god, a proof that he was at last about to interfere in the war to defend them.

Narr' Havas received the compliments of the Ancients. Then he ascended to Salammbô's palace.

He had not seen her again since the time when in Hamilcar's tent amid the five armies he had felt her little, cold, soft hand fastened to his own; she had left for Carthage after the betrothal. His love, which had been diverted by other ambitions, had come back to him; and now he expected to enjoy his rights, to marry her, and take her.

Salammbô did not understand how the young man could ever become her master! Although she asked Tanith every day for Matho's death, her horror of the Libyan was growing less. She vaguely felt that the hate with which he had persecuted her was something almost religious,—and she would fain have seen in Narr' Havas's person a reflection, as it were, of that malice which still dazzled her. She desired to know him better, and yet his presence would have embarrassed her. She sent him word that she could not receive him.

Moreover, Hamilcar had forbidden his people to admit the King of the Numidians to see her; by putting off his reward to the end of the war he hoped to retain his devotion;—and, through dread of the Suffet, Narr' Havas withdrew.

But he bore himself haughtily towards the Hundred. He changed their arrangements. He demanded privileges for his men, and placed them on important posts; thus the Barbarians stared when they perceived Numidians on the towers.

The surprise of the Carthaginians was greater still when three hundred of their own people, who had been made prisoners during the Sicilian war, arrived on board an old Punic trireme. Hamilcar, in fact, had secretly sent back to the Quirites the crews of the Latin vessels, taken before the defection of the Tyrian towns; and, to reciprocate the courtesy, Rome was now sending him back her captives. She scorned the overtures of the Mercenaries in Sardinian, and would not even recognise the inhabitants of Utica as subjects.

Hiero, who was ruling at Syracuse, was carried away by this example. For the preservation of his own States it was necessary that an equilibrium should exist between the two peoples; he was interested, therefore, in the safety of the Chanaanites, and he declared himself their friend, and sent them twelve hundred oxen, with fifty-three thousand nebels of pure wheat.

A deeper reason prompted aid to Carthage. It was felt that if the Mercenaries triumphed, every one, from soldier to plate-washer, would rise, and that no government and no house could resist them.

Meanwhile Hamilcar was scouring the eastern districts. He drove back the Gauls, and all the Barbarians found that they were themselves in something like a state of siege.

GUSTAVE FLAUBERT

Then he set himself to harass them. He would arrive and then retire, and by constantly renewing this manouvre, he gradually detached them from their encampments. Spendius was obliged to follow them, and in the end Matho yielded in like manner.

He did not pass beyond Tunis. He shut himself up within its walls. This persistence was full of wisdom, for soon Narr' Havas was to be seen issuing from the gate of Khamon with his elephants and soldiers. Hamilcar was recalling him, but the other Barbarians were already wandering about in the provinces in pursuit of the Suffet.

The latter had received three thousand Gauls from Clypea. He had horses brought to him from Cyrenaica, and armour from Brutium, and began the war again.

Never had his genius been so impetuous and fertile. For five moons he dragged his enemies after him. He had an end to which he wished to guide them.

THE BARBARIANS HAD AT FIRST tried to encompass him with small detachments, but he always escaped them. They ceased to separate then. Their army amounted to about forty thousand men, and several times they enjoyed the sight of seeing the Carthaginians fall back.

The horsemen of Narr' Havas were what they found most tormenting. Often, at times of the greatest weariness, when they were advancing over the plains, and dozing beneath the weight of their arms, a great line of dust would suddenly rise on the horizon; there would be a galloping up to them, and a rain of darts would pour from the bosom of a cloud filled with flaming eyes. The Numidians in their white cloaks would utter loud shouts, raise their arms, press their rearing stallions with their knees, and, wheeling them round abruptly, would then disappear. They had always supplies of javelins and dromedaries some distance off, and they would return more terrible than before, howl like wolves, and take to flight like vultures. The Barbarians posted at the extremities of the files fell one by one; and this would continue until evening, when an attempt would be made to enter the mountains.

Although they were perilous for elephants, Hamilcar made his way in among them. He followed the long chain which extends from the promontory of Hermæum to the top of Zagouan. This, they believed, was a device for hiding the insufficiency of his troops. But the continual uncertainty in which he kept them exasperated them at last more than any defeat. They did not lose heart, and marched after him.

At last one evening they surprised a body of velites amid some big rocks at the entrance of a pass between the Silver Mountain and the Lead Mountain; the entire army was certainly in front of them, for a noise of footsteps and clarions could be heard; the Carthaginians immediately fled through the gorge. It descended into a plain, and was shaped like an iron hatchet with a surrounding of lofty cliffs. The Barbarians dashed into it in order to overtake the velites; quite at the bottom other Carthaginians were running tumultuously amid galloping oxen. A man in a red cloak was to be seen; it was the Suffet; they shouted this to one another; and they were carried away with increased fury and joy. Several, from laziness or prudence, had remained on the threshold of the pass. But some cavalry, debouching from a wood, beat them down upon the rest with blows of pike and sabre; and soon all the Barbarians were below in the plain.

Then this great human mass, after swaying to and fro for some time, stood still; they could discover no outlet.

Those who were nearest to the pass went back again, but the passage had entirely disappeared. They hailed those in front to make them go on; they were being crushed against the mountain, and from a distance they inveighed against their companions, who were unable to find the route again.

In fact the Barbarians had scarcely descended when men who had been crouching behind the rocks raised the latter with beams and overthrew them, and as the slope was steep the huge blocks had rolled down pell-mell and completely stopped up the narrow opening.

At the other extremity of the plain stretched a long passage, split in gaps here and there, and leading to a ravine which ascended to the upper plateau, where the Punic army was stationed. Ladders had been placed beforehand in this passage against the wall of cliff; and, protected by the windings of the gaps, the velites were able to seize and mount them before being overtaken. Several even made their way to the bottom of the ravine; they were drawn up with cables, for the ground at this spot was of moving sand, and so much inclined that it was impossible to climb it even on the knees. The Barbarians arrived almost immediately. But a portcullis, forty cubits high, and made to fit the intervening space exactly, suddenly sank before them like a rampart fallen from the skies.

The Suffet's combinations had therefore succeeded. None of the Mercenaries knew the mountain, and, marching as they did at the head of their columns, they had drawn on the rest. The rocks, which were somewhat narrow at the base, had been easily cast down; and, while all were running, his army had raised shouts, as of distress, on the horizon. Hamilcar, it is true, might have lost his velites, only half of whom remained, but he would have sacrificed twenty times as many for the success of such an enterprise.

The Barbarians pressed forward until morning, in compact files, from one end of the plain to the other. They felt the mountain with their hands, seeking to discover a passage.

At last day broke; and they perceived all about them a great white wall hewn with the pick. And no means of safety, no hope! The two natural outcomes from this blind alley were closed by the portcullis and the heaps of rocks.

Then they all looked at one another without speaking. They sank down in collapse, feeling an icy coldness in their loins, and an overwhelming weight upon their eyelids.

They rose, and bounded against the rocks. But the lowest were weighted by the pressure of the others, and were immovable. They tried to cling to them so as to reach the top, but the bellying shape of the great masses rendered all hold impossible. They sought to cleave the ground on both sides of the gorge, but their instruments broke. They made a large fire with the tent poles, but the fire could not burn the mountain.

They returned to the portcullis; it was garnished with long nails as thick as stakes, as sharp as the spines of a porcupine, and closer than the hairs of a brush. But they were animated by such rage that they dashed themselves against it. The first were pierced to the backbone, those coming next surged over them, and all fell back, leaving human fragments and bloodstained hair on those horrible branches.

When their discouragement was somewhat abated, they made an examination of the provisions. The Mercenaries, whose baggage was lost, possessed scarcely enough for two days; and all the rest found themselves destitute,—for they had been awaiting a convoy promised by the villages of the South.

However, some bulls were roaming about, those which the Carthaginians had loosed in the gorge to attract the Barbarians. They killed them with lance thrusts and ate them, and when their stomachs were filled their thoughts were less mournful.

The next day they slaughtered all the mules to the number of about forty; then they scraped the skins, boiled the entrails, pounded the bones, and did not yet despair; the army from Tunis had no doubt been warned, and was coming.

But on the evening of the fifth day their hunger increased; they gnawed their sword-belts, and the little sponges which bordered the bottom of their helmets.

These forty thousand men were massed into the species of hippodrome formed by the mountain about them. Some remained in front of the portcullis, or at the foot of the rocks; the rest covered the plain confusedly. The strong shunned one another, and the timid sought out the brave, who, nevertheless, were unable to save them.

To avoid infection, the corpses of the velites had been speedily buried; and the position of the graves was no longer visible.

All the Barbarians lay drooping on the ground. A veteran would pass between their lines here and there; and they would howl curses against the Carthaginians, against Hamilcar, and against Matho, although he was innocent of their disaster; but it seemed to them that their pains would have been less if he had shared them. Then they groaned, and some wept softly like little children.

They came to the captains and besought them to grant them something that would alleviate their sufferings. The others made no reply; or, seized with fury, would pick up a stone and fling it in their faces.

Several, in fact, carefully kept a reserve of food in a hole in the ground—a few handfuls of dates, or a little meal; and they ate this during the night, with their heads bent beneath their cloaks. Those who had swords kept them naked in their hands, and the most suspicious remained standing with their backs against the mountain.

They accused their chiefs and threatened them. Autaritus was not afraid of showing himself. With the Barbaric obstinacy which nothing could discourage, he would advance twenty times a day to the rocks at the bottom, hoping every time to find them perchance displaced; and swaying his heavy fur-covered shoulders, he reminded his companions of a bear coming forth from its cave in springtime to see whether the snows are melted.

Spendius, surrounded by the Greeks, hid himself in one of the gaps; as he was afraid, he caused a rumour of his death to be spread.

They were now hideously lean; their skin was overlaid with bluish marblings. On the evening of the ninth day three Iberians died.

Their frightened companions left the spot. They were stripped, and the white, naked bodies lay in the sunshine on the sand.

GUSTAVE FLAUBERT

Then the Garamantians began to prowl slowly round about them. They were men accustomed to existence in solitude, and they reverenced no god. At last the oldest of the band made a sign, and bending over the corpses they cut strips from them with their knives, then squatted upon their heels and ate. The rest looked on from a distance; they uttered cries of horror;—many, nevertheless, being, at the bottom of their souls, jealous of such courage.

In the middle of the night some of these approached, and, dissembling their eagerness, asked for a small mouthful, merely to try, they said. Bolder ones came up; their number increased; there was soon a crowd. But almost all of them let their hands fall on feeling the cold flesh on the edge of their lips; others, on the contrary, devoured it with delight.

That they might be led away by example, they urged one another on mutually. Such as had at first refused went to see the Garamantians, and returned no more. They cooked the pieces on coals at the point of the sword; they salted them with dust, and contended for the best morsels. When nothing was left of the three corpses, their eyes ranged over the whole plain to find others.

But were they not in possession of Carthaginians—twenty captives taken in the last encounter, whom no one had noticed up to the present? These disappeared; moreover, it was an act of vengeance. Then, as they must live, as the taste for this food had become developed, and as they were dying, they cut the throats of the water-carriers, grooms, and all the serving-men belonging to the Mercenaries. They killed some of them every day. Some ate much, recovered strength, and were sad no more.

Soon this resource failed. Then the longing was directed to the wounded and sick. Since they could not recover, it was as well to release them from their tortures; and, as soon as a man began to stagger, all exclaimed that he was now lost, and ought to be made use of for the rest. Artifices were employed to accelerate their death; the last remnant of their foul portion was stolen from them; they were trodden on as though by inadvertence; those in the last throes wishing to make believe that they were strong, strove to stretch out their arms, to rise, to laugh. Men who had swooned came to themselves at the touch of a notched blade sawing off a limb;—and they still slew, ferociously and needlessly, to sate their fury.

A mist heavy and warm, such as comes in those regions at the end of winter, sank on the fourteenth day upon the army. This change of temperature brought numerous deaths with it, and corruption was developed with frightful rapidity in the warm dampness which was kept in by the sides of the mountain. The drizzle that fell upon the corpses softened them, and soon made the plain one broad tract of rottenness. Whitish vapours floated overhead; they pricked the nostrils, penetrated the skin, and troubled the sight; and the Barbarians thought that through the exhalations of the breath they could see the souls of their companions. They were overwhelmed with immense disgust. They wished for nothing more; they preferred to die.

Two days afterwards the weather became fine again, and hunger seized them once more. It seemed to them that their stomachs were being wrenched from them with tongs. Then they rolled about in convulsions, flung handfuls of dust into their mouths, bit their arms, and burst into frantic laughter.

They were still more tormented by thirst, for they had not a drop of water, the leathern bottles having been completely dried up since the ninth day. To cheat their need they applied their tongues to the metal plates on their waist-belts, their ivory pommels, and the steel of their swords. Some former caravan-leaders tightened their waists with ropes. Others sucked a pebble. They drank urine cooled in their brazen helmets.

And they still expected the army from Tunis! The length of time which it took in coming was, according to their conjectures, an assurance of its early arrival. Besides, Matho, who was a brave fellow, would not desert them. "'Twill be to-morrow!" they would say to one another; and then to-morrow would pass.

At the beginning they had offered up prayers and vows, and practised all kinds of incantations. Just now their only feeling to their divinities was one of hatred, and they strove to revenge themselves by believing in them no more.

Men of violent disposition perished first; the Africans held out better than the Gauls. Zarxas lay stretched at full length among the Balearians, his hair over his arm, inert. Spendius found a plant with broad leaves filled abundantly with juice, and after declaring that it was poisonous, so as to keep off the rest, he fed himself upon it.

They were too weak to knock down the flying crows with stones. Sometimes when a gypaëtus was perched on a corpse, and had been mangling it for a long time, a man would set himself to crawl towards it with a javelin between his teeth. He would support himself with one hand, and after taking a good aim, throw his weapon. The white-feathered creature, disturbed by the noise, would desist and look about in tranquil fashion like a cormorant on a rock, and would then again thrust in its hideous, yellow beak, while the man, in despair, would fall flat on his face in the dust. Some succeeded in discovering chameleons and serpents. But it was the love of life that kept them alive. They directed their souls to this idea exclusively, and clung to existence by an effort of the will that prolonged it.

The most stoical kept close to one another, seated in a circle here and there, among the dead in the middle of the plain; and wrapped in their cloaks they gave themselves up silently to their sadness.

Those who had been born in towns recalled the resounding streets, the taverns, theatres, baths, and the barbers' shops where there are tales to be heard. Others could once more see country districts at sunset, when the yellow corn waves, and the great oxen ascend the hills again with the ploughshares on their necks. Travellers dreamed of cisterns, hunters of their forests, veterans of battles; and in the somnolence that benumbed them their thoughts jostled one another with the precipitancy and clearness of dreams. Hallucinations came suddenly upon them; they sought for a door in the mountain in order to flee, and tried to pass through it. Others thought that they were sailing in a storm and gave orders for the handling of a ship, or else fell back in terror, perceiving Punic battalions in the clouds. There were some who imagined themselves at a feast, and sang.

Many through a strange mania would repeat the same word or continually make the same gesture. Then when they happened to raise their heads and look at one another they were choked with sobs on discovering the horrible ravages made in their faces. Some had ceased to suffer, and to while away the hours told of the perils which they had escaped.

Death was certain and imminent to all. How many times had they not tried to open up a passage! As to implore terms from the conqueror, by what means could they do so? They did not even know where Hamilcar was.

The wind was blowing from the direction of the ravine. It made the sand flow perpetually in cascades over the portcullis; and the cloaks and hair of the Barbarians were being covered with it as though the earth were rising upon them and desirous of burying them. Nothing stirred; the eternal mountain seemed still higher to them every morning.

Sometimes flights of birds darted past beneath the blue sky in the freedom of the air. The men closed their eyes that they might not see them.

At first they felt a buzzing in their ears, their nails grew black, the cold reached to their breasts; they lay upon their sides and expired without a cry.

On the nineteenth day two thousand Asiatics were dead, with fifteen hundred from the Archipelago, eight thousand from Libya, the youngest of the Mercenaries and whole tribes—in all twenty thousand soldiers, or half of the army.

Autaritus, who had only fifty Gauls left, was going to kill himself in order to put an end to this state of things, when he thought he saw a man on the top of the mountain in front of him.

Owing to his elevation this man did not appear taller than a dwarf. However, Autaritus recognised a shield shaped like a trefoil on his left arm. "A Carthaginian!" he exclaimed, and immediately throughout the plain, before the portcullis and beneath the rocks, all rose. The soldier was walking along the edge of the precipice; the Barbarians gazed at him from below.

Spendius picked up the head of an ox; then having formed a diadem with two belts, he fixed it on the horns at the end of a pole in token of pacific intentions. The Carthaginian disappeared. They waited.

At last in the evening a sword-belt suddenly fell from above like a stone loosened from the cliff. It was made of red leather covered with embroidery, with three diamond stars, and stamped in the centre, it bore the mark of the Great Council: a horse beneath a palm-tree. This was Hamilcar's reply, the safe-conduct that he sent them.

They had nothing to fear; any change of fortune brought with it the end of their woes. They were moved with extravagant joy, they embraced one another, they wept. Spendius, Autaritus, and Zarxas, four Italiotes, a Negro and two Spartans offered themselves as envoys. They were immediately accepted. They did not know, however, by what means they should get away.

But a cracking sounded in the direction of the rocks; and the most elevated of them, after rocking to and fro, rebounded to the bottom. In fact, if they were immovable on the side of the Barbarians—for it would have been necessary to urge them up an incline plane, and they were, moreover, heaped together owing to the narrowness of the gorge—on the others, on the contrary, it was sufficient to drive against them with

GUSTAVE FLAUBERT

violence to make them descend. The Carthaginians pushed them, and at daybreak they projected into the plain like the steps of an immense ruined staircase.

The Barbarians were still unable to climb them. Ladders were held out for their assistance; all rushed upon them. The discharge of a catapult drove the crowd back; only the Ten were taken away.

They walked amid the Clinabarians, leaning their hands on the horses' croups for support.

Now that their first joy was over they began to harbour anxieties. Hamilcar's demands would be cruel. But Spendius reassured them.

"I will speak!" And he boasted that he knew excellent things to say for the safety of the army.

Behind all the bushes they met with ambushed sentries, who prostrated themselves before the sword-belt which Spendius had placed over his shoulder.

When they reached the Punic camp the crowd flocked around them, and they thought that they could hear whisperings and laughter. The door of a tent opened.

Hamilcar was at the very back of it seated on a stool beside a table on which there shone a naked sword. He was surrounded by captains, who were standing.

He started back on perceiving these men, and then bent over to examine them.

Their pupils were strangely dilated, and there was a great black circle round their eyes, which extended to the lower parts of their ears; their bluish noses stood out between their hollow cheeks, which were chinked with deep wrinkles; the skin of their bodies was too large for their muscles, and was hidden beneath a slate-coloured dust; their lips were glued to their yellow teeth; they exhaled an infectious odour; they might have been taken for half-opened tombs, for living sepulchres.

In the centre of the tent, on a mat on which the captains were about to sit down, there was a dish of smoking gourds. The Barbarians fastened their eyes upon it with a shivering in all their limbs, and tears came to their eyelids; nevertheless they restrained themselves.

Hamilcar turned away to speak to some one. Then they all flung themselves upon it, flat on the ground. Their faces were soaked in the fat, and the noise of their deglutition was mingled with the sobs of joy which they uttered. Through astonishment, doubtless, rather than pity, they were allowed to finish the mess. Then when they had risen

Hamilcar with a sign commanded the man who bore the sword-belt to speak. Spendius was afraid; he stammered.

Hamilcar, while listening to him, kept turning round on his finger a big gold ring, the same which had stamped the seal of Carthage upon the sword-belt. He let it fall to the ground; Spendius immediately picked it up; his servile habits came back to him in the presence of his master. The others quivered with indignation at such baseness.

But the Greek raised his voice and spoke for a long time in rapid, insidious, and even violent fashion, setting forth the crimes of Hanno, whom he knew to be Barca's enemy, and striving to move Hamilcar's pity by the details of their miseries and the recollection of their devotion; in the end he became forgetful of himself, being carried away by the warmth of his temper.

Hamilcar replied that he accepted their excuses. Peace, then, was about to be concluded, and now it would be a definitive one! But he required that ten Mercenaries, chosen by himself, should be delivered up to him without weapons or tunics.

They had not expected such clemency; Spendius exclaimed: "Ah! twenty if you wish, master!"

"No! ten will suffice," replied Hamilcar quietly.

They were sent out of the tent to deliberate. As soon as they were alone, Autaritus protested against the sacrifice of their companions, and Zarxas said to Spendius:

"Why did you not kill him? his sword was there beside you!"

"Him!" said Spendius. "Him! him!" he repeated several times, as though the thing had been impossible, and Hamilcar were an immortal.

They were so overwhelmed with weariness that they stretched themselves on their backs on the ground, not knowing at what resolution to arrive.

Spendius urged them to yield. At last they consented, and went in again.

Then the Suffet put his hand into the hands of the ten Barbarians in turn, and pressed their thumbs; then he rubbed it on his garment, for their viscous skin gave a rude, soft impression to the touch, a greasy tingling which induced horripilation. Afterwards he said to them:

"You are really all the chiefs of the Barbarians, and you have sworn for them?"

"Yes!" they replied.

"Without constraint, from the bottom of your souls, with the intention of fulfilling your promises?"

They assured him that they were returning to the rest in order to fulfil them.

"Well!" rejoined the Suffet, "in accordance with the convention concluded between myself, Barca, and the ambassadors of the Mercenaries, it is you whom I choose and shall keep!"

Spendius fell swooning upon the mat. The Barbarians, as though abandoning him, pressed close together; and there was not a word, not a complaint.

THEIR COMPANIONS, WHO WERE WAITING for them, not seeing them return, believed themselves betrayed. The envoys had no doubt given themselves up to the Suffet.

They waited for two days longer; then on the morning of the third, their resolution was taken. With ropes, picks, and arrows, arranged like rungs between strips of canvas, they succeeded in scaling the rocks; and leaving the weakest, about three thousand in number, behind them, they began their march to rejoin the army at Tunis.

Above the gorge there stretched a meadow thinly sown with shrubs; the Barbarians devoured the buds. Afterwards they found a field of beans; and everything disappeared as though a cloud of grasshoppers had passed that way. Three hours later they reached a second plateau bordered by a belt of green hills.

Among the undulations of these hillocks, silvery sheaves shone at intervals from one another; the Barbarians, who were dazzled by the sun, could perceive confusedly below great black masses supporting them; these rose, as though they were expanding. They were lances in towers on elephants terribly armed.

Besides the spears on their breasts, the bodkin tusks, the brass plates which covered their sides, and the daggers fastened to their knee-caps, they had at the extremity of their tusks a leathern bracelet, in which the handle of a broad cutlass was inserted; they had set out simultaneously from the back part of the plain, and were advancing on both sides in parallel lines.

The Barbarians were frozen with a nameless terror. They did not even try to flee. They already found themselves surrounded.

The elephants entered into this mass of men; and the spurs on their breasts divided it, the lances on their tusks upturned it like ploughshares; they cut, hewed, and hacked with the scythes on their trunks; the towers, which were full of phalaricas, looked like volcanoes on the march; nothing could be distinguished but a large heap, whereon human flesh, pieces of brass and blood made white spots, grey sheets and red fuses. The horrible animals dug out black furrows as they passed through the midst of it all.

The fiercest was driven by a Numidian who was crowned with a diadem of plumes. He hurled javelins with frightful quickness, giving at intervals a long shrill whistle. The great beasts, docile as dogs, kept an eye on him during the carnage.

The circle of them narrowed by degrees; the weakened Barbarians offered no resistance; the elephants were soon in the centre of the plain. They lacked space; they thronged half-rearing together, and their tusks clashed against one another. Suddenly Narr' Havas quieted them, and wheeling round they trotted back to the hills.

Two syntagmata, however, had taken refuge on the right in a bend of ground, had thrown away their arms, and were all kneeling with their faces towards the Punic tents imploring mercy with uplifted arms.

Their legs and hands were tied; then when they were stretched on the ground beside one another the elephants were brought back.

Their breasts cracked like boxes being forced; two were crushed at every step; the big feet sank into the bodies with a motion of the haunches which made the elephants appear lame. They went on to the very end.

The level surface of the plain again became motionless. Night fell. Hamilcar was delighting himself with the spectacle of his vengeance, but suddenly he started.

He saw, and all saw, some more Barbarians six hundred paces to the left on the summit of a peak! In fact four hundred of the stoutest Mercenaries, Etruscans, Libyans, and Spartans had gained the heights at the beginning, and had remained there in uncertainty until now. After the massacre of their companions they resolved to make their way through the Carthaginians; they were already descending in serried columns, in a marvellous and formidable fashion.

A herald was immediately despatched to them. The Suffet needed soldiers; he received them unconditionally, so greatly did he admire their bravery. They could even, said the man of Carthage, come a little nearer, to a place, which he pointed out to them, where they would find provisions.

The Barbarians ran thither and spent the night in eating. Then the Carthaginians broke into clamours against the Suffet's partiality for the Mercenaries.

Did he yield to these outbursts of insatiable hatred or was it a refinement of treachery? The next day he came himself, without a sword and bare-headed, with an escort of Clinabarians, and announced to them that having too many to feed he did not intend to keep them. Nevertheless, as he wanted men and he knew of no means of selecting the good ones, they were to fight together to the death; he would then admit the conquerors into his own body-guard. This death was quite as good as another;—and then moving his soldiers aside (for the Punic standards hid the horizon from the Mercenaries) he showed them the one hundred and ninety-two elephants under Narr' Havas, forming a single straight line, their trunks brandishing broad steel blades like giant arms holding axes above their heads.

The Barbarians looked at one another silently. It was not death that made them turn pale, but the horrible compulsion to which they found themselves reduced.

The community of their lives had brought about profound friendship among these men. The camp, with most, took the place of their country; living without a family they transferred the needful tenderness to a companion, and they would fall asleep in the starlight side by side under the same cloak. And then in their perpetual wanderings through all sorts of countries, murders, and adventures, they had contracted affections, one for the other, in which the stronger protected the younger in the midst of battles, helped him to cross precipices, sponged the sweat of fevers from his brow, and stole food for him, and the weaker, a child perhaps, who had been picked up on the roadside, and had then become a Mercenary, repaid this devotion by a thousand kindnesses.

They exchanged their necklaces and earrings, presents which they had made to one another in former days, after great peril, or in hours of intoxication. All asked to die, and none would strike. A young fellow might be seen here and there, saying to another whose beard was grey: "No! no! you are more robust! you will avenge us, kill me!" and the man would reply: "I have fewer years to live! Strike to the heart, and think no more about it!" Brothers gazed on one another with clasped hands, and friend bade friend eternal farewells, standing and weeping upon his shoulder.

They threw off their cuirasses that the sword-points might be thrust in the more quickly. Then there appeared the marks of the great blows which they had received for Carthage, and which looked like inscriptions on columns.

They placed themselves in four equal ranks, after the fashion of gladiators, and began with timid engagements. Some had even bandaged their eyes, and their swords waved gently through the air like blind men's sticks. The Carthaginians hooted, and shouted to them that they were cowards. The Barbarians became animated, and soon the combat as general, headlong, and terrible.

Sometimes two men all covered with blood would stop, fall into each other's arms, and die with mutual kisses. None drew back. They rushed upon the extended blades. Their delirium was so frenzied that the Carthaginians in the distance were afraid.

At last they stopped. Their breasts made a great hoarse noise, and their eyeballs could be seen through their long hair, which hung down as though it had come out of a purple bath. Several were turning round rapidly, like panthers wounded in the forehead. Others stood motionless looking at a corpse at their feet; then they would suddenly tear their faces with their nails, take their swords with both hands, and plunge them into their own bodies.

There were still sixty left. They asked for drink. They were told by shouts to throw away their swords, and when they had done so water was brought to them.

While they were drinking, with their faces buried in the vases, sixty Carthaginians leaped upon them and killed them with stiletos in the back.

Hamilcar had done this to gratify the instincts of his army, and, by means of this treachery, to attach it to his own person.

The war, then, was ended; at least he believed that it was; Matho would not resist; in his impatience the Suffet commanded an immediate departure.

His scouts came to tell him that a convoy had been descried, departing towards the Lead Mountain. Hamilcar did not trouble himself about it. The Mercenaries once annihilated, the Nomads would give him no further trouble. The important matter was to take Tunis. He advanced by forced marches upon it.

He had sent Narr' Havas to Carthage with the news of his victory; and the King of the Numidians, proud of his success, visited Salammbô.

SHE RECEIVED HIM IN HER gardens under a large sycamore tree, amid pillows of yellow leather, and with Taanach beside her. Her face was

GUSTAVE FLAUBERT

covered with a white scarf, which, passing over her mouth and forehead, allowed only her eyes to be seen; but her lips shone in the transparency of the tissue like the gems on her fingers, for Salammbô had both her hands wrapped up, and did not make a gesture during the whole conversation.

Narr' Havas announced the defeat of the Barbarians to her. She thanked him with a blessing for the services which he had rendered to her father. Then he began to tell her about the whole campaign.

The doves on the palm trees around them cooed softly, and other birds fluttered amid the grass: ring-necked glareolas, Tartessus quails and Punic guinea-fowl. The garden, long uncultivated, had multiplied its verdure; coloquintidas mounted into the branches of cassias, the asclepias was scattered over fields of roses, all kinds of vegetation formed entwinings and bowers; and here and there, as in the woods, sun-rays, descending obliquely, marked the shadow of a leaf upon the ground. Domestic animals, grown wild again, fled at the slightest noise. Sometimes a gazelle might be seen trailing scattered peacocks' feathers after its little black hoofs. The clamours of the distant town were lost in the murmuring of the waves. The sky was quite blue, and not a sail was visible on the sea.

Narr' Havas had ceased speaking; Salammbô was looking at him without replying. He wore a linen robe with flowers painted on it, and with gold fringes at the hem; two silver arrows fastened his plaited hair at the tips of his ears; his right hand rested on a pike-staff adorned with circles of electrum and tufts of hair.

As she watched him a crowd of dim thoughts absorbed her. This young man, with his gentle voice and feminine figure, captivated her eyes by the grace of his person, and seemed to her like an elder sister sent by the Baals to protect her. The recollection of Matho came upon her, nor did she resist the desire to learn what had become of him.

Narr' Havas replied that the Carthaginians were advancing towards Tunis to take it. In proportion as he set forth their chances of success and Matho's weaknesses, she seemed to rejoice in extraordinary hope. Her lips trembled, her breast panted. When he finally promised to kill him himself, she exclaimed: "Yes! kill him! It must be so!"

The Numidian replied that he desired this death ardently, since he would be her husband when the war was over.

Salammbô started, and bent her head.

But Narr' Havas, pursuing the subject, compared his longings to flowers languishing for rain, or to lost travellers waiting for the day. He told her, further, that she was more beautiful than the moon, better than the wind of morning or than the face of a guest. He would bring for her from the country of the Blacks things such as there were none in Carthage, and the apartments in their house should be sanded with gold dust.

Evening fell, and odours of balsam were exhaled. For a long time they looked at each other in silence, and Salammbô's eyes, in the depths of her long draperies, resembled two stars in the rift of a cloud. Before the sun set he withdrew.

The Ancients felt themselves relieved of a great anxiety, when he left Carthage. The people had received him with even more enthusiastic acclamations than on the first occasion. If Hamilcar and the King of the Numidians triumphed alone over the Mercenaries it would be impossible to resist them. To weaken Barca they therefore resolved to make the aged Hanno, him whom they loved, a sharer in the deliverance of Carthage.

He proceeded immediately towards the western provinces, to take his vengeance in the very places which had witnessed his shame. But the inhabitants and the Barbarians were dead, hidden, or fled. Then his anger was vented upon the country. He burnt the ruins of the ruins, he did not leave a single tree nor a blade of grass; the children and the infirm, that were met with, were tortured; he gave the women to his soldiers to be violated before they were slaughtered.

Often, on the crests of the hills, black tents were struck as though overturned by the wind, and broad, brilliantly bordered discs, which were recognised as being chariot-wheels, revolved with a plaintive sound as they gradually disappeared in the valleys. The tribes, which had abandoned the siege of Carthage, were wandering in this way through the provinces, waiting for an opportunity, or for some victory to be gained by the Mercenaries, in order to return. But, whether from terror or famine, they all took the roads to their native lands, and disappeared.

Hamilcar was not jealous of Hanno's successes. Nevertheless he was in a hurry to end matters; he commanded him to fall back upon Tunis; and Hanno, who loved his country, was under the walls of the town on the appointed day.

For its protection it had its aboriginal population, twelve thousand Mercenaries, and, in addition, all the Eaters of Uncleanness, for like Matho they were riveted to the horizon of Carthage, and plebs and schalischim gazed at its lofty walls from afar, looking back in thought to boundless enjoyments. With this harmony of hatred, resistance was briskly organised. Leathern bottles were taken to make helmets; all the palm-trees in the gardens were cut down for lances; cisterns were dug; while for provisions they caught on the shores of the lake big white fish, fed on corpses and filth. Their ramparts, kept in ruins now by the jealousy of Carthage, were so weak that they could be thrown down with a push of the shoulder. Matho stopped up the holes in them with the stones of the houses. It was the last struggle; he hoped for nothing, and yet he told himself that fortune was fickle.

As the Carthaginians approached they noticed a man on the rampart who towered over the battlements from his belt upwards. The arrows that flew about him seemed to frighten him no more than a swarm of swallows. Extraordinary to say, none of them touched him.

Hamilcar pitched his camp on the south side; Narr' Havas, to his right, occupied the plain of Rhades, and Hanno the shore of the lake; and the three generals were to maintain their respective positions, so as all to attack the walls simultaneously.

But Hamilcar wished first to show the Mercenaries that he would punish them like slaves. He had the ten ambassadors crucified beside one another on a hillock in front of the town.

At the sight of this the besieged forsook the rampart.

Matho had said to himself that if he could pass between the walls and Narr' Havas's tents with such rapidity that the Numidians had not time to come out, he could fall upon the rear of the Carthaginian infantry, who would be caught between his division and those inside. He dashed out with his veterans.

Narr' Havas perceived him; he crossed the shore of the lake, and came to warn Hanno to dispatch men to Hamilcar's assistance. Did he believe Barca too weak to resist the Mercenaries? Was it a piece of treachery or folly? No one could ever learn.

Hanno, desiring to humiliate his rival, did not hesitate. He shouted orders to sound the trumpets, and his whole army rushed upon the Barbarians. The latter returned, and ran straight against the Carthaginians; they knocked them down, crushed them under their feet, and, driving them back in this way, reached the tent of Hanno, who was then surrounded by thirty Carthaginians, the most illustrious of the Ancients.

He appeared stupefied by their audacity; he called for his captains. Every one thrust his fist under his throat, vociferating abuse. The crowd pressed on; and those who had their hands on him could scarce retain their hold. However, he tried to whisper to them: "I will gave you whatever you want! I am rich! Save me!" They dragged him along; heavy as he was his feet did not touch the ground. The Ancients had been carried off. His terror increased. "You have beaten me! I am your captive! I will ransom myself! Listen to me, my friends!" and borne along by all those shoulders which were pressed against his sides, he repeated: "What are you going to do? What do you want? You can see that I am not obstanite! I have always been good-natured!"

A gigantic cross stood at the gate. The Barbarians howled: "Here! here!" But he raised his voice still higher; and in the names of their gods he called upon them to lead him to the schalischim, because he wished to confide to him something on which their safety depended.

They paused, some asserting that it was right to summon Matho. He was sent for.

Hanno fell upon the grass; and he saw around him other crosses also, as though the torture by which he was about to perish had been multiplied beforehand; he made efforts to convince himself that he was mistaken, that there was only one, and even to believe that there were none at all. At last he was lifted up.

"Speak!" said Matho.

He offered to give up Hamilcar; then they would enter Carthage and both be kings.

Matho withdrew, signing to the others to make haste. It was a stratagem, he thought, to gain time.

The Barbarian was mistaken; Hanno was in an extremity when consideration is had to nothing, and, moreover, he so execrated Hamilcar that he would have sacrificed him and all his soldiers on the slightest hope of safety.

The Ancients were languishing on the ground at the foot of the crosses; ropes had already been passed beneath their armpits. Then the old Suffet, understanding that he must die, wept.

They tore off the clothes that were still left on him—and the horror of his person appeared. Ulcers covered the nameless mass; the fat on his legs hid the nails on his feet; from his fingers there hung what looked like greenish strips; and the tears streaming through the tubercles on his cheeks gave to his face an expression of frightful sadness, for they seemed to take up more room than on another human face. His royal fillet, which was half unfastened, trailed with his white hair in the dust.

They thought that they had no ropes strong enough to haul him up to the top of the cross, and they nailed him upon it, after the Punic fashion, before it was erected. But his pride awoke in his pain. He began to overwhelm them with abuse. He foamed and twisted like a marine monster being slaughtered on the shore, and predicted that they would all end more horribly still, and that he would be avenged.

He was. On the other side of the town, whence there now escaped jets of flame with columns of smoke, the ambassadors from the Mercenaries were in their last throes.

Some who had swooned at first had just revived in the freshness of the wind; but their chins still rested upon their breasts, and their bodies had fallen somewhat, in spite of the nails in their arms, which were fastened higher than their heads; from their heels and hands blood fell in big, slow drops, as ripe fruit falls from the branches of a tree,— and Carthage, gulf, mountains, and plains all appeared to them to be revolving like an immense wheel; sometimes a cloud of dust, rising from the ground, enveloped them in its eddies; they burned with horrible thirst, their tongues curled in their mouths, and they felt an icy sweat flowing over them with their departing souls.

Nevertheless they had glimpses, at an infinite depth, of streets, marching soldiers, and the swinging of swords; and the tumult of battle reached them dimly like the noise of the sea to shipwrecked men dying on the masts of a ship. The Italiotes, who were sturdier than the rest, were still shrieking. The Lacedæmonians were silent, with eyelids closed; Zarxas, once so vigorous, was bending like a broken reed; the Ethiopian beside him had his head thrown back over the arms of the cross; Autaritus was motionless, rolling his eyes; his great head of hair, caught in a cleft in the wood, fell straight upon his forehead, and his death-rattle seemed rather to be a roar of anger. As to Spendius, a strange courage had come to him; he despised life now in the certainty which he possessed of an almost immediate and an eternal emancipation, and he awaited death with impassibility.

Amid their swooning, they sometimes started at the brushing of feathers passing across their lips. Large wings swung shadows around them, croakings sounded in the air; and as Spendius's cross was the highest, it was upon his that the first vulture alighted. Then he turned his face towards Autaritus, and said slowly to him with an unaccountable smile:

"Do you remember the lions on the road to Sicca?"

"They were our brothers!" replied the Gaul, as he expired.

The Suffet, meanwhile, had bored through the walls and reached the citadel. The smoke suddenly disappeared before a gust of wind, discovering the horizon as far as the walls of Carthage; he even thought that he could distinguish people watching on the platform of Eschmoun; then, bringing back his eyes, he perceived thirty crosses of extravagant size on the shore of the Lake, to the left.

In fact, to render them still more frightful, they had been constructed with tent-poles fastened end to end, and the thirty corpses of the Ancients appeared high up in the sky. They had what looked like white butterflies on their breasts; these were the feathers of the arrows which had been shot at them from below.

A broad gold ribbon shone on the summit of the highest; it hung down to the shoulder, there being no arm on that side, and Hamilcar had some difficulty in recognising Hanno. His spongy bones had given way under the iron pins, portions of his limbs had come off, and nothing was left on the cross but shapeless remains, like the fragments of animals that are hung up on huntsmen's doors.

The Suffet could not have known anything about it; the town in front of him masked everything that was beyond and behind; and the captains who had been successively sent to the two generals had not re-appeared. Then fugitives arrived with the tale of the rout, and the Punic army halted. This catastrophe, falling upon them as it did in the midst of their victory, stupefied them. Hamilcar's orders were no longer listened to.

Matho took advantage of this to continue his ravages among the Numidians.

Hanno's camp having been overthrown, he had returned against them. The elephants came out; but the Mercenaries advanced through the plain shaking about flaming firebrands, which they had plucked from the walls, and the great beasts, in fright, ran headlong into the gulf, where they killed one another in their struggles, or were drowned beneath the weight of their cuirasses. Narr' Havas had already launched his cavalry; all threw themselves face downwards upon the ground; then, when the horses were within three paces of them, they sprang beneath their bellies, ripped them open with dagger-strokes, and half the Numidians had perished when Barca came up.

The exhausted Mercenaries could not withstand his troops. They retired in good order to the mountain of the Hot Springs. The Suffet was prudent enough not to pursue them. He directed his course to the mouths of the Macaras.

Tunis was his; but it was now nothing but a heap of smoking rubbish. The ruins fell through the breaches in the walls to the centre of the plain; quite in the background, between the shores of the gulf, the corpses of the elephants drifting before the wind conflicted, like an archipelago of black rocks floating on the water.

Narr' Havas had drained his forests of these animals, taking young and old, male and female, to keep up the war, and the military force of his kingdom could not repair the loss. The people who had seen them perishing at a distance were grieved at it; men lamented in the streets, calling them by their names like deceased friends: "Ah! the Invincible! the Victory! the Thunderer! the Swallow!" On the first day, too, there was no talk except of the dead citizens. But on the morrow the tents of the Mercenaries were seen on the mountain of the Hot Springs. Then so deep was the despair that many people, especially women, flung themselves headlong from the top of the Acropolis.

HAMILCAR'S DESIGNS WERE NOT KNOWN. He lived alone in his tent with none near him but a young boy, and no one ever ate with them, not even excepting Narr' Havas. Nevertheless he showed great deference to the latter after Hanno's defeat; but the king of the Numidians had too great an interest in becoming his son not to distrust him.

This inertness veiled skilful manouvres. Hamilcar seduced the heads of the villages by all sorts of artifices; and the Mercenaries were hunted, repulsed, and enclosed like wild beasts. As soon as they entered a wood, the trees caught fire around them; when they drank of a spring it was poisoned; the caves in which they hid in order to sleep were walled up. Their old accomplices, the populations who had hitherto defended them, now pursued them; and they continually recognised Carthaginian armour in these bands.

Many had their faces consumed with red tetters; this, they thought, had come to them through touching Hanno. Others imagined that it was because they had eaten Salammbô's fishes, and far from repenting of it, they dreamed of even more abominable sacrileges, so that the abasement of the Punic Gods might be still greater. They would fain have exterminated them.

In this way they lingered for three months along the eastern coast, and then behind the mountain of Selloum, and as far as the first sands of the desert. They sought for a place of refuge, no matter where. Utica and Hippo-Zarytus alone had not betrayed them; but Hamilcar was encompassing these two towns. Then they went northwards at haphazard without even knowing the various routes. Their many miseries had confused their understandings.

The only feeling left them was one of exasperation, which went on developing; and one day they found themselves again in the gorges of Cobus and once more before Carthage!

Then the actions multiplied. Fortune remained equal; but both sides were so wearied that they would willingly have exchanged these skirmishes for a great battle, provided that it were really the last.

Matho was inclined to carry this proposal himself to the Suffet. One of his Libyans devoted himself for the purpose. All were convinced as they saw him depart that he would not return.

He returned the same evening.

Hamilcar accepted the challenge. The encounter should take place the following day at sunrise, in the plain of Rhades.

The Mercenaries wished to know whether he had said anything more, and the Libyan added:

"As I remained in his presence, he asked me what I was waiting for. 'To be killed!' I replied. Then he rejoined: 'No! begone! that will be to-morrow with the rest.'"

This generosity astonished the Barbarians; some were terrified by it, and Matho regretted that the emissary had not been killed.

HE HAD STILL REMAINING THREE thousand Africans, twelve hundred Greeks, fifteen hundred Campanians, two hundred Iberians, four hundred Etruscans, five hundred Samnites, forty Gauls, and a troop of Naffurs, nomad bandits met with in the date region—in all seven thousand two hundred and nineteen soldiers, but not one complete syntagmata. They had stopped up the holes in their cuirasses with the shoulder-blades of quadrupeds, and replaced their brass cothurni with worn sandals. Their garments were weighted with copper or steel plates; their coats of mail hung in tatters about them, and scars appeared like purple threads through the hair on their arms and faces.

The wraiths of their dead companions came back to their souls and increased their energy; they felt, in a confused way, that they were the ministers of a god diffused in the hearts of the oppressed, and were the pontiffs, so to speak, of universal vengeance! Then they were enraged

GUSTAVE FLAUBERT

with grief at what was extravagant injustice, and above all by the sight of Carthage on the horizon. They swore an oath to fight for one another until death.

The beasts of burden were killed, and as much as possible was eaten so as to gain strength; afterwards they slept. Some prayed, turning towards different constellations.

The Carthaginians arrived first in the plain. They rubbed the edges of their shields with oil to make the arrows glide off them easily; the foot-soldiers who wore long hair took the precaution of cutting it on the forehead; and Hamilcar ordered all bowls to be inverted from the fifth hour, knowing that it is disadvantageous to fight with the stomach too full. His army amounted to fourteen thousand men, or about double the number of the Barbarians. Nevertheless, he had never felt such anxiety; if he succumbed it would mean the annihilation of the Republic, and he would perish on the cross; if, on the contrary, he triumphed, he would reach Italy by way of the Pyrenees, the Gauls, and the Alps, and the empire of the Barcas would become eternal. Twenty times during the night he rose to inspect everything himself, down to the most trifling details. As to the Carthaginians, they were exasperated by their lengthened terror. Narr' Havas suspected the fidelity of his Numidians. Moreover, the Barbarians might vanquish them. A strange weakness had come upon him; every moment he drank large cups of water.

But a man whom he did not know opened his tent and laid on the ground a crown of rock-salt, adorned with hieratic designs formed with sulphur, and lozenges of mother-of-pearl; a marriage crown was sometimes sent to a betrothed husband; it was a proof of love, a sort of invitation.

Nevertheless Hamilcar's daughter had no tenderness for Narr' Havas.

The recollection of Matho disturbed her in an intolerable manner; it seemed to her that the death of this man would unburden her thoughts, just as people to cure themselves of the bite of a viper crush it upon the wound. The king of the Numidians was depending upon her; he awaited the wedding with impatience, and, as it was to follow the victory, Salammbô made him this present to stimulate his courage. Then his distress vanished, and he thought only of the happiness of possessing so beautiful a woman.

The same vision had assailed Matho; but he cast it from him immediately, and his love, that he thus thrust back, was poured out upon his companions in arms. He cherished them like portions of his own person, of his hatred,—and he felt his spirit higher, and his arms stronger; everything that he was to accomplish appeared clearly before him. If sighs sometimes escaped him, it was because he was thinking of Spendius.

He drew up the Barbarians in six equal ranks. He posted the Etruscans in the centre, all being fastened to a bronze chain; the archers were behind, and on the wings he distributed the Naffurs, who were mounted on short-haired camels, covered with ostrich feathers.

The Suffet arranged the Carthaginians in similar order. He placed the Clinabarians outside the infantry next to the velites, and the Numidians beyond; when day appeared, both sides were thus in line face to face. All gazed at each other from a distance, with round fierce eyes. There was at first some hesitation; at last both armies moved.

The Barbarians advanced slowly so as not to become out of breath, beating the ground with their feet; the centre of the Punic army formed a convex curve. Then came the burst of a terrible shock, like the crash of two fleets in collision. The first rank of the Barbarians had quickly opened up, and the marksmen, hidden behind the others, discharged their bullets, arrows, and javelins. The curve of the Carthaginians, however, flattened by degrees, became quite straight, and then bent inwards; upon this, the two sections of the velites drew together in parallel lines, like the legs of a compass that is being closed. The Barbarians, who were attacking the phalanx with fury, entered the gap; they were being lost; Matho checked them,—and while the Carthaginian wings continued to advance, he drew out the three inner ranks of his line; they soon covered his flanks, and his army appeared in triple array.

But the Barbarians placed at the extremities were the weakest, especially those on the left, who had exhausted their quivers, and the troop of velites, which had at last come up against them, was cutting them up greatly.

Matho made them fall back. His right comprised Campanians, who were armed with axes; he hurled them against the Carthaginian left; the centre attacked the enemy, and those at the other extremity, who were out of peril, kept the velites at a distance.

Then Hamilcar divided his horsemen into squadrons, placed hoplites between them, and sent them against the Mercenaries.

Those cone-shaped masses presented a front of horses, and their broader sides were filled and bristling with lances. The Barbarians

GUSTAVE FLAUBERT

found it impossible to resist; the Greek foot-soldiers alone had brazen armour, all the rest had cutlasses on the end of poles, scythes taken from the farms, or swords manufactured out of the fellies of wheels; the soft blades were twisted by a blow, and while they were engaged in straightening them under their heels, the Carthaginians massacred them right and left at their ease.

But the Etruscans, riveted to their chain, did not stir; those who were dead, being prevented from falling, formed an obstruction with their corpses; and the great bronze line widened and contracted in turn, as supple as a serpent, and as impregnable as a wall. The Barbarians would come to re-form behind it, pant for a minute, and then set off again with the fragments of their weapons in their hands.

Many already had none left, and they leaped upon the Carthaginians, biting their faces like dogs. The Gauls in their pride stripped themselves of the sagum; they showed their great white bodies from a distance, and they enlarged their wounds to terrify the enemy. The voice of the crier announcing the orders could no longer be heard in the midst of the Punic syntagmata; their signals were being repeated by the standards, which were raised above the dust, and every one was swept away in the swaying of the great mass that surrounded him.

Hamilcar commanded the Numidians to advance. But the Naffurs rushed to meet them.

Clad in vast black robes, with a tuft of hair on the top of the skull, and a shield of rhinoceros leather, they wielded a steel which had no handle, and which they held by a rope; and their camels, which bristled all over with feathers, uttered long, hoarse cluckings. Each blade fell on a precise spot, then rose again with a smart stroke carrying off a limb with it. The fierce beasts galloped through the syntagmata. Some, whose legs were broken, went hopping along like wounded ostriches.

The Punic infantry turned in a body upon the Barbarians, and cut them off. Their maniples wheeled about at intervals from one another. The more brilliant Carthaginian weapons encircled them like golden crowns; there was a swarming movement in the centre, and the sun, striking down upon the points of the swords, made them glitter with white flickering gleams. However, files of Clinabarians lay stretched upon the plain; some Mercenaries snatched away their armour, clothed themselves in it, and then returned to the fray. The deluded Carthaginians were several times entangled in their midst. They would stand stupidly motionless, or else would back, surge again, and triumphant shouts rising in the distance seemed to drive them along like derelicts in a storm. Hamilcar was growing desperate; all was about to perish beneath the genius of Matho and the invincible courage of the Mercenaries.

But a great noise of tabourines burst forth on the horizon. It was a crowd of old men, sick persons, children of fifteen years of age, and even women, who, being unable to withstand their distress any longer, had set out from Carthage, and, for the purpose of placing themselves under the protection of something formidable, had taken from Hamilcar's palace the only elephant that the Republic now possessed,—that one, namely, whose trunk had been cut off.

Then it seemed to the Carthaginians that their country, forsaking its walls, was coming to command them to die for her. They were seized with increased fury, and the Numidians carried away all the rest.

The Barbarians had set themselves with their backs to a hillock in the centre of the plain. They had no chance of conquering, or even of surviving; but they were the best, the most intrepid, and the strongest.

The people from Carthage began to throw spits, larding-pins and hammers, over the heads of the Numidians; those whom consuls had feared died beneath sticks hurled by women; the Punic populace was exterminating the Mercenaries.

The latter had taken refuge on the top of the hill. Their circle closed up after every fresh breach; twice it descended to be immediately repulsed with a shock; and the Carthaginians stretched forth their arms pell-mell, thrusting their pikes between the legs of their companions, and raking at random before them. They slipped in the blood; the steep slope of the ground made the corpses roll to the bottom. The elephant, which was trying to climb the hillock, was up to its belly; it seemed to be crawling over them with delight; and its shortened trunk, which was broad at the extremity, rose from time to time like an enormous leech.

Then all paused. The Carthaginians ground their teeth as they gazed at the hill, where the Barbarians were standing.

At last they dashed at them abruptly, and the fight began again. The Mercenaries would often let them approach, shouting to them that they wished to surrender; then, with frightful sneers, they would kill themselves at a blow, and as the dead fell, the rest would mount upon them to defend themselves. It was a kind of pyramid, which grew larger by degrees.

Soon there were only fifty, then only twenty, only three, and lastly only two—a Samnite armed with an axe, and Matho who still had his sword.

The Samnite with bent hams swept his axe alternately to the right and left, at the same time warning Matho of the blows that were being aimed at him. "Master, this way! that way! stoop down!"

Matho had lost his shoulder-pieces, his helmet, his cuirass; he was completely naked, and more livid than the dead, with his hair quite erect, and two patches of foam at the corners of his lips,—and his sword whirled so rapidly that it formed an aureola around him. A stone broke it near the guard; the Samnite was killed and the flood of Carthaginians closed in, they touched Matho. Then he raised both his empty hands towards heaven, closed his eyes, and, opening out his arms like a man throwing himself from the summit of a promontory into the sea, hurled himself among the pikes.

They moved away before him. Several times he ran against the Carthaginians. But they always drew back and turned their weapons aside.

His foot struck against a sword. Matho tried to seize it. He felt himself tied by the wrists and knees, and fell.

Narr' Havas had been following him for some time, step by step, with one of the large nets used for capturing wild beasts, and, taking advantage of the moment when he stooped down, had involved him in it.

Then he was fastened on the elephants with his four limbs forming a cross; and all those who were not wounded escorted him, and rushed with great tumult towards Carthage.

The news of the victory had arrived in some inexplicable way at the third hour of the night; the clepsydra of Khamon had just completed the fifth as they reached Malqua; then Matho opened his eyes. There were so many lights in the houses that the town appeared to be all in flames.

An immense clamour reached him dimly; and lying on his back he looked at the stars.

Then a door closed and he was wrapped in darkness.

On the morrow, at the same hour, the last of the men left in the Pass of the Hatchet expired.

On the day that their companions had set out, some Zuaeces who were returning had tumbled the rocks down, and had fed them for some time.

The Barbarians constantly expected to see Matho appear,—and from discouragement, from languor, and from the obstinacy of sick men who object to change their situation, they would not leave the mountain; at last the provisions were exhausted and the Zuaeces went away. It was known that they numbered scarcely more than thirteen hundred men, and there was no need to employ soldiers to put an end to them.

Wild beasts, especially lions, had multiplied during the three years that the war had lasted. Narr' Havas had held a great battue, and—after tying goats at intervals—had run upon them and so driven them towards the Pass of the Hatchet;—and they were now all living in it when a man arrived who had been sent by the Ancients to find out what there was left of the Barbarians.

Lions and corpses were lying over the tract of the plain, and the dead were mingled with clothes and armour. Nearly all had the face or an arm wanting; some appeared to be still intact; others were completely dried up, and their helmets were filled with powdery skulls; feet which had lost their flesh stood out straight from the knemides; skeletons still wore their cloaks; and bones, cleaned by the sun, made gleaming spots in the midst of the sand.

The lions were resting with their breasts against the ground and both paws stretched out, winking their eyelids in the bright daylight, which was heightened by the reflection from the white rocks. Others were seated on their hind-quarters and staring before them, or else were sleeping, rolled into a ball and half hidden by their great manes; they all looked well fed, tired, and dull. They were as motionless as the mountain and the dead. Night was falling; the sky was striped with broad red bands in the west.

In one of the heaps, which in an irregular fashion embossed the plain, something rose up vaguer than a spectre. Then one of the lions set himself in motion, his monstrous form cutting a black shadow on the background of the purple sky, and when he was quite close to the man, he knocked him down with a single blow of his paw.

Then, stretching himself flat upon him, he slowly drew out the entrails with the edge of his teeth.

Afterwards he opened his huge jaws, and for some minutes uttered a lengthened roar which was repeated by the echoes in the mountain, and was finally lost in the solitude.

Suddenly some small gravel rolled down from above. The rustling of rapid steps was heard, and in the direction of the portcullis and of the gorge there appeared pointed muzzles and straight ears, with gleaming, tawny eyes. These were the jackals coming to eat what was left.

The Carthaginian, who was leaning over the top of the precipice to look, went back again.

XV

Matho

There were rejoicings at Carthage,—rejoicings deep, universal, extravagant, frantic; the holes of the ruins had been stopped up, the statues of the gods had been repainted, the streets were strewn with myrtle branches, incense smoked at the corners of the crossways, and the throng on the terraces looked, in their variegated garments, like heaps of flowers blooming in the air.

The shouts of the water-carriers watering the pavement rose above the continual screaming of voices; slaves belonging to Hamilcar offered in his name roasted barley and pieces of raw meat; people accosted one another, and embraced one another with tears; the Tyrian towns were taken, the nomads dispersed, and all the Barbarians annihilated. The Acropolis was hidden beneath coloured velaria; the beaks of the triremes, drawn up in line outside the mole, shone like a dyke of diamonds; everywhere there was a sense of the restoration of order, the beginning of a new existence, and the diffusion of vast happiness: it was the day of Salammbô's marriage with the King of the Numidians.

On the terrace of the temple of Khamon there were three long tables laden with gigantic plate, at which the priests, Ancients, and the rich were to sit, and there was a fourth and higher one for Hamilcar, Narr' Havas, and Salammbô; for as she had saved her country by the restoration of the zaïmph, the people turned her wedding day into a national rejoicing, and were waiting in the square below till she should appear.

But their impatience was excited by another and more acrid longing: Matho's death has been promised for the ceremony.

It had been proposed at first to flay him alive, to pour lead into his entrails, to kill him with hunger; he should be tied to a tree, and an ape behind him should strike him on the head with a stone; he had offended Tanith, and the cynocephaluses of Tanith should avenge her. Others were of opinion that he should be led about on a dromedary after linen wicks, dipped in oil, had been inserted in his body in several places;—and they took pleasure in the thought of the large animal wandering through the streets with this man writhing beneath the fires like a candelabrum blown about by the wind.

But what citizens should be charged with his torture, and why disappoint the rest? They would have liked a kind of death in which the whole town might take part, in which every hand, every weapon, everything Carthaginian, to the very paving-stones in the streets and the waves in the gulf, could rend him, and crush him, and annihilate him. Accordingly the Ancients decided that he should go from his prison to the square of Khamon without any escort, and with his arms fastened to his back; it was forbidden to strike him to the heart, in order that he might live the longer; to put out his eyes, so that he might see the torture through; to hurl anything against his person, or to lay more than three fingers upon him at a time.

Although he was not to appear until the end of the day, the people sometimes fancied that he could be seen, and the crowd would rush towards the Acropolis, and empty the streets, to return with lengthened murmurings. Some people had remained standing in the same place since the day before, and they would call on one another from a distance and show their nails which they had allowed to grow, the better to bury them into his flesh. Others walked restlessly up and down; some were as pale as though they were awaiting their own execution.

Suddenly lofty feather fans rose above the heads, behind the Mappalian district. It was Salammbô leaving her palace; a sigh of relief found vent.

But the procession was long in coming; it marched with deliberation.

First there filed past the priests of the Patæc Gods, then those of Eschmoun, of Melkarth, and all the other colleges in succession, with the same insignia, and in the same order as had been observed at the time of the sacrifice. The pontiffs of Moloch passed with heads bent, and the multitude stood aside from them in a kind of remorse. But the priests of Rabbetna advanced with a proud step, and with lyres in their hands; the priestesses followed them in transparent robes of yellow or black, uttering cries like birds and writhing like vipers, or else whirling round to the sound of flutes to imitate the dance of the stars, while their light garments wafted puffs of delicate scents through the streets.

The Kedeschim, with painted eyelids, who symbolised the hermaphrodism of the Divinity, received applause among these women, and, being perfumed and dressed like them, they resembled them in spite of their flat breasts and narrower hips. Moreover, on this day the female principle dominated and confused all things; a mystic voluptuousness moved in the heavy air; the torches were already lighted in the depths of the sacred woods; there was to be a great celebration there during the night; three vessels had brought courtesans from Sicily, and others had come from the desert.

As the colleges arrived they ranged themselves in the courts of the temples, on the outer galleries, and along double staircases which rose against the walls, and drew together at the top. Files of white robes appeared between the colonnades, and the architecture was peopled with human statues, motionless as statues of stone.

Then came the masters of the exchequer, the governors of the provinces, and all the rich. A great tumult prevailed below. Adjacent streets were discharging the crowd, hierodules were driving it back with blows of sticks; and then Salammbô appeared in a litter surmounted by a purple canopy, and surrounded by the Ancients crowned with their golden tiaras.

Thereupon an immense shout arose; the cymbals and crotala sounded more loudly, the tabourines thundered, and the great purple canopy sank between the two pylons.

It appeared again on the first landing. Salammbô was walking slowly beneath it; then she crossed the terrace to take her seat behind on a kind of throne cut out of the carapace of a tortoise. An ivory stool with three steps was pushed beneath her feet; two Negro children knelt on the edge of the first step, and sometimes she would rest both arms, which were laden with rings of excessive weight, upon their heads.

From ankle to hip she was covered with a network of narrow meshes which were in imitation of fish scales, and shone like mother-of-pearl; her waist was clasped by a blue zone, which allowed her breasts to be seen through two crescent-shaped slashings; the nipples were hidden by carbuncle pendants. She had a headdress made of peacock's feathers studded with gems; an ample cloak, as white as snow, fell behind her,— and with her elbows at her sides, her knees pressed together, and circles of diamonds on the upper part of her arms, she remained perfectly upright in a hieratic attitude.

Her father and her husband were on two lower seats, Narr' Havas dressed in a light simar and wearing his crown of rock-salt, from which there strayed two tresses of hair as twisted as the horns of Ammon; and Hamilcar in a violet tunic figured with gold vine branches, and with a battle-sword at his side.

The python of the temple of Eschmoun lay on the ground amid pools of pink oil in the space enclosed by the tables, and, biting its tail, described a large black circle. In the middle of the circle there was a copper pillar bearing a crystal egg; and, as the sun shone upon it, rays were emitted on every side.

Behind Salammbô stretched the priests of Tanith in linen robes; on her right the Ancients, in their tiaras, formed a great gold line, and on the other side the rich with their emerald sceptres a great green line,—while quite in the background, where the priests of Moloch were ranged, the cloaks looked like a wall of purple. The other colleges occupied the lower terraces. The multitude obstructed the streets. It reached to the house-tops, and extended in long files to the summit of the Acropolis. Having thus the people at her feet, the firmament above her head, and around her the immensity of the sea, the gulf, the mountains, and the distant provinces, Salammbô in her splendour was blended with Tanith, and seemed the very genius of Carthage, and its embodied soul.

The feast was to last all night, and lamps with several branches were planted like trees on the painted woollen cloths which covered the low tables. Large electrum flagons, blue glass amphoras, tortoise-shell spoons, and small round loaves were crowded between the double row of pearl-bordered plates; bunches of grapes with their leaves had been rolled round ivory vine-stocks after the fashion of the thyrsus; blocks of snow were melting on ebony trays, and lemons, pomegranates, gourds, and watermelons formed hillocks beneath the lofty silver plate; boars with open jaws were wallowing in the dust of spices; hares, covered with their fur, appeared to be bounding amid the flowers; there were shells filled with forcemeat; the pastry had symbolic shapes; when the covers of the dishes were removed doves flew out.

The slaves, meanwhile, with tunics tucked up, were going about on tiptoe; from time to time a hymn sounded on the lyres, or a choir of voices rose. The clamour of the people, continuous as the noise of the sea, floated vaguely around the feast, and seemed to lull it in a broader harmony; some recalled the banquet of the Mercenaries; they gave themselves up to dreams of happiness; the sun was beginning to go down, and the crescent of the moon was already rising in another part of the sky.

But Salammbô turned her head as though some one had called her; the people, who were watching her, followed the direction of her eyes.

The door of the dungeon, hewn in the rock at the foot of the temple, on the summit of the Acropolis, had just opened; and a man was standing on the threshold of this black hole.

He came forth bent double, with the scared look of fallow deer when suddenly enlarged.

The light dazzled him; he stood motionless awhile. All had recognised him, and they held their breath.

In their eyes the body of this victim was something peculiarly theirs, and was adorned with almost religious splendour. They bent forward to see him, especially the women. They burned to gaze upon him who had caused the deaths of their children and husbands; and from the bottom of their souls there sprang up in spite of themselves an infamous curiosity, a desire to know him completely, a wish mingled with remorse which turned to increased execration.

At last he advanced; then the stupefaction of surprise disappeared. Numbers of arms were raised, and he was lost to sight.

The staircase of the Acropolis had sixty steps. He descended them as though he were rolled down in a torrent from the top of a mountain; three times he was seen to leap, and then he alighted below on his feet.

His shoulders were bleeding, his breast was panting with great shocks; and he made such efforts to burst his bonds that his arms, which were crossed on his naked loins, swelled like pieces of a serpent.

Several streets began in front of him, leading from the spot at which he found himself. In each of them a triple row of bronze chains fastened to the navels of the Patæc gods extended in parallel lines from one end to the other; the crowd was massed against the houses, and servants, belonging to the Ancients, walked in the middle brandishing thongs.

One of them drove him forward with a great blow; Matho began to move.

They thrust their arms over the chains shouting out that the road had been left too wide for him; and he passed along, felt, pricked, and slashed by all those fingers; when he reached the end of one street another appeared; several times he flung himself to one side to bite them; they speedily dispersed, the chains held him back, and the crowd burst out laughing.

A child rent his ear; a young girl, hiding the point of a spindle in her sleeve, split his cheek; they tore handfuls of hair from him and strips of flesh; others smeared his face with sponges steeped in filth and fastened upon sticks. A stream of blood started from the right side of his neck, frenzy immediately set in. This last Barbarian was to them a representative of all the Barbarians, and all the army; they were taking vengeance on him for their disasters, their terrors, and their shame. The rage of the mob developed with its gratification; the curving chains were over-strained, and were on the point of breaking; the people did not feel the blows of the slaves who struck at them to drive them back; some clung to the projections of the houses; all the openings in the walls were stopped up with heads; and they howled at him the mischief that they could not inflict upon him.

It was atrocious, filthy abuse mingled with ironical encouragements and imprecations; and, his present tortures not being enough for them, they foretold to him others that should be still more terrible in eternity.

This vast baying filled Carthage with stupid continuity. Frequently a single syllable—a hoarse, deep, and frantic intonation—would be repeated for several minutes by the entire people. The walls would vibrate with it from top to bottom, and both sides of the street would seem to Matho to be coming against him, and carrying him off the ground, like two immense arms stifling him in the air.

Nevertheless he remembered that he had experienced something like it before. The same crowd was on the terraces, there were the same looks and the same wrath; but then he had walked free, all had then dispersed, for a god covered him;—and the recollection of this, gaining precision by degrees, brought a crushing sadness upon him. Shadows passed before his eyes; the town whirled round in his head, his blood streamed from a wound in his hip, he felt that he was dying; his hams bent, and he sank quite gently upon the pavement.

Some one went to the peristyle of the temple of Melkarth, took thence the bar of a tripod, heated red hot in the coals, and, slipping it beneath the first chain, pressed it against his wound. The flesh was seen to smoke; the hootings of the people drowned his voice; he was standing again.

Six paces further on, and he fell a third and again a fourth time; but some new torture always made him rise. They discharged little drops of boiling oil through tubes at him; they strewed pieces of broken glass beneath his feet; still he walked on. At the corner of the street of Satheb he leaned his back against the wall beneath the pent-house of a shop, and advanced no further.

The slaves of the Council struck him with their whips of hippopotamus leather, so furiously and long that the fringes of their tunics were drenched with sweat. Matho appeared insensible; suddenly he started off and began to run at random, making a noise with his lips like one shivering with severe cold. He threaded the street of Boudes, and the street of Soepo, crossed the Green Market, and reached the square of Khamon.

He now belonged to the priests; the slaves had just dispersed the crowd, and there was more room. Matho gazed round him and his eyes encountered Salammbô.

At the first step that he had taken she had risen; then, as he approached, she had involuntarily advanced by degrees to the edge of the terrace; and soon all external things were blotted out, and she saw only Matho. Silence fell in her soul,—one of those abysses wherein the whole world disappears beneath the pressure of a single thought, a memory, a look. This man who was walking towards her attracted her.

Excepting his eyes he had no appearance of humanity left; he was a long, perfectly red shape; his broken bonds hung down his thighs, but they could not be distinguished from the tendons of his wrists, which were laid quite bare; his mouth remained wide open; from his eye-sockets there darted flames which seemed to rise up to his hair;—and the wretch still walked on!

He reached the foot of the terrace. Salammbô was leaning over the balustrade; those frightful eyeballs were scanning her, and there rose within her a consciousness of all that he had suffered for her. Although he was in his death agony she could see him once more kneeling in his tent, encircling her waist with his arms, and stammering out gentle words; she thirsted to feel them and hear them again; she did not want him to die! At this moment Matho gave a great start; she was on the point of shrieking aloud. He fell backwards and did not stir again.

Salammbô was borne back, nearly swooning, to her throne by the priests who flocked about her. They congratulated her; it was her work. All clapped their hands and stamped their feet, howling her name.

A man darted upon the corpse. Although he had no beard he had the cloak of a priest of Moloch on his shoulder, and in his belt that species of knife which they employed for cutting up the sacred meat, and which terminated, at the end of the handle, in a golden spatula. He cleft Matho's breast with a single blow, then snatched out the heart and laid it upon the spoon; and Schahabarim, uplifting his arm, offered it to the sun.

The sun sank behind the waves; his rays fell like long arrows upon the red heart. As the beatings diminished the planet sank into the sea; and at the last palpitation it disappeared.

Then from the gulf to the lagoon, and from the isthmus to the pharos, in all the streets, on all the houses, and on all the temples, there was a single shout; sometimes it paused, to be again renewed; the buildings shook with it; Carthage was convulsed, as it were, in the spasm of Titanic joy and boundless hope.

Narr' Havas, drunk with pride, passed his left arm beneath Salammbô's waist in token of possession; and taking a gold patera in his right hand, he drank to the Genius of Carthage.

Salammbô rose like her husband, with a cup in her hand, to drink also. She fell down again with her head lying over the back of the throne,—pale, stiff, with parted lips,—and her loosened hair hung to the ground.

Thus died Hamilcar's daughter for having touched the mantle of Tanith.

A NOTE ABOUT THE AUTHOR

Gustave Flaubert (1821–1880) was a French novelist who was best known for exploring realism in his work. Hailing from an upper-class family, Flaubert was exposed to literature at an early age. He received a formal education at Lycée Pierre-Corneille, before venturing to Paris to study law. A serious illness forced him to change his career path, reigniting his passion for writing. He completed his first novella, *November*, in 1842, launching a decade-spanning career. His most notable work, *Madame Bovary* was published in 1856 and is considered a literary masterpiece.

A NOTE FROM THE PUBLISHER

Spanning many genres, from non-fiction essays to literature classics to children's books and lyric poetry, Mint Edition books showcase the master works of our time in a modern new package. The text is freshly typeset, is clean and easy to read, and features a new note about the author in each volume. Many books also include exclusive new introductory material. Every book boasts a striking new cover, which makes it as appropriate for collecting as it is for gift giving. Mint Edition books are only printed when a reader orders them, so natural resources are not wasted. We're proud that our books are never manufactured in excess and exist only in the exact quantity they need to be read and enjoyed.

bookfinity™

Discover more of your favorite classics with Bookfinity™.

- Track your reading with custom book lists.
- Get great book recommendations for your personalized Reader Type.
- Add reviews for your favorite books.
- AND MUCH MORE!

Visit **bookfinity.com** and take the fun Reader Type quiz to get started.

Enjoy our classic and modern companion pairings!

Classic & Modern